Dear Reader:

The novels you've enjoyed over the past years by such authors as Kathleen Woodiwiss, Rosemary Rogers, Johanna Lindsey, Laurie McBain, and Shirlee Busbee are accountable to one thing above all others: Avon has never tried to force authors into any particular mold. Rather, Avon is a publisher that encourages individual talent and is always on the lookout for writers who will deliver *real* books, not packaged formulas.

In 1982, we started a program to help readers pick out authors of exceptional promise. Called "The Avon Romance," the books were distinguished by a ribbon motif in the upper left-hand corner of the cover. Although the titles were by new authors, they were quickly discovered and became known as "the ribbon books."

Now "The Avon Romance" is a regular feature on the Avon list. Each month, you will find historical novels with many different settings, each one by an author who is special. You will not find predictable characters, predictable plots, and predictable endings. The only predictable thing about "The Avon Romance" will be the superior quality that Avon has always delivered in the field of romance!

Sincerely,

WALTER MEADE
President & Publisher

Other Avon Books by
Victoria Pade

WHEN LOVE REMAINS

PASSION'S TORMENT

VICTORIA PADE

AVON
PUBLISHERS OF BARD, CAMELOT, DISCUS AND FLARE BOOKS

PASSION'S TORMENT is an original publication of Avon Books. This work has never before appeared in book form. This work is a novel. Any similarity to actual persons or events is purely coincidental.

AVON BOOKS
A division of
The Hearst Corporation
1790 Broadway
New York, New York 10019

Copyright © 1985 by Victoria Pade
Published by arrangement with the author
Library of Congress Catalog Card Number: 84-091241
ISBN: 0-380-89681-8

First Avon Printing, May 1985

AVON TRADEMARK REG. U. S. PAT. OFF. AND IN OTHER COUNTRIES, MARCA REGISTRADA, HECHO EN U. S. A.

Printed in the U. S. A.

WFH 10 9 8 7 6 5 4 3 2 1

To Jeff, who consoles my
insanities and supports
my eccentricities.

To Cori, without whom
I may never have written
a word.

And to Erin, who is my
famous rainbow.

Chapter One

September 13, 1849

"I have to go back, Ivy! I have to confess!" Alisa Todd's voice was soft, her words punctuated with a note of resigned determination.

"Don't be a ninny, Alisa!" Ivy Todd's voice was harsh, compassionless. "You would ruin us all with that, and I won't stand for it!"

Dense London fog wafted like a specter against the black sky as the carriage raced through quiet city streets. The driver slapped the reins against the backs of sturdy geldings, not understanding the reason for this hurried departure from the Todd family's country estate, but knowing well the dangers of two women traveling alone through the night, their barouche announcing a wealth all too many resented.

Within the carriage Ivy sat imperiously, garbed, even in haste, in a perfect traveling cape, gloves and a hat perched saucily to one side, while her younger sister wore a soiled riding habit, her wildly curling hair more unruly than usual, midnight-blue eyes wide as they stared into the darkness.

"When will you learn, Alisa?" Ivy chastised brutally. "Nothing worthwhile is served by your idiotic act of savior to the downtrodden! Now you can see the harm in playing rescuing angel!"

Alisa's chin tilted upward. Even through a complexity of emotions, her tone was one of strength in her convictions. "You may term it anything you like, Ivy. But there are some things no person should ever stand for, and beating a child is one of them!"

"That won't save your neck! His father is a Lord High Magistrate! He'll see you hanged no matter what your defense. It was pure stupidity not to mind your own business!"

"Given the same circumstances, I would do it again."

"That's very noble of you, Alisa." Ivy's sarcasm was thick.

"I should never have let you talk me into running from it." But fear rang clearly in Alisa's voice, belying her words.

The carriage stopped with a sudden jolt before the Todds' London town house. Ivy did not wait for assistance; she descended rapidly, pulling Alisa's arm as if she were a defiant child.

"Your running has just begun, dear sister!"

Only the faint glimmer of one candle, left each night for late-night homecomings, lit the entrance hall. The house was silent, deep shadows lending an eerie quality to familiar surroundings. Before Ivy and Alisa could renew their quarrel, a low, rumbling moan, emanating from the drawing room to the left of the foyer, broke the stillness.

Ivy's clipped footsteps crossed to the doorway. "Wonderful," she said snidely. "Is there no end this day to arrogant bastards causing me problems?"

Alisa stepped beside her sister. Ivy held the candle high, illuminating their American visitor of three weeks sprawled haphazardly on the settee, his long, muscular frame dwarfing the small sofa, one leg over the scrolled arm, the other on the floor, his head hanging precariously over the back crest rail. The smell of liquor was strong, and his moans lent credence to their assumption that the man was dead drunk.

"We'll have to get him to bed." Alisa sighed wearily. She had an inordinate internal strength, but the day's events had taken a great toll.

"I don't know why we should," Ivy grumbled. "The man has shown neither of us a speck of interest. In fact, he has ignored us as if he thought himself better! He deserves to be brought down a peg."

"He is also a guest in our home, and he needs assistance. Let's just get it over with." Alisa's tone was curt.

"As if we didn't have enough problems right now! You're still determined to play our lady of the good deeds," Ivy said with a huff, but joined her sister in hoisting the man, with difficulty, to a sitting position. "He's like lifting a bloody side of beef!"

Once on his feet, the man became semiconscious, carrying a portion of his own weight, enabling Ivy and Alisa to get him up the steep flight of stairs to the second level. Two candles were also left burning in the upper hallway. When they reached the landing, the man paused, staring oddly at Alisa.

"Ellen? Is that you?" he mumbled thickly, nearly incoherently.

Alisa did not answer him, knowing he was too far gone even to realize where he was.

The two small women fairly dragged the hulking man to his room as his ramblings continued. "Ellen, Ellen, how much I want you, damn you to hell!" A

heavy hand clumsily groped for Alisa's breast, finding it with amazing alacrity for someone so inebriated.

Alisa slapped his hand away with a stinging blow.

"Ah, damn you, Ellen," came the mumblings
again. "Not your games tonight! I hate pretending to
force you! It's a stupid game! I want you willing tonight! How I want you!" He groaned with an intimacy Alisa was embarrassed to hear as the two
women dropped him onto his bed.

Ivy pulled off his boots and swung his feet up onto
the mattress, the small smile playing around her
mouth the only clue to a dawning plan.

"I could shake you, you make me so furious,
Alisa!" Ivy raged as her sister paced their bedroom.
"You have only two choices. You can either trap
Christian Reed into marrying you and get safely out
of England, or stay and hang for murder."

"My God, Ivy! Hasn't enough damage been done
today? Granted, the Reed man is an arrogant Yan-
kee, but he doesn't deserve this."

"How long do you think it will be before Willis
Potts's body is found? We didn't drag him that far
into the woods. And when it is, his father will not
rest until he finds the murderer. Do you doubt that?"

"No, I don't doubt it," Alisa said softly, her arms
wrapped around her waist as if for protection. "But it
was an accident! I didn't murder him!"

"Who will believe that? The only witness was that
dim-witted boy who ran off, and he will surely say he
saw you there, arguing with Willis. When his body is
found with a knife in the belly, no one will believe
you're innocent. Lord Potts is a vindictive man. He
has never believed Willis to be less than the perfect

son, never seen even one of his faults. He is a power-ful magistrate, and you have no defense."

"But it was an accident, Ivy. What you suggest now is despicable and premeditated. It's vile!"

"Is it more vile than hanging for what happened today? Are you so ready to end your life?"

Suddenly Alisa's skin was clammy with the stark reality of the situation.

"Have you a better solution, Alisa?"

"You know I haven't." Her voice held resignation.

"Have you any other way out of England?" Ivy persisted vindictively.

"No," came the reluctant answer.

"Have you any doubt of what your fate will be if you stay?

"No!" She shot the word at her sister in angry de-fense of this attack.

"Then what will it be?" Ivy said smugly.

"It's an ugly plan, Ivy."

"It is a perfect plan. Papa is at his club, and the servants are all asleep belowstairs. We have only to make it appear that Christian Reed raped you in a drunken attack and fainted. I will say I saw him drag you into his room, that he was a madman, call-ing you Ellen. Whoever she is, he wants her badly, and you heard him say she likes to be forced. It's per-fect." Ivy's color was high with excitement. "I will convince Papa that we must avoid a scandal at all costs, that the best course is an immediate wedding followed by your departure for America. Now, what will it be, Alisa?"

Alisa gritted her teeth and made her decision. She was a fair and honest person, and it went against her grain to run from anything, let alone follow through with Ivy's planned deception. "I don't like it," she said flatly. "But I really don't have a choice."

"Good. Then come into the guest room. There is no time to lose!"

The guest room was deeply shadowed, the only light coming from the candles in the hallway. Alisa stopped in the doorway as she saw Ivy working carefully to remove Christian Reed's trousers without unduly jarring him.

Ivy's irritated sigh was the only sound. She held her voluminous skirts to quiet their rustle as she shoved Alisa back into the hall. Her whisper was stinging. "I will not do this all myself, Alisa. Remember that it is your problem, not mine."

"I can't undress the man," Alisa insisted in embarrassment. Putting Ivy's plan into action was difficult for her in every respect.

"You don't have to. I will take his pants off, and the rest doesn't matter."

"Be sure you cover him with a sheet."

"This is no time to fret about your innocence," Ivy whispered snidely. "Now do as I say! Muss your hair, tear the front of your dress and the skirt, then take off your petticoats, rip them and throw them around the bed." Her commands given, Ivy returned to the bedside of Christian Reed.

The man was a full head taller than most men, two heads taller than Ivy or Alisa. His build was muscular, massive in fact, which did not aid in the task of removing his breeches. Once this was accomplished, Ivy had no qualms about admiring his masculinity before she lightly draped the corner of the bed sheet over his lower half.

Alisa joined her sister, carefully directing her eyes

to Christian Reed's handsome face. She realized that she knew very little about the man. In the short weeks since he had arrived, she had paid him no more attention than he had her. She had thought him arrogant and perhaps vain because of his intense good looks; certainly he seemed a cold sort, but still she regretted the necessity of the deception she was about to perpetrate.

Ivy had no patience for such silliness as remorse. She eyed Alisa's gown with disgust and, without warning, turned her sister to face her. Her hands mercilessly tore Alisa's gown to shreds, leaving one breast totally exposed as well as both of her legs. Alisa reached instinctively to cover herself. Ivy was unperturbed. She pulled one of Alisa's hands free and drew a large hat pin from her pocket. With a victorious smirk, Ivy jabbed the weapon she had brought for just this purpose into the tip of Alisa's finger, smearing the blood onto the pure whiteness of the sheet beside the unconscious man.

She pushed Alisa on the bed. "You have just been raped, Alisa, try to summon some tears! Picture your neck stretched at the end of the hangman's noose." Ivy pinched Alisa's cheek viciously, to rouse her sister's tightly held emotions. With the stage set, she ran from the room.

Alisa heard her sister's voice rise as she descended the stairs, faking hysterics being one of Ivy's natural talents. Alisa grasped the remnants of her gown to preserve what little was possible of her modesty. She swallowed thickly and sighed, then squared her shoulders and set her jaw determinedly. There was no other way open to her. She could not accept losing her own life because of a cur like Willis Potts.

As the house erupted with the sounds of servants

responding to Ivy's convincingly emotional trills, Alisa looked down at her second victim of the day and spoke softly, "I'll make this up to you, Christian Reed. I promise you that."

Chapter Two

Angry sounds assaulted Christian Reed from far away. Light exploded behind his closed lids as his mind struggled to gain control. Suddenly, he was drowning. Consciousness dawned with the thrust of a lightning bolt as he sat up in bed, spewing water that had been doused on his face by Aldis Todd. The diminutive, aged man's face was alive with rage.

Christian's brain seemed painfully swollen. His massive hands reached to press his temples, and he fought for some semblance of lucidity amidst a woman's hysterical cries and Aldis Todd's shouting voice. He opened his eyes to the sight of Aldis Todd waving a small derringer beneath his nose.

His pale bluish-green eyes widened and rose in total disorientation to take in his surroundings. He was first aware of his lack of pants. One hand reached quickly to retrieve the sheet that threatened to expose him. The room was full of gawking servants standing just at the foot of his bed, leering. Christian's gaze moved to Ivy, who seemed to have gained control of her hysterics, and then to Alisa. He saw her ashen face, and her wide midnight-blue eyes, but his attention was drawn to her torn gown, and then the ripped petticoats scattered about the

9

bed, and finally, he noticed the fresh bloodstains on the sheet beside him. A groan of self-disgust issued from his parched throat. He had no memory of even returning here tonight. "What happened?" Christian managed, his voice a gravelly whisper.

Aldis Todd's jowly face grew crimson with fury. "What happened?" he shouted, apoplectically. "I'll see you rot in Newgate for this, you bloody bastard!"

"Papa!" Ivy, now remarkably serene, took control of the situation. "You must calm down. Dismiss the servants." Aldis Todd snarled at his employees, who reluctantly departed.

Christian was grateful for the dissipation of his audience. He ignored Aldis and the gun that still threatened him and spoke to Ivy. "Might I be allowed to dress before you explain to me what is going on?"

"Explain it to you? Dress?" Aldis screamed, "Do you think this is a social chitchat? You've raped my daughter! You can stay the way you are as evidence!"

Christian's eyes closed slowly, and his head shook from side to side as his worst fears were confirmed.

Alisa could not bear more of this humiliation. Her voice was low but strong. "Papa, please! I cannot stand to stay like this. Let us both at least dress."

Ivy added her persuasion. "Alisa is right, Papa. We must discuss this. We shall all meet in the library in just a few minutes."

Ivy clasped Aldis's arm firmly and led him to the door. Before he left, he turned to point his gun at Christian Reed's broad chest again. "Don't even think of trying to escape. I'll set two men to watch this door and bring you to me in twenty minutes." Then, to Alisa, who stood just behind him, Aldis vowed, "He'll pay for this, Alisa, I promise you. He will pay dearly!"

"He's a damned divorced man!" Aldis's shout pierced the air as Christian reached the library door.

A glass crashed against the stone hearth as Christian was admitted to the room. He stood proudly before the older man's desk, in control of himself once again. Alisa sat straight-backed in a chair near one wall, her head high, but unable to meet his eyes. Ivy stood behind her father's chair, one hand steadily on Aldis's shoulder as though she were forcibly keeping him in his seat.

Ivy's voice broke the silence as Aldis fumed in frustrated rage. "Since you seem to be unaware of your actions, Mr. Reed, I will tell you what you have done."

Christian stared evenly at the woman whose beauty had left him unaffected during his three-week stay there. He saw that she was enjoying this macabre scene, and it was hard to conceal his disdain of her.

"Alisa and I arrived home from the country late this evening. You were in the drawing room, slumped in a chair. Alisa noticed you and asked if you were all right. You became a mad man. You were calling her Ellen; over and over again you said you wanted her, that you knew she liked to be forced into your bed. She tried to leave, but you wouldn't allow it, raving that you would have her one more time. That you knew the game."

Alisa flinched slightly at Ivy's merciless repetition of Christian's words, her interpretation sounding even more vile.

Christian saw Alisa's reaction. A wave of guilt

stirred in him, but his countenance did not alter as Ivy continued.

"You dragged her past me, pushing me aside to pull her up the stairs. The guest-room door slammed before I could reach it, and you locked it against me. I heard you ripping Alisa's clothing and forcing yourself on her. I ran to wake the servants and to summon Father, but by that time it was too late."

Christian turned to Alisa; his voice was soft and deeply pained. "Is this true?"

Alisa could do no more than nod her head, pinning her gaze to a spot directly in front of her.

Now Aldis's voice boomed forth once again. "Of course it's true! I protected your reputation, I didn't even tell my girls about your wife Ellen, or any of the rest of your damn scandal. You should be shot! You're a damn defiler of women! I should never have allowed you in my home! God knows what your poor wife must have suffered at your hands! I should shoot you where you stand!"

"Papa." Ivy rebuked him as though he were a child. "You know what we discussed."

The older man grumbled. "I know it, but I don't like it. If it wouldn't do Alisa more harm, I'd shoot him right now."

Ivy continued, "You realize, of course, that Papa would be within his rights to do just that. Or he could call in the law and you could spend the remainder of your life in prison. Papa has many influential friends who would insure that you never got out." She paused to allow her words time to sink in. "However, that would not salvage the wreck you have made of Alisa's life."

Christian waited. He would not give Ivy the satisfaction of a comment.

"The only course that could save Alisa is marriage to you and a hasty departure for America." She flung the words at him in triumph.

Christian turned and crossed to Alisa, standing like a tower before her. His voice was low enough to reach her ears alone, ringing with remorse and contrition. "An apology is a feeble thing, Alisa, when the damage is this great. I take full blame and full responsibility. I will make amends in any way you want, any way at all. Is marrying and leaving England right away your choice?"

Alisa's lips parted slightly as she blew out her breath in relief. She had not expected kindness from this man, and it made her decision more difficult. Still, she had no other options. "It is what must be done. Yes," she said finally.

Christian turned back to Ivy. "Arrange for it, then," he said harshly. "I'll be in my room packing. I'll send a message to my ship to gather my crew. We will leave as soon as possible."

As his hand touched the doorknob, he paused. His eyes remained on the carved panel before him, and he spoke softly. "I am truly sorry, Alisa."

Chapter Three

Madness. Christian flung Alisa's torn petticoats to the floor and then ripped the soiled sheet from the feather tic. He dropped wearily on the bed, lying on his back with closed eyes to still some of the painful throbbing in his head.

It had to be madness.

Christian searched his memory for a clue to what had happened. He remembered leaving the house early in the evening to seek a brothel to ease his long-starved passions. He cursed himself now, for allowing a jovial group of men to draw him into their poker game instead of bedding the first whore he encountered. He had remained in the game and downed drink after drink, drowning memories he could not seem to escape even in an alcoholic stupor. He had not been so drunk since his early days as a whaler, and then he had the excuse of youth.

He remembered falling into the carriage after the game ended, but that was all, until he had been awakened by Aldis Todd.

Christian sighed in disgust and fury. "Instead of staying away from women, you've gotten yourself trapped into marrying another one!" he berated himself aloud. Madness indeed. There could be no other cause.

After Ellen, he had sworn never to become involved with any woman but an occasional whore. Never! Ellen had been a brutal lesson.

But then, he must have been mad to have been deceived by Ellen from the beginning. After eight years at sea, courting only the most adventurous danger, or perhaps foolhardy of what men could endure, he had met Ellen. She was beautiful, sweet-natured and guileless, he thought. He had loved her. No, he thought now, that phrase was too clean-cut to describe what he had felt for Ellen. Bewitched, enchanted, worshipful were more accurate descriptions. He was still amazed at his own blindness. She had needed marriage and money, and he had fallen prey to her wiles. It had taken over a year of marriage before he had discovered her legion of adulterous affairs.

Christian's brother had seen right through Ellen. Scott had tried to tell him, but Christian refused to believe his aspersions against her.

An anonymous note, leading him to find Ellen in another man's bed, opened his eyes to what she really was. He had listened outside the door to her telling her lover how she had cleverly deceived her husband. His love for her turned to gall. It had taken Christian three years to divorce Ellen. Three years of courts and lawyers and clergymen; of scandal and rumor and airing the juiciest details for all to pick apart like vultures over raw meat. And one damned evening of letting his guard slip had trapped him again.

Rage and self-contempt boiled up, stiffening his spine until he could not lie there and endure it. He rose with a fierce push from the bed, heedless of the pounding in his head. He moved to the washstand basin and splashed icy water over his face and neck.

This calmed his rage for a moment as his thoughts turned to Ellen's son and that day three months ago when she had finally come to take Nat with her after leaving him in the care of the nanny and nurse on the estate. It had been hard on Christian, harder than he had expected. After all, he reasoned, the boy was not his son, even though he had believed him to be for almost a year. Ellen's revelations the day he had found out about her left no question in his mind that she had duped him into believing the child was his, so he should have been thrilled to see the end of any connection with Ellen; giving up Nat accomplished that.

However, Ellen's return had a different effect: He discovered his desire for her was still strong, overshadowing his anger and contempt. With that realization had come the fear that he might succumb to her once again, or worse yet, that he might actually do what he had apparently done tonight to Alisa Todd. Ellen's sexual tastes had run to game playing. One of her favorites was to be forced by him while she pretended that she didn't want him. After their divorce, Christian had nightmares about it. Night after night, he would meet her, hating her and yet still wanting her badly. He would force himself on her, his subconscious enjoying the retribution of using her own ploy against her. He would wake when the deed was done, drenched with sweat, his body a mass of tense, taut muscles, his hands wanting to wring Ellen's neck for this power she still held over him.

He had come to London then to escape the gossip,

the stares, the turned faces, the whispers. Divorce was tantamount to the most heinous crime. Daughters were safely removed from his path lest he become interested in them, which would soil their reputations and immortal souls. Women looked at him as either the villain who drove lovely Ellen to sin or the pitiful victim of a scarlet woman. Men viewed him as foolish not to have simply shot Ellen and her lover where they lay. So before Christian lost his well-controlled temper, he decided to remove himself from the place that haunted his nights and tormented his days.

He laughed mirthlessly as he fell onto the bed once again. He had just begun to feel free of the past. How ironic, he thought, and again damned himself for holding his pent-up desires in check, precipitating the disastrous events of the evening.

The thought of his impending marriage hit him like the heavy blow of a meaty fist to his gut. But he was a man who accepted his responsibilities, no matter how loathsome. He would stay and marry Alisa Todd, but she would not get more from him. He would never again be vulnerable to any woman. He had no doubt that whatever made a man capable of love had died within him long ago. He would give Alisa his name as atonement for his black deed, but beyond that and his money, he was certain there could be nothing else for her.

Chapter Four

Alisa sat cross-legged on the daybed in her room. Her slender arms hugged her body, and she rocked back and forth as if the movement might somehow dispel her living nightmare.

Only two days past, Ivy had announced at breakfast that she could no longer bear the arrogant presence of Christian Reed, and meant to escape to their country estate. She had demanded Alisa's company, and Aldis, being forever pliable, had agreed. Alisa had not been duped by Ivy's tirade. She knew the true reason behind Ivy's anger. It was not Christian Reed's presence that incurred Ivy's wrath but his lack of interest in Ivy, an unforgivable offense.

Christian Reed was the nephew of Aldis's third wife, Deadra, a pale, limpid creature who hid away in her room, refusing admittance to any save Aldis, on rare occasions. Her existence was often completely forgotten in the household. Alisa had found it difficult to believe that Christian Reed, who was a large, strong, handsome man, could be related to Deadra in any way.

Ivy and Alisa had had little contact with Christian during his stay; he seemed disinclined to seek their company, preferring solitude. But even the brief time he was with the family was enough to spark Ivy's temper, for she expected all men to admire her considerable beauty. Within the past three months, she had been rejected by Owen Tanor, who deserted Ivy the moment he met Alisa. These two blows to her vanity had been unendurable, and she decided to remove herself and Alisa from the vicinity of both men.

As Alisa sat in her dark room, tortured by past events, she wished fervently that she had not allowed Ivy to force her to leave London. But since she always strove to avoid her sister's wrath and tantrums, she found it often easier to simply placate her.

Once in the country, Alisa and Ivy saw very little of one another, which suited them both, for they rarely enjoyed each other's company. Ivy's jealousy was an ever-present thorn, though Alisa could not understand it. Alisa had chosen to spend her time as always, in the woods, with paper and pen, sketching whatever pleased her well-trained eye.

Alisa closed her lids tightly, as though that might clear the events that came to her mind. Still the memory unfolded with a will of its own.

Willis Potts, the only son of their neighbor, the Lord High Magistrate, Walter Potts, stood in the road, holding a small boy about his neck in a grip so tight that the child's face was crimson. In his other hand, Willis held a small knife to the boy's ear, a line of bright red blood wetting the silver blade where it had begun to sever the ear from his head.

Alisa was consumed with a wild rage. She dropped her papers and pens, keeping only her walking stick, and screamed at Willis, "My God! What are you doing?"

"Get away from here, Alisa!" the small man warned, his eyes alight with eager anticipation.

"Let him go, Willis . . . now!" Alisa commanded harshly.

"This little bastard is my valet's son, and he has stolen something from me. I chased him through the woods, and he's lucky if I don't kill him. Now get the hell out of here!"

Alisa had seen immediately that there was no reasoning with the man. She moved with lightning speed, striking Willis in the side with a heavy blow of her walking stick. In surprise and pain, he eased his grasp of the boy's neck enough for the child to escape into a dense stand of trees. Seeing his prey flee, Willis Potts's rage had turned on Alisa.

"You bloody bitch," he snarled. "I'll teach you to meddle in my affairs!"

He lunged for her, but Alisa was more agile. She sidestepped his attack and hit him again with her stick, all of her weight and strength behind a blow to the back of his shoulders. She watched in horror as he tripped, his hands reached forward to catch himself, forgetting the knife he still carried. He slipped a second time, and his body fell onto the shiny blade with a convulsive flinch.

Alisa had rolled him to his back in dread. The knife was embedded at an angle from below his rib cage up into the left side of his chest, the hilt alone protruding from his blood-soaked vest. She searched frantically for a pulse and failed to find one. She pressed her ear to his nose, hoping desperately for a faint breath. With a cold shiver, Alisa realized Willis Potts was dead.

Alisa shook her head, trying to clear it of the horrible picture, but it was useless. She had run back to the estate house as if demons chased her, with the intention of sending for the constable and Lord Potts. Ivy had taken control of the situation, raving as always about Alisa's softheadedness. She convinced Alisa of the extreme danger in bringing in the law, in admitting anything at all. Instead they had ridden together to the morbid scene and dragged the cold, lifeless body into the woods. Ivy's plan then had been only to buy them some time before the body was found, time in which she could devise a way to save herself from the scandal of having her sister hang for murder. Ivy had no selfless thoughts.

When at last they returned to the estate house, Ivy's color had been high, her features animated, her voice rapid, as though she were enjoying the excitement. She had propelled Alisa into the carriage, plotting and planning the entire way back to London.

Alisa's eyes opened to the dawning September sun. Her mind was clear, but still she could find no better solution to the situation. She had to escape England. She could not remain and hang for murdering Willis Potts. The body was hidden, but sooner or later it would be discovered.

Alisa felt guilt, as well as remorse and fear, not only for Willis Potts, but also for the deception that had trapped Christian Reed. What else could she do? Alisa squared her shoulders in strength and determination. Marrying Christian Reed was her only salvation, the sole means for her to escape the gallows. She reasoned that she brought to the union a large, much-sought-after dowry. And, she vowed, she would be a good, amenable, undemanding wife, and she would never hinder whatever pleasurable pursuits Christian might choose after their marriage. She would repay the debt of forcing him to save her life.

Alisa breathed deeply to still her pounding heart. It was a despicable thing to do to an innocent man. It was more contemptible even than killing Willis Potts, for that had been an accident. Alisa knew there would be no escape from guilt. But she also knew she could not face the hangman's noose.

In a few hours, she would marry Christian Reed. She had no choice.

Chapter Five

Alisa stood rigidly through the ceremony that joined her in marriage to Christian Reed. The minister that Ivy had arranged for was a bit bleary-eyed and slurred the words he had difficulty reading from his book. His hair was combed neatly, but from its oily sheen, Alisa doubted it had been washed yet this month. It was a stark contrast to his white collar, which was so crisp that it appeared new.

Each word, each phrase of the ceremony echoed in Alisa's mind like an accusation. It seemed ludicrous to promise to love and cherish as she stood beside a man she neither knew nor loved. She fought a feeling of being dwarfed beside his height and iron-hard girth. She could not quite free her mind of the picture of his controlled features as she walked to him, the creases in his cheeks deepened by his clenched jaw. He was the picture of stoic acceptance. It was nothing more than an arranged marriage, she told herself.

She wished Christian were less handsome, less virile, less of all that made him a man. She suddenly felt a twinge of fear, of being at his mercy when he discovered her deceit. She could sense his implacable, iron will as she stood next to him. This was not a man who would easily forgive her, nor did she feel she merited easy forgiveness.

Christian was an extremely attractive man. Alisa's midnight-blue eyes studied him covertly from beneath thick copper lashes. He was at least three inches past six feet tall. His shoulders were broad enough to strain the well-tailored broadcloth of his black suit coat, its cut and quality speaking of the man's good taste. His legs were long and his waist narrow behind hands that were clasped together. His hands fascinated Alisa as she stared at them, seeing the golden hairs growing lightly at their backs; his fingers were long and powerful, his nails short and well manicured. She had no doubt that they could easily hurt or even maim, but she wondered if they could also soothe, comfort and caress. Her pale cheeks suddenly suffused with color. To draw her thoughts away from what it would feel like to have those massive, masculine hands upon her skin, she tried to view his face.

The man was amazingly handsome. His eyes were a transparent, pale bluish-green, the color of cool, clear seawater, beneath bushy eyebrows the same dark golden sand color as the wavy hair that framed his face. His nose was aquiline above a full, thick, meticulously groomed mustache. His cheeks were deeply creased with indentations that eased into a strong, square jaw. Full, sensuous lips finished an appearance that left Alisa just a bit breathless. She knew that this man would command adoring glances from the most exquisite women.

Though Ivy and Alisa resembled one another, Alisa had always viewed herself as less attractive than her sister. She knew that she was considered comely, but she had never had Ivy's inclination to spend hours dressing, adorning and coiffing herself. She only hoped she did not repulse the man she had entrapped in marriage.

She swallowed thickly as the minister pronounced them man and wife. Christian turned to her formally, his features so solemn, they seemed more fitting for a funeral. Alisa could not manage even a small smile; she stared wide-eyed up at her new husband in wonder. With slow, careful movements, Christian lowered his head to place a light, chaste kiss on the wild mass of curls.

"That's enough of that!" Aldis Todd's voice raged behind, still furious that Christian Reed would not pay for his crime.

Alisa heard Christian's indrawn breath as he stood like a stone statue, his jaw clenched visibly. As Aldis paid the minister and gruffly led him out of the house, Christian spoke to Alisa, ignoring Ivy, whose presence had become increasingly irritating to him.

"We sail at dawn tomorrow," he said stiffly. "I need to be on my ship until then to ready everything. If you would prefer, you can stay here and come out to the docks in the morning."

Aldis returned just in time to hear this. His blustery voice shouted before Alisa could answer, "That suits us all fine. I'll not have you taking my daughter in my own home again. But be warned, I'm sending three of my best men to watch your every move and to keep their guns on you. They will have orders to shoot you if it even looks like you're planning to run. I've already used what connections I have to keep your ship held at the dock until I give the word; a few comments in the right ears about what you might be loading in such a hurry accomplished that!

So don't even think about leaving your obligations behind you," Aldis finished smugly.

Christian's eyes were hard as he turned to face Alisa. He would accept his responsibility to her, but he was disinclined to portray the simpering penitent Aldis wanted. His guilt was a private matter, between himself and Alisa. He bowed formally before his new wife. "I will see you in the morning."

Alisa watched as Christian left her house. At least, she reasoned, consummating their vows would be postponed until she was safely out of England. Fear gripped her as she realized that Christian Reed would discover her virginity and the whole ugly deception in the middle of the cold waters of the ocean, where she would be totally defenseless.

Chapter Six

Dawn was just beginning to break as the Todd carriage stopped on the pier before the huge hull of Christian Reed's ship. Alisa was not a woman easily brought to tears, and so her farewell was quiet and solemn but dry-eyed.

Aldis descended first and, as Alisa gathered her reticule and the box that contained her pens, brushes and paints, Ivy lightly joined him on the docks. Alisa felt numb, as if all of her emotions had welled up to deaden her nerves. Calm resignation and her iron-clad inner strength propelled her this morning.

Aldis Todd was having difficulty believing the events of these past hours, and he knew only half of what had actually happened to his favored child. His voice was gravelly with emotion when he spoke to Alisa. "Have you hidden the money I gave you?"

"Yes, Papa," Alisa answered quietly, feeling suddenly like a small child.

The old man nodded brusquely. "Remember, Alisa, don't let him know you've got it. There is enough to feed and shelter you until you can find safe passage home, if need be. I know you, I know your stubborn pride and determination and that notion you have that you can take care of everything alone, but don't be putting up with anything from that man. If he doesn't treat you just as he should, you get back home. Will you promise me that?"

Alisa smiled wanly, touched by her father's words. "I promise you, Papa. You know I'd never tolerate a brute."

"Well, don't start now just because he's your husband! I don't feel right about this whole thing. Marrying you off to a man that's already abused you." The gray head shook, the brows drawing down into a deeply wrinkled scowl.

"I can take care of myself, Papa," Alisa reassured him.

"Hmph! If that was true, this whole thing would never have happened at all."

"Papa!" Ivy's voice interrupted impatiently. "Alisa will be fine. She's hardly a helpless little ninny, is she?"

Alisa wondered how Ivy could possibly appear so self-satisfied and smug after having hidden a dead body and trapped an innocent man into believing himself a rapist. Alisa had always known Ivy had no conscience, and now she actually seemed invigorated by it all. It was Alisa's turn to shake her head. She would never understand Ivy.

Christian Reed stood at the helm of his ship, watching the scene of parting on the dock below. He was plagued by self-disgust at the thought of having forced himself on any woman. It was a bitter brew to swallow.

His full brows puckered above pale eyes as he stared unabashedly at his second wife. As Alisa moved with her father toward the ship, Christian appreciated the pale skin framed in a wild mass of burnished copper waves falling to her waist in abandon. He remembered the intensity of those midnight-blue eyes beneath thick lashes, the small nose and gently curving lips the pale color of the season's first rose.

Still, Christian admitted as he watched Alisa walk up the gangplank, what attracted him to her most was the fact that she was unconscious of her own allure. She was exquisite, yet carefree and quietly untamed in comparison to Ivy's elaborately staged appearance and studied coquetry, which was reminiscent of Ellen. Christian far preferred Alisa, if he were ever to choose one woman over another again, which he was not. He told himself it was all an objective observation. Nothing more.

Christian moved to meet his wife and father-in-law as they boarded his ship. His heavy seaman's coat seemed to increase his already massive size. He nodded courteously to them, trying to bear in mind that Aldis had good cause for his contempt and distrust. "I would appreciate it if you would say your farewells and remove your guards. We must set sail with this tide as soon as possible."

Aldis's bluster was calmed by emotion, but his voice still held a note of strength. "I'm warning you now, Reed, you've treated my daughter badly, and if I had my way you'd rot for it. But seeing as that's not going to happen, I'll tell you this—and mark my words. If you ever do Alisa harm in any way, no matter how small, I'll hunt you down and you'll pay dearly for it!"

Christian was not a man to easily accept threats, but he held his temper in check. "I have no intention of harming your daughter more than I already have," he said evenly.

Aldis refused to comment, turning his back to Christian to face Alisa. "Remember, Alisa, remember where your home is." He kissed each ashen cheek gently and left hurriedly.

Christian waited, saying nothing as Alisa watched her father disembark. Not until he had entered his carriage and left the pier did Alisa sigh deeply and face her husband. Christian was surprised to see the lack of tears in a face etched with sadness. He was used to a woman's quick tears and hysterics; this quiet, resigned strength disconcerted him.

He cleared his throat, pulling his gaze away from eyes the same color of the sky in the darkness of night. He motioned to a young man who stood a short distance away. "Morgan will show you to your cabin. I'll be busy most of the morning, but as soon as we're at sea, I'll come below." He turned to the boy and said, "See to Mrs. Reed's needs and then get back on deck."

Again Alisa was left to watch his broad, departing shoulders. For the first time, she wondered just exactly what Christian Reed thought about this whole situation and, more importantly, what he thought about her.

Chapter Seven

Alisa followed the wiry cabin boy to the captain's quarters. She found it difficult to balance herself against the motion of the ship, finding the floor lower than her step anticipated, as it forced her stationary foot higher. Already the gentle swaying left her stomach in knots and her gorge rising. She worried that a new complication would be added to this already odd situation. She feared the horrible, debilitating seasickness that would rob her of what little remained of her dignity.

She quickly dismissed the cabin boy, hoping that when she was alone she could calm her worries and with them her stomach. The cabin was not large, holding only a carved desk, a table and chairs, an iron stove and a large trunk at the foot of a narrow bed. It was clean, the woodworking all polished to a high gloss and everything arranged to allow the most space possible. At that moment, Alisa was unconcerned with her accommodations, and sought to pry open the large porthole before she dropped to sit on the cushioned ledge beneath it. She fell back against the wall, hoping that breathing deeply of the cold air might settle her reeling stomach before her newly acquired husband discovered her embarrassing infirmity.

Hearing Christian's voice just outside the door, she sat up, erect. Her ashen face was a clue to the turmoil in her stomach, but she forced herself to appear well in control.

Christian stopped only a few feet into the room. "Why the hell is it so cold in here? Why wasn't a fire lit in the stove?" His eyes fell to Alisa, a scowl forming as he eyed her suspiciously.

"I was enjoying the sea air," she lied feebly, her voice soft with the effort to hold down her gorge.

Before Christian could utter a word, Alisa clasped one hand over her mouth and dove for the chamber pot against the wall. Neither determination nor complete embarrassment could force her stomach to retain its contents. As she retched in humiliation, Christian moved about the room against her fervent wish that he would leave. He dampened a cloth with water from a pitcher on the table and waited quietly for her to finish. Without a word, he handed her the cloth.

Her voice was barely audible as she remained kneeling on the floor, refusing to face him. "Would you please leave me to collect myself?"

"I will leave you to rest after I've seen you tended to properly."

Alisa was surprised by the note of compassion in his voice, but it did little to ease her shame. "I can tend to myself. Please!"

Christian ignored her plea and reached one large hand out to lift her gently to her feet. "It didn't occur to me that you might be seasick. If I had known, I would have sent someone to sit with you."

In vivid contrast to the gray pallor of her skin, two

bright spots of red blazed on her high cheekbones.
She could not meet Christian's gaze as he removed
her short jacket and led her like a child to the bunk.
"Lie down, Alisa. I have a draught that will help you
to sleep, at least."

She accepted the glass he pressed into her hand.
She felt him pull a heavy woolen blanket over her.
After rinsing the cloth, he again placed it gently on
her brow. He moved the chamber pot to the side of
the bed before he spoke again. "I'll send Morgan to
light a fire and empty the chamber pot. He will sit
outside the door; if you need anything, just call for
him. I have to be on deck."

Alisa's voice was soft, her eyes pressed tightly
shut. "I'm sorry, Christian. I didn't mean to be a
bother."

She did not see the hand that instinctively moved
to smooth her hair, but before it touched her, Christian thought better of the gesture and plunged it into
the pocket of his heavy coat. He said nothing more,
leaving Alisa alone with her mortification.

Long past the usual time that Christian usually
retired for the night, he stood at the railing, staring
out into the starless, black distance. He was reluctant to go below to his cabin and Alisa, though her
illness was not the cause. Not until he had found her
there this afternoon had he actually begun to realize
that he was married to her, owing her total allegiance and love he knew he would never feel again.
Seeing her there, in his bed, he had also felt the stir-
rings of an unbidden desire for her.

His overwhelming emotion was guilt. She seemed
such an innocent, the kind of inexperienced young
woman he had avoided all his life. He had always

sought women like Ellen, or even Ivy, who knew what they would get from him and what they wanted.

A deep frown pulled at his handsome features. He truly believed Alisa to be naive, but he also sensed a steely strength emanating from her. He could not help but think that she could handle whatever came her way. But Christian could not quite deal with his growing desire for the woman he had apparently defiled. He could not reconcile his desire and his guilt, and so he vowed to forestall consummating this sham of a marriage. Even more, he needed to placate the guilt he believed left him vulnerable, and to approach her only when he could view her in a completely unemotional way.

He mentally pulled a mantle of reserve around himself like a suit of armor and moved at last to his quarters. Guilt was a new feeling for him, one that he did not like.

Chapter Eight

"Please don't take any more off!" Alisa spoke in instant reaction to rousing from a deep sleep to find Christian undressing for bed. Panic struck at the sight of his bronzed, naked chest as his hands lowered to his breeches.

The cabin was dimly lit by only one candle on the desk. One bushy brow rose in surprise, but his features rapidly settled into indifference. His deep voice was patient and courteous. "I realize that I have caused you a great deal of disruption, Alisa. But the fact remains that we must share this cabin, for I have no intention of leaving it. I certainly don't want to shock you, but it is impossible for you to be completely spared the sight of me unclothed. I would think there would be no surprises for you, anyway."

Alisa said softly, "I don't think I am asking too much to be allowed a small bit of modesty, at least until we are better acquainted."

"It is not possible to become better acquainted than we were the other night."

"I prefer forgetting the entire incident and beginning this relationship as any two people might who have just entered an arranged marriage."

"This marriage is my punishment for a crime I

cannot even remember committing," Christian said flatly.

"Do you mean to punish me in response?"

"I don't consider your viewing me dressing or undressing as punishment. If you do, perhaps you should have sought refuge in a convent."

By now, Alisa's voice was loud as tension spurred her temper to rise above her ailment. "It is insufferably arrogant for you to believe viewing you unclothed is some sort of treat."

"Hardly that," he retorted sarcastically.

With a sudden lurch, the ship veered to one side and then righted itself again. Alisa's stomach responded violently. She barely reached the chamber pot before her churning, aching middle rebelled, though there was nothing left in it. It did serve to quell her anger and bring a semblance of sanity back to her as she fell against the mattress weakly.

Christian's anger, too, had cooled as he reminded himself that he was the villain here, not she. He prepared more of the draught he had administered in the afternoon, handing it to her in silence.

When Alisa had downed the entire contents, she said quietly, "I realize this is your cabin. If you would arrange for other accommodations I would be happy to move."

"Alisa"—Christian sighed her name—"I don't mean to be harsh. I am angry with myself, at my own weaknesses and the fact that I lost my control enough to do such a thing to you. It's a dark side of myself that I'm having difficulty accepting."

His features clouded, and his eyes moved from Alisa guiltily. "First of all, a sea voyage is a long and lonely journey, and you are far too tempting a morsel to men who will become increasingly more . . . hungry, shall we say. You would not be safe anywhere but in my cabin. Secondly, until we reach my home, which has many rooms to spare, there is no space open aboard this ship for you to move to. I give you my word that I will not lay a hand on you throughout this trip, so you needn't concern yourself with that. There will be time enough to consummate this marriage when we reach my home."

The medication had left Alisa too drowsy to argue. "This bed is not large enough for two people," she managed slowly.

He chuckled mirthlessly. "Under certain circumstances it can be done, but unless we encounter bad weather, I will hang a hammock and leave you the bunk."

"And if we encounter bad weather?" she asked, her eyes closed now.

"Then sharing the bed will not be an act deserving of punishment." He stared down at Alisa, hearing her last sigh before she dropped into a drugged sleep, wondering if she had heard his last words. A deep frown furrowed his brows as one large hand reached to smooth back a long, unruly strand of copper hair from where it fell across her cheek. He was impatient with himself, disgusted. He had thought love to be the most complicated state in which he had ever found himself. But this was far worse! Guilt, remorse, desire, fascination, all warred within him, but it was all encompassed in an overwhelming feeling of being trapped in a situation he would never have chosen for himself again, one that held only loathsome memories for him. He realized that he was hard-pressed not to resent Alisa for all of this, however undeserving she might be, simply because she was the instrument of his entrapment. Innocent or not, she was still the personification of a prison that he felt bound and punished him as surely as any cell.

Chapter Nine

A saltwater bath in a rain barrel was not Alisa's idea of a fastidious bath, but it was her only alternative. In the two days since she had boarded the ship, she had not even removed her traveling gown to sleep. Although she still felt dreadful, her stomach no longer attempted to rebel, so on her third morning at sea, Alisa decided she would feel better if she forced herself to rise, bathe and change her clothing. She was determined that if she could not altogether conquer her illness, she would at least fight it and strive to be more than an invalid on this voyage.

Having never bathed in anything but a tub, Alisa was at a loss as to the specifics of accomplishing her task. It had not occurred to her to ask Morgan for details when he brought the barrel in. So she set about devising her own system. The barrel was a large one, reaching nearly to her shoulders. A chair from the table worked nicely to aid her in climbing over the uneven edge into the steamy bath.

Alisa sighed, feeling the languorous magic that even warm salt water worked. She fought the urge to soak until the water turned cool, though it was an appealing thought. She had seen little of Christian since that first night, and she did not want him surprising her now. She worked quickly to lather the sweet-smelling soap, massaging deeply the muscles that ached from her long hours in bed. Next she soaped her long hair, scrubbing her scalp with a vengeance. Alisa could not remember having gone this long without a bath since childhood. She ducked under the water several times until her hair was rinsed and then wrapped a towel in a tight turban around her head.

Feeling pleased with herself, she decided it was time to leave her bath. Days of extreme illness and a complete lack of food had left her in a greatly weakened state. In fact, merely rising from her bed had sent her head spinning. The bath had refreshed and revived her. However, as she turned in a circle, she suddenly realized that she had not planned a way out, save to pull herself up onto the jagged edge and swing over onto the waiting chair. In any state of health, it would have been a difficult task because the barrel's edge was even with her shoulders. In her weakened state, it was impossible.

Alisa first tried facing the side and jumping as high as she could in hopes of rising far enough to hoist herself over. That failed. She tried kicking one foot up, trying to climb partially the inside of the barrel, but even its broad width would not accommodate her. She tried putting her back to the barrel's side, standing as far on her toes as possible to lift herself, again with a firm jump onto the edge. This, too, failed.

She sighed in frustration, leaning her forehead against the tall rim, cursing herself for not having considered this before she sank into the depths of the barrel. She decided that panicking was not going to solve her problem, and she breathed deeply, both to clear her thoughts and to summon every bit of her strength.

When Christian strode casually into the cabin, he found Alisa mumbling angrily to herself. "I didn't know you were feeling so much better," he said, his tone courteous but unemotional. He seemed unaware, or at least unconcerned, with her embarrassment at his intrusion on her toilette.

Alisa's face grew scarlet, for it was bad enough that he should find her completely naked in her bath. But she realized with a surge of embarrassment that she needed his assistance if she were ever going to be free of her wet prison.

She stared at Christian's broad back as he rifled through papers on the desk, apparently oblivious to her.

"Christian," she began, her voice matter-of-fact, for she would never whine or wheedle. "I'm afraid I have a bit of a problem."

Christian turned to face the barrel, seeing her cheeks flushed with color, deep midnight-blue eyes wide, almost challenging. He had been steadfastly avoiding the sight of her. One bushy brow rose, but he said nothing.

"I . . ." Alisa's voice cracked and was an octave higher than normal, so she paused to clear her throat. "I know it seems foolish, but I can't get out of here."

Christian's scowl was not reassuring. Alisa had no way of knowing her predicament left him as uncomfortable as it did her. "Why the hell didn't you put a bucket in before you got in?" His irritated tone did nothing to soothe Alisa; instead, it struck a note of anger in her.

"I have never before bathed in a barrel! I was not

aware of the practice, nor do I see how bailing the water out would help!"

Christian sighed deeply, turning his head to one side, eyelids dropping over pale bluish-green eyes in exasperation. "I will have to lift you out."

Alisa's eyes grew wider still. "Isn't there a ladder or something I could use? Or get a bucket and I will bail out the water, though I still don't understand how that will help."

Christian's voice rose slightly in his impatience at her ignorance. "You don't bail the damn water out! You put the bucket in upside down on the bottom of the barrel so you can sit on it while you bathe and step onto it to get out. You can't get the bucket in there now because you are taking up the space."

Alisa's thickly lashed lids closed slowly, and she wondered briefly if drowning might be preferable. "Surely there must be some other way."

"I can call in one of my crewmen if you prefer," he taunted.

Alisa's eyes opened, her chin raised. She refused to be ridiculed by his sarcasm. She unwrapped the towel from her hair, letting the dark russet curls fall in a heavy, wet mass down her back. With midnight-blue eyes glaring at him, she pushed the towel into the water and then wrapped the sopping cloth around her torso to give herself at least some modesty. "If it's the only way, please get it over with," she said finally.

She attributed Christian's ragged breath to fury as he lifted his large muscular frame onto the chair with one booted foot. Powerful hands reached beneath her arms, pressing each palm to her sides, where, to her dismay, he encountered the soft swell of her breasts through the tightly wound towel. With barely any exertion, he lifted her free, depositing her unceremoniously on the floor. Before Alisa could take a breath, he strode out the door, only to fling it open again and storm to his desk to retrieve the papers he had come for in the first place.

Before he slammed out of the cabin, his deep voice growled, "Next time use a damn bucket!"

Alisa jumped slightly at the sound of the crashing door, staring after it for several seconds. She could not decide whether she was grateful that he had neither gazed at her nearly bare form, nor allowed his hands to linger on her body; or if she was offended by his lack of interest and his ability to resist her womanly charms. Her response was to fling the wet towel from around her torso at the door.

Christian heard the soggy thud as he leaned against the wall outside the cabin, breathing deeply to gain control of himself, willing the hardness of his desire for her to soften again before he could face his men.

Chapter Ten

Alisa sat wearily on the bed watching Christian work at his desk. It seemed that she was doomed to stare at her husband's back through eternity. She wondered if he so despised the sight of her that he could not bear to face her. She saw clearly that he was reluctant to allow his gaze to touch her for more than a moment's time, and then only if it could not be avoided.

Alisa observed the broad, powerful shoulders as his thickly muscled arms moved over his desk. He was an extremely handsome man, and he piqued her interest more than she cared to admit.

When Morgan had served their meal, Alisa wondered if her husband would deign to speak to her. She reminded herself of her vow to be an undemanding wife but reasoned that simple civility and common courtesy were not asking too much.

Christian's deep voice interrupted her silent fuming as she pushed her plate away and slowly sipped the weak tea she had requested. "Have you eaten at all since we left London?" he asked conversationally.

"I seem to do best with nothing in my stomach," she replied in the same tone.

"I thought after this morning's romp in the bathtub that you were well."

Color heightened Alisa's pale cheeks, but blue eyes met his levelly. "I don't feel well, but I saw no reason to lie in bed throughout this voyage. I felt no better there."

One brow rose as Christian stared at her, his gaze assessing. "We'll be lucky to reach Connecticut by December, Alisa. You cannot live for more than two months without food. You're too thin already."

It was on the tip of her tongue to ask what difference it made to him, but she thought better of it. "I will try to eat something tomorrow."

"I will tell Morgan to have the cook prepare anything on board that appeals to you."

"Thank you," she answered, wondering how to negate this formality. Were she Ivy, Alisa thought, she could employ her talent for banal small talk. But as it was, silence reigned until Alisa opted to speak straightforwardly. "I know you resent me and this entire marriage terribly. I'm sorry for that," she said bluntly.

Christian sat back in his chair, his bluish-green eyes staring at her in surprise. After a time he spoke, his tone stilted with his apparent discomfort at this subject. "You have nothing to apologize for, Alisa. If I understand the situation correctly, you were only concerned for my well-being. You did nothing to provoke . . . the attack."

"I was not apologizing for that, but for the fact that you so despise this marriage and me."

"This marriage is my fault. It is little punishment for something that should never have happened. Were I your father, I doubt if I would have shown such restraint. It was an abomination for me to have responded to your solicitude in that way."

"Still, you resent it," she persisted, hoping that if he aired his feelings, the aloofness might be dispelled.

"Yes, I resent it," he admitted finally. "My experience with marriage was not one I relish repeating."

"Why did you seek divorce? Papa would tell me nothing of your past."

Christian's expression clouded; his countenance froze. "There is nothing you need to know about my first marriage except that it was legally dissolved."

"I am just curious about it," she said a bit defensively.

Christian leaned forward over the table, his threatening visage looming before her. "My first wife was a bitch and a whore. I disposed of her. Nothing else is your business, and I will not tolerate any questions or fishing for information on the subject. Is that clear?"

"What seems clear is that you must have something to hide to be so fiercely against speaking of it to your present wife."

Christian rose from the table in a cold fury. "My present wife"—his tone rang with disdain at those words—"should consider my wishes and practice wisdom in provoking a temper I should think she would be loath to incite again. Be warned, Alisa, my opinion of women is low, and at the moment, my patience is lower still."

Alisa's chin rose so that her stare met his evenly. "I am not afraid of you, Christian Reed," she lied.

"I would think you had learned well to fear me, Alisa Reed."

"Perhaps I have seen you at your worst," she retorted with false bravado.

"And then again, perhaps you haven't."

Chapter Eleven

Alisa awakened early on the fifth day at sea, finding herself alone in the cabin. As in each morning past, the hammock was removed from its position beside the bunk, and all traces of Christian were gone from the room. She sat up slowly, hating the ever-present nausea. If she moved cautiously, she was better able to control her constantly rising gorge, but only if she carefully avoided all but the blandest foods consumed in the smallest quantities.

She decided to dress and take an early-morning stroll. She donned a sedate brown velvet gown with a high ivory lace collar and cuffs. The longest task was brushing her hair, which reached to her waist in a full, wild mane of thick curls that defied even the hard bristles of her tortoiseshell brush. By the time the shining mass was free of any knots or tangles, Alisa's patience was spent. For her journey on deck, she simply caught her hair with a ribbon at the nape of her neck, leaving it to fall over the heavy woolen shawl she wore to ward off the chill that grew more noticeable each day.

As she left her cabin, she half expected Morgan to pounce on her like a wary cat from some place in the corridor. She realized that the cabin boy's duty was

51

to foresee the captain's wants and needs, but Alisa had the feeling that, among his jobs, Morgan had undertaken to appease her every whim lest she disturb Christian. She was not pleased with Morgan's role as buffer, as if she were some annoyance he tried to spare his captain.

Reaching the ship's deck without encountering Morgan pleased Alisa unaccountably, leaving her to think that boredom had reduced her to petty childishness. Dawn was only a scant hour old, and the air was crisp. Alisa's first breath cleared her lungs with the unexpected coldness. It felt more invigorating, because of her past days in a stuffy cabin.

As she walked slowly to the railing, she saw no one around and assumed that the crew was still abed. She began to wander among the coiled ropes and riggings, weaving amidst barrels, planks, rough crates and boxes stacked high, huge tarps and canvases rolled tight and masts rising to the just brightening sky.

As she roamed, she heard men's voices in the distance. She had little inclination to meet Christian's crewmen, but she craved the sight and sounds of other people. She did not at first realize what the group of men gathered around several barrels were doing. When she drew near, she saw they were in various stages of undress as some drew wet sponges from the barrels to wash themselves and others merely discarded soiled clothes for clean ones. The sight of a bare rump shocked her, and she gasped. The man hurriedly pulled up his trousers and turned in her direction.

A loud guffaw attracted the attention of the remaining men, who laughed boisterously and made ribald comments. Alisa took a few steps backward, not wanting to merely turn and run like a frightened rabbit. As she spun on her heel, she crashed face-first into the iron-hard girth of Christian's chest.

"What the hell is going on here?" he shouted, his face ablaze.

"Seems yer new missus come to pay a call, Cap'n!" one brave hand answered from the rear, to the raucous laughter of his mates.

"Alisa." Christian said nothing more than her name, but it was enough for her to sense his rage. Powerful fingers clasped her wrist painfully as he firmly dragged her across the deck, his crew's boisterous laughter echoing behind them, down the steps and through the corridor to their cabin. Christian fought the urge to fling her against the bed, but his anger impelled him to push her several steps into the room.

"That was unnecessary!" she breathed, midnight-blue eyes bright with a fury to match that which she faced.

"What the hell were you doing up there?" he demanded.

"I went for a walk!"

"You went for a walk." He mocked her words. "Do you have a penchant for being raped? Maybe once wasn't enough!"

"It was nothing more than an accident that I stumbled upon your men."

"You had no damn business being on deck!"

"Just what do I have business doing? Perhaps you would rather lock me away? I can't so much as speak to you, and certainly it is useless to expect even small talk from you. Your cabin boy hovers about this door trying to protect you from my unwelcome presence at every turn, sparing you from having to remember I exist. And now I am not allowed to leave this prison of a room to even go on deck. It's a wonder I have business breathing! You totally ignore me, and if you deign to speak, it's in monosyllables, without even looking at me! I am allotted as much attention as the rats that cannot be kept from infesting the hold, and not as much consideration! If you have chosen to punish me by denying my very existence, you are succeeding."

"I thought you were too ill to do anything *but* stay in this cabin."

"I may be seasick, but I am not dead. And how would you know anything at all when you act as though the very sight of me disgusts you? If this is how you treated your first wife, it's no wonder she sought someone else." Alisa regretted her words the moment they were spoken.

Christian's furious expression hardened into a mask of indifference that disturbed Alisa more than his anger. "Is it a husband's attentions you want, Alisa?" His voice was soft, silky, threatening her as he drew near one slow menacing step at a time. "Were your appetites awakened more than I thought by our encounter? I had meant to allow you some time to forget the incident, but since it seems you set out to find another man to repeat it, there is no need for my patience, is there? Certainly I will not refuse your needs and give you cause to practice the same deceits as my first wife. Did I awaken a whore's desires in you? It is something I do well, it seems." Christian stood just above Alisa, his pale bluish-green eyes holding hers mesmerized.

"N-no!" she stammered. "You don't understand. I needed only fresh air."

His only answer was a cruel smile as he lowered

his lips to hers in a fierce assault, his large hands at her shoulders pulling her tight against his broad chest, nearly lifting her from the floor. Her head was bent sharply back, though there was no pain. Instead his warm, slightly moist lips drew a response that she had never experienced from the safe, chaste pecks of her suitors. Fear was her first reaction, fear that the rape she had accused him of might indeed be committed. But she quickly realized that although he used his strength, there was no violence in him, only intense, turbulent emotion. Her inexperience and initial trepidations delayed her response, but within moments, her own lips parted, finding pleasure in the feel of his mouth on hers, and his body pressed against her, his hands supporting her arched back.

His tongue thrust its way between her parted lips and into her mouth, urgently searching. The strength of his forearm replaced the hands that had pressed her back, freeing one to cup her breast through the fabric of her dress. He filled his palm with it, kneading it in a way that sent shivers of delight down her spine.

She was lost in the kiss and a sensual delicacy that was new to her. She did not expect to be released with a suddenness that sent her reeling back against the near wall. Her eyes flew open to see Christian's tormented face. His hands ran through his dusky golden hair as his head shook in disbelief. "My God, Alisa! I'm sorry! I see now just how capable I am of using force on a woman. It won't happen again." He moved to the cabin door, but Alisa's voice stopped him.

"Christian," she said softly, wanting more of what had just passed between them. "I don't want to be forced, but I don't want to be ignored, either!" Her face flamed with the thought of what she wanted to say but couldn't bring herself to. "I'm sorry for the circumstances of this marriage, too, but can't there be something between refusing to acknowledge me and rape?"

"I don't know, Alisa. I know it's unfair to you, and I assure you, I will do my damnedest so that nothing like this happens again. But other than that, I'm not sure there is a middle ground." Christian turned from her but paused before he left the room. Once again he spoke without looking at her, as if he could not bear to meet her eyes. "Don't go out of this cabin without me, is that understood?" His voice was harsh, commanding.

"Yes," Alisa answered dejectedly. She was left with a slowly growing guilt at his pain and a frustration she was not sure she understood. She wondered what would happen when this marriage was consummated and Christian learned that his torment had been all for naught.

Chapter Twelve

In her sleep, Alisa did not at first understand the intense wave of nausea that fought its way to her throat, but consciousness dawned abruptly as her mind registered the fact that the meager contents of her stomach were about to depart. She fell from her bed, having long since stopped keeping the chamber pot beside the bunk. She fumbled frantically in the pitch blackness, barely finding it in time.

When she had finally stopped retching, she realized that the ship was in the throes of a fierce November storm. Alisa stood very carefully, working to maintain a semblance of balance and to control the awful feeling in her middle. Trying to find a candle or lantern, she got caught in the wildly swaying empty hammock that Christian usually removed when it was not in use. After several attempts, she finally managed to free herself. With shaking fingers, she struck a sulfur match and lit a small lantern on the desk.

In the dim glow, the cabin seemed alive, as everything that was not securely attached danced with the violent sway as the ship tossed like a mere toy.

Rain, snow, sleet and savage winds buffeted the large vessel for two days. Alisa had no sense of time passing as she alternated between violent illness and exhausted slumber, remaining amidst blankets on the cold floor, for she could not fight to maintain a place on the bunk.

She was only vaguely aware of the cabin boy's infrequent visits. She was too ill to worry that they all might find a watery grave so near the end of the voyage.

Just past midnight on the third night, Alisa was awakened in her cocoon of blankets on the floor by the silence in the aftermath of the storm.

The lantern Christian carried as he entered the cabin illuminated the small space brightly. He had not slept or eaten throughout those three days, and he looked every bit as exhausted as he was. He walked only two steps into the room when his gaze fell on the heap of quilts on the floor. Beneath them, Alisa's head was visible, her wide blue eyes sunk in deeply shadowed sockets in her pale face. He had worried about Alisa's seasickness as he waged war with nature, but Morgan had repeatedly told him how well Alisa was doing. Because he had witnessed her strength and determination, he believed his cabin boy. One sight of Alisa was enough for him to realize that Morgan had taken it upon himself to ease some of Christian's burdens with lies.

He knelt beside Alisa, one rough hand moving to her brow gently, finding it cool. "How long have you been like this, Alisa?" he asked, his concern ringing in his tone and etching his fatigue-lined face. His deep voice was soft, soothing, like a balm to Alisa's sorely strained body and mind.

"Since the storm began. I don't think I will ever be a sailor." She managed a feeble jest, wanting to maintain his warm kindness for that moment.

"I didn't know! Morgan told me you were faring well. I had no idea you were like this. Why aren't you in bed at least?"

"I couldn't stay there. Every time I slept, it seemed to toss me out onto the floor."

Christian smiled wearily. "This whole thing has been a nightmare for you, hasn't it?"

"I seem to move from one to another lately," she said before judging her words. Christian assumed only that she spoke of those horrors he believed himself to have inflicted upon her.

Strong, powerful arms slid beneath her as he lifted her easily from the floor. "You need to be in bed, Alisa. I'll see to it that you aren't tossed out again."

Alisa was too weak and too drained to wonder what he meant. She lacked the desire and the strength to fight his ministrations. He lowered her gently to the bunk, setting her near the wall behind it. Weakly, she watched him douse the lantern and peel away his wet clothing, his silhouette outlined in the faint light that filtered in from the porthole. He donned a dry set of seaman's long underdrawers, and then slid into the narrow bunk beside her.

"It's best if we share our body heat against the chill. I don't want you to get sicker than you are. And this way you won't wake up on the floor," he explained softly.

He pulled Alisa gently to his side, resting her head against one muscular shoulder; his massive arms encircled her to form an exquisitely warm cradle. Alisa sighed and allowed her own body to curl into his instinctively.

She did not understand what had brought about this change in Christian, but she far preferred it to the remote, coldly courteous sea captain of the past weeks. Her fervent wish was that somehow, in the storm, the reserved, aloof captain had washed overboard and left only the gentle, sensitive man she rested against now.

Dawn was barely breaking when Alisa rolled to her back in the guise of a stretch, careful to keep her side pressed lightly to Christian lest he believe she wanted to dissolve their closeness. Since Christian was of a like mind, he merely clasped his hands beneath his head, remaining otherwise immobile.

"Are you feeling any better, Alisa?" he asked kindly.

"Yes, I am better than I was during the storm, but I'm beginning to wonder if I will ever know what it is to be free of a queasy stomach."

A sudden frown creased Christian's handsome features. "I have never known anyone to be so ill for so long. Is it possible that you carry a child?" he asked in a tone so low as to be barely audible.

"No," Alisa answered a bit too quickly.

"Think about it, Alisa. It is a possibility, you know. It would be an unfortunate reminder of that night for us both, but if it's true, there is no sense in denying it. You do know how a woman tells if she is pregnant, don't you?"

Guilt and embarrassment swept over Alisa, his words a reminder of her ugly lie. Her voice matched his in softness. "It is only seasickness that plagues me."

An unmistakable sigh of relief came from Christian's lips. "Good. The memory of that night in your father's guest room is one I hope you can forget."

Silence fell; but after a time, Christian spoke.

"Did I alter great plans for your future?" he asked, curiosity and regret mingling in his voice.

Alisa was so pleased that his cold manner had not returned that a small, melodic chuckle escaped her lips and lightened the tension. "Nothing that was not a pleasure to leave behind." She paused, fearful of her own curiosity. "What of you?" she said hesitantly.

A mirthless laugh sounded. "I had no plans to marry again."

Alisa knew where this turn in the conversation might lead. She had learned well that Christian's first marriage had left lasting scars. To preserve the tenuous warmth, she tactfully changed the subject. "Tell me of your family. My stepmother hid away in her room from early in her marriage to my father. So we didn't know you existed until just before you arrived."

"My mother was nothing at all like Deadra. It's hard to believe they were sisters. Both of my parents died helping others through a smallpox epidemic eight years ago. Now there are only my younger brother, Scott, and our cousin, Nicholas Lamb. Actually, we think of Nicholas as another brother. He was orphaned as a child, and my parents took him in. He was my father's ward. We were all raised together."

"Do Scott and Nicholas live near your home?"

Christian laughed lightly. "Very near. They live in it." He paused suddenly, bluish-green eyes staring down at her sternly; his voice becoming suddenly threatening. "Scott and Nicholas will live in my house as long as they choose. I am firm in this, so be warned that it will serve no purpose to try to drive them out."

"Why would I want to drive them out? Are they vile?"

"Of course not. I simply want it understood from the beginning that it is their home as much as mine."

In the brightening cabin, Alisa saw his expression grow tense. He was once again the forbidding sea captain.

However, Alisa was not a woman to shrink back in cowardice; neither would she easily accept losing what ground she had gained. "Since it is I who am the outsider in your home, Christian, I would never think of evicting your family. Even if I were a cherished wife I cannot think why I should forbid them from living in a place that was theirs long before I arrived. I have many faults, but without provocation, I would never do such a thing."

Christian fought to bring his unaccountable anger under control, so as not to further disrupt the enjoyable peace between them. One bushy brow rose as he reached out to toy with a wild curl on the pillow above Alisa's head. "And what could your faults be?" he mocked gently.

"I am thought by some to be stubborn, strongwilled and outspoken. And I haven't the patience to primp for hours to make myself attractive," she finished defensively.

Christian laughed loudly, tugging gently on the burnished curl wrapped around his long finger. "Whose opinion is that?"

"My sister's."

"For what it's worth, I disagree. You're very attractive just as you are."

Alisa felt inordinately pleased, though she had

never before cared what any man thought of her. "What of your faults?"

"I have none." Her first glimpse of his mischievous smile was engaging, lighting his dazzlingly handsome features as he smoothed his bushy mustache with his thumb and forefinger.

"I can think of just a few," she retorted.

"In the interest of tempering your flaw of outspokenness, I won't ask you to list them." Christian reluctantly swung himself out of bed, pulling on his breeches before he stood.

"Now I shall have to add cowardice to it," she rejoined, pleased with their banter.

"I have to see to some things on deck. Are you up to sharing my breakfast?"

"No, but I would enjoy having my tea while you eat." Her face was alight with happiness as a wide grin spread his sensuous lips in answer. He pushed down on the thought that he should not be enjoying this woman's company. He remembered too well when he had last found such pleasure in a woman, and it had led to pure misery. But for just this moment, he told himself, he would relax and enjoy it.

Chapter Thirteen

As Alisa stood at the railing, she could see little of New Haven. They were docking at the farthest end of the Long Wharf, a wood and stone platform that thrust thirty-five hundred feet out from the waterfront.

She stood bundled in a long woolen cloak, her hands pressed inside a fur muff for warmth. She felt both relief and regret when the ship arrived at last that early December morning. Still plagued with nausea from the ever-present sway of the ship, she felt eased by the thought that she would finally be well again. Still, in the past two weeks, her relationship with Christian had just begun to blossom. She was afraid that leaving the close confines of his ship would destroy their tentative attraction with the diversion of friends, family and business.

After their one night sharing her bunk, Christian had returned to his hammock, still maintaining a certain formality that was no longer cold, but it seemed to deny the growing intimacy between them.

Alisa greatly feared the discovery of her lie. She reasoned that if she could conceal her virginity from him when they finally consummated their vows, she could maintain her secret, and perhaps they could move forward from that point into a normal marriage. She vowed once again that if that happened, she would work hard to compensate Christian for trapping him into an unwanted marriage to save herself from hanging as a murderess.

She pushed down the echo of Ivy's past words about the horrors of lovemaking. She refused to believe Ivy's fear-inducing stories of great pain. She reassured herself that she would be able to hide any slight discomfort, that too much was at stake.

No, she told herself, he would never discover her virginity. If only she could lure him to her bed.

Alisa was surprised by the first sight of Christian's home. None of his descriptions had done it justice. The enormous two-story mansion was set so far back from the street that it could barely be seen beyond the high brick wall that surrounded the perfectly tended grounds. Even in winter, the city pleased Alisa with its clean, whitewashed buildings and its air of pride. She also liked the sound of a clock chiming the hour as they were admitted through the gate.

Enormous old elm trees lined the drive to the house, with high bushes filling the space between each weathered trunk. The carriage followed the curve of the lane to stop directly before the house. It loomed, a red brick structure with whitewashed shutters framing all six windows on the first floor and all ten on the second. An oversize door sat at the back of a large covered porch, a carved balustrade enclosing it. A large fanlight window marked the exact center above the second level. As she climbed the five steps to the veranda, Alisa felt dwarfed both by the structure and by the man beside her. She stood straighter and raised her chin slightly as she entered her new home.

Christian handed their coats to the obviously surprised butler, giving him instructions she could not hear. A massive staircase, the bottom nearly the entire width of the room, rose before her to the second floor. Each step narrowed so that the top was half the width of the bottom. Its dark wooden banister was polished to a high gloss and bordered it on either side, edging several feet of the upper level left open to the entrance.

Dismissing the butler, Christian turned to Alisa. "I'll show you quickly around the house, and then I must return to my ship."

Did she detect a return of aloof disdain? Or was her own fear clouding her impression? Alisa's eyes met his evenly, searching for some sign where no expression at all was present. "If this is too tedious a task I'm sure I can find my own way."

"It will not take long," he answered curtly. The memories of his former wife made him uncomfortable. On top of this, he must somehow explain his hasty marriage to a family who knew of his vow never to repeat his mistake.

As she followed him through the house, Alisa was now certain that whatever ground she had gained in the past two weeks was lost again. She could feel Christian growing more remote, and her spirits sank. She would never allow him to know how much his rapidly changing moods affected her. She pulled her own mantle of reserve around herself, as much for protection as for appearance, as she tried to think only of the splendor unfolding before her.

The front parlor to the left of the stairs was a formal, imposing room with walls covered in hand-stenciled wallpaper from France. It was a room meant for entertaining; long sofas and many chairs lined the walls or formed more intimate groupings within the space. There were three chandeliers to light it and two fireplaces to keep away the chill. An arched door opened to an almost identical back parlor, which was used as the smoking room. An enormous ballroom and equally large formal dining room completed that side of the house.

Christian directed her next to the section on the right of the stairway. The drawing room at the front of the house here was far less formal. The walls were paneled and painted sage green, and the door frames and woodworking were all a warm beige hue. Shutters of the same paneling slid over the windows, blending identically into the wall on either side. Cupboards lined the space above the mantel to store an array of pewter plates and pitchers. The furnishings were all of polished oak, upholstered in deep green velvet and brocade. Farther back was the morning room, with a window-lined wall, brightening the pale yellow wainscoting that surrounded the room. The chairs encircling a large pedestal table were covered in a matching pale yellow.

The room that appealed to Alisa beyond all others was the library. It was an enormous space filled with book-lined shelves and brown velvet sofas and chairs. The hearth was a large, carved piece set between French doors on either side, which opened onto a wide terrace. Beyond that, Alisa could see brick-paved rows winding through a garden. She felt an immediate sense of security in this room, knowing it would be a refuge for her. It was as though this particular space welcomed her and made her feel less like an intruder.

The middle level of the house held ten bedrooms with adjoining sitting rooms opening off both sides of the wide center hallway.

The only room Alisa could not endure was the master suite. She found no fault in the quality of its furnishings, but when she first stepped through the doorway, she had an intense but inexplicable sensation of another woman's presence. She felt certain Christian had shared this room with his former wife. The thought of sleeping for even one night in the same bed they had shared was abhorrent to her.

Alisa lifted midnight-blue eyes to Christian and spoke with determination. "I cannot use this room."

One bushy brow rose in query.

"I cannot sleep in the bed that was used by your first wife."

"What makes you think I intended for you to sleep here?" he said cruelly, his own ugly memories of this room spurring him to strike out at her.

Alisa's face flamed with humiliation. "I assumed . . ." She could not finish.

Christian's voice was curt. "You may use any room you wish, Alisa, save those already occupied." He turned to leave without even a farewell, his own emotions at war.

Alisa did not want him to go, but her own pride forbade her doing more than delaying him with small talk. She forced her tone to sound indifferent. "Might I also have a room for a studio? My easel is large and I have a great many pens and brushes."

Christian barely turned to her, his eyes over her head at an invisible spot on the wall, his voice distant, as if addressing someone already dismissed. "The light in the attic is good. I'll send a servant to clean it and you can use that. I can't abide the smell of those paints." Without another word, he left, his large muscular frame moving with erect stiffness down the hall.

Alisa watched in dejection, thinking that the smell of paint was not the only thing Christian Reed could not abide.

Chapter Fourteen

Alisa woke feeling like little more than a wrinkle in the huge bed whose four massive posts reached nearly to the ceiling. She slid upward to brace her back against the smooth, undecorated headboard.

The room she had chosen for herself was as large as the master bedroom, the walls a soft blue-gray color like the stain of fresh blueberries in cream. The woodworking was pure white as were the heavy ball-fringed drapes that covered the windows. A small blue brocade-covered sofa sat before the white-paneled hearth at the opposite end of the room, and two tall wardrobes lined a wall to one side. A lovely carved dressing table with a washstand and a bureau rested against the fourth wall.

There was no question that this chamber could easily accommodate Christian as well. She sighed in tension and frustration. Hours after Christian had abruptly left her, he sent a message that he would remain aboard his ship to see to the unloading. The note had not even been addressed to Alisa, and she had neither seen nor heard from him since.

Alisa had seen no one in the past two days, discovering from servants that Christian's brother Scott and his cousin Nicholas were both away on business.

71

She was understandably uncomfortable in her new surroundings, neither mistress nor guest.

Alisa stared into the popping fire in the hearth, appreciating its warmth and the fact that Ann, her personal maid, had silently crept in to start it and left her a tray with steaming tea and English biscuits.

She sipped her tea but could not eat the biscuits. After dressing, she quietly left her room, moving down the hallway to a small door and up a short flight of stairs to the attic. True to his word, Christian's servants had cleared out the large, open airy space to be used for her studio. The attic was allowed full daylight from three dormer windows at each side. The smell of beeswax and lemon was evidence that the space had been freshly cleaned, and the walls were freshly whitewashed. In the center stood a large easel beside a table holding canvas, parchment, paints, brushes and pens, all in perfect order.

Everything stood untouched; for though Alisa had spent all of her time here, she had not been able to put one stroke to paper. Instead she paced the room, or rearranged it, or peered with regularity from each window.

Anger and frustration warred within her against a strong guilt. She told herself firmly that Christian owed her nothing, not even courtesy, and that she had no right to expect anything from him. She should be grateful, she railed at herself, and certainly forever amiable to whatever Christian required of her, even if it was to accept being totally ignored.

But her pride was strong, and so, she admitted, was her attraction to Christian Reed. Had he been a fat old man with a wart on his chin, she doubted that she would be so furious with his treatment of her.

She had never played the part of a simpering female, so now she had not a clue as to how to go about becoming attractive to a man who had only contempt for her.

She endlessly analyzed those two short weeks at the end of their voyage, trying to find any small hint of what had changed Christian's attitude toward her. She always came up at a loss and was furious with him for leaving her alone.

Sudden noise and bustle shook the huge house from its morguelike silence of the past days. The quiet had become an irritant in itself, so Alisa's attention was immediately alerted to the sound of Christian's deep voice booming from the entrance hall.

Her elation quelled her anger and even her guilt for that moment. She ran to her bedroom, forcing herself to breathe deeply to calm herself. Defiantly, she decided not to change her gown but compromised by freeing her hair to brush it and bind it back with a fresh ribbon at the nape of her neck. The face that stared at her from the mirror seemed much too thin and pale, so she pinched her cheeks and bit her lips to add color.

Then she left her room slowly, following the sound of Christian's voice to the morning room.

The door stood ajar, and before Alisa opened it, she heard the sound of an unrecognizable man's voice answering Christian's. When her own name was spoken, she stopped abruptly, unabashedly eavesdropping in hopes of discovering how she had displeased Christian on the day of their arrival.

"Married? Oh, my God!" exclaimed the unfamiliar

voice. "I thought you had learned your lesson with Ellen. You swore you would never marry again. What the hell possessed you to do it, and so soon at that?"

Christian's deep voice was low, sounding distinctly uncomfortable. "It was not my choice, I can assure you. You may as well save your judgment of me until you've heard it all, Scott; it gets worse."

"How can it get worse?"

"I was forced to marry her or spend the rest of my life in prison for raping her."

A long, shocked silence followed before Scott answered, "That's definitely worse. What the hell happened?"

"I don't know. I don't remember any of it. I was dead drunk. They told me I went mad, calling her Ellen, and I raped her. The evidence was overwhelming, and since I could remember nothing, I could hardly deny it."

"How could you have done something like that, Christian?"

"There's no excuse for it. But like it or not, I had to marry her. I owed her at least that."

"And do you like it?"

"No!" Christian's loud, firm denial shot through Alisa like the blade of a rapier. "Dammit, Scott, you know better than anyone how it was with Ellen. I would *never* have chosen to marry again."

"What do you intend to do about it?"

"Nothing," Christian said in disgust. "Endure it in as painless a way as possible. What else can I do? God knows I am responsible and deserve the punishment."

"I wish I knew what to tell you, Christian." The voice was full of compassion.

Alisa swallowed hard, wanting to flee back to her room. Disappointment overwhelmed her. She pushed open the door, her chin high, her shoulders straight. She would have to face these men sooner or later, and at least they would not know how deep her humiliation was at the thought that now another person was privy to her deception.

"Ann told me you were back, Christian," she lied, pride and dignity emanating from her. Midnight-blue eyes locked with bluish-green as if each searched for some answer to their problems in the face of the other. What they both saw was anger and pain.

The sound of a throat clearing broke the tension. "Aren't you going to introduce me, Christian?"

Christian looked away as if he could not face his wife. "Alisa, this is my brother Scott. Scott, my wife."

Alisa's gaze moved to Scott. He was as tall as Christian and nearly as muscularly built. His sandy brown hair and blue eyes showed a recognizable similarity to Christian's, and though his smoother features were strikingly handsome, they did not affect Alisa as did Christian's more angular ones.

Scott towered above her, his engaging smile warming her. "Welcome to the family, Alisa." He held a chair out for her, openly admiring her. "I can't sit and talk with you now, much as I'd like to. Unfortunately, I have an appointment. Later perhaps?" Alisa nodded, liking his pleasant manner, so different from his brother's.

Scott spoke to Christian then, his tone full of insinuation. "Alisa is a bigger surprise than your news, Christian. You neglected to mention how unlike your past acquaintances she is. Perhaps you should open your eyes; I think the fates have made a wiser choice than you think."

Chapter Fifteen

"Are you well?" Christian asked indifferently as Scott closed the door behind him.

Alisa stared at her husband evenly. "I'm fine, thank you." She fought the urge to demand explanations. Even reminding herself of her guilt did not cool her frustrated anger.

"I went upstairs to change my clothes a short time ago. I found them in the master suite," Christian said accusingly.

Her finely arched brows rose. "Where did you expect to find them?"

"Where are yours?"

"You said I was free to choose whatever room I wanted," she reminded him.

"I don't give a damn what room you've chosen, but why the hell weren't my things moved there, too?"

Now Alisa stared at him as if he were insane. "I had no idea you wanted that! Perhaps you should make your desires better known." It was a poor choice of words, she knew, but fury reigned over good sense.

Christian was taken aback, watching her intently for a time before he spoke again. His own raging emotions and the desire that coursed through him at the first sight of her seemed an imposing threat. "Regardless of my misdeeds in England, you are now my wife, in my home, and there are certain things I require of you."

Again Alisa's brows shot up challengingly, but she did not speak; her past resolutions to please him drowned in her growing anger.

"I will not be forced to watch you grow fat with someone else's bastard. I have no intention of allowing you the opportunity of filling your empty bed with anyone else."

"I wish you would make up your mind," Alisa railed, all of her past fury and frustration surfacing. "You distinctly told me aboard your ship that your home had many rooms to spare. Before you left the other day, you said you did not intend for me to share your room."

"What I said the other day was that I did not intend for you to use the same room my first wife had."

"Which is your room! Nothing led me to believe you meant to share mine. Now you act as if I have forbidden you admission and am planning intimate trysts with a dozen lovers. I never know what I will face from you! You swing from cold disdain and contempt, to kindness and compassion, to this anger-filled tyrant. Either punish me or don't. Hate me or love me, but I cannot bear this never-ending pendulum."

Christian's bluish-green eyes turned cold and hard; he stared at Alisa as if he despised her. "You have my name, Alisa, as well as my home, my money, my protection and your honor. It is not you that I hate, but this situation and all it reminds me of. Don't ever expect love from me, for you will be badly disappointed. It is the one thing that no one can ever force from me, or even find in me again, for it no longer exists."

Christian rose abruptly and stormed out of the room. The sound of the front door slamming harshly echoed throughout the house.

It was very late before Alisa wearily descended the small stairway from her attic studio. The house was dark and peacefully silent.

As so often in the past, Alisa sought her pens and brushes as the weapons to release pent-up emotions; she was absorbed for hours in drawing a handsome face distorted with cruelty, a face that closely resembled Christian's. Finally calm, she put her unflattering pictures behind a stack of canvases and decided to go to sleep. She assumed Christian had disappeared again without a word as to when he could endure her presence enough to return. Even though it was she who had trapped Christian, she felt more the prisoner.

Christian's tirade had left her with no doubts that any love between them was impossible. She could live with that, for she did not love him. The raw pain she had seen in Christian was the hardest thing to bear. Alisa knew that she had taken a deep, open wound and poured salt into it. In her ignorance and inexperience, she never guessed that Christian had been hurt so desperately by his first wife. Small wonder that Christian hid his vulnerabilities well and guarded his personal feelings and privacy with fervor. Alisa pictured herself as the child hurling knives at the injured giant without realizing the damage she was capable of. She was deeply ashamed of herself and had no idea of how to make amends.

She saw the light from beneath the door to her

room, thinking that Ann had once again built a fire
in the hearth, lit a candle at the bedside and pulled
back, the downy quilts in anticipation of her comfort.
She smiled slightly, thinking that even in such a
short time, these small touches had become a wel-
coming sight. Tonight especially she needed that
soothing balm for her frayed nerves.

She pushed the door open and stepped through it,
her gaze lifted to her bed. Her eyes widened in
amazement. Sitting propped in the center of the
large mattress, his broad, muscular chest and flat
stomach bare above the blankets, sat Christian.

Chapter Sixteen

Christian studied her as she stood just inside the doorway, her small frame dwarfed by the high ceiling and door. Her weary face was a pale, luminous oval overshadowed by the wide, midnight-blue eyes, and her burnished copper hair tumbled in a long, wild mass of tangled curls. He thought her beautiful and very appealing. Even though he was not happy to be married again, he was beginning to accept his indisputable attraction to Alisa and his intense desire for her.

His voice was deep, resonant, with no trace of his former anger. It held a sensuous tone that stirred something instinctive within Alisa. "In the future, madam, I expect you to be at my table for every meal, regardless of your appetite. I will not tolerate your fits of temper disrupting the routines of this household." Although it was clear that Christian meant what he said, his tone held a hint of self-mockery.

A tentative smile lit Alisa's features. "I should think this household is quite used to having its routines disrupted," she countered. He should not find fault with that unexceptionable observation. She was still unsure of his mood.

"Alisa," he said more seriously, "I apologize to you for this afternoon. You were right to be angry with me. I realize that since our marriage I have been moody. I spent this afternoon thinking about what you said. If you are willing, I would like this marriage to take a more normal course so that we both might find some peace." His smile was devilish, drawing the creases in his cheeks to deepen into the square line of his jaw.

"What did you have in mind?" she said simply, hoping she had not sounded as anxious as she felt.

"My belongings have all been moved here. The rest is better shown than explained."

Alisa was not unwilling to join her husband in bed, but modesty and innocence left her embarrassed. Even aboard ship, she had never undressed with Christian there, nor had she watched him disrobe. Her hesitation was apparent.

Christian's voice was soft and soothing. "I promise I won't do more than you want me to. Just come to bed."

Alisa's eyes lowered from his excruciatingly handsome face and his tousled hair, to his massive shoulders and biceps. She doused the candles in the room, relieved that the fire in the hearth was dying to smoldering ashes. She did not realize that the moonlight reflecting off the deep drifts of snow beyond the windows afforded Christian a perfect view of her as she undressed.

The silvery light enhanced her beauty; Christian's eyes devoured the vision of firm breasts bared for only a second before she turned from the bed. Petticoats fell one after another to reveal a small, well-turned rump above slim, tapering legs.

Alisa breathed deeply to still the pounding of her

heart. With her back to Christian, she slid beneath the sheet, surprised to find herself pressed against his large, iron-hard, naked thigh as he awaited her in the middle of the bed. Tension and embarrassment impelled Alisa to speak, her voice barely a whisper. "I thought you meant for this to be a platonic marriage."

"What gave you that idea?" His tone was low, thick with passion he had denied too long.

She didn't respond immediately, wishing she had not begun this at all. She opted for honesty. "I just didn't think you wanted me."

A deep, sensuous laugh sounded. "I've wanted you longer than I admitted even to myself. I did not want to force you in any way, and that still applies."

He rolled to his side, an arm arched on the pillow above her head, one powerful hand coming to rest at the side of her neck, feeling the pounding of the pulse there. Warm, moist lips lowered to hers, tentative, teasing, gentle. Alisa's eyes closed slowly as she yielded to his kiss and futilely willed herself to relax. His mouth savored hers, pressing just a bit harder, deepening the kiss and drawing her more surely into it. His hand played with the wild tangle of her hair, pleased to at last run his fingers through the silken curls that so intrigued him.

She moved her arms with conscious will to rest gently around Christian's broad back, her long, tapered fingers running tentatively across hard muscle. She was surprised at herself as one hand came to rest at the nape of his neck to press slightly and draw his mouth closer still, her own lips parting beneath his. His kiss expertly enticed her to yield all inhibitions, but just as she began to relax, she was startled to feel his large hand move from her neck downward to cup one firm breast. She stiffened, astounded by the light touch of a hand that could easily have crushed her. Kneading gently, he teased her nipple to a taut peak, causing violently pleasurable sensations that arched her body upward in instinctive demand.

His lips left hers, tracing a slow path along her neck, pausing slightly to feel the heartbeat that no longer pounded with fright. She reveled in the warm lips and lightly tickling mustache that nibbled her shoulder, wondering at the excitement his hand at her breast aroused in her. She lay back on a cloudlike cushion of wondrous new sensations.

Again Christian took her mouth with his, his desire rising to an intensity he had not anticipated. All thought had long been drowned in the surge of perfect sensual delight as his wife responded with a natural abandon he had never before encountered, or expected. He delighted in her soft caress, her hands cool as they explored his upper body with wonder; no perfunctory stroke, this. Its effect left him in a state of awe he had not experienced since his initiation into lovemaking.

She welcomed his mouth on hers, accepting his teasing tongue, though in her innocence she was not certain how to meet it. All thoughts had been erased by the tingling desire that coursed through her. She stiffened only slightly as Christian's hand moved to her flat abdomen and then lowered still farther, yet her yearning for all he offered quickly chased away any inhibitions. She welcomed his gently probing touch, which drew her with him to a need she did not understand but trusted him to fulfill.

He rose above her, spreading her knees easily with his muscular thighs, his lips finding the taut crest of her breast, sucking lightly to send a whole new tremor along her spine. He slowly moved his lower body to hers, and she felt for the first time his large, probing shaft of manhood near her most intimate spot. Instinct arched her hips to meet him, to aid his entrance. All fear washed away as her body sought the release only he could offer.

Christian could contain himself no longer, entering slowly at first, then lowering all of his weight to push home. He did not at first understand the barrier he met. He drove a bit harder, feeling Alisa draw away involuntarily. He lifted his head. Lines of pain etched in Alisa's brow. Her eyes clamped shut, her white teeth pressed tightly against her bottom lip. His jaw tightened in rage as he pushed himself just slightly deeper, meeting the unmistakable wall of a maidenhead intact.

He forcefully pushed himself away from Alisa. "You're a virgin!" The words were flung at her in contempt, a cold, harsh dousing of the desire he had aroused in them both.

Alisa's eyes opened to a face contorted in murderous fury. She could not meet his eyes; she could not speak. Nothing could excuse her terrible lie. She had deceived herself as well, thinking, in the ultimate moment, she could fool him. She deserved his wrath—and more. He had deserved the truth, long before he discovered it.

She pulled the sheet up to cover her nakedness, though nothing could hide the shame and humiliation she felt. Christian paced the deeply shadowed room, working to control his violent rage. After a time, he drew on his breeches, leaving his broad, hairy chest bare. He lit a candle and then stood at the foot of the bed, his contempt-filled eyes boring into her. A hard, mirthless laugh burst from his throat. "I can hardly wait to hear what story you can devise to explain this!" he shot at her as if reading her thoughts.

Alisa's voice held a quiet strength as she spoke, though she was unable to meet Christian's blazing bluish-green gaze with her own. "One of Papa's friends had asked for my hand in marriage," she began, inventing the lie as she went. "He was as old as my father, a fat, grotesque man. I told Papa I could not marry him, but he refused to acknowledge my wishes. I begged and pleaded, but he said Phillip Mathews was his dearest friend, that he owed him anything he asked. Even Ivy was on my side, but neither of us could convince him. We found you in the parlor that night and we helped you upstairs. You kept calling me Ellen and saying how much you wanted her and that you didn't want to force her again. Listening to you, Ivy concocted the plan of staging the rape. I knew Papa would never marry me off to Phillip Mathews if I weren't a virgin. I had no idea he would force you to marry me yourself. I thought he would just keep the whole thing quiet to avoid a scandal and perhaps simply make you leave England."

"Then why the hell did you agree to marry me? You could have stopped that."

"If I refused, Papa said he would use all of his influence to see you punished as fully as if you had committed murder. I couldn't sit by and see you imprisoned for the rest of your life, and if I confessed, all would have been lost."

"How noble of you. You married me to save me," he said sarcastically.

Alisa bowed her head under his caustic words. She

could never confess she was a murderess. "I married you to save myself. I'm sorry, Christian. But don't you see? I had no choice."

"I see that you had a hell of a lot of other choices than to trap me!" Now he paced again, furiously, like a caged animal ready at any moment to pounce. "When will I learn?" he asked himself. "Women are all lying bitches or whores or both! Am I the only gullible fool in the world that they all seek me as their victim?"

"Christian?" Alisa said softly, her voice filled with remorse. "I've earned your anger, but I honestly could do nothing else. Since we are already married and our vows are consummated, can't we put it all in the past and go on?"

"Consummated!" Christian shouted. "You are no less virgin now than before I had the misfortune of falling into this trap."

Alisa stared at him in terrified uncertainty. "Of course I am."

Again his laugh was harsh. "There is no physician in the world that would dispute your virginity upon examining you, madam. The act was not completed to that extent."

Now the blood drained from Alisa's cheeks, leaving two midnight-blue eyes the only color in her ashen face. "What will you do?" Her voice was a barely audible whisper.

Christian gathered his clothing, each stroke, each step a sign of unvented fury. When he did not respond, Alisa spoke again. "I never meant to bring you harm, Christian. I didn't realize how much you were against ever being remarried."

Christian stopped abruptly, glaring at Alisa with barely contained violence. He said nothing.

She pushed farther back against the headboard, an instinctive reaction to her husband's rage. Christian turned from her and strode from the room as though his control had snapped.

As the door slammed behind him, a sudden tremor ran through her. She wondered if she hadn't escaped the hangman's noose only to meet her fate at the hands of a man now bent on revenge.

Alisa heard the clock in Center Church strike five before the sound of Christian's loud furious voice drifted up to her from the front parlor of the house. She had not slept in the hours since Christian had left her; she had sat at her window staring out at the dark, frigid night.

Alisa decided she preferred facing Christian's wrath to this awful waiting and worrying. She pulled her black velvet robe closer, as though it would shield her, and went downstairs. Once again she stopped, to gather courage before entering the room.

Scott's voice, thick with sleep at this early hour but filled with compassion, tried to reason with Christian. "I wish you would just go upstairs and sleep on all of this, Christian. Get some rest. It won't look so bleak in the morning."

"She's a goddamned virgin! Haven't you heard what I've said? I didn't rape her! I married her for nothing, dammit! A virgin! I didn't wake you up to give me platitudes!"

"If she confessed to you, doesn't her honesty count for something?"

"She didn't confess willingly. I discovered her damned virginity when I tried to bed her."

"Then she's not a virgin anymore, Christian, and you can't have the marriage annulled."

"She sure as hell is! She's as much intact as she was on the day I met her. I stopped."

Scott cleared his throat. "You have amazing restraint."

"This isn't a damned joke, Scott! She's just another lying, conniving bitch! I believed I raped her, for God's sake. I thought I was a rapist. And then I find I never touched her. She's as bad as Ellen."

"They're not at all alike. You're too mad to see this clearly. Give yourself some time."

"Are you defending the bitch?"

Alisa's hand rose instantly to cover her mouth to silence her shocked gasp. She turned and fled back up the stairs. She had not thought Christian would announce it, even to his brother. Her humiliation was all-consuming. She ran like a frightened, wounded animal, in that moment feeling that she could not bear her burdens, her guilt and the degradation. She sought solace in the darkest corner of her studio and sat slumped, furiously trying to grasp hold of her racing emotions. She could not face anyone until she could once again control herself.

Chapter Seventeen

"He's gone, Alisa."

Alisa jumped at the sound of Scott's voice. She turned from the window at the front of her studio.

"Scott!" she murmured, embarrassment precluding further words, even after hearing the warmth and sympathy in his voice.

"Ann tells me you haven't eaten the whole time you've been here."

"That's a bit of an exaggeration," she managed softly, her eyes lowered.

"She also tells me you've been hiding up here all day, after you slept here last night." His tone was still kind.

She shrugged slightly. "Not hiding, exactly. This is the only place I feel comfortable right now."

"Well, I won't have any more of it!" His voice was brotherly, yet commanding. "I won't leave this room until you come with me. I have decided it's time we talk, and the drawing room is far better for that."

Alisa protested, feeling her face heat with color, but Scott would not be refused. He took her hand and gently pulled her behind him until he sat her in one tall wing chair in the parlor.

He moved to the sideboard to pour two glasses of

wine. As he handed one to Alisa, he said casually, "I know all about what's happened between you and Christian. Everything," he reiterated. "And I find your plot amusing and courageous, though a bit foolhardy, so please don't be embarrassed. Besides, you need someone to talk to, and more, you need someone to talk to you."

His manner was so natural that Alisa at last forced her eyes to lift to him. "Did you see Christian today?"

Scott's blue eyes were kind. "He left at dawn for a cabin we have in the mountains. Christian escapes there for solitude when he needs to sort out problems. While he's away, I thought I might educate you a little on what makes him tick right now."

Alisa's smile was wan. "I don't know that it will help."

Scott studied her, appreciating the sight and seeing how difficult it was for her to face him. Christian had said nothing about how he felt toward this wild-haired beauty before his anger had erupted. Scott drew his own conclusions.

"Christian is not an easy man to understand."

Scott laughed heartily. "I would guess that to be the kindest thing you can say about him at this moment. Actually, under most circumstances, Christian is not a difficult man, though he certainly seems to have set out to show you his worst side. As a rule, he is kind and compassionate."

Scott drank his wine, hesitating before continuing. He liked Alisa, he decided as he sat across from her. He found her quiet pride and dignity appealing. He also decided that this young woman might be good for his brother. "How much do you know about Christian's marriage?"

A deep voice from the entrance hall interrupted Alisa's answer. "I never expected you to use gossip to win a lady, Scott." The tone was teasing as a small man strode easily in to join them, obviously at home here. He bowed before Alisa, a mischievous glint in his deep black eyes as he took her hand and kissed it gallantly, his silver-blond hair falling over his brow. "But now that I see her, I can understand that nothing should be left untried in winning this one."

"It's too late, Nicholas. Alisa, this is our cousin, Nicholas Lamb. You will have to excuse him, he's our own private jester. Nicholas, this is Alisa, Christian's new wife."

Shock registered on the handsome face as silvery brows rose, and his square, boxy body fell with dramatic flair into the seat beside Alisa. "I am left speechless." He turned to Scott. "Surely you torment me with trickery."

Scott viewed his cousin indulgently. "At this moment no one wishes that more than I, except perhaps Alisa. But it is the truth, and he is not being kind about it. So if you will excuse us, I was about to be the benevolent brother-in-law, and it requires privacy. Please."

A careless shrug complete with comically raised brows was his answer. "Are you telling deep, dark secrets of which I am ignorant?" he said with exaggerated perturbation.

"Please, Nicholas, it has nothing to do with you, and certainly it's nothing you are unaware of already."

"It must be serious; even the butler has been exiled. I could stay and perform his tasks," he persisted, feigning the pout of a petulant child.

"We already have wine, thank you. Now get the

hell out of here." Scott's tone was friendly, affectionate.

Nicholas turned his back on Scott and spoke to
Alisa. "Beware, sweet Alisa, I shall expect equal
time to win your affection as your newest cousin."
Again he bowed low and left the room, pretending
dejection.

Even though Alisa had not spoken a word, her
spirits were lifted by Nicholas's clownish antics.

"You will get used to his drollery. But back to the
subject at hand. If I were to guess, I would say Christian has refused to tell you anything at all about his
first marriage."

"He told me it was none of my business."

"Tact is not one of his better qualities. Ellen is a
beautiful woman; it is perhaps her only virtue, but I
will admit that I am prejudiced. I was never fond of her.
In the eight years that Christian was at sea, Ellen
grew from a little girl none of us noticed, into a young
woman few could resist. Unfortunately, she could not
refuse any man who found her attractive. In my opinion, it's a sickness with her; she needs a never-ending,
constantly changing stream of fawning men around
her. When Christian came home, he was one of the few
men in New Haven she had not conquered. So of course
she set her trap to ensnare him. Even I did not realize
until later how much she needed Christian at the
time."

Scott paused, staring into his glass. "I told him
what I thought of Ellen when he announced his en-
gagement. We argued bitterly. Christian was convinced that I was jealous."

"That must have been very difficult for you."

Scott laughed wryly. "It was miserable! Even after
his wedding, things were cold between us for a long

time. It wasn't easy for me to watch him. I have never seen a man so in awe, so full of worship for a woman so undeserving of it. If I believed in witchery, then surely that would account for it. He saw nothing but perfection in her. By the time they returned from their honeymoon, she was pregnant."

Alisa's eyes widened. "I didn't know there was a child."

Scott's head shook sadly. "Yes, Nathan. We call him Nat. He was born seven months after the ceremony. Ellen said he was premature," Scott said sardonically, smiling at Alisa's shock. "Of course that was a polite lie, but I had hoped that at least the baby was a product of Christian's time with her before the wedding. God, he loved that baby!" His head shook with regret. "Christian believed Nat was his child. He ignored Ellen's, shall we say, excursions, accepting her excuses. I expected him to kill her. I really thought that at any time she was going to push him too far and he would kill her. I never knew how he found her, I only know that he did, in bed with a lover, and I guess she must have told him about Nat then. He never confided the details. Ellen felt pretty sure of herself; she didn't think he would do anything by then. Actually, Christian surprised us all by divorcing her. I've never seen anyone so hurt, though he swore he didn't love her anymore. I believed him, but I think the worst of it was finding himself so vulnerable to her, so blind. It's a frightening thing to be so completely duped."

Alisa's voice was quietly remorseful. "I did the same thing."

Scott smiled affectionately. "Not quite. You tricked him, but not with his eyes open. I think if you give him some time he will come to realize that."

"When will he be back?" Knowing the details of Christian's past intensified her own guilt again.

Scott shrugged. "I can't tell you that because I don't know. I don't think he had really worked through everything in his mind about Ellen before this whole thing with you started. I'd say he has a lot of thinking to do, and even more calming down."

Panic surged through Alisa. "I want to go to him," she blurted out more in reaction than in common sense.

Now Scott's eyes widened in surprise. "That's not wise, Alisa."

"Maybe not, but it's what I have to do. I can't stand just waiting while it all festers and grows worse in his mind."

"I don't think you realize how fierce Christian's temper can be. Besides, Alisa, if he had wanted to see you he wouldn't have gone to the cabin. He needs time alone now."

"He ran off like a wounded animal, Scott, but even the strongest lion needs his wounds tended. You can't change my mind." Her determination was obvious.

"It's foolish, Alisa! The cabin is high in the mountains, near our country house, actually. At this time of the year, you could be snowed in without even a warning."

"All the more reason. This will be made worse if his rage feeds on it. Surely I deserve a chance to defend myself. I have to go!" she ended firmly.

"And how do you think to get there?"

"You're going to take me."

Chapter Eighteen

"Get her the hell out of my sight, Scott! You had no business bringing her here!"

Christian stood on the doorstep of a small cabin fashioned of weathered, rough-hewn boards. Both powerful hands rested in his narrow buckskinned hips, and his bluish-green eyes blazed with rage from beneath bushy brows.

Alisa slid from her saddle with practiced ease. "I forced Scott to bring me against his will."

"At gunpoint or knife?" he said caustically, but his glance did not leave Scott, who remained astride his mount, amused by the scene.

"I didn't think you would want her trying to find you alone."

"I doubt that she would have gone far before turning back," Christian growled.

"You underestimate her, Christian."

"That has been all too obvious. Matchmaking is not a role that suits you."

Scott laughed, unintimidated by his brother's wrath. "The match was made long before I had anything to do with it."

Christian glared at Scott for a long moment before

turning to Alisa. "Do us both a favor and go back the way you came. You are not welcome here."

Alisa drew her belongings from behind the saddle, facing Christian above the ungainly bundle. Midnight-blue eyes met his without wavering. "I am staying, Christian."

Scott laughed boisterously now, reining his horse around to leave. "You might as well fight it out up here, Christian. She's a determined little thing. At least you won't have servants to gossip about it." Scott's laughter filled the air long after he was out of sight, leaving Alisa and Christian facing each other in the chill mountain air.

Without speaking, Christian moved to a large woodpile and began furiously assaulting the immense logs with an ax. His rage was almost tangible as corded muscles stood out in his neck and powerful forearms flexed hard where they were exposed beneath the rolled sleeves of his flannel shirt. Alisa entered the cabin, leaving behind the sound of wood splitting and splintering in rapid succession.

The cabin was clean but rustic. Its only room contained a large table with an odd assortment of chairs around it. A stone hearth took up one complete wall; on another was an all-white cupboard containing food and all of the utensils for cooking and cleaning. A shiny rifle braced against one side, and a washtub hung from a hook on the other. Two obviously handmade chairs waited before the fireplace, one a rocker, the other a ladderback with plump cushions tied to the seat and back for comfort. Christian's heavy coat hung from a rack to one side of the only door; on the other side was a tall ladder, the only access to a loft half the size of the lower room.

Alisa tried futilely to maneuver her awkward bundle up the ladder before finally opening the heavy tapestry bag and choosing what she could manage to carry with her. The loft held four narrow beds, all lined in a neat row against the wall. At the near side stood a washstand and basin, at the far side another fireplace, much smaller than the one below. Since it was obvious by the unmade state of the bed nearest the hearth that Christian slept there, Alisa deposited her belongings on the cot beside the washstand, leaving their sleeping arrangements divided by the two unused cots between.

She was surprised to find that she liked the cabin. She had never in her life spent time in a place so lacking all the comforts she had taken for granted, but it had an undefinable, homey quality that appealed to her. She smiled at the thought of what Ivy would say if she saw this place, and the thought of her sister's horror made it all the more endearing to her.

Leaving her velvet riding jacket on against the chill, Alisa carefully climbed back down the ladder for a second armload of her belongings. She jumped in startled fright when the cabin door flew open abruptly, slamming against the wall behind it. From her place kneeling on the floor, she looked up to see Christian, his massive arms filled with the wood he had chopped. Ignoring her, he crossed to the hearth and let his bundle fall unceremoniously into a box between the cupboard and the fireplace.

Alisa spoke, her voice strong, for she would not be cowed. "I saw no wardrobe in the loft. Where shall I hang my clothes?"

Christian lowered cold eyes to her, his jaw clenched to deepen his creased cheeks. He stared at her for so long that Alisa began to doubt he would answer her at all. Then he snapped sarcastically, "It hasn't arrived from France yet." He paused, all his contempt for her etched into his handsome face. "The few hooks on the walls are all there is. Your delicate sensibilities are bound to be offended here; most of the amenities are blessedly absent." His scorn deepened as his gaze dropped to the clothing in her lap. "Don't tell me you are so dim-witted that you brought only your best gowns with you. Did you think you were coming to your father's country estate?"

Alisa's face paled with the reminder of her last trip there. But pride ruled, and she raised her chin defiantly, though she spoke in strong, unheated tones. "I brought my warmest clothing. I was not aware it was improper."

"There is nothing proper or improper here, madam. Unless you consider what propriety lies in freezing to death. I don't suppose my addlepated brother had the foresight to equip you adequately."

"I'm sure I'll be fine. I'm quite comfortable now."

Christian exhaled impatiently. "This is warm! I promise you will not be so comfortable when it snows and even a tear will freeze as it falls to your chin."

"I'm sure that's an exaggeration."

"Are you? Just keep in mind that it was your choice to come here."

Christian grabbed his rifle with a vengeance and strode out of the cabin, slamming the door behind him. Alisa sighed deeply, realizing he was going to make this as difficult as possible for her.

Her heaviest woolen shawl did not protect her at all against the chill that permeated every corner of the cabin the moment darkness fell. Christian had returned after dark, prepared a simple meal of dried meat Alisa could not eat and fresh bread Scott had brought in a box of other foodstuffs.

Christian refused to speak to her. He successfully ignored her, giving the impression that he was not even aware of her existence. It was an adept ruse. In fact, he could not force her from his thoughts, though his anger was all-encompassing and he wanted only to punish her.

It was not late when Christian climbed the ladder to the loft. Alisa had decided to allow his anger to cool and give him time to get used to her intrusion into his secluded domain. She knew that broaching the subject of her deception at that moment could only cause the hot volcano boiling within him to erupt. She fought hard to quell the fear that when his wrath cooled, he would decide he preferred to rid himself of her. She did not want his anger to rule that decision, so she silently endured his repudiation.

She waited until she heard him sink into his bed before she changed into her nightgown, and finally climbed the ladder again for bed. A bright fire blazed beside Christian's cot, and his solemn profile stared into the flames as if oblivious to his roommate. She wished fervently for some clue as to how to make amends. She only hoped that patience would prove the best course.

Tension, the early hour and cold all worked against her attempts to fall sleep. A heavy wool blanket and an extremely thick, downy quilt were not sufficient to keep the chill at her end of the room from tormenting her. She did not understand how a roaring fire at one side could throw so little heat to the other. When her teeth began to chatter uncontrollably, she pulled the heavy blankets up over her head, hoping Christian would not hear it.

She jumped with fright when, without warning, he flung all of her covers away in one fast swipe. "How the hell am I supposed to sleep with that racket?" his deep voice boomed.

"I'm doing the best I can," Alisa managed through wildly clacking teeth.

One large hand reached the hem of her nightgown and flipped it up to her knees, exposing bare feet. "I don't suppose you brought anything but those idiotic silk stockings," he said flatly.

"I don't own anything but silk stockings," she retorted truthfully.

"Of course not." His tone was sarcastic again. "Get out of that damn bed and into mine."

Alisa's eyes widened with a question Christian answered before she opened her mouth. "I have no intention of sleeping with you. I'll take the one beside it," he growled impatiently.

Alisa ran to his bed, which was still warm from his body. She watched as he strode to the bed nearest her, his long underwear covering every inch of his muscular, perfect male body like a second skin. She pushed down on the thought of that large, powerful form curving around her in delicious, warm comfort.

Christian leaned over her, his hands reaching beneath the bed to pull a trunk from it. He opened the top. "I thought so," he growled to himself, pulling a pair of woolen socks out and flinging them at Alisa. "These are some of Nicholas's clothes from when he was a boy. They should fit you, if you're inclined to sacrifice your vanity for warmth. But if I were you I'd wait to wear the rest until morning to be sure you're not sharing them with some form of life even lower than yourself."

His scathing remark withered any thought of thanking him. As she gratefully pulled on the musty-smelling stockings, Christian added a log to the fire and pulled the quilts from the two unoccupied beds, dividing them equally between his cot and hers before he dropped with an irritated sigh into his bed.

Alisa relaxed as warmth finally crept over her, but sleep eluded her. She stole a tentative glance at Christian. He was lying on his back, his hands cupped beneath his head, staring up at the ceiling. His strong, square jaw was clenched; his eyes did not blink.

"I truly am sorry, Christian," she whispered, in the hope he might break his enforced silence.

He did not speak, or turn his head to look at her. Alisa knew at that moment that he hated her, and although she did not blame him, it caused her an odd stab of pain.

Chapter Nineteen

Alisa sat huddled before the fire, sipping her morning tea and wondering where Christian was. She had heard him rise an hour earlier and waited until she knew he was dressed before leaving her warm bed for the frigid cabin. The steaming tea warmed her from the inside while the fire worked on her back. She could see the early December sun's rays from the two small windows and hoped for a warm day to wash the newfound treasure of Nicholas's old clothes.

Christian entered the cabin, closing the door behind him. His heavy fleece-lined coat was buttoned to his neck, the collar pulled up about his ears, leaving his thick, wavy hair to fall over it.

Alisa thought that he made an appealing sight, this ruggedly handsome mountain of a man, except that his face held an expression of scorn. She watched him place a bucket on the table and return his coat to the rack without once looking at her. She was mildly surprised to see him pour milk from the pail.

"I didn't know you liked milk," she said hesitantly.

"There are a number of things you don't know about me." His voice was cold, remote.

It went against Alisa's nature to ignore his cutting tone, but she fought her anger, realizing it would solve nothing. "What do you do up here during the day?"

Christian's handsome head turned in a deliberately slow motion, clearly showing his irritation as though she had interrupted something vitally important. "I do whatever strikes me at the moment, so I will be spending as much time as possible away from this cabin and you."

She held herself in check with the thought that he was acting like a child. She decided to return to quiet patience before she lost control of her own temper. "Is there a way for me to bathe?" she said some time later, a note of dejection creeping into the mundane question.

Christian stared at her curiously, moved for just a moment by the real emotion in her voice. Then he steeled himself against her by remembering her deception. She was no different from other women he had known. His anger fused into a white heat. His voice was harsh as he answered her, his gaze averted from the all too attractive picture she presented. "The tabletop slides free; the bathtub is below it. You will have to haul water from the river south of here until it freezes, then you will have to melt snow." He stood abruptly and left the cabin, as though he could not bear the sight of her for another moment. But it was not from hatred as much as from temptation.

Alisa spent the entire morning attending to her bath. She was left to her own devices to find buckets first, and then the river. She trekked tediously back and forth for water, heated it, then struggled with the large, heavy tabletop to get to the bathtub.

Her afternoon was spent building a fire outside of the cabin and finding a washtub large enough to boil water to scrub the old clothing from the trunk in the loft. She was much too slight to wear the pants and shirts, she discovered, but she was grateful for the long underwear and woolen stockings that could be worn beneath her gown, and for two sweaters she could use to ward off the chill.

The sun rose high as she stood stirring her soapy brew. Unexpectedly, she was too warm. First her shawl came off, then the short jacket from her riding habit. As perspiration formed, she unfastened the top buttons of her wool gown, folding the high neck inside to allow a V-shaped opening to cool at least her throat.

Washing, rinsing, and wringing the garments was back-breaking, tedious work that left her in awe of what was required for this sort of life. She had never considered herself pampered, but she realized now that she had been naive and swore she would never again take any servant for granted.

When at last she had finished, she regretted the order in which she had done the day's tasks, for she longed for another bath. Instead she used what little water was left and, moistening a cloth, drew it around her neck, down the open bodice and inside between her breasts. She was completely unaware of Christian standing several feet away, stopped abruptly in his tracks as he returned with his day's catch of fish.

Her face was raised to the sun's warming glare, long, coppery lashes resting against cheeks brightened with a healthy glow. Her small tongue ran lightly over dry lips in an unconsciously sensual motion, deepening their pale rose color.

Christian's jaw clenched, but he could not force his gaze from his wife, following the thin column of her creamy throat to the porcelain skin of her chest and resting for a tormenting moment on the small rise of two perfect breasts. Christian felt himself harden with desire. He called himself every kind of fool, disgusted that he should be attracted to this treacherously deceitful baggage. He closed his eyes tightly, breathing deeply to quell his yearning for her. He would never again be ruled by emotion for any woman. He would never again be vulnerable.

Control was hard-won. Christian strode past Alisa and into the cabin, appearing for all the world as if he were oblivious to her presence.

It was well into the night, and Christian could not clear his mind or his senses enough to sleep. He stood before the fire in the loft, sipping brandy and staring at Alisa. She slept easily after her unaccustomed toil, curled beneath downy quilts with only her face and one fragile hand visible.

Christian was plagued with the realization that his hatred of her was dissolving, though his anger was still a full draft of bile within him. Hating her had made it all easier. His desire for her and his righteous fury left his emotions warring. Even Ellen had had a more urgent reason for her initial deception than Alisa; certainly pregnancy was a greater impetus than the threat of marriage to an old man.

Still, some unbidden voice argued, Ellen had never shown the slightest sign of remorse, never attempted to compensate for her trickery. Ellen had never, not even in the end, so much as apologized. Yet he was responding to all of Alisa's attempts at atonement with abuse and more punishment than he had ever inflicted on Ellen.

The contradiction raged within him, for her beautiful, innocent-looking face did not coincide with the picture he worked to maintain in his mind of her self-serving, contrived trickery.

Christian stoked the fire and finally dropped into his bed. He did not know how he was going to resolve this, but he was wary of desire clouding his decision, and regardless of how hard he fought it, his wanting her was racing apace with his rage.

Chapter Twenty

Alisa had spent three days in the cabin. Three long, empty days and three longer, emptier nights. She thought that if Christian intended to drive her mad, he was succeeding. He did not speak to her unless forced, he did not look at her, he did not acknowledge her in any way. Frustration and anger were rapidly overcoming Alisa's decision to wait patiently until his ire cooled.

On the fourth day Alisa and Christian awoke to a blizzard. The wind turned the white snow into an opaque, swirling curtain that held them captive in the small space. They spent the day sitting before the hearth for warmth, save for Christian's brief forays out to split wood or milk his cow and tend the horses. Throughout the day and evening Alisa viewed Christian's attitude as a challenge she would meet, and matched his silence with her own, trying to convince herself that if she treated this as some sort of game, her endurance might increase.

By late that night, Alisa admitted defeat and decided as she lay in her bed that anything was preferable to the uncomfortable silence. She turned her head to look at Christian on the cot beside hers, seeing his eyes open, staring at the ceiling as he did

111

each night. "When will we talk about this?" she asked finally.

"Have we something to discuss?" he answered ironically, never wavering from his study of the beams above them.

Alisa met his sarcasm with her own. "Would it make you feel better to beat me or shoot me in retaliation?"

Christian paused as if contemplating the possibilities before answering. "I have never before shot or struck a woman, though I have known several who deserved it, you among them."

"Your perfection is astounding," she said in mock defeat. "One would think you have never made a mistake in your life."

"I have made two very large ones, and both of them were marriage."

"And the rest of your life has been faultless. Are all of your actions beyond reproach? Have you never lied or deceived a single person, have you never needed something badly enough to do whatever was necessary? Perhaps you are a saint!"

Christian's face turned slowly to her. "My past errors are not up for discussion here. What's important is that I have never taken it upon myself to selfishly disrupt another person's entire life. It hardly compares with a minor lie or trick, does it?"

Sufficiently chastised, Alisa sighed. "I was unaware that I am the gravest punishment a man can endure."

"It's too late for martyrdom, Alisa."

His ridicule ignited her temper. "What do you want from me? Is even a pound of flesh too little payment for my misdeeds?"

"I want nothing from you." Christian's gaze was

cold, his voice steel-edged. "Except perhaps my freedom, and that I will take if I decide to."

"Have you never worked to make the best of a bad situation?"

"Often. I have just spent three years working to be rid of my last wife!"

Knowing nothing productive was being served by this argument, and feeling her own frustrated anger growing boundless, Alisa pulled the quilts up about her shoulders, punching her pillow with more force than it warranted.

"I did not take you to be a man who hides from his problems rather than facing them." Alisa realized instantly that her own cowardice in doing just that should have stopped the words before she voiced them. More unwise words were never spoken, for she found herself grasped on the shoulders by hurtful hands and lifted from her bed to stare into the fierce, dangerously angry eyes of her husband.

"Coming from a lying little bitch who decided I should be the pawn in a childish game with her father rather than standing up to him, you should know all about that! I didn't come up here to hide from my problems. I came to keep from killing you! I swore to God that if ever another woman played me for a fool, she would pay with her life. Don't for a minute believe that I can ever take your deception lightly, for nothing turns my stomach more. You've forced your way into the lion's den; now you had damned well better pray you come out of it alive. The kindest thing that can come of this for you is to find your little ass on a ship back to England." He pushed her back to her pillow, snapping her head with the force.

Fear coursed through her, but she responded to

this attack nonetheless. Her voice was quiet but strong. "I promise you that everything that led to this marriage causes me more shame than anything I have ever done. Had I any other option in the world I would have taken it. I did not do this to gain some hold on you. It was pure desperation for which I was and am willing to do whatever you want of me to compensate. You act as if I gloat over some victory over you when, in truth, I live in absolute humiliation to have sunk to depths I never thought possible for me."

The genuine pain and remorse that rang in her voice caught Christian's attention, but still his fury was great. "Don't expect sympathy from me."

"I expect nothing from you but the contempt I deserve. You cannot punish me more than I punish myself, nor hate me more than I hate myself! There was no pleasure in having deceived you, even though I knew nothing of your past marriage. I know you don't believe it, but I have always prided myself on being an honest person. There is nothing I condemn more than deceit, and no one I condemn more than myself for having perpetuated the worst of it on you." Ugly, painful feelings that she had forced down deep inside of her were rushing to the surface uncontrollably.

She fought wildly against the surge of long-denied emotions that threatened to raise hated, humiliating, foreign tears to her eyes.

Christian's piercing bluish-green gaze seemed to bore through her; his voice was deep, his tone suspicious. "And yet you did all of this, caused us both so much pain simply to escape your father's wishes that you marry some old crony?"

"I'm sorry! I'm sorry!" her voice sang with her fast

weakening control. "I know you can't understand. But to me it was a great cause. If I didn't think clearly, or if it seemed more desperate to me than it was, it is because I was afraid. It seemed hopeless."

She lost the battle as tears fell and sobs racked her. She could not remain under Christian's questioning scrutiny; she could not bear to show such vile frailty to him. She lunged from her bed and ran to the ladder, seeking any escape. Once below she whirled in a frenzied search for a place to hide until she could gain control of herself. She sank into a corner, her face buried in her hands.

Christian now stood near, watching her, torn between his own rage and an aching desire to comfort her, seeing clearly a grief for which he could not account. His voice was low, his fury under control once again. "Do you want to tell me what is really going on, Alisa?"

"Oh, God, no. Please. You know what's going on. Leave me alone! Please!"

Christian sighed as he lost his own battle. "Damn," he muttered as one large, powerful hand curved gently around her thin arm, pulling her from her corner and into his embrace.

Alisa was beyond reason now, overwhelmed by waves of hysterical sobbing. Her body sought the solace Christian offered with a will of its own, desperately needing the comfort, heedless of what problems still separated them. Christian's broad shoulders curved around her like a protective cocoon, muscular arms encircling her, holding her so close they seemed fused together, one massive hand cupping her head as his face lowered to the silken curls, whispering words of solace.

She fought for control, despising tears as a weakness others used to manipulate any situation, mortified that her emotions had brought her to this; and he was witness to it. That thought brought an abrupt cessation of her tears. She eased her body to an independent stance, wiping her cheeks briskly with both hands to erase the evidence that shamed her.

"I'm sorry. I didn't mean to do that. I seem forever to be apologizing to you."

He watched her closely, seeing the effort required for her to compose herself and wondering at a strength he had never before witnessed in a woman. He did not speak, nor move from a position that left her imprisoned between the wall and his mountainous girth.

Finding no way out, Alisa said softly, "Please, Christian, can't we just forget this ridiculous display?"

As he watched her, Christian felt certain that she was hiding something from him. "I will tell you one thing, Alisa, and think it over seriously. There is no secret that is not eventually discovered, and the longer the deceit lasts, the more dire the consequences." He turned from her then and climbed the ladder to the loft.

She could not follow her husband's lead to her solitary bed. Instead she sat huddled in the rocking chair, fear washing over her in waves. She spent the remainder of the night staring into the darkness, wondering if she should leave while she could, before Christian either sent her back to England or, worse than that, discovered her secret himself.

Chapter Twenty-one

A deep layer of snow still covered the earth when Christian returned from his afternoon's hunt in the forest. He carried only his rifle and an empty sack slung over his neck and one shoulder. He stared up at the darkening sky, seeing that the night would be starless beneath dense clouds and that more snow would fall before morning. The thought of spending another day snowbound in the cabin with Alisa was appealing to him. After hours spent thinking about her, when his mind should have been concentrating on hunting, he understood why. His anger was slowly dissolving, though deep resentment over her trickery would linger a long time to come. But his cooling temper had allowed him to make a decision about the future.

He went first to the small barn to feed the two horses and his cow. His body was chilled all the way through, and he was anxious for the warmth of the cabin.

Christian's tall chestnut stallion raised a velvety nose to his master as if in question, but no other animal greeted him.

His first thought was that an intruder had done something horrendous to Alisa and then stolen the horse and cow from the barn. Anger rapidly replaced fear as Christian discounted this theory, knowing well that no thief would steal a small mare and a cow and leave a stallion. He could only conclude that Alisa had left, taking the mare to ride and the cow to sell.

He flung his empty hunting sack to the ground, a string of curses perking up his horse's ears as he ran from the barn.

He kicked the cabin door open with a vengeance and then slammed it behind him, tossing his gun to the tabletop where it slid to the opposite side before stopping, precariously balanced half on, half off. He ripped his coat off and then climbed the ladder to the loft. Not until he stepped onto the upper level did his eyes move to the farthest bed where Alisa sat beneath a quilt staring at him as if he were insane.

Christian stopped for a moment, not quite understanding why his wife was here. Then his anger took over. "Where the hell is my cow?" he demanded bluntly.

Alisa sipped from a mug she held at her side before speaking, her cheeks a healthy pink glow, wide eyes meeting his evenly. "I'm sure that vicious beast is in the barn."

"A cow is not a 'vicious beast,' and she is not in the barn! Neither is your mare, for that matter. What did you do with them?" he raved, but still Alisa was unruffled, again drinking from her cup.

"I didn't do anything with them. I went out to the barn this morning and that cow tried to kill me."

Now Christian watched her intently, thinking that she seemed odd. He sat on his own bed. His tone was impatient, his bushy brows drawn. "Cows do not kill people, Alisa. What happened?"

"There was a rat in the barn. A horrid, ugly black thing! It startled me, and then your cow charged at me with flaring nostrils. I barely missed being trampled to death!"

"I suppose you screamed and scared the poor animal."

"Not nearly as much as that 'poor animal' scared me." She exhaled a short, indignant sigh.

"You're drunk!" Christian shouted, catching a faint whiff of brandy sweet on her breath.

"Drunk?" she said dryly. "No, I don't think so." She smiled at him tentatively. She was not quite drunk but not quite sober, either.

Christian consciously tried to calm himself. "What happened after the cow charged you?"

Midnight-blue eyes widened innocently over her cup, which Christian realized still contained some brandy. "I ran back here and I haven't left the cabin since."

"Leaving the barn door wide open, no doubt. It's a wonder we have even one horse left," he said to himself, then, "Why are you sitting in bed drinking brandy?"

"Because there wasn't any wine."

"Of course." He hadn't the patience to pursue this. He stood, thinking how warm and alluring she seemed. "Have you eaten today?"

"I wasn't hungry."

"I don't suppose the fact that you can't cook had anything to do with it," he muttered wryly. "Come downstairs and I'll fix you dinner."

A brilliant, oblivious smile was his answer, but as Christian watched Alisa stand on unsteady legs and weave her way to the ladder, he decided she could not safely descend it. Without a word he picked her up and flung her over his shoulder unceremoniously, setting her down in a chair at the table below.

Alisa felt wonderful as she watched Christian move around the small space, heating what remained of a stew he had prepared the day before. The sight of him was more heady than the brandy.

As they ate Christian said, "Why were you looking for wine? Surely you didn't need to drink the day away just because of a little scare from a harmless cow."

A blush suffused her cheeks. "I didn't feel well," she said simply.

Christian didn't question this, feeling too disconcerted by the unceasing stare of those damnable blue eyes. Alisa's gaze did not even waver to look at what she was eating.

"Do you drink wine often to feel better?" he said a bit disdainfully, irked by her power to unnerve him.

Again her face colored. "Only at certain times." Her glance lowered momentarily, but all too quickly returned to study him.

Christian exhaled a long, slow breath. He decided she was too drunk either to be able to talk or to act normally. He would simply have to endure it.

By the end of their meal, he could stand no more of her perusal and opted for an early bedtime. Knowing Alisa was no more capable of climbing the ladder than before, he reluctantly lifted her to his shoulder once again. Without thinking, he rested one large hand on the small, round backside that was so near to the side of his face, feeling how the soft, warm curve fit his palm perfectly. The fast stab of desire brought full realization to him of just what he caressed, and he pulled his hand away as if burned. He ascended the ladder in record speed, and Alisa found herself abruptly dropped onto her bed before she knew what was happening.

"Dress for bed and be quick about it," Christian growled as he returned to the lower level.

Once in bed, he stared up at the ceiling. His hope that Alisa would fall asleep immediately was crushed as her melodic voice drifted to him softly from her cot.

"I know you hate me, Christian, and you have good reason, but sometimes I think I see something different in your eyes." Her words were gently slurred, and she felt no inhibitions. It was a nice release from a tension that had been present for so long, and she did not question it.

"What do you see?" Christian answered, knowing the liquor spoke.

"I see kindness and gentleness, compassion. I don't think you're always the stern sea captain, but I fear you don't know how to be any different with me."

"Is that right?"

"Before all of this, in London, I saw you perform a kindness for a small child, and I began to wonder if there might be a little sensitivity in the arrogant Yank. But then on your ship, I was surprised to find you can be even meaner and colder than you were in England. I far prefer Christian Reed to the sea captain. He is a fearsome beast."

"Go to sleep, Alisa," Christian said softly.

"You know, Christian," she said sweetly, ignoring his command, "I liked it when you made love to me. It was really quite nice. I'm sorry it ended as it did." Her words rambled almost as if she spoke to herself. "It was nothing like Ivy said. It was all lovely until the last. You left me terribly disappointed. Does it always feel so good, I wonder? Or is it even better when it's finished properly?"

"Dammit, Alisa!" Christian bolted from his bed, knowing he could not endure the strange effect she was having on him, and certainly not when the conversation turned to making love.

He stormed to the ladder, growling back at her, "I'll be downstairs. Go to sleep."

Alisa sighed in contented innocence and did just that.

Chapter Twenty-two

Alisa woke to a gentle nudge as Christian stood beside her bed, a steaming cup of tea in his hand. His expression was warm and kind, leaving Alisa immediately suspicious.

"I thought that after last night you might enjoy your tea before rising."

Alisa stared at him quizzically for a moment, half-expecting him to pour it over her. She eased herself to a sitting position with a light flinch, holding the quilts up to her neck. "Thank you," she said, accepting the proffered cup. "What do you mean, 'after last night'?" Alisa's memory was hazy, she did not remember anything but conversation passing between them, and she could not recall exactly what she had said.

Christian smiled, a wide handsome grin that made her fear that she had embarrassed herself again. He saw her concern and laughed, sitting on his own bed, beside which waited a cup of coffee. "I simply meant that you spent the night drunk."

Alisa relaxed back against the wall behind her cot. "I had never tasted brandy before. In fact, I've never had anything stronger than wine," she said by way of explanation.

"Are you feeling better this morning?"

Alisa's cheeks flamed. "Yes, thank you. Why are you here?" She sought to change the subject rapidly.

One bushy brow rose in query. "It's snowing again. Besides, after yesterday's attack, I couldn't leave you to face rats and wild cows, should they return, now could I?" His voice held a note of teasing, and Alisa was terribly disconcerted. She fervently wished she could remember what had passed between them the previous night to lighten his attitude to such a degree.

"I'm sorry about the cow. I know how you enjoy your milk." Alisa watched him intently as he smiled, a wide, bright grin beneath the bushy mustache.

"It isn't important. I'm only glad you weren't hurt. When I first got back, I was afraid someone had taken them by force."

Silence fell as they each drank from their respective cups, but still Alisa's wary eyes watched him surreptitiously. "Is something wrong, Christian?"

"In what way?"

She shrugged uneasily. "You're not surly," she managed, unsure of how to put into words his changed mood.

"I told you it was unimportant. There are more where that one came from."

"No, I don't mean just the cow. I mean everything."

"I thought you preferred this to the 'stern sea captain,' as you put it last night."

Alisa blanched. "What else did I say last night?"

Christian laughed, raising only one brow. "You were very enlightening." He stood and left the loft, chuckling all the way.

* * *

The entire day was lovely. Christian devoted every minute to entertaining her, talking to her, teasing her. It aroused Alisa's suspicions as she sat up in her bed that night; she feared that at any moment the irascible sea captain would return to ship her off to England. She could not fathom what she might have said the previous night to alter his behavior this drastically.

She heard Christian climbing the ladder to the loft. She watched him warily, seeing his warm smile and the glint of mischief in the bluish-green eyes as he met her wondering blue stare. He undressed slowly, his gaze locked with hers.

As he discarded the last of his outer garments, Alisa forced her eyes away, feeling a stirring of emotions that left her uneasy. She found Christian too handsome, too appealing and much too unpredictable.

Alisa was startled to see him at her bedside when she had assumed he had already entered his own.

"Would you like a glass of brandy?" he asked, holding the bottle up in one hand.

"No, thank you," she answered unsteadily. She sensed that there was yet another change in the air between them. It was nothing more than a feeling, an indiscernible, inexplicable feeling, but suddenly she was very much aware of Christian's intense masculinity.

He poured himself a glass of brandy and sat on the side of her bed, facing her. It seemed a natural act for him, as if he had done it a hundred times before. Alisa's pulse quickened, but she wasn't certain if it was from fear or attraction.

"Are you sure you wouldn't like just a sip?" His voice was low, sensual.

"Did something happen between us last night that I don't remember?" she asked bluntly, wondering at the rich tone in her own voice.

Christian smiled, a tilted half-grin that lifted one side of his sandy-colored mustache higher than the other. "If something had happened between us last night, you would have remembered it." The creases in each cheek grew deeper, his bluish-green eyes sparkled. "You did enlighten me to a very interesting secret, however."

She held her breath in sudden fear that she had exposed her darkest secret. Did he hate her so much that he was delighted to send her to the gallows? She could not speak, but Christian answered her shocked expression with a light chuckle.

"Don't you remember that you told me how much you enjoyed my lovemaking?"

Alisa's breath burst from her lungs as if she had been hit. Relief and embarrassment flooded her, her face blushing crimson as long-lashed lids closed over her eyes. "Oh, no," she breathed.

"Was it true?" he persisted, obviously toying with her.

Alisa sighed, opening her eyes to stare unwaveringly into his all too attractive face. She wanted him. If it meant brazenly acknowledging her past pleasure in his arms, she reasoned that it was not a high price to pay.

"Was it true?" he repeated after her long pause.

She shrugged, her voice soft. "I can't believe I said it, but since I suppose I did, yes, it's true."

He slowly set his glass on the floor. With deliberate movements of sensual grace, he eased his torso toward Alisa, only his lips touching hers at first in a soft, delicate kiss. Still uncertain of what to expect from him, Alisa remained braced against the wall behind her bed, accepting his kiss without leaning forward to meet him. Still, she closed her eyes and enjoyed the warm, slightly moist feel of his lips on hers.

He raised a hand to the side of her neck, a light caress that caused her pulse to quicken even more as his fingers worked their way up into her hair. He pulled her nearer, deepening his kiss and demanding a response Alisa wanted to give. Her last rational thought was how much nicer this was than the fighting; she tasted the brandy on his tongue as it teased her mouth.

She raised her hand to his hard chest, lightly resting on the steely muscles. His other arm encircled her, pulling her up against him as they sat facing each other on her bed. Her back arched so that taut nipples pressed into him. His kiss was a deep, heady wine, more intoxicating than the brandy from the previous night, and she drank with building pleasure. She reveled in his warm embrace, dwarfed by his size and strength in a way that was delightfully sensual.

The hand in her hair moved slowly to her shoulder, and she regretted it since she could not fully enjoy the sensation through heavy woolen underwear and flannel nightgown. Still, her pleasure in his kiss was far too great to interrupt. When his hand moved lower still, cupping one firm breast in that kneading, teasing way that she remembered, sudden realization struck, and with a groan she fell back against the wall, abruptly ending all that she had been so enjoying.

"No, Christian. You can't," she said, a disappointed sigh.

Christian's frown was not pleasant. His own desires had been raging, and having made his decision about their future, he had anticipated this moment with relish. "Why can't I?" he asked in a voice hoarse with passion and ringing with irritated impatience.

"It isn't what you think," she moaned, her face crimson. She saw the suspicion in his eyes.

"Why don't you tell me what it is?" he challenged.

"I'm not well," she managed, closing her eyes to escape his penetrating stare.

"You were fine all day."

"I am fine!"

"Make up your mind."

"I'm indisposed!"

"Meaning?"

"Oh, Christian! Surely you should know about this." She breathed impatiently, mortified to be forced to blurt it out. "It's a very particular time for me; we can't . . . be intimate." One of her hands covered her eyes as her face heated with humiliation.

After a moment Christian pulled her hands from her eyes. "I'm sorry, Alisa. I should have realized. There is nothing to be embarrassed about. It's not a surprise to me. A disappointment, I will admit, but not a surprise." He lifted her chin with two curved fingers. "Would you like some brandy now?"

"Yes, I think I could use a little bolstering about now."

Christian poured a small amount into the second glass he had brought, handing it to her. He sighed in frustrated resignation. "I had every intention of sharing this bed with you tonight, but it would be much too painful to do it platonically." He stood, kissing the top of her unruly curls gently, and then moved to his own cot.

They sipped brandy in silence for some time, until Alisa could no longer contain herself. "Christian?" she said hesitantly, fearing his answer. "If you meant to consummate our vows tonight, does that mean you've decided to continue the marriage?"

A tense pause stretched on uncomfortably. When at last he spoke, his voice was grave, all of its past lightness and teasing gone. "Yes, Alisa, but to be truthful, it is not because it pleases me."

"Why, then?" she asked softly.

Another long silence preceded his answer. "Allowing the vultures to pick my bones clean is not something I relish repeating, whether it be through divorce or annulment. And as you pointed out yourself, remaining married saves me from becoming the target of yet another conniving woman."

"I see." It was not a flattering answer, deflating all of her high hopes. "Perhaps it will be better this time," she ventured.

Christian faced her, his scowl dark and ominous. "You may as well know one thing from the start, Alisa. If it isn't better, if I ever find you are unfaithful, I'll do what I should have done the first time."

Alisa stared at him, waiting.

"I found her in bed with her lover. I should have killed them both right then. If it happens with you, I won't hesitate."

There was no question that he meant what he said.

Chapter Twenty-three

The snow continued throughout the week, a steady, light powder falling from gray clouds to form a thick blanket covering everything. Huge pine branches sagged low beneath their heavy crystal burden, some snapping under the weight.

Although she felt uncertain of their relationship during these days of enforced companionship, Alisa enjoyed their time together. Christian was very charming when he chose to be, as well as knowledgeable and interesting. They talked for long hours at a time, played chess, took quiet walks in the snow-laden forest and shared equally the chores of tending the cabin. Alisa was pleased to find that they were quite compatible. She discovered that she liked Christian, that she enjoyed more about him than simply his undeniable attractiveness.

Christian had been surprised by the pleasure he had found in his wife's company in these past days, at times forgetting that she was a woman and he a man; he simply enjoyed being with her as he would any good friend. It was something he had never before experienced with any woman. He found it odd but not nearly as disconcerting as the possessiveness he had discovered in himself. He was reluctant to leave the cabin at any time without her, wanting her presence continually in a way he had not felt even with Ellen at the height of his love for her. Always before he had reveled in time alone, so it was strange to find himself never wanting to be away from her. He felt an intense aversion to the very thought of returning to civilization and sharing her with other people, as well as leaving her to tend his normal routines. This was something new to him, made odder by the fact that it was separate from his immense desire for her.

He fought against the fear that he was becoming vulnerable to her already, assuring himself that this would all pass, that it was nothing more than the novelty of her, for in his life and experience, Alisa was unique. He reasoned that he was well equipped with an armor of memories to ward off any dangers she might present.

One early evening on Alisa's final trip to collect snow for a long-awaited bath, she saw Christian leaning against the barn door studying her, a wicked grin on his handsome face, his arms crossed over his broad chest. Straightening her shoulders, she went to him with her request.

"Might you go hunting or fishing or something for about an hour's time?" she asked, smiling brilliantly up at him.

One brow rose in mock suspicion. "There is not a great deal that can be done out here after it gets dark. Are you trying to be rid of me, madam?"

"Yes, as a matter of fact. I want desperately to have a bath."

"It won't disturb me in the slightest for you to bathe." He feigned ignorance.

"But it will disturb me greatly for you to be in the cabin while I do."

"And if you find yourself in need of a back-scrubber?" he teased.

"I shall manage just fine. Please?"

Christian shrugged elaborately. "Am I to be offered the same courtesy for my bath?"

"I have never intruded on you yet, have I?"

"Much to my regret. Nor have I on you."

"Yes, but until now you were nowhere near this place when I chose to bathe. It has hardly been a matter of restraint on your part."

A glint lit his eyes. "My life seems full of disappointment lately."

Alisa's face flushed scarlet. "But will you stay out here?"

"Only if I'm forced."

"You are! I'll call for you when I'm finished."

By the time Alisa sank into the large bathtub, darkness had engulfed all but the small space lit by the roaring fire in the hearth.

Alisa had just begun to lather her skin when the cabin door opened abruptly. "Christian!" she shrieked, sinking far below the water's surface, her face coloring.

Christian closed the door, standing for a moment with his back against it before moving to take off his coat. A slow, sensual smile lifted the corners of his mouth as his eyes stared at her, his desire plain.

"You agreed to stay out until I finished!" she accused.

"I said only if I was forced, and I suddenly realized that no one was forcing me." Long fingers began to unbutton his shirt as he walked to the foot of the tub, his intent unquestionable. His voice was deep, soft.

"As I stood in that cold barn, I couldn't help but think how good a bath sounded to me. So I counted the days, and it seemed to me that there shouldn't be any obstacles standing between us now. Are there?" He pulled his shirt free of his trousers, shrugging from it to reveal the broad, hard expanse of his chest and shoulders. Sandy-colored hair curled across it, narrowing to just one thin line down the flat stomach, disappearing behind breeches that his hands already worked to unfasten.

Abruptly, Alisa realized where her gaze had traveled and that far too long a silence had followed his question. Her voice was unnaturally high, her words spoken too quickly. "I'll be finished in just a minute if you want to use the tub."

A low chuckle rumbled from his throat. "I can't wait any longer, Alisa."

Her eyes widened as he pried off his boots and then dropped his pants to reveal muscular legs and the long, hard proof of his desire for her. She cleared her throat, pushing her eyes swiftly back to his handsome face, wishing that she could relax. She had wanted this to happen, but somehow she had pictured it beneath the cover of total darkness and heavy quilts.

He stood directly before her, his large body a tower of hard muscles, tanned skin and dusky hair. She could not help but admire the steely contours and perfect proportions.

"You haven't answered my question." His voice was low, sensual.

She swallowed, trying to remember what he had asked, for her mind held only thoughts of his magnificence and what it stirred in her. "Question?"

"Are you still indisposed?"

Her eyes closed, and she breathed deeply, trying to get a rein on her racing emotions. "No," she whispered simply.

One sinewy leg lifted over the edge of the tub, and the other followed before Alisa had come to grips with what was actually happening. Christian sat facing her. He lifted her legs up over his on either side and pulled her toward him.

His voice was a soothing, beckoning whisper. "You're not afraid, are you?"

Alisa tried hard for even a wan smile. "Not exactly afraid," she said, tension lending a slight quiver to her tone.

"What, then?" His lips lowered to her shoulder, first one, then the other, in a kiss so light, so slow she barely felt it.

"I don't think I can talk," she managed in stilted, forced words as she fought to relax.

Christian laughed lightly, a rich sound. His lips reached the side of her neck, lingering for a moment. "Don't be embarrassed, Alisa. I've seen you before . . . and felt you. And the memory is too distinct to resist for any longer."

His mouth touched her with light kisses, first her upper lip, then her lower, then each corner in turn before warm, moist lips savored her whole mouth in short kisses that left her wanting more. Long lashes drew down as she tasted his lips and they teased hers, felt his massive hands on her arms, gently, barely touching her, from her wrists to her shoulders and then across her bare back.

Christian sat back, smiling again at the sight of her exquisite face in repose. "Lay your head back."

She obeyed, his kiss a reminder of how much she wanted this man. She fought her embarrassment as

Christian drew the lathered sponge across her body
in deliberately slow strokes, his hands never touching her in what seemed like a torture in itself. She
felt her breathing deepen, her pulse grow rapid, and
she thought he was driving her mad with wanting
him. Every inch of her body cried out for him, to be
held by him, caressed by him, kissed by him. The
merciless sponge seemed too rough as he drew it
across nipples grown taut and sensitive with desire
for him; too hard and impersonal across her inner
thighs.

"Are you teasing me?" she whispered, surprised
by the sensual sound of her own voice.

"Only a little," he breathed as his lips again found
hers, more demanding in a deep, drawing kiss.

He stood then and pulled her with him, the full
length of their bodies pressed for only a moment before he wrapped her in a rough towel, again a terrible torment when her skin cried out for the warm,
wet feel of his. Powerful hands rubbed tenderly as
soft kisses rained on her face, his breath a hot whisper on her eyes, her nose, her cheeks.

With a deep growl of passion Christian suddenly
flung Alisa over his shoulder and swatted her rump
with a resounding slap.

He moved to climb the ladder. "It's past time we
got on with this, lady!"

Chapter Twenty-four

The cold air of the loft and Alisa's unusual position flung over her husband's shoulder quelled her ardor. Small hands grasped the damp towel at her breasts to preserve what modesty she could, though she realized it was ludicrous at this point.

"Put me down!" she demanded in a tone more beseeching than firm.

"Not until there's a bed to put you on!" Christian retorted, unaffected by her squirming. His free arm reached to pull two feather tics from the narrow beds, dropping them on the floor before the hearth. Only then did he swing her to lie on the soft mattresses pushed together to form a more accommodating pallet for two people.

Alisa's hands worked fast to hold the towel closed at her breasts and hips, wide eyes watching Christian's nude form as he quickly built a fire. He was a magnificent man. Her senses were stirred by his perfect male body, long, lean, muscular. The sight alone caused a prickly wave of desire across the surface of her skin. When he lay beside her, a quivering sigh escaped her as the length of his body fit against hers.

He was on the side opposite from the hearth, to allow Alisa the full warmth of the fire and himself a perfect view of her beauty in relief against the blazing blue, yellow and orange of the flames. He raised a hand to smooth her wild burnished copper hair from her cheek, then to move lightly across each arched brow, touching just the tips of thick lashes over eyes so dark blue that they seemed nearly black. The back of his hand ran gently down her cheek, feeling the velvety smooth softness. Heavy lids dropped halfway over bluish-green eyes that held her mesmerized. She could feel the soft breeze of his breath on her face, then his warm lips lowered to hers in a kiss at first light and tentative, then, as if he had unleashed a portion of his passion, deeper, demanding, drawing her response back once again to building desire.

His hand rested at the side of her neck, his thumb tracing her jaw line in a lulling motion that relaxed her. His tongue teased her mouth as his other hand rested above her head, toying with a silken curl and massaging her temples with barely felt strokes. She forgot the towel and raised her hands to Christian's broad shoulders, encircling his iron-hard body, gently caressing the muscles that rippled there.

His hand at her neck lowered in a devastatingly slow path to one firm, upthrust breast, kneading tenderly as his thumb and forefinger first brushed the taut nipple, then grasped it in a delicate pinch that sent sparks along her spine. Taking her breast full in his hand, he squeezed gently, leaving her lips to lower his mouth to the extraordinarily sensitive crest. His warm, moist tongue tantalized it, teasing in exquisite pleasure, chasing away inhibitions. He took her nipple between his teeth, tugging slightly, only to release it to the hot torment of his tongue again, kneading, sucking, rousing a desire that arched her unconsciously closer to him in answer.

His hand lowered, rubbing the flatness of her stomach and then tracing the curve of her hip to pull her more firmly against his hard shaft, its steely length leaving Alisa all too aware of his urgent desire for her. His hand traveled down her thigh and then up again on the sensitive inside. A hot trail of desire erupted in Alisa's most intimate spot, so that when at last he touched her there, a soft moan of pleasure rolled in her throat. His strong fingers gently teased the silken web of her delight, tenderly driving her mad, parting her to seek a spot that instantly drove her to arch still farther in response, gently entering her, teasing her, leaving her open and moist for him.

He rose above her, his knees easily spreading hers. His lips took hers again in a fierce, devastating kiss full of his own raging passion and burning desire for her. His long, hard manhood probed, taunted, tormented before he entered her, slowly at first, then drawing out, entering and withdrawing again and again until Alisa thought she would die from the need to feel his full length within her. In one fast stroke, he broke through the telling membrane, sending a sharp pain that drew Alisa's breath in rapidly, tensing her body beneath him.

Whispered, incoherent murmurings filled her ears as Christian kissed her again, slow, tantalizing kisses, his hand working magic at her breast once again in quick reminder of what she had been feeling before, raising her desire instantly past the pain. His hips moved again when he felt her yield, her body softening, moving in an instinctively arousing way beneath him, until he could no longer restrain himself.

The first few thrusts, though slow and careful, burned until Alisa's body eased open to perfectly encase him in a way that left them each racing toward something she was ignorant of; and then her body exploded with sensation, every inch of her flesh tensed in a pleasure more exquisite than she had known existed. High, soft moans escaped her as her head drew back, her lips parted and soft hands clasped Christian's back with a strength born of passion. Just as the delicious sensations began to ebb, she felt Christian's body tense, driving himself so deeply within her that for one brief moment she thought her own peak might return. She felt the muscles in his back and arms like corded steel, moving her hands to the rock-hard muscles of his buttocks, holding him, helping him to dive as far into her as he could until each of their bodies relaxed, melting together into liquid, languorous pleasure in the aftermath of a perfect act.

Christian rolled to his side, pulling Alisa closely into his embrace as if he would feel incomplete without her pressed to him. "Are you all right, sweet?" His voice was gravelly.

Alisa smiled up at him, a soft, alluring sight. "Yes, are you?"

Christian laughed. "I'm not sure. You're quite a surprise."

"I can understand your saying that the last time, but I can't imagine what shocked you now," she said innocently.

"No, I don't suppose you can." He sighed into her hair, pulling her closer still but not saying more. The surprise was the depth of his pleasure, something he could not explain. He fought threatening feelings, holding the thought that what had just passed between them was nothing more than simple enjoyment of something that was his due.

After a long silence, Alisa spoke quietly. "I'm sorry about being a virgin, Christian."

"I'm not unhappy to be your first, Alisa. I think teaching you all about making love may prove to be my favorite task."

"Am I forgiven for following you up here, then?"

Christian paused a long time before answering. "Perhaps just for that."

"I suppose it's a start."

"Why the hell did you come up here?"

Alisa shrugged, staring at her hand where it rested on his furry chest. "I was afraid that if you were left alone for too long, this whole thing would fester in your mind and seem worse than it already was." She felt his arm loosen slightly from around her.

Christian's voice was deep, a harder edge to it than moments before. "Did you think you could convince me that it was less than it was?"

"No," she answered hesitantly, not understanding what was happening between them. "I simply hoped to convince you that we might have a future together regardless of the cause that joined us." Her words were slightly impatient with the unaccountable frustration she felt.

"So you thought to come here and seduce me." His words dropped flat and heavy.

Alisa rolled from his side, covering herself with a quilt, feeling suddenly too exposed and unprotected. Her temper rose. "If you will only think about it, you will discover that it was not I who did any of the seducing here."

"Do you expect me to believe that you followed me to this small cabin knowing we would be isolated here, alone together, and you believed this marriage would remain unconsummated? It seems more likely that you knew I could resist the temptation you presented for only so long."

Heat ran through Alisa's blood, but passion was not the cause. Her features were taut with outrage. "I will admit to deceiving you into this marriage, but I will not accept the blame for what has just happened. I came up here meaning to settle this between us, but I did not use my body like some harlot to buy it!"

"Didn't you? Whether you intended it or not, you have succeeded, haven't you? The vows were consummated, and your position is secure."

"You bloody bastard!" Alisa's voice was barely a whisper as she sat beside him, holding the quilt to her breast, staring with unbelieving eyes at him. "You had decided not to annul this marriage before any of this happened. How can you, in all of that honesty you so value in yourself, accuse me of luring you into consummating our vows so that you couldn't seek an annulment?"

Christian knew he was being irrational. But unreasonable anger ran through him, and he felt as if Alisa, in some inexplicable way, had won a victory over him. He flung the quilt from his body and stood, pulling on his robe angrily.

Alisa's temper flamed with his silence. "Since I've accomplished what you think I set out to do, there isn't a need for any of this to be repeated, is there? Keep your distance from me, Christian Reed. I wouldn't let you touch me again if my life depended on it!"

Cold, hard, bluish-green eyes stared at her over his shoulder. "What makes you think I would want to?"

Chapter Twenty-five

Damn!

Christian silently cursed himself as he stood in the frigid night air, staring up at a starless sky through pine trees bowed with snow. He had pulled on his pants under his robe and left the cabin. He was disgusted with himself. What had happened to his sanity, his control, his reason?

Alisa had not deserved what he had said to her, and he knew how hurtful his words had been.

Of course she was right! He had made the decision to continue the marriage and then sought the consolation of her body. He had a right to distrust her, to resent her for her trickery, but tonight's outburst was unfounded and unreasonable.

How could he explain it to her? How could he tell her that there were moments when he was obsessed by the thought of being vulnerable to any woman in any way? That simply enjoying her left him feeling like a bear caught in a trap? She was right—he had seduced her, and now they both reaped the rewards of the past. He could not yet trust; he could do nothing but offer her remote formality again.

* * *

Alisa felt as if she had been lured by the soft, glowing warmth of a fire only to have the flames strike out when she least expected, to burn her. Rage and pain filled her like hot sparks in her blood. She wanted to scream and break things and throw a tantrum no child could match. But she decided she had degraded herself quite enough, she could not allow Christian to see how badly he had hurt her. She erected barriers of her own.

With her robe fastened firmly about her naked body, Alisa worked in a fury, stuffing her belongings back into the tapestry bag. She would not return to England—she was not that brave—but neither would she endure this private hell Christian had devised. She would not stand for such abasement. She had done enough penance for her lie.

"What are you doing, Alisa?" Christian stood braced against the wall at the very top of the ladder to the loft. His scowl was dark and ominous.

Alisa did not pause in her frenzied packing. "I'm leaving at dawn," she answered flatly.

"How do you intend to do that?"

"I'll walk."

"You'll be lost before you're gone an hour."

"I'll manage."

"That's ridiculous."

Blazing dark-blue eyes raised to meet his; dignity and pride emanated from her diminutive form. "I have tried to please you, but there is no pleasing you. Make no mistake about it, I am capable of doing anything I set out to do. I am leaving."

"What do you think will be accomplished by that?" Christian's tone was low, dispassionate.

"I tried to be what you wanted, I tried to make up for the wrong I did you, but there is only so much punishment I am willing to accept from you for that. You will unfortunately still be a married man, but you will be free of the plots of conniving women. We need never see each other again."

"I won't agree to that," he said flatly, but he wondered at the level his own anger was reaching at the thought. Still, he held it in check.

"I don't care whether you agree to it or not. I refuse to be eternally punished by you! I will not suffer your moods any longer. You cast me as either the cherished bride or the hated villainess according to your whim, and never with any warning! Well, we've both gotten what we need from this."

Christian laughed without mirth as he walked slowly toward her. "I need nothing from you."

"And that is exactly what you will get from now on. You will have the protection of marriage without the burden of the unwanted wife! It should suit you!"

"You are not leaving!" Christian's voice rose loud.

Alisa stared at him levelly, her determination evident. "You can't stop me!" Her tone was quiet, strong.

His large hand shot out with lightning quickness, grabbing her reticule and tossing it over the edge of the loft. The creases in each cheek grew deep as his jaw clenched and his eyes bored through her. "You are not leaving," he repeated.

"Why?" Alisa taunted. "Haven't you finished your punishment? I should think that this evening's entertainment was the ultimate retaliation. Or do you mean to kill me as you threatened?"

"Tonight was not some damn punishment. You wanted to be my wife and, by God, that's what you're going to be!"

"Why? Do you find pleasure in tormenting me?

No, I almost forgot, you find no pleasure in me at all, do you? It was a well-orchestrated performance. You have my admiration for your talents, but I will not stay for the encore."

Powerful hands clasped her shoulders painfully, and Alisa stared up into a countenance of the blackest rage, but her own fury was an equal match and she felt no fear.

"You'll stay, my sweet, treacherous little bitch! You'll stay until I'm finished with you. I decide when you'll go and only then will you find yourself back in England."

"I'll never go back to England!" she shouted without thinking.

One bushy brow rose. "And what do you think to do here with no family and no money? Walk the streets, perhaps?"

Alisa slapped his arrogant cheek with force, her voice knife-edged with sarcasm. "You've already said you don't want me. What difference does it make if someone else does?"

Christian spoke through clenched teeth. "No other man will ever touch you!"

"What difference does it make to you? You were forced to marry me, you despised me even when you believed yourself responsible for your fate. Knowing I was the cause only deepened your hatred. I should think you would count it as a blessing to pass me off onto someone else."

Christian shook her just once. "I may not have chosen you, but you're mine now! And goddammit, you are not leaving!"

His mouth took hers in a fierce, hard kiss as powerful hands held her tightly to his chest, her breasts pressed flat. Alisa pushed against him in a futile attempt to free herself, her small strength nothing compared to his large, muscular body.

He was filled with an overwhelming desire for her, a need to possess her, to prove she was his. His body hardened and throbbed with a white-hot need he had never before known.

Alisa's fury and pain turned rapidly into a desire that nearly matched Christian's, though she fought against the rising tide in her blood. A tiny voice in her mind reminded her of his hurtful words. She pulled her mouth from his, her head thrown back more in agony than in anger.

"You don't want me," she said, a low, hoarse, pain-filled sound.

"I want you too much," he grated as again his lips met hers, his hand holding her head imprisoned.

She wanted to fight him, she wanted to injure that arrogant male pride, she wanted to prove he held no power over her. But she wanted him, and as his massive hands held her melded to him, all else seemed unimportant.

His lips left hers to bury themselves in the deep hollow of her throat as he lifted her up into his arms. Their mutual hunger engulfed the rage.

Christian knelt on the feather tics before the now-cold hearth. His arms moved to slide beneath Alisa's robe, slipping it from her shoulders to fall free of her body. His large, powerful hands ran across her skin. His mouth fell to hers, his tongue no longer tentative or teasing but searching, demanding, meeting hers in bold thrusts as he shrugged from his own robe and breeches.

The first meeting of bare flesh induced a gasp of pleasure as her hands reached for him, curling about his broad back to press its granite-hard, bulging muscles. When his hand reached her taut breast, her body thrust upward; and when the searing moistness of his mouth took it fully, sucking, nipping, tormenting, she moaned for more. His hand left her breast to the single delight of his tongue and teeth and lips, reaching without preamble to the curling triangle between her slim thighs and then lower still, exploring her satin warmth for just a few fleeting moments before he rolled to cover her completely with his immense, magnificent girth.

Her legs opened to him in sensual invitation. His rigid length sought entrance into her warm, moist intimacy. A stinging pain instinctively made her tighten her muscles firmly around him, but her discomfort was quickly replaced by the exquisite feeling of him full within her. She met his thrusts, striving equally with him to reach a crest, each sleek body clinging to the other in a union of timeless perfection.

When at last passion was slaked, Christian rolled to his side and, as he had before, clasped Alisa tightly to him. His whisper broke the silence. "Alisa . . ." he began, but two slender fingers pressed his lips to stop him.

"Don't talk, Christian," she breathed. "Your words hurt too much."

"I'm sorry for that," he said almost inaudibly.

Her only answer was to curl close in his arms, and each found an exhausted slumber.

Chapter Twenty-six

Christian awakened slowly with no thought of shattering this feeling of genuine contentment. He was filled with wonder at the night's lovemaking. He had never experienced such a flawless blending of passion. Alisa demanded only that he sate her desire. Her joy in his body was heady. Too many times his encounters had been perfunctory, a bartering for money, favors, or enhancing a reputation.

And then, there had been Ellen. Only now did Christian realize what a talented actress she was. Ellen had never seemed to want more from him than his own pleasure, the picture of the selfless lover. Yet in the end, she had been no different. She had needed his money, his name, his position. She had played the role so well that only now, in comparison with Alisa's response, did Christian realize the emptiness in it. Everything about Ellen had been a fake.

He sighed, breathing the clean, sweet scent of his wife's hair as she slept in his arms. He admitted it was impossible to keep himself remote from her as he had planned the previous night. It was threatening and disconcerting to find himself so affected by her, and worse yet, by the thought of her leaving. But she presented no danger, he rationalized. Only if he loved her could she actually injure him, and he felt safe from that foolishness.

In her sleep, Alisa curled more deeply into the warm shelter of his body, an innate sensuality in even this small movement. Christian smiled to himself, enjoying the feel of her. One hand lightly caressed the silken skin of her back and the gentle roundness of her buttocks. He reminded himself that soft feelings for a woman were treacherous. He sighed and eased his body from around Alisa, so as not to wake her.

Once out of bed, Christian pulled the quilts up to her shoulders. As he donned his clothes, he watched her sleep. Even now she seemed a bit untamed. He found her more intriguing than any other woman he had ever known. Her indomitable spirit challenged him. Her beauty was natural, and she was unaffected by it. She did not use it to accomplish her ends. She had humility and grace. And she was a wonderful companion.

Christian forcibly stopped himself from continuing this litany of Alisa's virtues. It sounded as though he were in love with her. But his capacity to love had been exhausted long ago. He viewed it as a depleted cache, a spring gone dry. His interest in Alisa was harmless, his desires for her understandable, for what man wouldn't want her? He felt a certain relief in having convinced himself.

He moved to awaken Alisa, confident in the knowledge that his heart was unassailable, his emotions under impenetrable control.

"I don't understand why it was imperative that we leave the cabin the moment you decided," Alisa complained as she wrapped her arms more tightly around Christian's broad body. She was in imminent danger of losing her seat on the horse, and her temper at their spur-of-the-moment departure.

Christian shrugged, the movement of his muscular back, in rhythm with their mount, sending a slight thrill through her. "There wasn't any reason to wait. I'll have to send a servant up to get our things. We couldn't burden this horse with more than the two of us," he explained easily.

"When did you decide it was time to leave the cabin?" Alisa was trying to understand this impulsive move.

"It occurred to me this morning that Christmas is less than a week away, and I prefer celebrating it as always."

"And how is that?" Alisa had forgotten the holiday was so near. In the turmoil of the past weeks, she had little thought, save a solution to her problems with Christian.

Christian's handsome face peered at her over his shoulder, the grin beneath his bushy mustache forming deep crevices in each cheek. "We spend it quietly, at the country house." A glint of mischief suddenly sparked in his eyes. "Hold tight, it's too damn cold to keep this slow pace."

Christian nudged his well-trained mount into a fast trot, anxious to reach the warm comfort of the place he considered home.

The first sign of civilization was two huge stone slabs supporting a gate of heavy cedar slats opening at the center to lead to a long, winding, tree-lined road beyond.

Finally, the house came into view in the distance. It was a huge Georgian mansion with a pillared front on which thick vines grew up the columns and across the roof to form leafy green arches in the summer. The portico sheltered a veranda, which opened off the front parlor and overlooked a wide brick terrace and perfectly manicured gardens. The porch was supported by brick arches that formed a protected gallery below, adjoining the terrace. As they drew near, Alisa could see that the arches made a brick tunnel over a cobbled floor.

The house contained forty-two rooms, as well as a large stable and servants' quarters. Alisa was awestruck as she entered the oversize front door, to find herself facing a grand staircase in the entrance hall. It reached straight up three floors, deep landings marking the second and third levels.

Christian's pride and affection for this place was obvious as he led her from one magnificent room to another. Nothing in this house held the austere formality of the one in New Haven. It was decorated in perfect taste to afford the warmest, most comfortable ambience possible. Alisa instantly fell in love with it.

"Did the same person decorate this house and the New Haven one?" she asked curiously.

Suspicion clouded Christian's features. "My mother did both originally. Does something displease you?" His question was an accusation. She was bewildered by his abrupt change in mood.

She forged ahead, expecting to offend him as it seemed she always did. "I meant nothing, except that this house and half of the other are lovely. But the formal rooms seem so stiff and stuffy, they don't fit with the coziness of the rest."

"And what would you change?" he challenged.

Alisa felt as if she were suddenly facing an inquisition; she opted for honesty. "I would not alter this place in any way. And the other I would not touch, either, save for those rooms I mentioned, but even that is unimportant. They are your homes, Christian. I would not presume to change anything."

Christian's smile was slow, warm, further disconcerting her. "The rooms which you dislike in the house in town I allowed Ellen to decorate. She abhorred the rest of that house and all of this." There was a bitter note in this disclosure, which made Alisa wonder if each time a drastic change came over him, he was recollecting something about his former marriage. She did not like the feeling that at any moment she might stir some memory and be punished for something said in innocence. "I am not your first wife, nor am I anything like her, and I do not appreciate having to guard my every word lest you believe my motives the same as hers!"

Christian scowled darkly, one bushy brow rising. "Your shrewishness seems quite similar. And since you know nothing of Ellen, you cannot judge whether you are alike or not."

"Since you know virtually nothing about me, neither can you!"

"I know very well that you prefer deceit and trickery to the truth, and that is very much like Ellen."

"I don't 'prefer' them. I was in a position that forced me to use them."

"So was she. It's hardly enough to soothe your victim."

"My victim needs no soothing; he wallows in what is past and what wrongs were done him."

They stood facing each other in the upper hallway of the third floor; her voice was raised loudly while Christian's was controlled, level, remote.

"Wallowing, is it? Perhaps you should have

chosen some dimwit who would not remember your treachery beyond the moment it trapped him."

"Perhaps I should have. Certainly had I known I would be punished not only for my own misdeeds but for your former wife's as well, I would not have chosen you."

Christian's voice was suddenly low. "Why did you choose me, Alisa? Any man would have served the purpose."

Alisa was struck dumb for a moment, her thoughts racing. "I didn't choose you, Ivy did," she answered after a pause, averting her eyes from his. "There was not another man that my father would have believed capable of doing the deed. I have never been a compliant person, and he would have known that a lesser man would have come out of it more damaged than I." She had to convince him.

"Why the hell didn't you just run off and marry some suitor? Wouldn't that have been easier?"

"There were no suitors," she said in a voice so soft that it was barely audible. Then she remembered that this argument was not about her misdeeds but his, and anger flowed anew. "You have adeptly changed the subject. But the fact remains that I will not be blamed for someone else's crimes against you."

Christian stared down at her. "You've committed enough of your own, I don't need to 'blame' you for someone else's. You're hardly the innocent being accused wrongly."

"I am guilty of one crime against you. As of late, I am most certainly innocent of what you accuse. Or has your memory faded again since just last night?"

"As I said, your shrewishness is much like Ellen's." Christian turned from her and walked to the end of the hallway. With one hand already on the banister, he added, "I was going to wait until tomorrow to go into New Haven to tend to some business, but I've always found that the best way of dealing with feminine tantrums is to remove myself. Pick whatever rooms appeal to you. I'll be back in a few days." He took one step down and then turned back to Alisa. "And don't try to leave. Every servant in the place will be warned not to allow it, and I'll set a man to watch you. The aces are all in my hand now, and I intend to use them to my advantage."

Alisa's shriek of frustration echoed behind him as he left and brought a smile to his handsome features.

Chapter Twenty-seven

For three days Alisa fumed. She chose her bedroom, a beautiful haven of reddish browns and russets, with thick velvet drapes framing carved lintels over each window, and hand-sewn quilts in cream and russet colors on the huge bed that stood nearly waist high. She found no solace in overseeing the servants' preparation of a large room on the third floor, which was to be her studio. Her temper cooled a bit with the arrival of newly purchased paints and inks, parchments and canvases. The note that accompanied them was written in Christian's large, dark scrawl, instructing her to keep herself busy until he returned, and it was signed with only his name. The arrogance of this brief missive induced a fresh surge of anger.

When Scott arrived two days before Christmas, Alisa was not yet in a pleasant mood, though she tried to appear polite to her brother-in-law. He again found her in her studio arranging her supplies.

His voice startled her. "Do you spend all of your time at this, Alisa?" His tone was warm.

She managed a taut smile in return. "I haven't much else to do."

Scott laughed lightly. "Do I detect a note of hostility?"

Alisa sighed. "Not for you. I didn't mean to take my anger out on you, Scott."

"I didn't expect to find you in this mood. Christian came back to New Haven in high spirits. I assumed everything had worked out well for you."

"As well as is possible in view of your brother's penchant for holding grudges."

"Making you suffer for your trickery, is he?" Scott laughed.

The thought of what had passed between them in the cabin brought a blush to her lovely features. "Let's just say he is not forgiving."

"Give him some time. Whether you know it or not, I think he's softening toward you. I heard him arrange for your Christmas present."

"A shackle and chains, no doubt."

Again he laughed, finding her very appealing. "Not quite. Are you giving him a gift?" Scott's friendliness was irresistible, and Alisa welcomed the camaraderie he offered.

"I can think of only one thing to give him. Actually, it's something I owe him, but I don't know how to go about getting it."

"I don't have anything to do between now and Christmas. I'd be glad to help, if I can."

Midnight-blue eyes glowed as Alisa accepted his offer. She wondered if merely arranging to transport something Christian already owned could be considered a gift.

Alisa truly liked Scott. His company was extremely pleasant; his natural warmth always put her at ease. But the newness of their relationship, as well as the tenuous, uncertain one between her and Christian, left Alisa still feeling like an outsider. Because of this, after sharing an enjoyable few hours with her brother-in-law decorating the Christmas tree in the huge drawing room, she refused his invitation for wine. She needed the time to complete her payment to Scott for his help with Christian's gift.

She stayed closeted away in her studio until late on Christmas Eve, putting the final touches to a portrait of Scott, working carefully with a pen unsuited to the task. Christian had neglected to include pens and brushes with her supplies, so she was left to use what was on hand. Scott had decided that a portrait of himself was sufficient payment for the small service he had provided.

When at last Alisa judged the picture complete, she placed it beneath the tree. As she climbed the stairs to her room on the second level, she wondered if Christian intended to return at all, for it was well past midnight. She was surprised to find her anger gone and in its place a weighty disappointment that he had not returned to spend Christmas with her. It was not comforting to think of herself as such bitter medicine that he would avoid a family tradition to be free of her company.

The first wave of homesickness washed over Alisa with the feeling of being heartily unwanted, if not despised. Through all that had happened in the past months, she had rarely thought of her family in England. Now she suddenly felt devastatingly lonely, longing for the uncomplicated companionship of her family.

She wearily opened the door to her room. Her eyes grew wide at the unexpected sight that awaited her. The room was awash in the golden glow of dozens of candles in every crevice and on every firm surface that could accommodate them. The reflection of all the small flickering flames in the tall cheval mirror completed the effect. On the floor in front of the hearth was the large mattress swathed in quilts.

Alisa's surprised glance traveled the room, resting on Christian's broad back as he bent to light the last few candles in the far corner. All of Alisa's dark feelings fled to be replaced by a glow as warm as that which filled the room.

At the soft sound of the door closing, Christian turned to face his wife, a wide grin pulling his mustache and deepening the indentations in his cheeks. "Merry Christmas, Alisa," he greeted her, the low, rich tones of his voice kindling pleasure in her breast.

Alisa returned his smile. "What is all of this?" she asked softly, a quizzical frown creasing her features.

The sight of her beauty made him realize why he had been so impatient to get back. She stood bathed in candlelight, the burnished copper mass of curls glimmering as they fell about her shoulders and arms. He shrugged negligently, reluctant to show eagerness.

"I was plagued all the way home by the picture of you lying on the floor in the glow of the fire. It seemed like a nice way to spend Christmas Eve."

Alisa moved away from the door, walking slowly around the room to see the extent of an effort that unaccountably touched her with tenderness. "I didn't think you were coming back," she said, the simple statement hardly conveying the desolation she had felt.

"I told you I'd be here in a few days."

Alisa shrugged, not understanding what she felt in the air around them. There was no animosity, only an indescribably sweet tension. "But by this time of night I didn't expect you."

"Are you sorry to see me?" he asked tautly.

"Surprised but not sorry. I would hate to have my gift go to waste."

They stood facing each other, separated by the entire length of the room. Christian smiled lazily and stepped slowly closer. "It seems I am forever returning to find we do not share a room."

"It hasn't seemed to hinder you."

He laughed lightly, moving still nearer. "Do you mean it to?" His voice was filled with sensuality, every movement of his large, masculine body visually arousing.

"You always leave me in suspense. I'm never sure what to expect from you."

"And so you ban me from your room?" His smile was languorous.

"It doesn't look as if you've been banned from here."

"Then why aren't my things here?" Christian stood only a few feet from her.

"As I said, I never know what to expect from you. I didn't know if you intended to share my room."

"How could there be any doubt?"

He stopped only inches from her; she tilted her head back to maintain her view of his handsome face. They did not touch.

She laughed lightly. "I've learned well to doubt

everything. I seem always to be teetering on the verge of igniting the flames."

"That's definitely true, but the flames you ignite are not always my temper."

His head lowered to hers, taking her lips in a soft, sensual kiss that lasted only a brief moment.

"Now, for instance," he whispered, "what warms my blood has nothing at all to do with anger."

Again he kissed her, a bit longer, a bit deeper.

"What does it have to do with?" Her voice was soft, her eyelids moving slowly open after his kiss.

Christian laughed, a low rumble in his throat. "It has to do with how your hair falls freely to your waist like some silken waterfall; it has to do with those damn blue eyes that are too dark to be real, and with lips that demand to be kissed without ever speaking. It has to do with the memory of how your bare skin feels against mine, of the sweet smell of you and the sweeter taste. It has to do with the way it feels to be inside you."

He inhaled deeply as his lips again took hers, this time with more force, his tongue exploring her mouth, but still his hands did not reach her.

She felt entranced by the spell he wove so expertly around her.

"I think I should be offended that you neglect my mind and think only of my body," she murmured teasingly.

He kissed the hollow of her throat, his tongue flicking lightly. "I can never disregard what makes the rest function. Unless it chooses now to spar with me, then I shall be forced to ignore it." His mouth sucked gently on the side of her neck just below her ear.

Alisa sighed, giving herself over to the desires he

was arousing in her. Her voice was a whisper as she bent her head to ease his way. "I was very angry with you."

He nibbled lightly on her earlobe, his breath warm against her skin. "One of us seems always to be angry with the other."

His large hands moved to the buttons fastening the front of her gown, loosening them without touching the satin flesh beneath.

"Why do you think that happens?" she breathed.

"I think it has to do with the fact that you're a tart little termagant." His hands slid under her gown to free her of it.

"Or perhaps it's your quick, hot temper."

"Perhaps," he conceded, shrugging free of his own shirt, leaving his hairy chest bare. "Have you always been so difficult to get along with, my lady?"

"Always." She smiled sensually, her eyes caressing him. "Have you?" she countered.

"Certainly."

He lowered her many voluminous petticoats to fall about her feet, leaving her clad in only her chemise. Bluish-green eyes lowered to her breasts where they pushed against the light fabric, but his hands worked to remove his own trousers.

"Do you think we shall ever get along?" She felt the heat of his body so near, yet not touching her.

"Only if you are tamed," he answered as the last article of clothing dropped to the now large pile around their feet.

"And what of you, my fierce sea captain? Shall you be tamed as well?"

His kiss traced a fiery path to just above her breast, his tongue teasing.

"Never!"

He pulled her arms up to rest on either side of his neck. Her hands turned in to rub his nape softly, toying with the waving hair.

"Then we are destined to war," she breathed huskily.

He picked her up into his arms and stepped over their clothes and onto the mattress.

"But not tonight," he growled into her shoulder.

He laid her gently down and then joined her, one long leg crossed over the copper triangle where her thighs joined, pressing just enough to light the fire that he had so carefully been building in her. His mouth took hers now in a demanding kiss, his tongue jutting freely to meet hers. One massive hand reached her breast, already taut and aroused, so that even the lightest caress sent chills along her spine. She felt his hard manhood against her side, inviting her to push against him. He groaned at the contact, his kiss deepening in response to the fierce desire racing through him.

Discovering that she could contribute to his pleasure was an intriguing surprise. Her hands felt him, traveling the full expanse of his muscular body, exploring granite-hard ridges and the tangled hair at his chest. Light fingers followed that hair but stopped at the flat, firm stomach, uncertain as to what she was allowed beyond that.

Christian moaned in near agony, tearing away from her lips. "No, don't stop!"

His massive hand reached hers, guiding it lower until she discovered that nothing was forbidden, that the softness of her hand aroused Christian to a level where she could feel the devastating wave of passion and a desire too great to be refused. She liked the silken feel of him and his response to her hands stroking him.

Christian's mouth took her breast in delightful torment as his own hand explored her lower parts, until neither could endure another moment without their bodies joining. They raced together to a peak of ecstasy that exploded in nearly the same second as they held each other in a crushing embrace.

Chapter Twenty-eight

In a household without children, Christmas morning arrives quietly. Christian left Alisa to dress while he and Scott distributed gifts to the servants. He assured her that the family would not congregate around the tree for at least an hour more to open their packages.

Alisa's gown was a deep, rich hunter's-green velvet, the high neck edged with crisp white lace that also fell in four lines down the tight-fitting bodice and circled the wide skirt in three rows around the bottom. A wide taffeta sash in a brilliant red, white, and green plaid encircled her narrow waist, ending in a large bow at the base of her spine. The sleeves were large puffs that stood in gathers high above her shoulders and were caught again at her wrists by wide cuffs trimmed in the same white lace as the neck.

Alisa had worn this gown and sash on the Christmas just past. It had been a gift from her father, brought with him from a trip to Scotland. That memory raised another short surge of homesickness, but she quickly chased it away.

She spent the remainder of her time brushing the tangled mass of her hair and arranging it in a loose knot at the crown of her head, though several stray wisps refused to be contained at her ears and the back of her neck. She sighed when she had finished, fearing her arrangement was too plain.

She hurriedly left her room, only to collide with a very dapper-looking Nicholas, his silver-blond hair falling casually across his brow as black eyes widened in surprise at the sight of her. He bowed gallantly, his smile rakish.

"You are a lovely vision, sweet Alisa. I don't think Christian deserves another gift for the rest of his life. I know I would be willing to accept you as my only Christmas present."

Alisa laughed lightly at his banter. "And your honeyed words are gift enough for me, though I fear you're teasing me."

He held out his arm for her to take as they proceeded down the hall. "If you think so, then all of the mirrors in your room must be broken." He pulled her hand up to his mouth, gently kissing it. "You are a vast improvement on the scenery here, I assure you." The twinkle in his dark eyes left her still believing he jested.

That was how Christian found them at the foot of the grand staircase. A scowl darkened his features as he possessively moved between them to take his wife's arm.

"Be warned, Nicholas," he said, half-teasing, half-serious. "This fair package is mine alone!"

Nicholas's hands clasped his chest above his heart. "Have pity, Christian, it's Christmas morning. Allow me at least the joy of looking."

Christian led the way to the drawing room, speaking over his shoulder. "Look, yes, but never touch."

As they entered the parlor, Scott came quickly to welcome Alisa, his smile warm. "Merry Christmas, Alisa." Though her hand was still held firmly in the crook of Christian's arm, Scott clasped her shoulders and surprised her with a kiss, then turned a mischievous grin to his brother. "That was the only thing I really wanted for Christmas."

Christian frowned at his wife. "I can see that I will never be able to leave you alone with these two lechers."

But Alisa simply smiled brilliantly, thoroughly enjoying the attentions of these handsome men.

As Christian sorted through the wrapped packages beneath the tree, Alisa's eyes followed him. He was dressed in a navy-blue coat and breeches, both tight-fitting to accentuate his muscular frame. His vest was dark-blue brocade that hugged his narrow waist snugly. He wore a shirt of crisp white silk with collar points that stood up, and a neckcloth wound around his throat. Alisa marveled at his well-groomed handsomeness, knowing he had spent very little time to accomplish it.

Everything was opened in one flurry of colored papers and ribbons before Alisa realized that the slow, careful, separate unveiling of each person's gifts that was her family's tradition was not observed here. She had not opened even one gift while everyone around her was already finished and shouting their thanks. Within moments all eyes rested on her.

Alisa laughed gaily. "You're all like little boys who can't wait to see what Santa's brought."

"You'll have to forgive us, Alisa," Scott said.

"Since Mother's been gone, we have not had the calming presence of a lady."

Christian cleared his throat in mock consternation at his brother's pointed barb, but his tone was kind when he spoke to her. "You're the only one left, Alisa. Open yours."

Alisa supposed that her careful unwrapping made them impatient, but she would not be hurried. From Nicholas she received a large box of French bonbons, which delighted her, and from Scott, a hand-tooled riding crop.

"I thought perhaps you might need that to defend yourself," Scott said, his gaze markedly on Christian.

Alisa's final package was a long, flat wooden box with only a card that read "Christian." When she opened its lid, she found a varied assortment of pens and brushes with the most beautiful hand-carved and polished handles she had ever seen. They were exquisite. She raised midnight-blue eyes to Christian, almost quizzically, for she had not expected anything so thoughtful and certainly not something so unique.

He returned her smile, their eyes locked for a brief second. "Didn't you think it odd that I sent you everything but these?" His voice was soft, for her ears only.

"I thought you had simply overlooked it. I've never owned any so lovely, thank you."

A knowing chuckle from Scott interrupted. "She does very well without those fancy things, Christian. Did you see my portrait?"

Without waiting for an answer Scott pulled the picture from behind the tree to display it to Nicholas and Christian. It was the very likeness of Scott in black ink on parchment. Captured there was his sensitivity, his warmth, even his humor in the small lines around his eyes. There was nothing of the usual stiff, posed, formal portrayal of most portraits.

Christian studied the picture proudly held before him. He turned a raised brow toward his wife and then to his brother.

"It seems the two of you have spent quite some time together," he commented in a neutral tone.

"I should say so!" Nicholas exclaimed, oblivious to Christian's meaning. "Why, something so finely done would take long hours. It is absolutely magnificent."

"Hardly that!" she murmured, embarrassed.

Christian's gaze was piercing. "I had no idea you were so talented, Alisa. Or so taken with Scott."

"Back off, Christian," Scott interjected. "I asked her to do the picture as payment for your Christmas gift. That's all there was to it."

Nicholas watched the three now, seeing a tension he had been unaware of before. "Surely you can't see anything in this but her great ability with a pen, Christian."

"Is there more to it?" Christian asked Alisa, who was mortified to be the center of this new outburst.

Before she could answer, Scott's voice interrupted in a more jovial tone.

"Go on, Christian, you haven't seen your gift yet. Let her show it to you."

Alisa was grateful for the reprieve. "I'll get my cloak," was all she said as she left the room, avoiding the eyes of the three men there.

When Alisa was well out of hearing, Scott faced his brother in irritation. "You're a damn fool, Christian! What the hell got into you?"

Christian sat back against the chair, staring at the floor rather than meeting his brother's glare. "Old memories, Scott," he said in a low, barely audible tone.

"She doesn't deserve to be treated that way."

"She doesn't need you to defend her, either!" Christian shot back.

Scott frowned, searching his brother's features as if he found something there he had never seen. "This isn't like you, Christian. Let go of what happened in the past and open your eyes to what you have now, before you ruin it."

Christian sighed heavily and pushed himself from his seat. "I assume I'll need a coat," was his only answer as he followed Alisa.

Scott shook his head and he, too, left the drawing room, saying nothing to Nicholas, who sat watching it all in interest.

"I sure as hell wish I knew what was going on," he said to himself, knowing he would not rest until he found out.

Alisa and Christian walked in silence to the stables. The air was crisp and silent save for the crunch of each step on fresh snow.

Alisa stared straight ahead, her chin high, her arms crossed to hold her cloak closed around her. Christian watched her surreptitiously from the corner of his eye, not knowing whether she was furious or simply as dispassionately removed as she appeared.

Just before they reached the large, whitewashed wooden structure, Alisa spoke, her head never veering from its rigid frontward stare, her voice as icy and impersonal as the world around them. "Have you always been such a big oaf, or is it a new facet of your personality for my benefit alone?"

In the time between leaving Scott in the drawing room and joining Alisa, Christian's reason had returned, and his quick suspicions dissolved with it. He spoke in a normal tone. "The portrait was very good. My first impression was that it was too good to have been done by someone without feelings for her subject."

Midnight-blue eyes flashed up at him suddenly. "I do have feelings for your brother. Warm, friendly feelings. He is the only member of the Reed family that has treated me with kindness, understanding or consideration. There is nothing beyond friendship between us. Perhaps your anger is due to the fact that you abandoned me once again in a strange place with people I don't know, with not a clue as to what my position in your household is, and Scott disrupted your punishment by keeping me company and offering me a perfectly innocent diversion."

Christian's jaw clenched, and he stared over her head for a time, realizing that she was nearer to the truth than he cared to admit. He was angered by the thought of Scott enjoying Alisa's company when he had been without it. He said only, "I did not leave you here as punishment. I had things to tend to in New Haven."

"For a man who has spent so much time harping about honesty, Christian Reed, you are a remarkably good liar."

"Am I?" He stared down at her, his brows furrowed into a deep frown, but his mouth twitched as if suppressing a grin.

"You are also insufferably arrogant, and I will thank you to spare Scott, Nicholas and me the embarrassment of such a display in the future. No one appreciates being witness to other people's marital arguments."

"Is that so?" Now he broke into a full grin, obviously amused by her tirade.

It served to fuel her anger, and she had a strong desire to double up her fist and surprise his smirking face with a punch in the stomach. "Yes, you are, and yes, that is so!" she fairly shouted in answer to his irritatingly smug question.

"I will tell you one thing in all honesty, Alisa Reed." He seemed suddenly to be enjoying himself. "A tongue-lashing in this frigid clime is not my idea of a Christmas gift, and I sure as hell know that you don't need help from Scott in presenting it to me."

Alisa turned to face the house again. "As a matter of fact, I have lost all desire to give you anything."

A large hand halted her retreat as he grasped her upper arm and pulled her close to the side of his chest. "You wouldn't want me to go back to thinking something 'improper' happened between you and Scott, would you? You had better show me the proof of his aid."

Midnight-blue eyes flashed up at him. "I don't care what you think!"

"But if you run back to the house like a scared rabbit without showing me my gift, many will be witness to our discord." His gaze left her and moved to the house.

Alisa's eyes followed his to find Scott and Nicholas peering from one window, and any number of servants from the others. Her eyes closed in embarrassment. "I think I prefer fighting in the cabin without an audience."

"We could always return there." He spoke low, his

mouth pressed to her ear as if voicing endearments. He appeared to be quite in control while she raved.

Alisa hissed in a soft, jeering tone, "But then I would have to endure your close company again. I prefer the audience!"

He laughed low. "I know that to be a lie." He pulled her to stand in front of him. "Now, let's show them that we have resolved our differences, shall we?"

Alisa smiled sweetly up at Christian, for all the world appearing to be placated by her handsome husband. "Then you're not above a little deceit of your own?"

"I've found my solution, Alisa, make no mistake. It's a simple matter of not leaving you alone. Besides, since you consider the lack of my company to be a punishment, I wouldn't think of depriving you."

Alisa's smile faded, and she pulled her arm from his grasp. She would not return to the watching eyes of the household, but neither would she let him goad her. Instead, she marched into the stable several feet ahead, to the sound of Christian's victorious laughter.

The cow that waited in the barn with a red ribbon tied around her neck stood unaffected by the two people staring at her. Alisa ungraciously gestured toward it, refusing to speak. She positioned herself a good distance from the animal and her husband.

Christian laughed heartily, delighted with his present. He untied the bow and swatted the animal's hind quarter, in appreciation, just above the Reed brand. Then tying the ribbon in a bow around Alisa's collar, he gently coaxed her back to the house.

Chapter Twenty-nine

Alisa stood with her back to Christian as she unpinned her hair from its loose knot. Christian watched her openly as he discarded his clothing piece by piece.

Alisa had not spoken to him throughout the day and evening, though her wit and light chatter had entertained and entranced both Nicholas and Scott. Christian knew the tactic only too well and refused to allow it to rile his temper.

Alisa had untied the plaid sash encircling her waist and Christian was just removing his trousers when they heard the sound of a loud commotion. Male voices rose in bellowing rage, accented with the heavy crash of something hitting the side of the house.

"Dammit," Christian muttered impatiently, pulling on his boots hurriedly. He raced from the room, his broad chest bare.

Alisa heard the other bedroom doors open as Scott and Nicholas ran fast on Christian's heels toward the angry voices. With her hair flying in wild disarray, Alisa followed them down the huge staircase and through the kitchen. Even before she got outside, she could distinguish the sound of fists meeting flesh in meaty thuds.

She stepped through the door after Scott and Nicholas, seeing two men battling with ferocity. Already one face was bloodied, clothing was torn, and a large stone vase on the brick path was shattered. The strong smell of liquor assaulted her nostrils.

One man was much larger than the other, though he seemed the more abused as his small, wily opponent shouted obscenities. The larger man suddenly produced a knife, snarling that he would not lose to a runt.

"Dammit, Bart, that's enough!" Christian's voice was loud and commanding as one long, bare arm reached to wrap around the smaller man's waist to pull him, kicking and screaming, from his attack.

Alisa's glance was riveted to the larger man as he veered, ominously losing his balance. He teetered twice as if he would catch himself, but his inebriated state was his undoing. His body lost all control and he fell forward, his hands flailing in his drunken clumsiness.

Alisa's eyes grew round and wide as she stared in horrid memory. In her eyes, the man falling seemed slower than he possibly could have been, as if every movement of his descending body was exaggerated. Before he even reached the ground, her mind had taken over and what she saw was Willis Potts falling to the ground of the deserted road. She heard none of what was actually being said around her; she saw only the widening red puddle beneath Willis Potts's body. She heard a woman screaming, loud, terror-stricken shrieks. She did not realize it was her own voice that screamed in horror.

All eyes turned to her. Her face was a gray

sheen, and a glassy glare covered her terror-widened eyes.

Christian flung his prisoner toward Nicholas. "Take care of this mess," he shouted to Scott, who knelt beside the large, prostrate man who was just pushing himself up onto his hands and knees, the knife lying harmlessly beneath.

Alisa did not even feel Christian's arms lift her to rest against his chest; she was unaware that he carried her back to their room and set her gently on her feet again.

Christian shouted her name over and over again, shaking her shoulders in an effort to reach her through her screams.

Reality dawned as the sound of her name being called came through to her. Her hands pressed more firmly against her mouth, her eyes cleared of their glazed stare.

But the terror remained reflected in her exquisite features. Christian reacted instinctively, pulling her into his embrace, holding her tightly against his body, his arms wrapped around her, his shoulders curved to protect her from something he did not understand. He knew that the brawl downstairs had not caused this hysteria.

"Sh, sh, Alisa. It's all right. You're safe," he murmured, his tone deep and comforting, drawing Alisa's senses back into sanity.

Her small body shook with the tremors of fear, and dry midnight-blue eyes tried hard to focus on her surroundings. Her cheek pressed into the warm mat of furry hair on Christian's chest.

It took a long while before she calmed down. In all that time, Christian remained holding her, smooth-

ing the silken tangles of her hair, whispering soothing words of comfort.

"I'm sorry, Christian. I'm so sorry," she repeated
over and over, still not completely aware of the time
and place.

"What are you sorry for, Alisa?" he asked softly.

The sound of his deep voice was a welcome balm to
her shattered nerves. She wanted to remain forever
in his arms, protected by his massive, powerful body,
soothed by the richness of his voice as it sounded at
that moment. The cocoon of his body formed such a
safe haven, the only refuge where she felt truly safe.
But when total reality dawned, Alisa knew that
there would be no haven, no refuge if Christian
learned she was a murderess. As she fought for control, long, fingered hands rested for a moment on the
muscular hardness of Christian's chest, and then she
pushed herself reluctantly from his arms.

"I'm sorry for being such a ninny," she said
unsteadily, refusing to lift her gaze to those bluish-
green depths that saw too much. "I've seen fights before, but never where a man was killed."

Christian studied her, seeing her confusion, her
fear and her attempt to conceal it. Bushy brows drew
down in a deep frown, but his tone was still low,
soothing. "No one was killed, Alisa."

"Oh!" A note of panic sounded in her voice. "I was
afraid the man who fell on his knife had died."

"He got up after he fell." He watched closely, her
words confirming his certainty that she had been re-
acting to something other than what had happened.

"I must not have seen that," she said uneasily.

"What did you see?"

Alisa moved across the room now, her hands
wringing in agitation. "I thought I saw the man

killed. I didn't see him sit up, I must have looked away then. I'm glad he didn't die," she hedged.

"I don't think you saw any of what went on downstairs. I don't think you even knew where you were."

"How could that possibly be? I was just upset by the incident. There's nothing else to it."

"I think you're lying to me, Alisa," he said evenly.

"You always think I'm lying!" she shot back.

"Regardless of how we came together, Alisa, I am your husband," he said softly, his genuine concern ringing clear. "I would not let you suffer your demons alone."

She could not be harsh with him. "It's nothing, Christian. Please, can we not talk about it anymore? It embarrasses me to have put on such a display," she said honestly.

Christian sighed but said nothing. He removed his breeches and boots and got into bed, bracing his head on clasped hands to watch Alisa disrobe. She donned her nightgown, never once turning to meet his gaze, and then climbed onto the high mattress very near to the edge. She tried futilely to suppress the tremors that again shook her.

"Won't you tell me your secrets, Alisa?" he beckoned one last time.

Her voice was a whisper. "There aren't any." The lie burned in her throat like bile.

One strong arm reached beneath her back, pulling her to his side. "If you won't confide in me, at least let me hold you."

She moved eagerly into his arms, her head falling to his muscular, hairy chest.

Christian held her tightly, still feeling her need for comforting, one hand pressing her head so firmly against his heart that she could hear its every beat.

The strength in his hands, in his arms, even his pulse consoled her anew and left her feeling well protected.

Christian was now positive she was hiding something. Instinct told him what she concealed was not threatening to him but something that tormented her alone. He wanted to help her, but there was no way unless she confided in him. Her quiet strength was a rare quality he respected. He admired the fact that she strove to conquer her demons alone. He could only offer solace.

He held her so tightly against him, he feared his own strength might hurt her, one sinewy leg thrown over her hips, so that she lay partially beneath him. After a long time, he felt her relax as if finally reassured she was safe. That much he could do for her.

Only then did he allow himself to sleep.

Chapter Thirty

"Are you all right, Alisa?" Scott stood behind her chair in the dining room, placing a warm hand on each shoulder.

She jumped, startled, not yet having fully recovered her composure from the past night.

"I'm sorry," Scott was quick to apologize. "I thought you heard me come in."

Alisa forced a laugh, trying not to embarrass herself further. "It's not your fault, Scott. I'm afraid I was daydreaming."

He sat beside her, patting her hand gently before stirring sugar into his morning coffee. "Have you recovered from last night's brawl?" His tone was friendly, putting her at ease as always.

"I'm fine, thank you. How is the man that fell?"

"He's bound to have one hell of a headache today, but he'll be all right. The other man is our overseer. He's a good worker, but his small size makes him feel the need to prove his strength. After holiday celebrations, I'm afraid, he tends to pick fights. I'm sorry it bothered you so much."

"It was silly. I'd rather forget all about it."

His smile was kind, accepting her dismissal in a way that made her grateful. "And where is my iras-

cible brother? I can't believe he's left you to breakfast alone."

"He was here a few minutes ago. He said he had to
see to the animals before we left for the city."

"Did he like his Christmas gift?"

Alisa blushed becomingly. "I don't really know."

Scott laughed. "He's still being difficult, is he?
Just have patience a while longer. I have confidence
in you. You'll win in the end, or my brother has lost
his wits."

Christian appeared in the doorway. He poured
himself a cup of coffee from the pot on the sideboard
and moved to sit on Alisa's other side. "Just what do
you believe my wife will win over what remains of
my wits?"

Scott smiled mischievously at Christian, unperturbed by his brother's barbs. "We are all hoping she
wins back the less surly Christian of before."

Christian pushed back into his chair, balancing on
only two of its legs, one arm across Alisa's seat. "My
reputation grows by the minute. Let's see if I have it
all understood. I am irascible; bad-, quick- and hot-
tempered; mean; a stern sea captain; a fearsome
beast; an oaf; and now surly as well."

Scott laughed. "Is that all? Alisa must be a master
of patience if she has called you only that."

Scott stood and smiled at Alisa as he moved to
leave the room. "You have my admiration for your
self-control."

"So long as it's from a distance," Christian
warned, only half-teasing.

"Always, Christian, always. Far be it from me to
woo the wife of a fearsome beast." As Scott passed
Alisa's chair, he pulled Christian's arm up by one
finger and then let it drop heavily back again. "Care-

ful, Christian, don't lose the battle too early and rob me of my entertainment."

Scott left the dining room, but not without first noticing that Christian removed his arm and replaced it on the table beside his cup. Scott's laughter sounded down the hallway.

Christian's eyes turned slowly to Alisa. They really had not spoken yet this morning, for she had still been asleep when Christian left their bed. He thought this morning that she seemed like fine china, too easily broken, too vulnerable, and he felt a resurgence of protective feelings.

"Do you want to talk about last night?" he asked softly.

Alisa studied her teacup. "Scott explained what happened. He said the man who fell will be fine."

"And what about the lady who was so frightened she nearly curled inside of my skin in her sleep?"

Her color grew high. "I'm sorry if I disturbed you. You should have awakened me."

Christian's piercing bluish-green eyes watched her closely, intensifying her discomfort. "That isn't what I said, Alisa."

"I don't know why you won't let this drop, Christian. It was not important. I merely got a little upset at watching two men beat each other up."

"A *little* upset?" he repeated with gentle sarcasm. "The only thing you could possibly have seen was one man fall. If that terrorized trance you were in is considered a *little* upset, I sure as hell hope I never see you *really* upset."

"Perhaps I'm overly sensitive to violence."

"Or perhaps you haven't told me something about your past."

Now midnight-blue eyes shot to him, spurred by

her own fear and embarrassment. "You adamantly refuse to tell me anything about your past, yet you harass me for something nonexistent in mine."

Still Christian remained calm, seeing her panic at the threat of revealing whatever it was she tried so diligently to conceal. "My past doesn't send me into a state like you were in last night, Alisa. I think anything that frightens you so badly should be talked about."

"Your past haunts you, Christian. In fact, it haunts us both, yet I am left ignorant of it. There was no need for you to be involved in what happened to me last night, yet I cannot escape the effect of your memories."

"Should I have left you screaming out back? Would you have preferred that I didn't hold you or comfort you or ease your fears? Should I have left you to tremble alone beside me in bed?"

"And in payment for all of that, do you expect me to fabricate some horrific story about my childhood to appease your curiosity?"

"I expect only a truthful explanation, Alisa."

"Will you offer me the same? Will you tell me about your first marriage and your wife and all that happened to you and what you felt then and feel now?"

"No, I won't," he said softly, but firmly all the same. "I only want to know what haunts you so that I can help you, Alisa," he added gently.

"I could say the same, Christian. I only want to know so that I can save us both from more problems unwittingly caused by my lack of knowledge."

"It's something I must deal with alone; telling you would help neither of us."

"That is true of me as well," she said softly.

"Then you admit that there is something you're not telling me."

"No," she denied too quickly. "I only meant that such silly fears as plagued me last night are best dealt with by myself."

"I see. Then next time I will leave you to sort it out alone, ignore your screams and trembling. I'll just walk away and leave you to it."

Alisa's shoulders drew back, her chin raised only a bit. "I appreciated what you offered me last night, Christian. But I can't give you in payment something that doesn't exist. If your comfort is not offered freely, then perhaps it's better if you don't give it at all." Alisa's words were stiff, forced from her when in fact she was not sure how she could have managed the torment in her mind without Christian's drawing her back to reality.

Christian stared at her, seeing clearly the strength needed to pull the words from her throat. It only fueled his curiosity.

Alisa sat alone in the black-velvet-upholstered carriage, waiting to embark on the journey back to New Haven. In the hour since breakfast, Christian had barely spoken to her.

Her gaze flew to the carriage door as one boot appeared, but she was disappointed when the body that hoisted up behind it was Nicholas and not Christian. His smile was broad, but it was not the face she wanted to see.

Nicholas sat directly across from her, his black eyes unwavering. "Christian has decided to ride his horse into New Haven. I was going to do the same and allow you two the privacy of the coach, but when I discovered that sweet Alisa was to be left without a companion for the trip, I couldn't bring myself to do it. Is my company welcome or should I honor my horse after all?" His expression was kind and teasing.

Alisa returned his smile, wondering why Christian must be so difficult when neither Nicholas nor Scott presented any threat to him. "I'd be pleased to have your company."

"Wonderful. I've been terribly jealous of your attentions to Scott." His grin was crooked, and Alisa laughed at his jest.

Nicholas settled his lap robe evenly about himself and then turned his attention wholly on Alisa. "I have a dark secret I have been dying to share with you since yesterday morning," he said in exaggerated confidence.

"That long?" One finely arched brow rose, and Alisa decided she quite liked Nicholas's joking manner.

"I have always wanted to paint," he said, as if revealing something shocking. "No one knows. I have forever hidden everything I have tried to do. I am not nearly as talented as you, Alisa, but would you consider helping me?"

Alisa saw that he was serious. "Why have you hidden it?"

Nicholas's handsome silver-blond head drew back as if to see her better. His tone was light. "My dear Alisa, I was raised with Christian and Scott. I spent years battling with them much as Bart did last night, trying to prove that though I was smaller, I could still whip them. The last thing I ever would have admitted was that I liked to draw pictures. I would have found the need to defend myself so many more times, I doubt I would be alive today to talk with you."

Alisa smiled sympathetically. "Was it very difficult for you to be raised with Scott and Christian?"

Nicholas laughed. "I had all of the advantages they both did." But there was something underlying those words that suggested he had gotten less. It must be her imagination; yet his humor did not reach his eyes.

"Are we to keep your penchant for painting a secret?" She asked lightly to dispell her ominous feeling.

"If we do, can we have clandestine meetings and secret rendezvous?" he teased in return, and everything was as before.

"No, we can't!" she said laughingly.

"Then I will have to settle for letting the world know I actually like to paint, even though I'm short."

"Will you need to fight to prove your manhood then?" she countered.

A lecherous grin stole over his handsome features. "Certainly not! I have better ways to prove it now."

Alisa's face colored, but she laughed, finding him amusing and entertaining company. "How shall we arrange your lessons, then?"

"At your convenience, of course. I serve as aide to Scott and Christian, overseeing their interests when they're away and assisting them when they are home. As long as either or both of them is around, I usually have a great deal of spare time. So whenever you think you can abide my company, I'd be delighted to join you."

"At the moment I'm afraid I don't have any tasks at all allotted to me, so I should be spending a great deal of time in my studio just to fill my days. You are welcome to come anytime you're free."

Nicholas acted extremely pleased, almost as if he had just been granted a victory, and no hint of teasing was evident.

Chapter Thirty-one

Alisa undressed for the night in the room that was the color of blueberries and cream. Christian had not even spent one full night here with her, and she wondered now if what happened between them in this room would weigh on his mind as it did on hers.

She had not seen Christian in these past hours. She was very irritated by the fact that her husband felt no compunction about deserting her at any time and without explanation. She could not help but feel that it was a denial of any ties between them.

She wrapped a heavy robe over her nightgown and, pulling a pillow and quilt from the bed, turned down the lamps and left the room. She moved quietly down the back stairs, seeking the library at the rear of the house.

She decided that if she were to be nothing more than a fixture here, it was time to accept that and please herself. She would not argue over it, for somehow she forever lost those struggles, nor would she beg or wheedle him for attention.

Determination rose high within her that Christian Reed had seen the last of her efforts to win him. From this moment on, she would do whatever suited her, in whatever way she chose, and Christian Reed could go to hell!

She laid a fire in the paneled hearth of the library, enjoying the mixed smell of polished wood and leather-bound books. She set her pillow and quilt on one of the velvet sofas before the fireplace and then set about choosing a book.

James Fenimore Cooper had been an early favorite, and so she welcomed a volume of *The Pilot,* remembering fondly how it had inspired her to dream of a life at sea as a child. With book in hand, she settled comfortably on the sofa, her legs crossed at the ankles beneath the heavy weight of the quilt. She sighed in contentment, feeling as if she had resolved a difficult problem. For the first time in months, she did not wait for the sound of Christian's return.

After reading awhile, Alisa closed her book, blew out the candle behind her and lay flat on the settee, relaxed for sleep. The fire was low in the hearth, leaving the room very dark so that she could see the light flakes of snow that fell in the garden beyond the French doors on either side of the mantel. It was a peaceful sight, crystalline flakes drifting to the ground against a black sky, their path so slow, it seemed that they floated.

The hue and cry that disrupted the house did not affect Alisa's reverie. She recognized Christian's bellowing voice as he shouted for her but chose to remain as she was. She would no longer be readily available to him, nor would she be intimidated by his wrath. It was time, she decided, that she stood up for herself, regardless of her past misdeeds.

It was a long while before anyone thought to look in the library. When Scott opened the doors, his attention was caught by the dying embers in the hearth before he realized that Alisa lay comfortably on the sofa watching the snow.

"Are you all right?" he asked softly as he came to stand behind the settee.

Alisa smiled up at him warmly. "I'm fine, thank you."

Scott returned her smile then, amused. "You know I'm going to have to tell him you're in here."

"Of course," she answered evenly, unperturbed.

Scott chuckled as he left the room. "Good luck, Alisa."

Alisa merely returned her gaze to the white world beyond the French doors.

"What the hell are you doing in here? Didn't you hear everyone calling you?"

"Hello, Christian." Alisa ignored his angry words, her eyes never veering from their perusal of the storm.

He strode in front of the window, blocking her view. His hands were planted on each narrow hip as he stared down at her through blazing bluish-green eyes. "I repeat, what the hell are you doing in here?"

"Without your boorish shouting throughout the house I would have been asleep by now," she answered calmly, peering at Christian as if he were inconsequential.

"Last time I checked, there were any number of beds upstairs."

"There still are, to the best of my knowledge."

"Then why are you sleeping here?" The creases in each cheek ran deeply to his clenched jaw.

"I did not want to disturb a servant to prepare a different room for me tonight. I'm quite comfortable here, actually."

"Are we playing a game, Alisa?"

"I certainly am not."

"Explain to me exactly what is going on." Christian's rage grew hotter in answer to her composure.

"You have chosen my role here, Christian. I have merely decided on a few details that are within my rights. Nothing is going on, nor is there any game. I accept my position and I am simply acting accordingly."

Christian crossed his arms over his chest, each bicep bulging, his weight resting on one hip and his head cocked slightly to the right. "What the hell are you talking about?"

Alisa remained unaffected. "You are unhappy to be married again and are obviously upset by my presence in your life. You can endure the situation only by removing yourself from my company as much as possible, which I assume is why you decided to leave the cabin so abruptly and then the country house as well. I really have tried to please you, but I can accept my failure in that. You can abide me only as some fixture within your household and can allot me only the barest of common courtesies, but that, too, I can accept. What is within my right is control over my own body. I will not accept your use of me in bed, much as you avail yourself of anything that offers you the baser comforts of life. I will not allow myself to be used to simply satisfy your lust. And so, I will no longer share your bed or your room."

"Is that so?"

"It is," she said firmly.

"In other words, you mean to use my name, my money, my home, and everything else that comes with being my wife and refuse me the only thing I ask in return?"

"I will oversee your servants, clean your house

myself if necessary, scrub your floors, cook, launder, market for you, entertain your guests; in short, do anything you ask of me. But I will not share your bed." There was no challenge in her words or her expression, but neither was there any doubt that she was steadfast in her decision.

"The use of your body is my right as your husband."

"Not if I refuse."

"It does not necessarily require your consent."

"I'm well aware of the existence of rape. I believe that is how we came to be here in the first place."

"Is that how you want it?" he threatened.

Alisa was unruffled. "You won't accomplish it without the biggest battle of your life, and I promise you that I will hurt you in any way I can, to avoid it. You would not come away unscathed, nor would you find much pleasure in it." Her tone was a simple statement of fact, her determination indisputable.

"Don't push me too far, Alisa. You may find more than you bargained for."

"I am not pushing you at all, Christian. You will have anything you want from me, but you will not have me in your bed."

"Where do you intend to sleep?" he asked through clenched teeth.

"You said yourself, there are any number of beds upstairs. Tomorrow I will have one readied for me."

An evil grin spread his mustache. "In my house you will share my bed or you will not be allowed any. I will personally see to it that every bedroom door is locked to you but mine."

Alisa stared at him levelly. "Do whatever you think you must."

"What do you hope to win by this?"

"Nothing. I explained it to you clearly. I can accept your treatment of me in everything, Christian, but I will not be a whore for you at any price."

"Then I suppose we shall see which of us is more stubborn."

Chapter Thirty-two

It was not late when Alisa woke the following morning. She stretched languidly, well content with her decision of the previous night. She rose, donned her robe and gathered her quilt and pillow. Again she used the back steps, for she had no desire to meet Scott or Nicholas in her night clothes.

Out of curiosity, she tried the door to each bedroom she passed as she moved down the hallway to the master suite. She found every door locked securely, though she had not doubted Christian's threat. She tried the knob of the oversize door to Christian's room. It, too, was locked tight.

She sighed and tapped lightly. When no one came, she leaned near and softly called her husband's name. She was startled when Ann's voice answered from behind her.

"He's long gone, Miss Alisa."

Alisa turned to face the woman, smiling at her. "Would you unlock this door so I might dress, please, Ann?"

The older woman cleared her throat uncomfortably, "I'm sorry. I can't. Mr. Reed called us all in at dawn this morning, even young Mr. Reed and Mr. Lamb were there. He made it very clear what would happen if anyone opened a bedroom door to you or gave you a stitch of clothes. We will lose our jobs here. He even threatened the other two men, if they was to help you, either. I haven't seen Mr. Reed so mad since the other missus was here." She shook her head, emphasizing her astonishment.

Alisa kept a tight check on her rising temper. Her chin lifted, her spine straightened. "Is there not a room in the kitchen where the servants may wash if they desire?"

"Yes," the woman answered, uncertain if even this was a breach of the strict orders decreed this morning.

"Then I shall bathe there. You may wash my nightgown and dry it by the fire. I will sit in the kitchen in my robe until that is finished."

Alisa did not await an answer but walked erectly back down the stairs she had climbed minutes before, her determination intact.

Alisa was in the drawing room as the sun set behind dark gray clouds, not knowing whether she would be dining alone. She sat regally in a wing chair, her bare feet flat on the floor in front of her, the high, ruffled collar of her nightgown visible above the round neckline of her deep blue velvet robe. Her hair fell freely around her shoulders, untangled with the help of a brush she had found in the washroom off the kitchen.

The day had been long; the harshest blow was finding that Christian had also locked her studio. With that move, he unwittingly cut her off from access to money that would have aided her in fighting him.

She breathed deeply when she heard the front door open to admit all three men at once. She had hoped Scott and Nicholas would not come home for dinner. Since she refused to cower, she sat facing the entrance to the drawing room, her hands resting on the wooden arms of her chair. Conversation stopped abruptly as the three men entered and saw Alisa waiting.

"Gentleman," she said casually in greeting, meeting their eyes evenly.

Nicholas walked to her, bowing gallantly, a glint of mischief in his black eyes as he took one hand to press to his lips. "You look terribly fetching, sweet Alisa. My compliments."

"Thank you, Nicholas," she answered sweetly.

Christian scowled fiercely, realizing his cousin's observation was all too true. His temper was further exacerbated.

Scott took a deep breath as if to strengthen himself, and stepped to the sideboard. "Dammit, Christian, at least be sporting enough to allow her a gown."

"No." Christian's voice was commanding, stern, his eyes on his wife. "Alisa knows my terms."

"Well, I don't know about you, Nicholas, but I'm in need of a drink if we are to be treated to this much-too-alluring sight all evening," Scott said, pouring himself a tall Scotch.

Alisa's gaze did not falter from Christian's, but she spoke sincerely to Scott. "I would not embarrass either of you. If you prefer, I'll dine in the kitchen."

Scott brought her a glass of wine, smiling warmly down at her. "I am long past embarrassment. Nicholas is right, you are lovely just as you are. I, for one, would join you in the kitchen if you refuse to pleasure us with your company."

Alisa accepted the proffered wine gratefully from her brother-in-law.

Christian turned from pouring his own drink and raised his glass to her in silent toast, one brow arched, his lips rueful beneath his mustache, as if to say she had won this round, but he had not yet lost the battle.

The night grew late and Alisa grew weary. Nicholas had long since excused himself for bed, and as Scott seemed intent upon the same course, she bade her husband and his brother good night and left them. She went first to the kitchen to gather her quilt and pillow from a shelf in the washroom and then returned to the library, anxious to end this day. She was surprised to find the door to that retreat locked to her, and it took a great effort to keep hold of her temper now.

She walked back to the drawing room, feeling the cold chill of the hardwood floor beneath her feet. She did not speak to Scott, who paused in his own leave-taking, but marched directly to Christian, standing before him poised and dignified though dwarfed by his enormous size.

"The library is not a bedroom," she said flatly but without animosity, knowing any venting of her anger would please him.

Christian smiled leisurely. "It seemed quite cozy last night."

"So I am not to be allowed the use of that room, either?"

"It would seem that way."

Alisa said no more, moving to the much less comfortable brocade sofa, dropping her pillow at one end and spreading her blanket with one flick of the wrist.

Scott stepped farther back into the room, a frown marring his features. "Come on, Christian, this is taking it too far. She'll freeze in this open space without a fire burning all night, and you damn well know it."

"Mind your own business, Scott," was his mild answer.

Still Scott persisted. "At least let her use the library."

"No!"

"Dammit, Christian, this is ridiculous!"

"Get the hell out of here, Scott, and leave us to what is a private affair."

"It's not private when you leave her only the open sections of this house without even a gown or shoes to wear."

Christian's gaze was threatening, his voice low. "We fought once over a woman. I thought we agreed never to do it again. I warn you, Scott, you are out of line."

Alisa could not mutely watch this happen; she could not be the cause of a rift between the two men. "Please, Scott, I am well able to care for myself. Go on to bed."

Scott was torn, hesitating for a long moment as he stared at his brother in indecision and disapproval. After a time he shook his head in disgust, his voice the same tone Christian had used. "Remember one thing, Christian. I was right then and you paid dearly for not listening to me." Scott departed, and Christian turned to Alisa, who ignored him and slid beneath her quilt. She left her robe on over her nightgown against a chill that already permeated the large, open room.

"What is it you want from me, Alisa?" Christian's voice was deep and irritated.

Midnight-blue eyes looked up at him evenly. "I want nothing from you, Christian. It is you who have turned this into some sort of battle of wills. If you allow me a bedroom and my clothes, you will find that nothing is changed between us."

"Except that you refuse me my rights as a husband."

"Yes, but that is a small thing. I would refuse you nothing else," she said simply.

"What brought you to this decision?"

"I told you, Christian. You choose to act like a bachelor, coming and going as you please, when you please and for whatever length of time you please. I certainly can't follow you as I did to the cabin, forcing myself on you. I can accept that you don't want my company. But I am not a woman to sit with bated breath, never knowing what I am to expect from you. And I could not live with myself if I spent my time doing nothing but awaiting you only to serve you in bed. I will not be anyone's whore. Return my belongings and allow me a room and we shall both go on about our lives as we see fit. Perhaps you could look on me as a sister."

"A sister?" he said in disgust. "You're my wife, dammit!"

"You don't want a wife, Christian. We both know that, and I can't change it."

"Do you think this tactic will turn me into some simpering, fawning husband who never leaves your side?"

"I would not want that in you or in anyone else."

"But you're angry because I don't pay enough attention to you, isn't that it?"

"No, I am not angry, nor do I want undivided attention. I want the freedom to come and go as I please, just as you're doing, and without awaiting your whim."

Christian stared at her for a long moment, assessing her. "You're adamant in this?"

"I am."

"You deny me my rights as your husband?"

"Only in bed, but, yes, I'm afraid I must."

"All right then, Alisa. I can have one of my ships ready to sail in a week. You trapped me into this marriage. I can't annul it, nor will I seek another divorce, but I will not support you, nor keep you here when I am refused the only thing I ask of you as my wife. I am sending you back to England to your father."

Alisa stared with wide eyes at Christian. "Is it so important to you to degrade me by making me your private harlot?" Panic ran through her as she realized she had backed herself into a corner. It did not occur to her that Christian was bluffing, for he had unwittingly hit upon her one weakness.

Christian watched her, confidence and arrogance in his posture as he glared down at her. He shrugged. "You got what you wanted out of this, Alisa. Did you really think you could have it all your way? The well-staged plot that trapped me into this union was successful, but if you thought me simple or pliable because of it, you were mistaken. I will not be refused what is my right and what is little payment for what you've gained. You will be my wife in any way I choose and at any time I choose, or you will not be my wife at all." His handsome head cocked slightly to the right in query. "What will it be? My bed or back to England?"

Alisa stared up at the ceiling, fuming, knowing she had lost more than she had set out to gain. Her own strong will rebelled, and finding herself without options now was galling.

She sat up abruptly, refusing to speak or even look at her husband. Her rage and frustration were vented in the fierce grasp of her pillow and pulling the quilt roughly from the settee. She climbed the stairs, never looking at Christian, her back straight, breathing deeply to gain control of herself.

Christian's stride was unhurried. His face held a satisfied expression, his lips only barely turned up at the corners beneath his mustache. He unlocked the door and pushed it wide, one long arm stretched into it, and he bowed, a mocking gesture Alisa refused to acknowledge.

She dropped her bundle on the bed and unfastened her robe, her pale lips tight. She climbed onto the high mattress and lay on her back, her hands pressed flat on either side, her eyes staring up at the ceiling once more. If she was to be used, she decided, she would at least not aid him in it. He would have his due, and she would not fight, but she would not respond, either.

Christian followed her into the room, seeing all that her actions conveyed. His gaze did not leave her as he undressed, thinking that she was exactly wrong in her assumption of why he avoided her. It was not that he abhorred her company, but that he enjoyed it too much. He felt the need to prove to himself that he could do without her. His threat to send her back to her father had scared her. He had no intention of following through with it. He wondered if there was more to her capitulation than not wanting to be exiled in shame back to England.

He doused the lamps and joined Alisa in bed, lying on his back, hands clasped behind his head, making no move toward her at all. Alisa's impatience and anger grew as she waited . . . and waited, and still Christian did not even look at her.

"Are you availing yourself of your rights tonight?" she said at last, sarcasm thick.

A long, silent moment passed before Christian's head turned with deliberate slowness, his piercing bluish-green eyes amused. "I told you it would be when *I* chose."

Alisa rolled to her side, her back to her husband. She doubted that the bite of the gallows rope was less chafing than what she felt at that moment.

Chapter Thirty-three

By January's end, Christian was marveling at Alisa's stubbornness. He was beginning to believe he might perish at any time from an excess of courtesy.

As he sat alone with her in the drawing room one night, he watched her openly, his senses filled with the lovely sight she presented. She sat intently sketching before the hearth, her legs curled under her, the wild mass of burnished hair falling over her shoulders as her hand worked quickly with a pen from the set he had given her at Christmas.

In the month since he had forced her to return to his bed, Christian had not yet "availed" himself of his rights, as she sardonically put it. In that way, she had won a victory, too, because he had no doubt that if he tried to make love to her, he would find her as cold as the proverbial fish, and he would not give her that satisfaction. Instead he waited, determined to prove his will was stronger, though it was becoming increasingly harder to ignore his desires for her.

Alisa felt Christian's eyes upon her, and it pushed her hand to a greater speed trying to outrun the excitement his glance could raise in her blood. She had never suspected that her punishment of him would become a greater burden to her. Never in her life had she longed for a man's touch, a man's kiss. But now she felt such desperation to have him touch her that she feared she would shame herself by ending this game in a most unladylike attack on his person. She wished fervently that he would allow her a graceful way out of the situation, yet each night her own stubborn will prevailed, and she goaded him again with the question that deterred him from doing what she most wanted.

Alisa looked more closely at what she was doing now, a hot blush spreading across her cheeks as she viewed what had come from her pen almost of its own volition. There before her was a picture of a man and woman in a very close embrace, their mouths a bare whisper from touching. She had drawn herself and Christian in a portrait that spoke of sensuality and an intimacy that betrayed her true feelings, the feelings she hid even from herself.

Christian's interest was piqued by the color in her face. A large hand shot out and grabbed the parchment from her lap before she could rescue it.

"You're a boorish clod," she said without guarding her tongue, her face now suffused with scarlet. "If you had any manners at all, you would give that to me."

Christian chuckled lightly, his eyes appreciating what he held in his hands and all it revealed. "Your talents amaze me, Alisa. And your memory is quite good, too, it seems." Gleaming eyes moved to her, an amused quirk to one side of his lips. "Perhaps you would like to avail yourself of your rights over me?" he asked in mockery of her words to him each night.

Midnight-blue eyes locked with his. "You forget, sir, I have no rights at all."

Bushy brows drew down into a feigned frown as he glanced to the picture again and then at Alisa. "A bit of an itch, then?"

She lunged for the parchment, but Christian was far quicker, and he held it up, out of her reach.

"You blithering oaf. I'm sure you'd like to think so."

But again Christian foresaw her intent and raised the paper well above his head, and Alisa fell against his long, hard length, losing her balance as she reached for it. His other arm encircled her waist, holding her pressed firmly to him, one arm trapped at her side, the other grasping his shoulder. His hips arched up against her intimately.

"Why, Alisa"—he feigned astonishment—"I had no idea you were so aroused!"

"It isn't lust that fills me, it's contempt," she gritted, trying to wiggle free of his grip. But he only held her tighter, leaning back so that her feet left the floor and her entire body aligned against his.

He peered at the drawing high above her head. "No, it doesn't appear to be contempt. I think you're confusing being filled with something and a *need* to be filled. Could that be?"

"You are foul!" Alisa swung one leg back to kick, but Christian's legs were spread wide, and all she accomplished was swinging seductively against his groin.

"You are an impatient little thing, aren't you?"

"Put me down, you arrogant ox!" she spat, her color high. "I hate you!"

Christian laughed, squeezing her so tightly that the air went out of her lungs. "Are those two hard little knobs pressing into my chest caused by hatred? I don't think so. If memory serves, I've felt that response a time or two beneath my hand . . . and my mouth," he taunted.

"Give me the bloody picture and let go!" she shrieked, squirming to loosen his hold. She felt him grow hard against her.

"Very nice." His voice was low, husky. "You do that as well as you draw."

Alisa stiffened suddenly. Over Christian's shoulder she saw Scott standing in the entrance, a broad grin on his lips. She groaned, dropping her forehead to the back of the hand that was still on her husband's shoulder.

Curious, Christian turned to look into the amused countenance of his brother. "You picked a hell of a time to come home, Scott."

"Actually, I'm sorry I didn't get here earlier. Looks like I missed quite a fracas."

Christian lowered Alisa to the floor but only long enough to swing his other arm, picture and all, behind her knees, to pick her back up.

"If you will excuse us, Scott," Christian said with exaggerated courtesy, "I think we will finish this upstairs." His insinuation was clear.

"Put me down!" Alisa ground out softly through gritted teeth.

"I'm afraid I can't do that," Christian said, his words directed toward his brother. "Scott is unmarried, and I would hate to shock him with a show of what comes up between a man and his wife."

Her embarrassment was complete as Scott's loud laughter followed them up the staircase to the room they shared. Inside, Christian sailed the picture to the floor but kept Alisa captive. He crossed to the bed, climbing onto it on his knees to lower Alisa to the mattress and himself on her, to pin her beneath him.

She raised freed hands to strike out, but he was quicker and grasped them both at the wrist, pulling them up above her head, where it required only one of his massive hands to contain them. His handsome face was only inches above her. He pushed his hips against her in a way that made it very clear his desire had not waned.

"Aren't you going to ask me if I'm going to 'avail' myself of my rights?" he taunted.

"I'd rather go back to England!" she shot back, fury and desire warring within her.

His free hand ruthlessly pulled down the bodice of her gown, popping buttons and ripping her chemise below. His hand slid to a full, ripe breast, the nipple raised taut and hard. "Would you, Alisa? Could you find some insipid Englishman to do this for you?" He took her nipple between his thumb and forefinger, rolling it and squeezing gently.

She fought the heat coursing through her veins. "Englishmen are gentlemen," she retorted senselessly.

He laughed, a deep, throaty sound. "So it's a gentleman you want, is it? Some simpering little fop who will do whatever you say while you order him around like a whipped puppy?"

"Yes," she tried to say firmly, but it came out a groan as his hand worked at her breast, teasing, taunting, kneading.

"You're still a damn liar," he growled as his mouth fell on hers hungrily, his tongue searing hers in the kiss that she had hungered for. His hand left her breast to be replaced by his mouth, and Alisa moaned softly, arching, yielding her body to sweet torment as he took first the hard crest between his lips and then the whole of her throbbing breast into his sucking, demanding mouth.

His hand lowered to the waistband of her gown, grasping all of her petticoats. With one firm jerk he tore them away, baring her lower torso to his searching hand. He found what he sought, and her hips curved to the magic of his probing fingers.

He released his hold of her wrists, working madly to free himself of his own clothes, ripping anything that didn't come loose immediately. His lips came down hard on hers in a deep, impassioned kiss filled with torment and desire.

She forced her hands to the granite muscles bulging at his shoulders to push him away, but instead they slipped beneath his shirt, aiding him in its removal. She tried to remember why she should resist, but her body sent waves of pleasure through her that spoke louder than her feeble idea of resistance. She knew he was right; she needed desperately to be filled by him.

Their hands caressed each other's flesh at a fevered pace as intense passion ruled. His naked body covered hers, the long, hard shaft of his manhood seeking entry. Her hips arched to welcome him, feeling that he could not enter her quickly enough. Her breath drew in sharply as he pressed himself deep within her and then drew partway out again. It was divine agony as every nerve cried out, her hands clutched his rippling back, feeling his need as great as her own.

"Christian!" The shout from beyond their bedroom door was like ice water thrown over their entwined, unsated bodies. They lay perfectly still, hoping the intrusion might disappear if no movement or sound came from them.

"Christian!" Again Scott's voice sounded, his fist beating on the door.

Christian's tone was savage, each word shouted with slow precision. "What the hell do you want?"

The sound of Scott's throat clearing preceded his answer. "I'm sorry, but there's a servant from Ellen's house downstairs. He says it's an emergency, and I think you had better come down."

Christian pulled away from Alisa, holding his breath in an attempt to keep himself from killing his brother. "I'll be right there," he ground out through clenched teeth. He lunged from the bed, pulling on a shirt and breeches with ferocity.

Alisa's small white teeth bit the tip of her tongue lightly as she realized what was happening. She curled on her side, pulling up the quilt to cover her nakedness, knowing a frustration deeper than anything she had ever felt.

Chapter Thirty-four

Alisa awoke early the next morning to find herself alone in bed. Christian had not returned.

Nor did he appear for two more days and nights. No word was sent, no message to tell her what he was doing, where he was, though she assumed he had gone to his former wife. Alisa was left in confusion and doubt, assaulted by ugly suspicions.

On the third morning she was awakened by the sound of Christian gathering clothes from his bureau. She pushed herself up in bed, blinking her eyes to clear them of sleep.

"What are you doing?" she asked softly, her voice thick.

Christian did not pause in his task, nor did he look at her. His voice was impatient. "Go back to sleep, Alisa, I didn't mean to wake you."

"Where have you been?" she persisted, her voice echoing with pain in this unguarded moment.

But Christian was in a hurry, intent on his chore. "I haven't time to talk to you now," he growled. "It doesn't concern you." And he was gone again, leaving her with no more knowledge than on the night he had answered his former wife's summons.

He returned late that same night, rousing Alisa

only accidentally as he bumped into the corner of the bed. He said nothing, but dropped down beside her, fully clothed, and instantly fell into a deep, exhausted sleep with one arm across his eyes.

Alisa sat up against the headboard, staring down at her husband's shadowy features. She sighed, not knowing whether to be annoyed, worried or raging mad. As she inhaled, her nostrils caught the faint odor of a fragrance not familiar to her. She felt a sinking sensation in the pit of her stomach. There was now no question how she should respond.

She sat in a chair facing the bed, wearing her robe over her nightgown and a crotcheted shawl over that. Across her lap was an afghan on which rested her clasped hands. She was the picture of serenity, all but her eyes, as she waited for her sleeping husband to awaken.

The feeble winter sun rose high in the sky before Christian rolled to his side and came awake with a quick jolt. He braced himself up on one elbow, pressing his eyes with his thumb and forefinger. Sensing Alisa's presence, Christian spoke as he swung his legs to the floor. "What time is it?" he asked in a voice hoarse with sleep.

"Past ten," she answered coldly, not moving.

"Dammit! I shouldn't have slept so late!" He stood then and hastily began to change his clothes.

"Are you going to explain to me where you have been for the past three days . . . and nights?"

Christian sighed impatiently. "I'm late already, Alisa. If you're spoiling for a fight, it will have to wait."

"Late for what?" she demanded.

"It's none of your damn business." Christian's temper was short, fatigue still etching his face.

"Your former wife must be a demanding lover," she accused venomously.

"My former wife?" he said as if confused, then, "Ellen isn't even in New Haven."

Alisa's laugh was short and mirthless. "Do you expect me to believe you were called to an empty house by her servants?"

Christian had almost finished dressing. "I don't give a damn what you believe. Right now I don't have the time to spare while you play fishwife." The door slammed behind him.

Alisa was enveloped in a wave of fury, pain and an emotion unfamiliar to her: blinding jealousy.

Three weeks passed. Alisa knew no more than on the night Christian had so prematurely left their bed. Each night he returned home well past midnight, falling into an exhausted slumber the very second his head touched the pillow beside her. He always rose before dawn to dress hurriedly and leave. If Alisa woke and questioned him, his answer was always the same: It was not her business.

Alisa did not see Scott, either. The servants explained that he was overseeing all of the Reed holdings alone, since Nicholas had been sent to New York.

Alisa's suspicions strengthened, and her frustration escalated as she imagined Christian becoming involved again with his former wife, so besotted he could easily abandon her anytime Ellen beckoned.

She needed to act, even if it meant finding Christian in a compromising position. A confrontation was preferable to visualizing them together every day. At least she'd know.

She ordered a carriage to take her to Ellen's house,

only to find that Christian had left firm orders that she was not to be allowed to go there. This increased her determination.

When Nicholas returned, Alisa decided he might offer her the means to accomplish her ends.

"Ellen's house? Why would you want to go there?" Nicholas's shock was obvious. He had already left for New York when all of this began, so he was completely in the dark.

Alisa sighed, uncertain what might cause him to refuse her as everyone else had. Still, she opted for the truth. "Christian was called there a few weeks ago, and since then he is acting very strangely." Alisa paused, seeking the right words. "I know your allegiance is to Christian, but I must know what is happening there. If you will only get me a horse and show me the way, I will tell him I stole the animal and found it myself. Please, Nicholas. I need your help. You're my only hope."

Nicholas's face clouded; his handsome features became serious. He seemed lost in his own thoughts, more than simply weighing a decision. "Christian is with Ellen again?" he murmured to himself softly.

"Yes! And no one else will even tell me where her house is. I can't sit here a moment longer."

"Are you absolutely certain he is seeing Ellen?" he asked, a dark, ominous frown marring his brow, his concentration intense now.

"I think he must be. He told me she was not even in New Haven, but he could have lied to me."

An instantaneous, relieved smile spread his lips. "Of course!" he said as if memory dawned. "I knew there was something not quite right about this. I had heard that Ellen was away; her second husband died recently, and she had to settle his estate, I believe.

You must be mistaken, Alisa." Nicholas's teasing manner reappeared. "You must be imagining things. I'm sure Ellen is gone."

"Then why would her servant summon Christian, and why has he been so absorbed ever since? Perhaps she came back and seeks to renew her relationship with Christian. If she is widowed, it leaves her free again, doesn't it?"

Nicholas laughed lightly now. "After what passed between them, I doubt that anything Ellen wanted of Christian would be forthcoming, let alone absorb him."

Alisa's frustration grew boundless. "Then show me the place to satisfy my suspicions. What harm can be done if what you say is true?"

"Ah, Alisa, it's a waste of time, I assure you. It's something I know better than anyone."

Alisa's wide blue eyes narrowed, her color was high, her determination evident. "I swear to you that if you don't help me I will walk the streets of this city shouting until someone does."

Nicholas laughed uproariously. "You are delightful. I believe you would do just that. All right, Alisa, I will take you there to show you your suspicions are unfounded. You will see that this conspiracy you think is whirling around you is only in your mind." His expression became a bit remote again as he spoke to himself. "I'm certain Christian knows better than to ever have anything to do with Ellen again."

Chapter Thirty-five

The night air was cold and damp, the streets wet and puddled from an early spring snow. A hazy fog wafted near the ground, concealing the wheels of the chaise that Nicholas drove. New Haven was quiet in the early evening hour, save for the rare carriage that passed and the *clop* of hoof beats.

Alisa sat beside Nicholas silently, her heavy woolen cloak wrapped around her, her hands clasped beneath the lap robe that covered them both. Her pulse raced, and for the first time she feared what she might find at Ellen's house. Suddenly the pictures in her mind of Christian sharing intimacies with another woman left her unsure of her course. Still, she fought her fears. Knowledge was better than waiting and wondering and imagining.

It took them half an hour to reach the modest yellow clapboard house amid a row of dwellings similar in structure.

Nicholas stopped the chaise. Light was visible on both levels of the house. It was obvious to both Alisa and Nicholas that Ellen had returned. The deep frown reappeared on Nicholas's features.

"Maybe it's better if I go in alone, Alisa," he said ominously, his eyes never wavering from the house.

Alisa took a deep breath and squared her shoulders. Her heart pounded in trepidation. "No, I came to find out what's going on and I mean to." She tore her eyes from the house. "If you would rather go back home it's all right. I'm sure Christian can arrange a way back for me. I promise I won't let him know you brought me."

Nicholas's smile was forced, but he attempted to lighten the mood by teasing her. "My sweet Alisa, do you offend me with doubts of my courage? I may be lacking in height, but that is no indication that I lack valor as well." His gaze returned to the house, his voice again serious and low. "Besides, I could never leave without learning the conclusion to this mystery."

Alisa did not wait for any assistance in lowering herself from the carriage. She approached the inviting house slowly.

Her knock on the oak door was firm. An aged butler opened it, raising one brow in query. "I am here to see Christian Reed," she said flatly, refusing to be intimidated by the man.

The butler's other gray brow joined the first in lofty scrutiny of her as he continued barring her entry.

Nicholas cleared his throat then, attracting the old man's attention.

Recognition dawned in the wrinkled face. "Mr. Nicholas! I didn't see you. It's been some time, sir." Only then did he step aside to allow them into the house.

Nicholas whispered teasingly, "Now aren't you glad you brought me?" The question did not distract her from hearing the unmistakable sound of Christian's voice coming from up the flight of stairs directly in front of them. She did not wait for the butler to announce her, or for Nicholas to accompany her. She moved as if in a trance, to see for herself what went on in the rooms upstairs.

She paused on the landing above as Christian's voice grew louder. She could not distinguish his words, only that he spoke without pause and that no other voice responded. At the far end of the dim hallway, a door stood ajar and light emanated from behind it. Alisa swallowed thickly, wondering what she would do if beyond that door Christian lay in bed with his former wife, entwined as he had been with Alisa on the night he was summoned, holding her as he had Alisa, kissing her, caressing her. . . .

Her hand stopped in midair as she was about to push the door wide, for she realized Christian was not talking to someone, he was reading, his voice rising and falling, exaggerated inflections accenting it.

A move slightly to one side gained her a clear view of the bed at the far end of the room. Christian sat in a rocking chair beside it, only his broad back facing Alisa. The bed covers were mussed, but no one rested there, and Christian's girth blocked the view of anything directly in front of him. His wide expanse of shoulders was curled slightly forward, and his left elbow was propped on the rocker's arm. His head was lowered, the dusky, golden hair waving against the steely back of his neck.

The picture in her mind of how she would find Christian was so drastically different than what was before her that it took several minutes for her to reconcile it.

As she stood there, Christian's voice trailed off in mid-sentence, his head cocked slightly to one side and lowered. Then his right arm slowly eased a book to the floor beside him. He stood, careful not to let the rocker sway behind him, to gently bend over the bed. His long, thick arms lowered a small body to the pillows; one bare foot kicked up involuntarily before Christian pulled the blankets up.

She watched Christian push the covers underneath the mattress, smoothing them across the small lump the child made in the bed. A large, powerful hand went carefully to the brow, easing beneath the wispy blond hair to rest there for a moment. Then he kissed the very top of the small head before he lowered the wick in the lamp.

The instant Christian turned to the door, he saw Alisa. An ungentle hand clasped her upper arm painfully, swinging her away from the bedroom and pulling her with him down the stairs and out of the house. Ignoring Nicholas and the butler, Christian propelled Alisa across the yard, flinging her up into the waiting chaise. He slapped the reins across the horses' backs with a vengeance, spurring them into a fast gallop that tipped the carriage precariously.

Alisa clung to the side of the chaise with one hand, her other clasped around the seat's edge like a claw. The night air was frigid against her cheeks, stinging her eyes and pushing her hair back from her brow.

No more than twenty minutes elapsed before Christian pulled the horses to a halt before their house. He shouted for his groom and clasped Alisa's arm as he pulled her behind him, not pausing until he thrust her into their bedroom.

Alisa reeled, fighting for her balance. She fell backward into the tall bed. The expression on Christian's face looming above her was so violent that for the first time in her life, she feared she was about to be struck.

Chapter Thirty-six

She stared in horror as Christian visibly warred with himself for control. Her confusion grew apace with her fear, for she could not understand why her finding him with a child should enrage him.

He breathed deeply, trying to calm himself, his fists clenched at his sides. He turned to the small table that held a brandy decanter and glasses. After three long drafts of the amber liquid and several more minutes spent staring at the wall before him, he turned to Alisa, his jaw clenched tight. His bushy brows nearly met over his nose, his frown was so fierce. When he spoke, it was in deep, measured tones.

"Will you never respect what I ask of you?"

Her fear dwindled, to be replaced by anger. "Not when you require blind obedience without explanation. You did not *ask* anything of me, at any rate. You simply charged out of here to answer a call from your former wife with nothing more than a shout to me that it was not my concern."

"It wasn't your concern," he ground out. "Dammit! You have no business barging into places you don't belong."

"Meaning you do belong in the house of the woman you divorced?"

"I had no choice." Christian again drained his glass. He was irrationally angry and he knew why. Alisa had witnessed a deeply buried, well-guarded weakness that he did not want to admit even to himself. It was easier to deny it if only he knew it existed.

Alisa had unwittingly stumbled upon the only wound still raw from his time with Ellen: his feelings for the small boy he had believed to be his son. Alisa watched the play of emotions on Christian's features. It served to cool her own temper. She moved from the bed to sit in the chair across from him. She saw the lines of exhaustion etched in his face and wished desperately that he would let her ease his pain. But she knew he would not let her approach now. She had nothing to lose by demanding the explanation she was due.

"You left me with nothing but my imaginings. What could I think but that you had renewed your relationship with Ellen?"

Christian sighed. For some reason he did not understand, he decided to clarify the situation for her. Besides, he was too damn tired to argue. "I told you Ellen is not even in New Haven," he began wearily.

"I tried to believe that, but you smelled of perfume."

"Her whole damn house reeks of the stuff. I didn't work years to be free of Ellen, only to have an affair with her, Alisa. Be reasonable!"

"What else was I to think when you ran to answer her summons?"

"It was not her summons, it was a servant from her house. He was sent by the nanny she employs for

Nat." He hated going into all of this. "Nat was born while we were married, but he is not my son."

"Scott told me there was a baby and that you believed him to be yours for a time."

"Scott has a big mouth. Did he also tell you that Ellen left Nat here during the entire three years I sought the divorce?"

"No. Didn't she want him?"

"Who the hell knows! The woman is a selfish bitch. She didn't come for him until just before I left for England. By then, she had hooked another unsuspecting fool into marrying her, and Nat went to live with them. The man was old and fancied having Nat as his son. I suppose Ellen used the boy as bait."

"You kept her son for three years?" Alisa said in amazement.

Christian's glance shot to her, as if she were accusing him of stupidity. "Of course I kept him," he shouted. "What the hell would you expect me to do, auction him off?"

She remained calm; this was obviously a very sore spot. "I only meant that another man would have hated the baby and not allowed her to leave it," she said, trying to soothe him. "You care greatly for the child, don't you?"

Christian's forefinger repeatedly smoothed his mustache in agitation, and his eyes stared into space. "Someone had to, didn't they?" was the most he would admit to.

"Why did they come for you that night?"

"He was sick . . . dying! He needed a diseased appendix removed."

"Where is his mother?"

"Nobody knows. The old bastard she married died,

and she's off seeing how much she can get out of it. 'Settling the estate' is the polite term. She's been gone two months, and no one is sure where the hell she is. She only said she'd gone 'south.' I sent messages to every place I could think of, but she obviously didn't receive them or didn't care. There isn't any family, so the servants didn't know what to do but turn to me."

"Is that where you've been this whole time?"

"He's only four years old, dammit. He deserves someone more than a servant around when he's sick."

"I don't begrudge you spending time with a sick little boy, Christian. I only wish you had told me. Did it ever occur to you that I might have been able to help?"

"That would have been amusing, wouldn't it? The present Mrs. Reed caring for the child of the former Mrs. Reed with poor Mr. Reed, who probably still thinks the boy might be his? No, now that the crisis is past, I've arranged for his care until Ellen returns."

Alisa was struck by the realization that, regardless of the sordid details, Christian still had a strong tie with the past, in the child if not in the woman. For the first time, she wondered if he truly hated his former wife as he said, or if divorcing her had been a reaction to pain she could only inflict by virtue of his deep feelings for her.

"Do you think the child is yours?" she asked almost inaudibly.

"Lord deliver me from women who think I'm a fool!" he exclaimed to the ceiling. "Nat is not my son. Before I surprised dear Ellen with her lover, I heard her bragging about how clever she had been, trapping me into marrying her to give her bastard a name. Apparently, the real father was not as wealthy as she had believed, and so she set her trap for me." His self-disgust rang clear. "That moment was my last as a dupe. Until I met you, of course. But even then I was at least unconscious." His bitterness was almost tangible.

"If I could undo what I have done to you, Christian, I would. It seems now that I was very much a child when we met, oblivious to anything but myself and my own problems. I honestly did not know how deeply you were wounded."

These words focused his attention back on her. He studied her quizzically, for the first time believing what she said, that she suffered genuine remorse for her actions.

"If you had known, Alisa, would you have gone after someone else?" he asked softly.

She sighed and shrugged helplessly. "No matter what you believe, Christian, I had no other choice."

Christian found it curious, after all this time believing her as treacherously corrupt as Ellen, that he now perceived she could have been as much a victim of circumstances as he.

"Tell me your secrets, Alisa," he beckoned once again.

For a moment, she was tempted, wanting him to understand that her reasons had been so much greater than he thought.

"No secrets, Christian."

He knew she was lying as certainly as he knew she had spoken the truth before. "I must seem a terrible ogre to you," he said.

"Sometimes," she agreed. "And I must seem childish."

"Strong-willed, perhaps, and stubborn as hell. But not childish."

He stood then and reached out a hand to her. "There has been enough talk tonight, and enough anger. More than dredging up bad memories, I need sleep; it's been many nights since I've had enough." There was no promise of anything more.

But when Alisa climbed into bed beside him, he pulled her immediately to his side, not questioning the feeling of contentment and comfort he gained from her presence there.

Alisa's voice was soft, reluctant. "What do you feel for Ellen?" she whispered.

"Hatred. Nothing more," he answered firmly.

Alisa wondered if perhaps he spoke too firmly. She did not speak again, thinking sadly that sometimes the distance between love and hate was not even the width of a hair.

Chapter Thirty-seven

"Ivy!" Alisa was shocked to enter the drawing room to find that her visitor was her sister. "What in the world are you doing here?"

Ivy sat regally in a wing chair as if she were a queen sitting at court. "Hello, Alisa. I was under the impression that this is the land of opportunity, and so we have come to seek our share."

The late June afternoon was warm, and Ivy dabbed delicately at her upper lip. She was dressed elegantly, as always, in a mint-green and white traveling gown, a high lacy collar no doubt adding to her discomfort. She wore a large matching hat, tilted to one side of her perfect, elaborate coiffure. A long white feather swooped nearly to her shoulder in back.

"I would not refuse a cool drink," Ivy said pointedly.

Alisa ordered lemonade and then sat across from her sister. "Is Papa here, too?" she asked eagerly, recalling Ivy's use of *we* and *our*.

Ivy said haughtily, "No, he will die in England sitting alone atop his pile of money, the stingy old idiot."

Alisa sighed, any joy she had felt at seeing her sister dissolved with this reminder that Ivy's personality had not changed. Alisa was already irritated with her. "What are you doing here?" she repeated, suspicion raising its ugly head.

Ivy's eyes scanned the room slowly as she sipped her drink. "Very impressive," she said to herself. Then to Alisa, "I was unaware that your boorish husband was quite this well off. I half expected to find you living in some little cabin in the midst of a forest."

Alisa said noncommittally, apprehension rising rapidly, "You still have not answered my question."

Ivy sighed peevishly. "It's quite a long story, actually. You did know that I am married and have a child?"

Alisa's eyes grew wide. "How would I know that? Neither you nor Papa wrote!"

"I thought Papa probably had by now, to complain, if nothing else. He asked me not to write; he was certain it would be painful for you in light of your feelings for Owen."

"Why don't you tell me everything from the beginning."

"If I must. I was with child when you left, Alisa. Unfortunately, I was forced to marry Owen Tanor. You see, he was enamored of me all that time you so foolishly believed he loved you."

"I knew you fancied him, Ivy. I'm happy for you," Alisa said perfunctorily, ignoring Ivy's barb.

"Don't be. It appears you got the better of the two." Again her pale blue eyes assessed the room. "I thought Owen had a fortune and a future and that I would be comfortable. Instead, his family business has failed miserably and I find he hasn't a penny.

That is why we are here." Ivy paused, her eyes narrowed. "Papa refused to help us. He said he hadn't the inclination to support us and would do nothing for us but pay our passage here. I see we made a wise decision. Obviously, you can put us up, and certainly dear Christian must have enough holdings to offer Owen a well-paying position."

Alisa sat back in her chair as if the wind had been knocked from her. She knew only too well Ivy's disruptive influence. Christian would not be happy to find Ivy, whom he had disliked, as well as her husband and child, descending on his household. Certainly her own position here was still much too insecure for her to feel free to offer Christian's hospitality without even consulting him. Though in the last two months, she had begun to believe she might win his affection, Ivy's presence could well destroy the little ground she'd gained.

She breathed deeply, trying futilely to quell the surge of panic in her breast.

"I would like to help you, Ivy, but you must understand that my marriage has not been an easy one. Christian discovered our deception. He was terribly unhappy about it, to say the least. I could not offer his house to you as things stand. If you will give me some time, perhaps I can persuade him to give Owen a job and then you can set up housekeeping for yourself."

Ivy was unperturbed. "You don't understand, Alisa. We had only enough money to sail here. Our ship docked this morning. We have nowhere else to go, nor money to pay for lodgings of any kind."

"I still have the money Papa gave me when I left London. I'll give you that. It's more than enough to get you started." Alisa was grateful she had not touched that sum hidden in her studio.

"You expect me to make some hovel my home while you live in this?"

"It's the best I can offer."

"Oh, no, Alisa. You can offer much better. This place is big enough for us all, and I have no intention of living anywhere else."

"It is not my place to offer it, Ivy," Alisa said firmly, a note of anger creeping into her voice.

"You will simply have to arrange it, Alisa. Have you forgotten so soon how you came to be here in the first place? You owe me this."

"I will give you the money from Papa, Ivy. It is not a small sum."

"You force me to be blunt, Alisa. Either you arrange for us to live here or dear Christian will learn today that his wife is a murderess and that the only reason you married him was to escape the gallows. I don't suppose that little tidbit has come up in your conversations, has it?"

Alisa knew it was coming. She had always known Ivy was not above using any ammunition to gain what she wanted.

"I will have to speak with Christian, at least, before you move in."

"Then I hope he is upstairs, for Owen and the baby are waiting in a very hot carriage out front, and I have no intention of joining them."

Alisa's fingers tapped nervously on the carriage seat beside her. She did not even see the lush green beauty of a June day in New Haven as she rode through the elm-lined streets.

Alisa was garbed in the same calico gown she wore

working in her studio, its skirt smudged with a rainbow assortment of colors. Her heavy mane of curls was gathered with one ribbon atop her head, left to fall cascading down the back in wild disarray. Her thoughts were absorbed in what she would say to Christian when she found him.

She had no choice but to allow Ivy and her family to stay, but she could not wait until Christian arrived home for the evening meal and simply surprise him with their presence in his home. Instead, she set out to find him, knowing he had planned to spend the day checking factory production and inventory.

One of his factories manufactured the finest carriages in New Haven, and it was there that she was left pacing a sparsely furnished office while a quiet man with one eye that wandered curiously to the side assured her he would bring Christian to her.

"What's wrong?" Christian's tone was concerned as he hurried into the small space. The sight of Alisa's pale face and smudged gown did not relieve his fear.

"Nothing is wrong," she said quickly. "I needed to talk to you."

Christian frowned deeply, sensing Alisa's uneasiness. "Sit down, Alisa. I'll get you a glass of water," he said brusquely.

"I don't want any water. I'm sorry to bother you, Christian."

"Why don't you just calm down and tell me about it."

Alisa paused, unable to meet his eyes. "Ivy arrived unexpectedly a few hours ago," she said bluntly, waiting for a comment. "I honestly didn't know she was coming."

"It's nothing to be upset about, Alisa," Christian

said calmly. He disliked Ivy intensely, but he hardly begrudged her the entire city of New Haven.

"It isn't that simple." Alisa's agitation was obvious. "She has a husband and a baby," she said, still not making any sense to Christian, though his brows rose in surprise.

"She made short work of that, didn't she?"

"They're planning to live in your house," she blurted out.

Christian was silent for a time, wondering if Alisa's reaction was repugnance of the situation or fear of his own response. "I see," was all he said, choosing to bide his time in order to gauge Alisa's feelings before speaking.

"I'm sorry. I didn't invite them. But, you see, they have no money, her husband lost everything."

Christian said, "What is it you're trying to tell me, Alisa? Are you unhappy to have them in our house, or just worried that I will be?"

"Are you?"

Christian shrugged. "I don't like Ivy; I never have and I think you know it. But she is your sister. If you want them in our house, they are welcome, but if you prefer that they stay elsewhere, I'll pay for them to leave."

"No," she answered too quickly, "Ivy wants to stay in your house."

"Isn't it your home, too?"

"I don't know. Is it?"

Christian laughed lightly. "I don't understand why you're so upset, Alisa."

She sighed and finally fell into the large chair behind the desk. "It's just that I feel pulled between the two of you. I don't really want Ivy here, and I know how you feel about her, but as you said, she is my sister. I don't feel that I can refuse her help," she said wearily, hoping it was sufficient explanation.

"What exactly does Ivy want from you?"

"She wants to stay in the house and hopes you might employ her husband."

"I think I can do that."

Somehow Alisa's relief was not total, for it suddenly occurred to her that Ivy had not mentioned how long she intended to stay in Christian's home.

"Is it what you want? If you prefer, you can tell her I refused to let them stay and will pay for whatever they need until they're settled."

She shook her head. "I think it's best for now to let her stay. Can you find Owen something to do?"

Christian smiled at her, seeing she was not consoled nor more easy than when she had begun, and he wondered why. Still he kept his uncertainty to himself. "He can start to work tomorrow if he wants."

Alisa rose to leave, wishing he would pull her into his arms; she felt a need for his comfort and a reassurance that she had a place in his life. Her smile was wan. "Thank you, Christian. I'm sorry about all of this."

Christian, too, felt the urge to hold her, seeing how distraught she was, but the relationship between them was still too tenuous. He crossed his arms over his chest instead of holding them out to her. "Will you be all right?" he asked.

Alisa's only answer was a forced nod. Somehow anything being all right seemed impossible now.

Chapter Thirty-eight

Alisa left Christian to his evening grooming while she went to entertain their new houseguests. As she passed the room that had been designated as the nursery, Owen called her name, summoning her company as he sat feeding the baby, Jonah.

Alisa's smile was courteous as she entered the room and for the first time peered at her nephew.

"He's so tiny!" she commented in surprise.

Owen gazed down at the infant in his arms fondly. "Too small, I fear. I was against leaving England when we did. He was but two weeks old."

Alisa was sympathetic. "I know how Ivy is when she sets her mind on something."

Silence fell for a moment as Alisa watched the scene that struck her as unusual. His apparent devotion and gentleness with the infant touched her.

Owen Tanor was not a large man, perhaps a head shorter than Christian, and very thin. He was pleasant looking, with deep-brown hair the color of shiny mink and vibrant green eyes. His mouth had a sensuous tilt that Alisa had never noticed before, perhaps through her own naiveté.

Owen placed the baby to his shoulder to burp him. She noticed that his handling of the tiny bundle was confident, experienced, and judged that Ivy did not tend much to her child.

"You're very good with the baby. I don't think I could deal so well with him."

Owen smiled a bit ruefully. "Ivy was very unhappy to be unable to bring a nurse along with us. She hasn't much patience with Jonah."

"Ivy has never had much patience with anything."

"Except her toilette. I didn't realize anyone could spend so many hours grooming herself."

Alisa sensed resentfulness in his tone, and a hint of bitterness.

"It's hard to believe you are sisters," he continued. "You aren't a bit alike, are you?" His green eyes studied her intently as one hand gently patted the baby's back.

"I suppose there must be some similarities."

His face turned serious, his glance intense. "I thought you were at least a little fond of me, Alisa. I never understood what happened. You rushed into marriage and left England all before I had even heard of Christian Reed. Ivy only laughed when I questioned her about it. She would never explain it to me."

"I suppose you could say Christian swept me off my feet." She took refuge in the cliché.

"Didn't you realize how I felt about you?"

"I thought we were friends, Owen," she answered uncomfortably.

"I thought we were more than that."

"That's all past now. You have Ivy and Jonah."

"And you have Christian."

Alisa turned to leave before this conversation became any more embarrassing, only to see her husband standing in the doorway. She wondered how long he had been there.

"Have you met Owen?" she asked too hurriedly.

"We met downstairs when I came in," Christian said flatly.

Alisa breathed deeply. "We shall see you for dinner in a few minutes, Owen," she excused herself, joining a frowning Christian in the hallway.

"I didn't know you were well acquainted with Ivy's husband," he said conversationally as they descended the stairs.

"We were friends. Ivy was always fond of him," she said truthfully, hoping Christian had not overheard Owen's words.

Christian said no more but watched his wife much too closely for her comfort.

"Well, well, well." Ivy's tone was breathy as she approached Alisa and Christian at the entrance to the drawing room, her eyes moving slowly from Christian's face down the entire length of his body and back again. "You do look different than I remember you, Christian." Ivy smiled insinuatingly at her sister's husband and ignored Alisa. Christian's countenance remained impassive. The first sight of Ivy reminded him how unappealing he had found her. He was unaffected by her subtle, seductive invitation.

"Hello, Ivy," he said coldly, in a tone of indifference that Alisa found amusing in answer to what she saw all too clearly was Ivy's intent.

Christian turned to his wife, smiling warmly. "Would you like a glass of wine, love?"

Alisa appreciated the rare endearment. "Thank you, yes."

Ivy turned to Alisa, her tone overly sweet. "I don't know how I overlooked that man in England. Had I realized he was so attractive and so rich, you would have really found yourself in trouble, Alisa. I would never have given him over to you." She laughed, a low, confident sound, as she turned from Alisa to where Christian stood near the butler.

She watched in irritation as Ivy put all of her feminine wiles into work on Christian, bending forward to offer him a clear view of what was bursting from her bodice, laughing coyly at his words and lavishing giddy flattery on him. Alisā thought she must be irresistible, but Christian seemed impervious to Ivy's ploys.

He seized his escape at Owen's entrance, though he only moved to Alisa's side on the settee as he greeted the man. "Alisa tells me you're looking for work, Owen. Is that true?"

Owen's face grew slightly red, his feeling of debasement obvious. "Yes, I've come into some hard times, I'm afraid."

"If you're interested, I need a man at the carriage works to do bookkeeping and paperwork. The pay is good, if you'd like to give it a try."

Owen smiled sheepishly. "Thank you. It's a generous offer."

"Then you can start work in the morning."

"Wonderful!" Ivy's tone was syrupy. "How shall I ever thank you, Christian?"

"I gave the job to Owen, Ivy. You have nothing to thank me for."

Ivy's smile insinuated that she wanted more from Christian than her words conveyed at the moment. "I do have one request for myself, though."

Owen glared at his wife, looking like he had just swallowed something vile.

Christian's eyes raised to Ivy as she again stood before him, her skirts pressed against his knees. "What is it, Ivy?"

"Might I have the use of one of your servants to tend the baby? I simply cannot cope with him alone; he's such a trial to me," she said, pouting.

Owen's voice cut through the room with disdain and sarcasm. "Yes, by all means. Jonah has the audacity to expect to be fed and changed, and yes, even held. And he has no consideration for Ivy's three-hour toilettes. Do you know he actually spit up on her gown once? The child has no manners. I can't imagine why we keep him."

Thick tension filled the air, leaving Alisa intensely uncomfortable. Ivy stared at her husband with venomous hatred in her pale-blue eyes, a sneer on her lips.

"You forget yourself, Owen, dear. Keep in mind that I've done your begging for you! Without me you'd be in the streets."

Christian cleared his throat, rising and offering a hand to Alisa as he spoke. "A maid for the baby is no problem; the staff can adapt to a *temporary* situation," he said pointedly.

Ivy's expression changed with the talent of an accomplished actress. She smiled delightedly at Christian. "You're so kind. That way I'll be free to spend more time with Alisa. I'm looking forward to a long, long visit."

Chapter Thirty-nine

Alisa was startled at the sound of a knock on her studio door. After three weeks of Ivy's presence in her home, Alisa's nerves were taut, her temper short. She breathed a sigh of relief that it was Nicholas who entered and not Ivy. She recalled that Ivy never knocked before barging into any room. Nicholas's handsome face contorted in distaste. "It's like an oven up here. How can you bear this heat, let alone work?"

Alisa laughed lightly, mopping at her forehead and then the back of her neck and her throat with a moist cloth. She wore a light gingham dress, but perspiration stains dampened the fabric.

"Alisa!" Nicholas began in mock sternness, his arms akimbo. "I expect you to have better sense than to remain in the attic in the middle of July."

"The heat is preferable to the company of my sister, I assure you."

"She isn't so bad," he defended. He appreciated Ivy's fawning attention. In fact, all three of the men in the Reed household received their share. Owen seemed to be the only male Ivy despised.

"I didn't come to talk about Ivy, at any rate. It occurred to me that this is a fine day to take you to see the gallery at Yale. I've been remiss in not doing it sooner. Will you come?"

"Just let me change, I'll be ready in ten minutes."

Nicholas was the perfect guide, his wit adding levity to his extensive knowledge on the subject of art. Alisa wondered how he knew so much about something he claimed was no more than a hobby. She decided that it was perhaps better termed as a hidden passion.

In her intense pleasure and interest, Alisa did not realize the amount of time they spent in the gallery. She was enthralled by her first view of American art as well as absorbed in her companion's detailed expertise. When they left the building to find the sun nearly set, she became frantic. Nicholas could not understand her agitation. But he knew nothing of her sister's game.

Since Ivy's arrival, Alisa rarely found a moment's peace, for a brief respite cost her dearly afterward. Ivy was a demanding houseguest. She was petulant if Alisa was not at her beck and call, harassing and haranguing her sister just for spite. Sometimes Alisa believed Ivy upbraided her for entertainment. It was an unfair match because Ivy always reverted to her threat to inform Christian of Alisa's past. Before, Alisa had won her fair share of sibling battles, but she was now at a decided disadvantage.

To top it off, Christian was forced to be courteous to this intruder who expected her slightest whim to be met with alacrity. All too often Christian found no servant available when he called, his meals altered to suit Ivy's time and tastes, his sleep disrupted by loud arguments between Ivy and Owen and even his favorite brandy confiscated for Ivy's own use.

She acted as if she were holding court, prancing and primping, posing before him in a dance she believed seductive, while Christian wanted to throttle her. Alisa was left in the exact center, her own temper stretched to its limits while she was goaded by Ivy and faced Christian's justly irritated, disgusted complaints. The tenuous relationship Alisa and Christian attained before Ivy's arrival was in shreds.

"Goddammit, Alisa! Where the hell have you been?" Christian raged as Alisa entered their bedroom, short of breath from her mad dash up the stairs.

"Don't raise your voice, Christian. You'll wake the baby."

"It's my damn house, isn't it?" He loomed before her, stark naked, a sight that aroused feelings in her she could not make obvious.

She turned from the disturbing vision of Christian's masculinity. Her voice was soft. "Please put something on and tell me calmly what the problem is now."

"Where the hell have you been?" he repeated, ignoring both of her requests.

"Nicholas took me to the Yale gallery."

"That's the problem," he shouted irately. "You abandoned the house to your sister."

Alisa sighed, her own temper igniting. "There is nothing for me to abandon! I do nothing here."

"You are mistress here. Not Ivy."

"What has she done now?"

"I arrived home to find her baby screaming with no one in attendance because every servant in the place was seeing to some task for Ivy. I had to tend to the little bugger, who wet all over the front of me.

When I finally managed to quiet *her* son, I discovered our evening meal would not be served for hours yet, because her majesty had a late lunch and ordered *my* dinner to be postponed. Then I rang for my bath. That was at least an hour ago, and as you can see, I have yet to be allowed even that!"

Perhaps it was the effect of too much strain over the past weeks, but Christian's raging account of the day seemed funny. One small hand pressed her lips; her other arm wrapped about her middle as she turned to face the wardrobe.

"What is it that you find amusing, Alisa?"

Thinking she had gained control, she faced him, suppressing a smile. "Did you actually tend to the baby?"

"What the hell else was I to do?"

"I'm sorry, Christian," she managed as she began laughing again. It was the final blow to Christian's sorely stretched temper. He pulled on his clothing angrily.

"What are you doing?"

"I'm getting the hell out of this house! Before I return, you had damned well better do something about your sister. Remind her that she is a guest here and that a guest is a person whose visit eventually ends. I've had enough of this visit for two lifetimes!"

His patience had come to an end as she knew it would. She had to buy time, to placate both Ivy and Christian. "I'll talk to her right now. There's no need for you to leave."

"I'm damned tired of this, Alisa. I warn you, you do something or I will arrange to be away from here until you do."

"Where are you going?"

"There are any number of places I frequented before our marriage where I am still welcome. I know I can get a bath, a glass of brandy and company that is more relaxing and entertaining than any I can find here."

"And where is that?" she asked angrily.

One bushy brow rose arrogantly. "Why should you be concerned with the wherabouts of a man you married to save yourself from life with an old lecher? After all, I've provided you with what you wanted and your sister with what she wanted. So what the hell difference does it make?"

The door slammed closed with a force that shook the walls. Alisa fell back into a chair in frustration and defeat.

Chapter Forty

Alisa stood outside of Ivy's bedroom door, hearing the sound of water splashing as her sister enjoyed Christian's bath. Knowing Owen was not yet home, Alisa decided to emulate Ivy's tactics and storm into the room without knocking. Ivy was unperturbed as she lounged back in the tub, staring at Alisa as though she were a minor nuisance.

"You have gone too far, Ivy."

"Me?" Ivy arched a brow in feigned innocence.

"I'm sure you heard Christian shouting."

"I did hear his voice bellowing, but I paid no attention. It didn't concern me."

"It concerned you, all right! It was all about you."

Ivy soaped her arms, uninterested in Alisa's words.

Alisa refused to be put off by this ploy. "When are you moving out?" she said bluntly.

Ivy shrugged. "I like it here."

"I'm sure you do. This is not your home, and you are fast wearing out your welcome."

"Then you had best fix that, hadn't you?"

"No." Alisa's voice held a quiet strength Ivy was familiar with. It generally meant her defeat. Her eyes narrowed at Alisa's audacity.

"Do you need reminding *again* of the information I could use to destroy you?"

"I don't ever need to be reminded of it. You are a guest here . . . a *temporary* guest, and you had better remember that. Leave the running of this household alone. That includes mealtimes and all of the servants, save the one poor wretch that is your personal maid. You will have to conform to the routines; they will not revolve around you. And you will begin to look for another place to live tomorrow. Is that understood?"

"Understood . . . and unheeded."

"I think it's time you thought of one thing, Ivy. If you go to Christian with your story of my past, it will no doubt destroy my marriage. But when I go down, so do you and your family. You will lose everything you have already gained. Christian is thoroughly disgusted with your intrusion here and your behavior. So you remember that if I lose, you lose."

"Is that so?" Ivy spat. "I just may tell your husband the truth and then take your place."

Alisa laughed genuinely. "You really should have paid attention a moment ago. He holds nothing but contempt for you, Ivy. He's seen too much of your selfishness."

"That's only what you're hoping. Maybe we will just have to put it to the test."

"You do that, Ivy. You just do that."

Alisa did not realize that Ivy considered the gauntlet had been thrown down, and she never refused a challenge.

Sleep was impossible for Alisa, who was disturbed by her arguments with Ivy and Christian, as well as the temperature. She donned a lightweight robe and stole quietly from her room and down the back stairs.

The house was silent. She moved through the dark library and out into the garden. The wide brick terrace was inviting, and Alisa perched sideways on the low brick wall surrounding it. Just beyond, in the garden, was a tall fountain with a cherub holding a pitcher aloft from which water fell to a small basin and then a larger one.

The soothing sound of cascading water eased Alisa's tensions somewhat. She drew her feet up onto the wall, her arms hugging her knees. Her hair was tied up into a knot to free her neck of its hot mass, and small tendrils fell about her face.

She heard steps in the library and reluctantly turned to view her intruder as he paused at the French windows.

Owen smiled warmly at her. He wore a silk dressing gown, his hands thrust into the pockets casually. "I hope you don't mind if I join you," he said tentatively. "I saw you from my room, and you looked so inviting I couldn't resist."

Alisa felt a wave of sympathy for him. "Is Ivy asleep?"

His laugh was mirthless. "No. She persuaded Nicholas to take her out in the carriage in search of some entertainment. Actually, I think his room would have sufficed, but that would have seemed too tasteless even for Ivy."

"I'm sure you're wrong, Owen." Alisa felt the need to comfort him, for she suspected what he said was true. "Ivy has always loved to live frivolously and needed parties and people."

"And men."

"I wish I knew what to tell you. I don't."

"It doesn't matter anymore. The worst of it is that there isn't even money to ease the misery. Were things as they used to be, Ivy and I would simply reside together and lead separate lives."

"Perhaps she will tire of this in time."

Owen smiled at her, sitting at her feet on the ledge. "It will never get better, Alisa. There's no need to pretend. I accepted that on the trip over here. She told me it was too soon after the baby for me to return to her bed, yet I found her with the ship's captain; apparently it was not too soon for him. I haven't bedded her since, and I doubt if I ever will again."

"I'm sorry," she murmured, staring out at the fountain.

"No, I'm sorry. I shouldn't have told you such a thing." Silence fell for a moment. "I'm also sorry you married Christian."

"Christian is a good man," she said.

Owen sighed. "And I am a cad to be saying these things to his wife. I owe him a great deal. He's been kind to me, and he's also treated me with respect. He never made me feel like the charity case I am. He's a better man than I. I've watched him dive into the dirtiest job, something no one in my family ever did. Perhaps if they had, we wouldn't have lost everything. We always thought ourselves above menial tasks. He has the respect and admiration of every man I've met. Mine, as well." Owen stood reluctantly. "I had better go back upstairs before I dishonor and disgrace myself."

Alisa watched him leave, feeling sorry for him. There was nothing left of her old affection for him. She wondered, in comparison, how to define her feelings for Christian.

She denied that it was love, especially tonight

when she feared he had sought another woman's company. But she had to admit that there were powerful emotions roiling around in her.

"Don't tell me we're going to do this again." The object of her musings stood leaning against the frame of one of the library windows, his arms crossed over his chest.

"Are you still spoiling for a fight?" she asked derisively.

"I wasn't until I found your former paramour coming out of the library in his nightclothes. Or perhaps he is your *present* paramour. I see that you are dressed for the occasion, too."

"We are not all as loose-moraled as you." Her brow arched in accusation.

"What were you doing, Alisa?"

"What were you doing, Christian?"

"Bathing."

"With whom?"

"With a bottle of brandy and a rare steak at the Connecticut Arms."

"I wasn't aware it was a bathhouse."

"It isn't and you know it. Had I realized you were so well occupied, I would have accepted the doorman's offer to procure me some company."

"I am down here because the bedroom is stifling. Anyway, why should you care who admires a wife you don't want?"

"Was he 'admiring' you?" Christian's voice rose only slightly.

"Were you alone?" Alisa matched his tone in strength.

"Yes, dammit!"

Alisa turned her head to face the fountain again.

"Actually, Owen was out here admiring you. He was regaling me with your merits."

"Did that disappoint you?"

"I'm getting used to being overlooked."

"Are you?" His bluish-green eyes traveled over her slowly. "Looked over, but never overlooked." His voice was thick with innuendo. "I don't suppose Owen was informing you of their pending departure?"

"No, he wasn't. I spoke with Ivy."

"Did you tell her to leave?"

"I told her it was time she looked for a house of her own and that while she remained here, she was to abide by your rules."

"That should do next to nothing."

"Go away, Christian. I came out here for a little peace and quiet. I've battled enough for one day."

The sound of a door slammed loudly on the second floor as Ivy's voice shrieked at Owen. Simultaneously, the startled baby wailed, and the stillness was rent with harsh, grating noise.

Alisa's head shook slowly in defeat, her eyes closed in frustration. There would be no more peace now for hours and she felt embarrassingly responsible for the bad behavior of her sister.

Christian let out a short, exasperated breath, his eyes traveling to the upper windows. He pushed away from the door abruptly, crossing to Alisa to pull her from the ledge.

"Tomorrow, offer your sister a separate room from her husband."

Without another word, he dragged her behind him, leaving the terrace and walking with determination down a brick-lined path through the garden.

"Where are we going?" she asked, angrier still to be treated like this.

"You need a little cooling off before I heat you back up."

The offensive sounds from the house grew muted where the trees grew ense at the far end of the estate opposite from the stables. The change in temperature was a welcome relief as Christian entered this private forest, and Alisa's curiosity was fast exceeding her anger.

A small clearing appeared, a near perfect circle in the trees where silver moonlight illuminated a pond so still it seemed more a mirror reflecting the full moon and each sparkling dot in the clear summer sky. Here, the air was cool and fragrant with the perfume of wild flowers.

Christian swung Alisa to a rock and tore off his clothes with sensual abandon. He reached for Alisa's wrists, pulling her to her feet again. A mere second was all he wasted in stripping her of nightgown and robe, leaving his wife dressed only in the moon's silver glow.

His face lowered to the sensitive spot where her neck and shoulder met, kissing lightly, his tongue flicking across her smooth skin. Then his mouth raised to hers in a soft, gentle, arousing kiss as one large hand cupped her breast lightly, his thumb teasing the nipple to a taut peak of desire. He ended the caress and picked her up in his arms. The feel of his bare skin against hers was delightfully titillating.

His deep, throaty laugh echoed around them as he waded into the pool. Alisa gasped as her backside met the cold water. Christian found the center of the shallow depth, the surface reaching just to his chest.

"Can you swim?"

"Of course!"

"Maybe tomorrow you can return for that. There's no time for it now." His arms suddenly opened, dropping her into the pond like a boulder.

Alisa opened her eyes in the black depth, finding Christian's legs, braced far apart like two tree trunks. Small hands circled each thick ankle as Alisa tried to pull him under. Christian merely laughed, his balance never disturbed. He bent and reached into the water, pulling her back above the surface.

"You're an audacious little guppy to attack a whale!" His hands rose upward, from her sides, each palm pressing against the side of her breasts, pushing each mound together as he stared down at them. "Playing in the water is not what I had in mind." Again his mouth lowered to hers, his tongue teasing. "I will have what I came here for, and only then will you play . . . if you can."

His lips took hers, fiercely demanding everything. One of her arms encircled his broad shoulder, taking some of her weight from the muscular arm that braced her thighs. Her other hand caressed the side of his neck, feeling the corded tendons there. His tongue searched her mouth, meeting hers as it matched his game. Her hand traveled down from his neck, across his shoulder and down the iron-hard bulge in his bicep to his chest. She felt his nipple grow taut, and she delighted in playing with it as her lips reveled in his kiss.

His head raised, and his powerful arms lifted her slightly so that his mouth could reach her breast; a surge of tingling sparks flew down her stomach to that spot between her thighs with the first hot, moist touch of his mouth full upon that exquisite mound drawing it deeply into the depths of his mouth, sucking, then biting gently the hard peak that could not get enough of him.

Her head fell back, and she arched to meet him, as if they could not be close enough to satisfy her need.

He slowly lowered her legs, leaving her breast still yearning for more of what he offered. Again his mouth fell to hers, in a bruising kiss, his tongue thrusting into her mouth much as she longed for his manhood to enter her lower region. One massive hand returned to her breast for only a moment's torment before it followed a path down her flat stomach, still farther beneath the water, toying with the softly curling hair there. She moaned in a torture of yearning for him to touch her between her legs. When he did, her breath drew in a deep gasp of pleasure as she felt her own flesh open to him, want him.

Her hands ran from his shoulders to his chest and all the way down, grasping his long, hard member with both hands, one curved along the shaft, the other exploring, discovering his response to light fingers tracing the tip, teasing. A deep, guttural groan rumbled from his throat as his hips arched toward her. He nibbled lightly on her neck, her shoulders, weaving a torturously slow trail back to her breast. He drew it deeply, deeply within his mouth as his hand worked its magic below, parting her, a gentle finger drawing forward, finding her ready for him. Both powerful hands ran to her ribs, again cupping her breasts as his palms pressed them, lifting her to slide up his huge, muscular body as if she weighed nothing. He kissed her again, urgently, whispering his instructions as his mouth trailed down to the valley between her breasts, burying his face between the two soft, glistening mounds pressed there.

She wrapped her legs around his waist, desperate to feel him full within her. Buoyed by the water, she easily accomplished what he demanded, and he slid her back down his chest, his hot, hard shaft probing for entrance. He eased her with careful slowness onto it, allowing only the very tip to penetrate her as he moved his hips toward her, then lower still, slowly, slowly, until at last she felt his huge length deep within her, so deep that she felt him pressed against her womb in a new, divine sensation.

He moved then, his hips pushing upward, into her as he gently guided her to match each thrust. She was lost in sensation, the cool water around her, the exquisite tingling as her nipples brushed against his hairy chest with each movement, the deep, fullness of his hard shaft filling her to the limits of her endurance, that extremely sensitive spot his finger had aroused before, rubbing against the hard bone of his pelvis; all joined and grew and grew, striving to reach that peak of intense, matchless satiety. Short, high bursts of sound pushed from the very center of her being, mingled with his deep groans of pleasure as he, too, found that perfect ending, every muscle in his body a taut chord of ecstasy. His head fell back as release freed his lungs to once again breathe deeply. Alisa's head fell against his heaving chest.

In that moment Christian felt every sense satisfied in a way he had never before experienced in his life.

He pressed a light kiss into the unruly tangles of her head. His hands moved to her sides again, and he pulled her upward until they were parted, and then, with one arm behind her knees, he lifted her into his embrace and left the water.

He did not pause to gather their clothes, nor did he put her down, but strode casually back to the now quiet, dark house. To her relief, they did not encounter anyone, and Christian refused to stop until he reached their bed, laying her gently on it and then joining her there to pull her possessively into his arms. Their bodies had been cooled enough by the water that staying closely entwined now was still comfortable.

After a time Alisa gave in and asked the question that would give her no peace. "Were you with someone else tonight, Christian?"

He laughed, a low, languid sound. "Still so naive, my love? No, Alisa. Had I been with anyone else tonight we could not have done what we just did."

Alisa breathed deeply to gain courage. "Were you faithful to your other wife?" she ventured fearfully.

"Painfully. Right up to the last," he answered without rancor. His face turned into her hair, breathing deeply of the clean scent of her. Kissing her lightly, he whispered, "And to this one, too."

Chapter Forty-one

"Stop it! Stop it right this instant! Do you hear me, Jonah?"

Ivy's shrieking voice carried through the quiet afternoon. Hearing her nephew's name, Alisa ran from her bedroom. She was used to Ivy railing at everyone else, but her sister rarely entered the baby's room.

"Ivy, don't!" Alisa commanded, seeing her sister standing beside the cradle, her hand raised to strike the tiny infant whose wails echoed in the hot stuffy room.

She moved quickly to pick the baby up, holding him protectively to her breast. "My God, Ivy! Would you hit a baby for crying?"

Ivy's anger turned on Alisa, her eyes narrowed, her expression venomous. "It's your fault! I've spent these past weeks not disrupting the routines of this house as I was ordered. Your precious staff is short-handed today, and some ninny decided to use the nanny to tend the house, leaving me to care for him," she shouted, her tone revealing her outrage.

Alisa glared back, as angry as Ivy. "I am the ninny that decided that. After all, he is your child!"

"I don't want him," she spat. "I've abided by the rest of your idiotic rules, but I will not take a hand with that brat. Owen can take him to the carriage factory for all I care."

"You are despicable, Ivy."

"I don't care what you think, Alisa. I never have. If you're so concerned about the brat's welfare, then you tend to him. It's only fitting that the murderer of his father should have to care for him." Ivy's color was high, her pale-blue eyes blazing with fury.

"I thought Owen was the father."

"Ha!" Ivy's hands were in fists pressed to her waist. "I had been meeting Willis Potts secretly for months. He was an amusing diversion."

Alisa merely shook her head in disgust. "But Owen believes the baby is his."

"Maybe he does. Maybe he doesn't. I don't really care. He believed it at the time, that's why he married me. I've certainly come to regret that! I'd rather he take this little bastard and leave me in peace."

"What would you do then, Ivy?" Alisa's question was thick with scorn. "Who would support you? Perhaps you had better think about what advantages Owen offers you and be kinder to him."

"He offers me nothing. He is excess baggage to me and not a thing more." Ivy smiled viciously. "My biggest mistake was in not seizing Christian for myself and letting you have dear Owen."

"It's too late now. You would be wise to make the best of what you do have."

Ivy laughed caustically. "I wouldn't be too sure of that, Alisa. I've always been more woman than you could hope to be. If I set my mind to it, you may yet find yourself with Owen. He's almost as dull as you are; after all, it would be a perfect match. And then you could play mother, too." With a wicked laugh, Ivy swooshed from the room.

* * *

Six weeks had passed, and Christian had been gone more than he had been home. He was absorbed in negotiations for the sale of one of his whalers in New York.

Since the day she rescued Jonah from his mother's temper, Alisa had been spending her mornings with the small baby. She was driven to compensate for what his natural mother denied him. It seemed cruel to leave the infant shut away with only a servant. She found that the baby filled a gap in her life while Christian was gone on business, filling her hours with uncomplicated joy. It surprised her, for she never thought of herself as maternal. It was, she supposed, yet another feminine attribute she lacked.

Yet she found Jonah, at five months, very amusing and endearing. He laughed aloud at her contorted faces and silly noises, delighting in the rattle and rag doll she bought for him, and was fascinated with the movement of his own hands. He cooed at her seriously, his eyes wide, or shrieked in glee for her. Alisa cared greatly for him and began to wonder what it would be like for her and Christian to have a child.

On Christian's first morning back, Alisa sat playing with Jonah on the bed in the nursery, musing on the subject. She was unaware that he stood watching from the doorway.

His bushy brows were drawn together in a pensive frown. During his time away, he had discovered an intense longing to be back with her, even if it meant tolerating Ivy. It disturbed him greatly, for he realized it was more than a simple craving for her in bed. He was plagued by the picture of her in his mind at the most inauspicious times, distracting him from business matters. His mind recreated the sound of her laughter, the feel of her silky skin. He would dream of her, only to come fully conscious and realize with a wave of disappointment that she was not there.

As Christian stood now and watched Alisa playing with the baby, a dark memory came unbidden: the sight of Ellen tending Nat at this same age, a picture that had warmed him with contentment and left him believing his life was perfect and would remain so. It had been brutally shattered only months later.

How could he trust that Alisa would be different, he wondered painfully; in this guise of innocence was a woman who had deceived him as fully as had Ellen.

"Christian! I didn't hear you come in," Alisa said gaily, her smile warm and beckoning.

He moved to stand beside the bed, staring down at the baby he thought quite homely. He held out a long, thick finger to the infant, who seized it with delight.

Alisa spoke again, not noticing Christian's mood. "I was waiting for you to wake before I had breakfast. Are you home to stay?" she asked bluntly, for she had decided that if he left New Haven again, she was going to accompany him if it meant following him.

Christian's tone was formal. "My business is complete, if that's what you mean."

"Then you won't be going away again?"

"Not in the foreseeable future."

Her eyes captured his, gleaming with emotion. "I'm glad," she whispered, telling more about how much that pleased her than effusiveness could.

Christian sighed, resigning himself reluctantly to

his desire to be with her now, unable to maintain his aloofness with her. "Have you missed me?" he asked a bit gruffly.

"On occasion," she teased, her glance resting on the baby between them. "I have been busy with Jonah."

Jealousy struck Christian, adding to his emotional turmoil. "I hadn't pictured you as enamored of babies, Alisa."

"Neither had I. It's come as a surprise to me, but I really enjoy him."

Alisa tickled Jonah and nuzzled his side until he shrieked. "Would you mind a baby of our own, Christian?"

Silence fell heavily between them. "Are you pregnant, Alisa?" he asked at length.

She swallowed thickly, disappointed. "No, I'm not. I merely wondered how you would feel about it."

There was another pause, then he answered in a remote voice, "I learned all too well the first time I thought I was a father that babies are easily passed off onto those they don't belong to. I can't see a child as anything but a source of trouble."

Alisa was struck more deeply than she would have him know. Her voice chilled considerably. "Most babies are born to their rightful fathers. Were I to have a child, it's sire would not be in question. Perhaps if you have such feelings, you should take a separate bed, then there will be no child at all and you needn't be troubled."

Christian was coming to know Alisa well. He knew his words were painful to her, and she used her anger to hide it. But he was pushed by his own demons. "Babies are an unfortunate result of pleasure. I will not be refused your bed, Alisa, not for any reason. If my seed strikes fertile ground, I have the resources to employ nurses and nannies and later boarding schools to solve the problem."

"That is not how you were raised. What if your father had felt like that?"

"My father acted according to his experiences and I to mine."

"You should have married Ivy, then. It seems you share a similar selfishness. I hope there never is a child, Christian, because no baby of mine will be treated that way. I would take it away from you before I would stand quietly by and allow the same treatment my sister believes fitting for her son. You don't deserve to have a child of your own any more than Ivy does."

Christian rose abruptly. Alisa had struck a sharp blow of her own. "Are you certain you're not pregnant, Alisa?" he said harshly, wondering why she felt so strongly so suddenly.

"I'm quite sure. And grateful for it, too," she said through gritted teeth.

"Then there is really no point to this conversation, is there? But since your sister has come into it, I think she has stayed here long enough. I want you to get her the hell out of this house before she or any of her family causes more problems. Is that understood?"

"It's understood, Christian. But don't blame this innocent for your past ugliness. No matter who he belongs to, he isn't the cause of your problems."

"Are you coming down to breakfast?"

"I've lost my appetite as well as any desire for your company. This room and this baby have been a respite for me in the past weeks. It seems I am still in need of one."

Christian left then, angry at Alisa but furious with himself.

All of Alisa's joy in Christian's being home dissolved. Her spirits plummeted.

But it was morning yet, only the beginning of a day destined for great unpleasantness.

Chapter Forty-two

"What do you think you're doing?" Alisa shouted from the top of the short staircase into her attic studio.

Ivy stopped, turning on Alisa as if she were the intruder here instead of Ivy. "Good! Now you can just tell me where it is and save me the time looking."

She stood in the center of the large, open room, amidst the disarray of her quest. Paintings and drawings were flung across the floor, as were clean parchment and canvas; brushes and pens had been dumped from their cups; jars of paint rolled about the tabletop and to the floor.

"You have no right to be in this room!" Alisa shrieked, utterly at the end of her tether with this wanton disregard of her privacy.

Ivy ignored Alisa's rage, confident in herself and her weapon over Alisa. "I want that money you took from Papa."

"You have already had more from me than you deserve, Ivy."

Ivy was not one to accept refusal of her demands. "You owe me your life, dear sister. You will never finish paying that debt. Now give me that money."

"You may have it only when you get out of this

house. There is no other reason I will ever give it to you."

"I will leave this house only when I can go to its equal. I accepted your terms before, Alisa; I stopped interfering with the sacred routines of this mausoleum, rather than chance Christian's evicting me. But I will not leave here until I am ready. And when I need nothing more from your husband, you will be the only one left with something to lose! Then my knowledge will do you the most harm."

"I always knew you were vile, Ivy, but even I am surprised by how thoroughly."

"That money is Papa's. I have as much right to it as you, and I want it. I've invited a guest for dinner this evening, and I refuse to have her see me in the same gown again. The dressmaker has finished one I ordered, but she will not allow me more credit. Now give it to me."

"No!" Alisa fairly shook with anger and outrage, venting not only her frustration with Ivy but also with Christian. "I am sick to death of being the pawn in this house."

"I want that money, Alisa. Either I will have what I want or I will destroy this whole sham now." Ivy flung a large sheet of parchment at Alisa, who ducked easily.

It was caught by a wide-eyed Scott, who stood just behind Alisa in the doorway.

"It's customary to call in a judge and seconds in a duel," he said as his glance slowly took in the mess around Ivy's feet. "Can I offer assistance?"

Alisa was humiliated at having this scene witnessed, and she feared how much Scott had heard. Ivy remained glaring at her sister challengingly.

"I'm sorry, Scott. It's a silly squabble." Then, turning back to Ivy, Alisa said in a calm, strong tone that prevented further argument, "You will not find what you seek, Ivy, because it's not here. I told you what you have to do to obtain it. Nothing will alter that."

Ivy's eyes narrowed evilly; her voice was low. "You may have won this for now, Alisa, but beware. I will not be the loser for long, and you will find yourself very, very sorry." She walked to where Scott still stood, heedless of what she crushed with each step. Before she left, she turned a vindictive smile to her sister. "My dinner guest will no doubt be of great interest to you, Alisa. I've invited her with you in mind."

Scott came into the room as the sound of Ivy's footsteps died away, picking up everything in his path. He smiled sympathetically at Alisa. "Have you and Ivy ever gotten along?" he asked kindly.

"No," Alisa admitted softly. "I apologize for that childish scene." She could not face him, so she began cleaning up also.

They worked mutely for a moment before he said, carefully choosing his words, "Ivy and I seem to have silently agreed to ignore one another, so she doesn't disturb me. Nicholas is fond of all beautiful women, so I think he likes having her here. But if she disturbs you so, Alisa, why don't you ask her to leave? This is your house."

"I have tried," she answered simply. She could neither tell the truth nor have him believe that she wanted Ivy to remain here.

Scott handed Alisa what he had collected of her crumpled drawings. "I heard most of what was said, Alisa," he told her honestly, seeing the fear that grew with his words. "I'm not as closely involved with you as Christian is, so I doubt that whatever

Ivy is holding over your head would affect me. I might be able to help you."

It was useless to deny what he had already heard, but Alisa could not bring herself to tell her husband's brother what she had done, no matter how sympathetic he was. Tears filled her eyes, but Alisa would not allow them to fall. "I can't, Scott," she managed simply.

Scott saw the wetness glistening in those beautiful dark-blue eyes. "Your silence gives her a strong weapon, Alisa. I think Ivy is a merciless adversary. You are among friends here, you know, and whether or not he admits it, I think Christian has come to care for you. Not one of us would stand by and watch you hurt."

Alisa shook her head rapidly in denial. It was difficult to quell the weakness his tender words caused in her. She turned from him, tempted to capitulate in the face of his kindness. She breathed deeply until she could control her voice.

"Thank you, Scott. I truly appreciate all you have offered me. But it's better if I deal with Ivy alone."

He watched her a moment longer. "All right, then. But remember what I've said. If for some reason you don't want to go to Christian with this, you can still come to me."

Alisa sat alone in the sitting room adjoining the master suite, waiting as Christian dressed for the evening meal. Ivy had let everyone know this was to be a formal dinner to entertain her guest, so Alisa wore a gown of black lace over flesh-colored taffeta, which gave the bodice the alluring effect of open tatting over bare skin, the neckline fell gently from creamy shoulders the exact color of the gown's lin-

ing. The three-tiered skirt was full, the back longer
to form a train.

Alisa was unaware of her own beauty, her
thoughts absorbed in how to handle her predicament
with Ivy. It was imperative that she do something or
she would forever be her sister's victim. She did not
notice her husband as he entered from the con-
necting doorway.

Christian was breathtakingly handsome in a white
linen suit, black satin vest and white silk shirt. His
cravat was black satin, and a gold chain crossed his flat
middle to the small watch pocket in his vest.

Christian studied Alisa. He did not like to see her
pensive and subdued. He had hoped that this morning's argument had been forgotten.

Alisa raised her eyes as Christian came farther into
the room. She was not unaffected by the sight of his
masculine, virile attractiveness, though she wished
she were. She did not return his wide grin, nor did she
acknowledge his compliment on her appearance.

Instead she said bluntly, "I would like to spend
some time in the country. Is that permissible?"

"When did you need ask my permission?" he
teased, hoping to lighten her serious mood.

"Then you have no objections?"

"Is this another ploy to escape my bed, Alisa?"

"There are many things I need to think about,
Christian, and I can't do it here."

"Am I banned from accompanying you?"

Alisa knew she should resist him, perhaps offend
him if that would keep her from conceiving a child he
was already determined to hate, but she knew she
could not. Her willpower was no match for her feelings for him. "I need to be away from Ivy for a time.
It doesn't matter if you come along."

"Hardly a warm invitation."

"I'm afraid it's the best I can do. I know well that I can't keep you from my bed, nor even remain cold to you when you . . . want me. But I cannot freely and gladly accept you when there is the possibility of my conceiving and your treating our baby in the manner you described."

"Dammit, Alisa! Why is this an issue if you aren't pregnant? It just isn't important." Christian was unhappy with himself for making such a severe statement in anger, but he would not rescind it.

"It's important to me, though I don't know what to do but pray no child of mine is ever born to you."

Her bitter words were a blow to Christian, and he sought refuge in harshness. "That is the only way it won't happen, because I will not be refused what I desire most from you, Alisa."

Tension filled the silence between them, and then Alisa said, "Then you will not stop me from going to the country?"

Christian shrugged. "I was going there next week to see to the harvesting and bringing the cattle down for winter. But there is no reason we can't leave tomorrow if you prefer."

Alisa ignored the arm he offered. "Fine. I'll be ready then."

They descended the stairs in silence, each at opposite sides of the banister. They had just reached the bottom when Scott appeared, an odd expression on his face. He opened his mouth to speak, and then closed it again as high-pitched laughter sounded behind him.

He stood aside to allow them to pass, and only then did he speak, his voice a low tone directed at Christian. "Be prepared, Christian. You're in for a shock."

Chapter Forty-three

"Ellen!" Christian's surprise registered in his voice.

Ivy's light laughter drew Alisa's glance from the beautiful woman who walked seductively toward Christian.

"Hello, darling!" The familiarity brought Alisa's attention back to Christian as the statuesque woman stood before him, smiling sensuously, her large breasts pressed fully against a revealing décolletage.

Christian stared at Ellen, and Alisa detected no distaste in his expression. She felt plain looking beside this exquisite beauty. Ellen had chestnut hair that shone like a sleek stallion's, perfectly, elaborately coiffed. Her eyes were a rich hazel color beneath thick, long lashes. Each alabaster cheek was deeply dimpled, adding a coy sweetness to her smile.

Alisa could not help thinking what an attractive couple they were, Ellen the magnificent female counterpart to Christian's extraordinary handsomeness.

"I hope you don't mind me being here too much, darling." The rich voice tore through Alisa's musings. "Ivy and I met at the dressmaker's. When I told her how much I wanted to see you to thank you for caring for Nat when he was ill, she suggested I come to dinner. I'm afraid I just could not resist seeing your expression."

"I hope it was worth the trouble, Ellen," Christian said evenly. His tone was the remote, aloof one Alisa hated, but now she believed it was a ruse to conceal his feelings for this woman.

Christian continued, "Ellen, this is my wife, Alisa. I'm sure Ivy spoke of her sister."

Alisa was unnerved when Ellen turned that same warm smile to her. "Ivy has spoken of you. I'm happy to meet you, Alisa. I'm afraid I must apologize to you for being here. I know it's an awkward situation." She seemed genuinely sympathetic to Alisa's feelings.

Alisa worked to gain control of herself, drawing from an inner strength and dignity. "You have caught me a bit off guard. Ivy kept you quite a secret."

Ivy spoke, still looking only at Alisa. "It was too delicious to tell. I would never ruin such an amusing scene."

Alisa was grateful for Scott's intervention then, since she felt at a disadvantage. Christian still stared at Ellen, lost in his study of his beautiful former wife and apparently unaware of anything else.

Scott clasped Ellen's arm. "It's time we went in to dinner. I think I can escort both Ellen and Ivy."

Alisa did not eat, nor did she speak through the meal that followed, feeling Ivy's vengeance fully. Ivy and Ellen chatted on in a continuous stream of subjects that Ivy initiated for Alisa's benefit. Ellen reminisced about her meeting with Christian, their honeymoon in New Orleans, and a variety of amusing anecdotes about their marriage. Listening was agony for Alisa, for it gave far too much substance and form to Christian's past. He avoided all comment, but that did not ease Alisa's mind. She again felt like an unwanted wife.

Scott made several attempts to change the subject to more common ground, but it was futile in the face of Ivy's determination and Ellen's enjoyment.

After dinner, Ellen refused coffee and, to Ivy's disappointment, ended the evening early. Alisa politely said her farewells and climbed the stairs, not waiting to hear Christian's parting words to the other woman, nor allowing Ivy her final vitriolic comment.

She paced her bedroom in fury and pain. She had no desire to face Christian as she was, her control near to snapping. When she heard the front door close, she decided to seek the library as refuge. She was surprised to find Christian in the hallway just a short distance from their room. She had expected him to stay until the moment Ellen departed, if not offering to escort her home. Christian's calm, quizzical stare only fueled her anger.

"I'm in need of a book. Don't wait up for me, I may be some time in choosing one," she said irately, not waiting for his question.

"Your talents lie with pen and brush, Alisa. The stage will never be your forte."

Christian clasped her arm and pushed her gently back into the bedroom. He closed the door behind them, unmoved by Alisa's rage as she stood in the center of the room, her hands clenched into tight fists at her sides. He leaned back casually on the closed door, his muscular arms crossed over his chest.

"I can understand your being mad as hell at Ivy,

but why are you mad at me? Ellen's presence here was as much a shock to me as to you," he said quietly, calmly.

"I didn't say I was angry with you. I said I wanted a book." She fairly shook with the effort to control herself.

"We have been together long enough for me to recognize when your anger is aimed at me. I simply want it explained."

"Do you?" she said sarcastically. "I should think it would be obvious. I have just spent the evening with your former wife, listening to a boring account of what a delightful marriage you had. How should I react? Would it be suitable for me to say, 'What a lovely woman my predecessor is. It sounds like you had a wonderful life together. You were certainly enthralled by her. What a shame the courts destroyed your happiness!'?"

Christian smiled slowly, watching her in that aloof way she detested. "I was not 'enthralled' by her, Alisa. And I found no more pleasure in her embellished stories than you. And I did nothing to encourage her."

"You didn't stop it, either."

"What should I have done? Thrown her bodily from our house? This seemed like the best course. Ivy's satisfaction in the whole thing was lessened this way; she would have preferred that both of us have a tantrum, don't you think?"

"Do you expect me to believe you ogled the woman to defeat Ivy?"

Christian was unaffected by her raised tone. "I did not 'ogle' her. Did you see things that were not there tonight? I showed Ellen cold courtesy, nothing more."

"You couldn't take your eyes off her. Scott had to suggest dinner and drag her away while you stared at her mesmerized."

Christian chuckled. "I admit my guilt there. I did stare at her but not for the reason you think."

"I suppose you were astounded by her homeliness."

"Tonight is the first time in over a year that I have seen Ellen. I was struck by the fact that I felt nothing for her. Nothing. I saw her in a new light. I saw all of her shallowness, all of her selfishness, and I was amazed to find she had no effect on me, not even anger."

"Of course not. You save it all for me. Now she is blameless, innocent, and I am guilty for every wrong ever committed against you by that woman. Now that you have me to blame, you use me to vent all of your bitterness. Even to the point of caring for her child while threatening any I might have."

Christian was struck by the possible truth in her words.

"You aren't guiltless, Alisa. Your deceit added to my bitterness. You've earned your share."

Alisa's frustration was mountainous. She shrieked through gritted teeth, "It always goes back to that! God, how tired I am of it. It was one act compared to so many of hers, and yet I am always judged as an equal offender. There is nothing I wish more at this moment than that you had annulled this marriage." Her semblance of control cracked. "I hate you! And I hate everything my life has become! I hate being the victim of Ivy's greed and treachery and your bitterness and distrust and contempt! You're both the same. You think you have me backed into a corner, that you can rule me with guilt."

Tears fell unheeded; she felt totally defeated. "Divorce me! Annulment is impossible now, but you got one divorce, I'm certain you can arrange another. Surely you have grounds great enough to accomplish it again."

Alisa's tears affected Christian, for he knew she never cried.

"Dammit, Alisa," he muttered under his breath as he pulled her into his arms.

Alisa fought him, small fists pounding against his iron-hard chest. "I hate you! I hate what you can do to me!" She moaned amidst sobs that wracked her body.

Christian ignored her words and her feeble blows, forcing her to rest against him, to be comforted by his powerful arms encircling her.

After a long while, when Alisa's sobs had turned to only tears, Christian spoke into her hair, his voice calm, quiet. "I don't mean to punish you for my past, Alisa. I think you're right; too often I do. I'm no longer sorry you're my wife, so it's all the more wrong of me to punish you. I don't mean to be cruel to you. I never mean to be. It just seems that sometimes I'm driven by a rage that leaves me blind to the truth. I am sorry for that, and I will try not to let it happen anymore. But you aren't really mad at me tonight. You rail at me when I'm unfair, but how long will you let Ivy go on without standing up to her? You're doing what you accuse me of; you're punishing me when it's Ivy that deserves your wrath."

Alisa pushed herself from his arms, her strength an armor around her once again. "You always win, don't you? Even when you concede, you win," she said bitterly, knowing she was still caught firmly in the trap between Christian and Ivy.

"Are we at war, Alisa?"

Her chin rose defiantly, knowing that lowering her defenses was too dangerous to risk. "Sometimes I think so."

Christian's handsome head shook sadly. "You're wrong in that. Very, very wrong."

Chapter Forty-four

Alisa sat quietly through the carriage ride to the country estate, staring from the window at the brilliant gold, red and yellow leaves of fall shimmering on thick branches in a cool autumn breeze.

Christian watched her from the opposite seat wishing he could read her thoughts. She had not spoken ten words to him since the past night, but he felt certain it was a result of whatever tormented her and not anger at him.

Instead of his wife's company at breakfast, Christian had suffered Ivy's. She had enlightened him to a fact that stirred his curiosity.

"Ivy tells me you have quite a large sum of money hidden away." Christian broke the silence between them conversationally.

Alisa's eyes shot to her husband, filled with sparks of anger. "Ivy has never been known for her tact."

"Then you don't deny it?"

"It's true; why should I deny it?"

"Where did you get it?"

"I am not a thief, if that's what you think."

Christian sighed patiently. "I hardly think you that, Alisa. Especially when you won't touch the money I give you freely."

Alisa fought against losing her temper. "My father gave it to me when I left, to buy safe passage home if you mistreated me. He was understandably worried about my future with you."

"I see." He paused.

"Why did Ivy tell you about it?" she ventured hesitantly, fearing what else her sister might have disclosed.

"Why didn't you tell me about it?" he countered.

"It is money I was to use if I needed to leave you; I did not think it wise to reveal its existence."

"You knew the truth about the circumstances of our marriage, Alisa. I did not attack you, you have never been in danger, nor had any reason to fear your treatment at my hands."

"You hated me, Christian. Even before you discovered my lie. That did not make you the model husband. I am still not certain I will not need to escape you."

"That's ridiculous," he said softly.

"Is it?"

"Has your life been such hell with me?"

"At times," she answered stubbornly.

"Do you honestly want to leave me?"

Alisa looked away, peering again from her window at the countryside rolling past. "Sometimes my future with you seems bleak," she said truthfully, but her tone spoke of disappointment at the prospect.

"I don't mean for it to be. I think we can have a good life together, Alisa."

Alisa realized the magnitude of this statement, as well as his admission the night before about his not being unhappy to have her as his wife. "I hope so, Christian. I find it is what I want."

Silence fell as neither could bring themselves to offer more than that. Then Alisa remembered, "Why did Ivy speak about the money?"

Christian sighed. "She wanted me to force you to give it to her. She said your father had told her he meant for Ivy to have it."

"She lies."

"I'm sure she does."

"What did you tell her?"

"I said I had no knowledge of the money, but that you are an honest person, and I felt sure you would do the right thing with it."

Alisa flushed. "Thank you," she whispered.

Christian studied her closely, gauging. "She said I had no idea how dishonest you really are." He watched every drop of color drain from her face. He knew at that moment that whatever secret Alisa kept from him was Ivy's weapon.

"Alisa," he began in a deep, soft voice filled with compassion. "You know that I would never have chosen to marry again. But the fact is that you are my wife, and have been for over a year now. I am not looking for a reason to change that. But it's obvious to me that whatever you're keeping from me is far more dangerous in Ivy's hands than it could ever be in mine."

Alisa wanted to believe him. But she knew too well Christian's drastic mood swings, and she felt no security with him, regardless of his words.

Alisa shook her head firmly, in answer to more than her words said. "I don't keep the money to leave you, Christian. I told Ivy that I would give her the money only when she leaves your house. But she wants it for new gowns. I'm sure she meant to cause trouble between us because I refused her and she hoped to raise enough doubts for you to force me to give it to her. There isn't more to it." She turned to look out of the window again, for she could not blatantly lie while facing him.

But he knew. He was not angry that she kept her secret at all costs, for whatever she held from him no longer mattered. What tortured him was bitter disappointment that she trusted him so little. He said no more, deciding instead to work at winning her confidence, never questioning why gaining Alisa's trust was of paramount importance to him.

Chapter Forty-five

Autumn was Alisa's favorite season in Connecticut. Temperatures were mild as the sun shone brightly each day. The countryside sparkled with nature's last burst of color, all warm, golden hues, russet elm leaves, red maples, gilded wheat spears, and dark green vines that sprouted plump orange pumpkins. The sky was a clear, pale, perfect blue. It was a dynamically beautiful conclusion to the scorching summer's heat, a final explosion of umber and ocher and rust.

Alisa was uncertain if the weather had eased her thoughts and fears or if the two-week respite in the country was the cause.

Her color returned to its normal, healthy radiance as she relaxed. The change was so drastic, Christian was convinced that Ivy should be evicted immediately on their return to New Haven.

Alisa sat beneath one of the brick arches that covered the lower gallery, sketching the elongated man-made tunnel they formed.

Christian's approaching footsteps gave her a warm feeling. She liked him best as he had been these past weeks, calm and affectionate.

He paused beside her, wrapping her largest and

warmest woolen shawl around her, his massive hands remaining at her shoulders.

"Will you come away with me?" he said in a deep voice.

"I thought I already had." Alisa laughed.

"I mean right now. Will you put this away and come with me without question?" His smile was beguiling.

Alisa laughed lightly. "Are your intentions honorable, sir?"

"Absolutely not."

"Then of course I will."

Christian placed her art materials in the hinged seat of a deacon's bench nearby. Then he took her hand and led her to the stable where his horse awaited them; a large rolled bundle was tied across the stallion's back with a huge picnic basket hanging from the side. Christian took the reins in his free hand, and they set out on foot, frightening a wild deer eating the last apples that had fallen to the ground in the garden.

"What have you planned?" Alisa's curiosity was piqued.

"No questions!"

They walked, hand in hand, along countryside still alive with the colors of fall. Just beyond the house, they passed huge, vine-covered elms whose perfectly symmetrical branches were all but bare. The leaves on the ground were so deep that Alisa and Christian's feet were buried; they kicked up rustling bursts of gold and rust with each step. They came to a stream where still more leaves floated along the slowly flowing, clear water. They crossed a bridge of reddish-brown sandstone and then followed the river upstream beneath huge sycamore trees that leaned over the water, the gnarled branches like old, protective hands.

They rambled in companionable silence, enjoying the peaceful splendor around them. Christian's long fingers rubbed Alisa's hand unconsciously. He paused once to shake leaves from the fringe of her long shawl.

Dusk was falling quickly now; the air grew cold and moist. Alisa was grateful to reach a small stone house standing alone on the edge of a forest that rose up the side of a small mountain behind.

"Spooner's Cottage," Christian announced.

"What is this place?" Alisa asked as they entered a door barely higher than her head; Christian was forced to duck low to pass through it.

"I told you. It's Spooner's Cottage."

The place smelled of lye, beeswax and lemon. Christian lit a fire that had already been laid, and bright flames quickly illuminated the small space. He sat on the hearth, one long arm stretching wide as if displaying what was nothing more than stone walls, a fireplace and a lone, narrow bed.

"This, my sweet, was formerly used by our overseer, when we grazed cattle on the fields near here. But that was before I was born, when this was the farthest reach of the Reed holdings. Since that time, it has been used by many an ardent couple in need of a bit of privacy."

Christian stood, stalking her slowly.

"Have you been planning all of this?"

"Only since this morning when Scott sent a message that he and Nicholas would arrive tonight. I sent the servants to clean the place. I simply could not share you yet, so you will have to forgive me. I never before felt my life and my homes so crowded as I find them now."

Alisa circled the small room, as if inspecting it, trying to gauge his mood. Then she sighed deeply, her breasts heaving against the linen and lace of her blouse. "It seems I have no choice in the matter." She unfastened the buttons of her high collar with deliberate slowness. She wanted him, and the change of scene excited her.

But no more than it did him.

His clothes were off within seconds, and he lay flat on the narrow cot, watching her shed layer after layer. When she wore only one petticoat and the thin veil of a chemise, she crossed to his side.

She smiled seductively at him, pulling the ribbon from her burnished copper hair and shaking it to fall freely down her back and shoulders. She loosened her chemise, leaving it open between breasts that pushed against the thin fabric, but before she shed it, she cupped her hands around her neck and swept the thick mass of curls forward to cover the firm globes. Only then did she drop the chemise. She pushed the last petticoat past her hips but sat beside Christian at the same moment, refusing him the sight of her completely bare.

He groaned in impatience, pulling her to rest across his broad, hairy chest. "If you don't quit stalling, I'm going to proceed without you."

"If I'm not needed, then . . ." She pushed herself away from him, only to find powerful hands keeping her captive.

"And I thought you would be kind instead of cruel."

He pulled her down to him, his mouth reaching up to hers in a kiss already urgent, his tongue invading the recesses of her mouth in a delicious assault she was only too willing to return. The taut, sensitive crests of her breasts rubbed lightly against the coarse mat of hair at his chest, tormenting them both with their need to feel bare flesh pressed closely together.

She lay beside him, the narrow width of the cot making it necessary to place half of her body atop his, one small thigh riding over one bulging, muscular leg, the warmth between her own thighs pressed to him to the delight of both.

His hand slid from her shoulder, brushing away her heavy hair to grasp her full breast, first gently, then more firmly, his thumb teasing her nipple lightly, then squeezing it between two fingers, pulling it slightly and then releasing it. One powerful arm pulled Alisa's body farther up his long length until he could take her breast in his mouth, sucking, drawing, taunting with the hot lick of his tongue.

Her hands ran through the soft waves of his hair, holding him more closely to her breast; the movement of his mouth sent shivers of delightful sensations along her spine and through her middle to that spot where his hand now played, parting, entering, drawing forward. She moved to lie completely on top of him.

He grasped the backs of her thighs, pulled them open to straddle him, pressed his hips upward so she could feel his long, hard shaft. His hands cupped her small buttocks, holding her still as his manhood probed, teased, sought entry and then pressed deeply into her. A low moan rolled from his throat as her warm, moist sheath surrounded him.

He guided her hips, matching each thrust perfectly as she rode him; she was filled to the very limit by the exquisite union of her small body with his massive one.

She peaked first, an explosion that seemed to go on and on and on, as her body rubbed perfectly against him.

She opened her eyes, drinking deeply of the sight of him beneath her. His handsome face was taut, a muscle pulsating in his temple; the creases of each cheek deepened as his jaw hardened in response, his head slightly back, his neck a thick cord of tense muscles, his shoulders and biceps bulging to their limits, glistening with the light sheen of sweat. She felt him pull her hips closer to him, embedding himself deep within her with a low, rhythmic groan. His body began to relax a moment later, and his breathing slowed to a normal pace as he fell deeply asleep.

Alisa lay curled comfortably into Christian's naked body, staring at the dying fire. Sometime during three lovely romps of lovemaking, he had managed to bring in a basket of food and blankets. The food still sat untouched.

She thought he was asleep again, so his deep voice in the stillness startled her. "After hours of the purest joy, how can I find such a scowl on that beautiful face?" he said softly.

"I have never been beautiful," she answered a bit peevishly.

"I know you aren't blind, so that must be Ivy speaking. You are beautiful, Alisa. I find I can never quite get my fill of looking at you." He paused, pushing her hair from her cheek tenderly. "What plagues you?" he whispered, kissing her head and leaving his lips resting there.

"Did you bring Ellen here?"

"No. Never. She hated the country and thought the country house a medieval hovel. She would not have stayed in this place for a second. I never wanted her here. I know how you feel about sleeping anywhere Ellen did. I would never have brought you if she had been here."

Still she did not soften.

"What is it?" he repeated.

Alisa sighed and shrugged. "Jealousy, I suppose. I've never felt it before." She paused, uncertain if she should admit her thoughts to him. She decided it could do no more harm than it was, festering silently within her.

"Until I met Ellen, I rarely thought of her. She wasn't real to me. I saw too clearly her beauty, the way she looks at you and smiles at you. Now I can't seem to chase away the picture in my mind of you holding her like this, kissing her, whispering to her, sharing everything just the same." She breathed deeply. "It hurts. And it somehow cheapens it," she whispered.

Christian sighed raggedly. "Oh, God, Alisa. I'm so sorry," he breathed. "I've had a lot of women. I can't lie and pretend I haven't. But I have never known a woman like you, in bed or out. I never realized making love could be such a sharing of pleasure. Before you, I had never been made love to, and certainly I had never had an equal partner in it. It was never this way with Ellen, or with anybody else, either. The motions were the same, I wish I could tell you they weren't, but what we share is new to me, special to me in a way nothing before ever was. Believe me, Alisa, I could never accept less now, and no one else could give me what you do."

Alisa was eased by his tender words. He was awed by the depth of feeling that impelled him to reassure her with passionate words while he was still blinded to the truth.

Chapter Forty-six

The morning was nearly gone by the time Alisa and Christian left the cottage. He was in no hurry now as he paused several times to pull Alisa into his arms for long, passionate kisses beneath the golden autumn sun. He dropped the reins, smacking his stallion's hindquarter with a resounding slap that sent him galloping home ahead of his master.

"Why did you do that?" Alisa said unhappily.

"What difference does it make?"

"I was going to feed the birds and squirrels from the picnic basket."

"There was plenty there to feed them," he concurred.

"I know. I was going to do it so the kitchen staff wouldn't find it all left and know what we did."

Christian laughed heartily, a pleasing sound to Alisa. "It's too late now. But I doubt if it will shock them."

He stopped in the midst of a small clearing in the forest. She looked around them curiously. "Why did you stop?"

"I was giving serious thought to tumbling you here."

"Oh, no!" she said, backing away from him. "I can't!" she said firmly.

His bushy eyebrows both arched in acceptance of what he saw as a challenge. He pursued her stealthily.

"Of course you can. I've already kept Scott waiting; he can bide his time a bit longer."

Alisa's back came up against the huge trunk of a maple tree, but Christian was too near for her to escape it. He leaned toward her with a hand at each side of her head, his lips lowered to hers in a low, sensual kiss Alisa responded to unwillingly. Then small hands pushed at his chest, and she moaned in disappointment.

"Truly, Christian. I cannot. This is not a jest."

"Will you lie and say you don't want me?" he taunted, his lips taking hers again and again, short, teasing kisses that drove her mad.

"Christian," she said fiercely, "please!"

"Give me one good reason not to, Alisa."

"Because," she said, coloring becomingly, "I can barely walk as it is," she finally blurted out. "Once more and I won't make it to the house."

Christian laughed boisterously. "I'm sorry, sweet. I didn't think about that. You have been sorely abused. If you had only spoken sooner, you could have ridden the horse." He laughed again at the deepening crimson of her cheeks. "No, I don't suppose that would have helped, would it? Well, then, I did the damage, I should bear the burden." He scooped her up into his arms as though she weighed nothing.

No amount of pleading, cajoling or nagging could prevail upon him to set her back on her own feet; he seemed to enjoy her futile attempts to wiggle free, laughing at each new tactic she used to persuade him. To further her mortification, Scott stood in the entrance hall as Christian bounded from the kitchen with Alisa still firmly in his embrace.

"What happened? Are you all right, Alisa? Where the hell have you been all night?" Scott asked, his concern amusing Christian.

Alisa closed her eyes in humiliation.

Christian answered before she could find her voice. "It seems we were waylaid in Spooner's Cottage, Scott," he answered jovially. Passing his brother to climb the grand staircase, he added over his shoulder, "Alisa assures me she will be fine after a soak in a hot tub and in this I must trust her judgment."

Scott laughed, his worry appeased. "Abusing your wife again, are you, Christian?"

"Up until half an hour ago I wasn't getting any complaints," he called back. Both deep male voices joined in laughter to Alisa's complete embarrassment.

It was late before Christian came to bed that night. He and Scott had cloistered themselves in the den for the entire evening, leaving Alisa and Nicholas in companionable conversation and a game of chess. Alisa had seen just a glimmer of resentment in Nicholas's eyes as the two Reed men excused themselves, and it had left her unaccountably angry with her husband.

"Was your business so important?" she accused from their bed as Christian undressed.

"Yes, it was," he answered with a quizzical note.

"Was it some secret council?"

"No." His bushy brows drew together as he raised

his glance to her. "But you would have found it tedious and dull, so I thought you'd be better entertained by Nicholas," he said, misinterpreting her anger.

"I didn't want to hear any of it, but you might have had the courtesy to include Nicholas."

"For your information, Alisa, had we been discussing anything that concerned Nicholas, he would have been included, but seeing as how it was a subject he has no knowledge of, it would have bored him as much as you."

"You said it was business!"

He breathed deeply to curb his rising temper. "In January of 1849, Scott and I joined a group of other men to form the New Haven and California Joint-Stock Company. We recruited a party of fifty-four men in various occupations and sent them to the Sutter's Mill gold fields to practice their trades. Scott and I were discussing the report that just came from those men. It is a dealing that Nicholas had absolutely no part in. Does that satisfy you?"

Alisa was duly chastised. "Still, you might have at least invited him."

"What the hell is going on? For a good number of years we three have been doing very well with both our business and personal relationship without your intervention. So what is your complaint?"

"Did it ever occur to you that you and Scott exclude Nicholas?"

"This is absurd, Alisa. Has Nicholas complained to you?"

"No." She lied to protect him, for he had spoken to her in confidence, telling her of his resentment at being treated like an employee and his dream that it might be proven that he was really Christian and Scott's brother. His denigration of himself as the

Reed's "house pet" showed a side of him that Alisa doubted anyone had seen before. His proposal that she should be the one to ease his torment frightened her just a little. He could not be serious, yet there was a note in his voice that quickly changed at her disbelieving reception of his words.

She had determined to find a way to apprise Christian of Nicholas's feelings without betraying his secrets and had broached the subject with a great deal of trepidation. Christian's impatience justified her feelings.

"Then what the hell is the problem?"

"I think you're being unfair to him."

"Do you?" Christian's temper was hot. "And what makes it any of your damn business?"

"I care for him."

"Are you having an affair with Nicholas?"

"Of course not. That is pure foolishness. Why would I want him included in your private business tête-à-têtes if that were the case? I'd be thrilled with your absence and his presence, then, wouldn't I?"

Christian pushed himself away from her and circled the bed to his own side. "Then why the hell are you concerned with Nicholas all of a sudden?"

"I think there's more to him than you give him credit for."

"You're imagining things, Alisa. We were all raised to know what our futures held, and it has suited each of us just fine. Nothing holds Nicholas here. If he were unhappy, he could change things, but as far as I know, he is perfectly content."

Alisa lay flat in bed, turning to her side away from Christian. His suspicions eased, and his temper cooled. "I prefer your feelings for Scott and Nicholas to Ellen's hatred of them. But there is no cause for concern, Alisa. Nicholas is hardly treated like a servant, for God's sake."

"Nor like an equal partner," she pointed out.

"He is not an equal partner." Christian's patience was forced. "My father left Nicholas a large sum of money to do with as he pleased, but all of the Reed holdings belong to Scott and me. As far as I know, Nicholas has never had the need to touch his inheritance."

"Money is not always the most important thing, Christian."

"What is it you think Nicholas wants?"

"I don't know," she said finally. "But I think you should be more conscious of your treatment of him. It's possible that you have come to take him for granted, isn't it?"

Christian laughed. "I suppose it's possible. If it eases your mind I will watch myself," he promised. "Are you happier now?"

"Yes," she conceded, though doubts about Nicholas's true feelings still concerned her.

"Then get the hell over here and prove there's no cause for me to suspect all those hours you spent together painting!"

Chapter Forty-seven

Alisa sat close beside Christian in the carriage, watching the light November snow fall beyond. She was as quiet on this return trip to the city as she had been leaving it.

Christian's strong arm rested across the back of her shoulders. "Why so thoughtful, Alisa?" he asked quietly.

She sighed. "I'm sorry we're going back."

"It was your decision to be in New Haven for Thanksgiving," he reminded her.

"I know. It's just that things between us are nicer in the country."

"That doesn't have to be true."

"It isn't a choice. It simply happens and you know it."

"I don't think it would if Ivy wasn't in our home."

"You see. It's already starting."

"Why don't you let me handle Ivy?" he offered, watching her closely.

Alisa's expression tensed instantly. "No, I will deal with her."

Christian paused, studying his wife and again feeling intensely protective of her. "What if I buy her a house and pay for a staff? Would she move out then?"

Alisa brightened slightly. "She might. But that is a great expense."

He pulled her closer to him, squeezing her tightly. "It's worth it to me."

"I'm sorry, Christian. I never meant to cost you so much."

He laughed. "You cost very little, Alisa. My money is yours as well."

"No, it's your money. It would be different if you had married me because you wanted me . . . loved me. Then you would have chosen to share your life and everything else with me. I took enough from you when I tricked you out of your freedom. If Ivy weren't being so difficult, I would refuse this offer, too."

"You aren't taking anything, Alisa," he said quietly but with a cooler edge, resenting that she would not share this burden, at least. "I offer it freely. And believe me, I consider any expense incurred to remove Ivy to be money well spent."

Alisa sat in silence. She felt Christian's slight withdrawal and heard a faint aloofness in his words. Her spirits plummeted.

Christian saw her dejection. "You're determined to be unhappy today, aren't you?"

Alisa mentally shook herself, seeing he had intended to please her. "I'm sorry." She smiled up at him more warmly. "Tell me about Nicholas's childhood. He told me that he fought a great deal with you and Scott as boys."

"That's an understatement. He was the meanest little monster I've ever known."

"He said he had to prove his strength and manhood because he was so short."

"It was more than that. He had to prove he didn't need us or want anything we had. But he always had everything Scott and I did. It was as if he was determined to show us he didn't care about anything at all. My father said he thought it was just the opposite, that Nicholas wanted what we had so badly that no matter what he was given, it always seemed to him that his portion was less. Sometimes Scott and I felt Nicholas was favored in order to prove to him that he wasn't being cheated or overlooked." Christian shook his head at the pictures in his mind. "As we grew up, he turned from his wanting my toys to his wanting the same girls."

"Did he plague Scott, too?"

"Not as badly. I don't think Scott's temper was riled as easily as mine, so he wasn't as entertaining a target."

"Was Nicholas ever excluded from your family?" Alisa was thinking of how Nicholas had made his feelings of ostracism very clear to her.

"No. What an odd question, Alisa. I told you we have always considered him our youngest brother. My mother doted on Nicholas more than either of us. She said Nicholas needed more than we did, whatever the hell that means."

Alisa said no more. She thought that Christian's mother had been a very perceptive person, and Alisa understood the woman's words well.

Chapter Forty-eight

Alisa jolted awake when her head slipped from the high back of the rocking chair as she dozed in the nursery.

"Go on to bed, Alisa," Owen Tanor's voice whispered to her from his seat near his son's cradle.

Alisa smiled, embarrassed to have fallen asleep. "What time is it?"

"Past midnight. I'll sit up with him tonight; you've been in here every night since you got back from the country. Jonah's asleep, and his breathing is much better. I can tend him alone. I'll call you if he worsens."

Alisa stood, pressing a cramp from her lower back. "Are you certain you want to go to Hartford tomorrow, Owen? Christian will send Nicholas if you'd rather stay with the baby."

His head shook. His face was etched with lines from the past ten days of worry and fatigue they had spent sharing the care of the desperately ill child. "It's really something I must take care of. Christian has already allotted too much of my work to others. The doctor said Jonah is better." Owen's hands clasped her shoulders. "I couldn't have managed without you, Alisa. Thank you." He bent slightly to kiss her forehead, wishing he could do more, aching to do more.

"Do you intend to spend the entire night in here again?" Christian's deep, angry voice interrupted the caress as he stood in the doorway, his scowl dark and ominous.

Alisa drew away from Owen guiltily. "I'm coming right now," she said.

Alisa could feel Christian's heated stare as she preceded him to their room; every muscle in her body ached with weariness. She knew Christian's patience had been stretched thin as night after night she stayed with Owen in the baby's room, offering her former suitor as much comfort as she could while Ivy acted as though nothing were amiss.

"That was a touching little scene." Christian's tone was barely controlled as he stood with his arms crossed over his chest. "I think this little escapade has gone far enough."

Alisa shed her clothing and donned a soft nightdress. "I don't know what 'escapade' you're talking about, Christian, and I'm too tired to argue with you."

"You weren't too tired to accept your lover's kiss and bid him a fond farewell."

"What you saw was hardly a lover's kiss!"

"Just what the hell is going on, Alisa?"

She climbed into bed, sinking into the downy mattress and pulling a heavy quilt to her shoulders. "You know Jonah is very ill, Christian. The only thing going on is his care. How can you be suspicious of that?"

"Easily, under the circumstances. I haven't seen you for two straight hours since we left the country. You've been closeted away in that room day and night with a man any idiot can see feels more for you than he does for his wife. Now I find you in the bastard's arms. I think you have pushed this situation too far." His bluish-green eyes blazed with rage as he stood beside the bed glaring at her.

"Please don't do this," she pleaded weakly, feeling a desperation foreign to her. "I am needed there, Christian. Owen doesn't have the knowledge to care for the baby alone. He's prostrate with worry over Jonah. He is a very sick child!"

"It's Ivy's place to be with them, not yours," he shouted. "If the situation is so damn bad, then your sister should curtail her socializing and stay with her family. But then this is such a perfect excuse for you to be alone with Owen, isn't it?" His tone was vicious.

Alisa saw a hatred in his eyes that frightened her. His own ugly memories were clouding his vision of innocent circumstances. When she spoke, her voice was quiet but genuinely sincere.

"Open your eyes, Christian, and see me, Alisa. Not Ellen. Your former wife and I are not the same person. You give me all that I could ever want, more than I hoped for. I have never given you reason to suspect me, for I have not even thought of another man since our marriage. Please . . . please don't do this to either of us when there is no cause. You make me suffer for something I haven't done, but you punish yourself at the same time. Let go of your damned past! I don't know what was wrong with Ellen that left her blind to what she had in you. You insult us both with these unbased suspicions. It's you I want, Christian, no other," she ended almost inaudibly, for it was a difficult disclosure to make to a man she feared might never feel the same.

Still Christian stared at her, wanting to believe all she said but worried that this could merely be a well-played ruse.

"This is difficult to believe when you spend so little time with me," he said more calmly.

"If you will recall, we had this argument before, only it was I complaining about being ignored. What I am doing is necessary."

"The child isn't yours, Alisa." Christian's anger was somewhat soothed, even through his doubts.

"He's my nephew, and his mother doesn't care about him. Did you not do the same thing for Ellen's son?"

Christian admitted defeat. "All right, dammit. You have me there. But remember that Nát was all alone; Jonah has Owen. I begrudge your attention to the father, not the child."

He reached for her, pulling Alisa into his arms where she curled willingly into the contours of his body.

"It seems the worst is past. Owen is leaving for Hartford in the morning, if you recall."

"It's hardly appeasing to be told you won't be spending so much time with the man only because he won't be available."

Alisa laughed slightly at that, grateful to have bridged a gap she feared she didn't understand. "What will appease you?"

"I expect your company tomorrow night in this room, from the moment I arrive here until I leave again in the morning. And I had damned well better have your exclusive, undivided attention to convince me."

Alisa closed her eyes as sleep stole over her, too tired to feel anything. "I think that can be arranged."

She fell asleep without hearing Christian's sigh, never knowing that he realized how torn she actually was.

Chapter Forty-nine

Alisa lay awake in Christian's arms, hearing the tower clock strike two. Sleep eluded her as she failed to chase the thoughts from her mind that had risen with the climactic end to their lovemaking. She eased slightly away, not wanting to disturb Christian's peaceful slumber, but his arms tightened about her, intent even in sleep to keep her close to him.

She settled her head back to his chest, hearing his slow, even breathing and the rhythmic beats of his heart, comfortable in his embrace. Her smooth brow was furrowed as she pondered feelings within her that were new and strange.

She felt vulnerable to Christian, and for the first time in her life she felt emotionally fragile. It required very little from Christian to crush her like some soft petal beneath his fist. Never had it occurred to her that any person could hurt her as deeply as she now knew Christian could.

This was not how she envisioned love, for that seemed to render its victim giddy and senseless, and she did not feel that. Instead she found herself on some erratic pendulum, always swinging precariously from joy, elation and contentment to deep fear, pain and worry, all of which were so unlike her.

If this was love, she decided disdainfully, it was worse than she had ever imagined, for it held such a powerful force over her, something she could not control with logic or reason. She felt defenseless against this man who had sworn to her that he was incapable of love.

Surely this could only be bearable if he felt the same worry, the same fear, the same vulnerabilities. But if she alone felt this, Alisa fretted, then she would be forever at his mercy and she knew it would be unendurable.

"Miss Alisa! Please wake up, Miss Alisa!"

Alisa's thoughts were interrupted by a soft knock at the bedroom door and the voice of the young maid who acted as Jonah's nurse.

"What the hell?" Christian grumbled, angry at the disturbance.

Alisa pushed herself from his arms, almost grateful to be diverted from her troubled musings. "I'm awake, Christian. I'll see what it is. Go back to sleep."

One hand followed the line of her back as she moved from him. "Don't be long," he said thickly, never opening his eyes.

Alisa drew her heavy velvet robe over her bare skin and eased the door open to slip into the hall. The young maid waited there with wide, fearful eyes.

"I'm sorry, Miss Alisa, but I didn't know what to do. That baby is so sick. He's just awful! He's wheezin' so bad I didn't know what to do!"

"Did you send for the doctor this afternoon as I told you?"

"Miss Ivy wouldn't let me. She said he wasn't that sick."

"Where is his mother?" Alisa asked disgustedly.

"I heard her come in a little while ago, but she said I better never disturb her for nothin'. She said tendin' that baby was my job, and if I bothered her with it, she'd get rid of me." The girl's fear of Ivy was plain. "But I'm scared for him now."

"I'll go to see him, Missy, and you send my sister to his room." She patted the maid's arm reassuringly. "Don't worry. My husband employs you, not Ivy. Your job is safe."

Alisa left the dubious girl then, to hurry to her nephew's bedside.

The room was hot and steamy as Alisa had instructed. She saw the large kettle of water boiling over a well-stoked fire. Even before Alisa moved to the small cradle, she heard Jonah's raspy breathing. He was so small for his seven months; his lips were blue, as were the creases around his nose and eyes. Genuine alarm ran through her.

She lifted the limp infant, feeling the burning heat of his skin, and she fought a wave of panic. She sat in the rocking chair near the hearth and held his shoulders elevated slightly, discovering that his breathing came a bit easier.

The young maid returned minutes later, her distress an indication of Ivy's irritation at being disturbed. Alisa's voice, raised slightly in fear, instructed her, "Go downstairs and send someone to fetch the doctor immediately. It's an emergency!"

Missy did not hesitate, fleeing just as Ivy appeared in the doorway, her elaborate evening gown still in place. Her face contorted with distaste. "Why is this

room so stuffy? I told that moronic maid to stop boiling water in here!"

"The baby needs this steam to breathe, Ivy!" Alisa
spoke angrily. "Did you make her stop it?" she accused.

"Of course I did. I can't see how boiling the brat in
this room could help."

"But you thought refusing him a doctor would?"

"The twit told me you wanted a doctor, but neither
of us knew who was to pay for his services. It seems
you overlooked that."

"You refused your own sick baby a doctor because
of money?"

Ivy's expression turned victorious. "If you weren't
so selfish, I wouldn't have. But you've kept Papa's
money all to yourself, along with all of Christian's. I
decided if you wanted a doctor to see the brat badly
enough, you could pay for it."

"I can't believe what you're saying, Ivy. Don't you
care anything at all for your own child?"

Ivy wrinkled her nose. "I can't bear illness. You
know that, Alisa. What exactly do you want from
me?"

"Nothing," Alisa spat in disgust. "Get out of here.
You nauseate me."

Ivy shrugged and left, perfectly happy to escape
the sickroom.

By the time the doctor arrived, Jonah was strug-
gling weakly for each rattling breath. Jonah's illness had developed into pneumonia in both tiny
lungs. The old doctor prepared Alisa for the worst, as
the two alone kept vigil in the steamy bedroom, the
wheezing sound a horrible, repetitive chant all
around them.

The tower clock struck six, and then silence fell.

The doctor checked Jonah one final time before covering him with his blanket. He took Alisa's hand and pressed it gently.

"I'm sorry, Mrs. Reed." He led Alisa with him through the silent house, sitting with her in the drawing room. "Would you like me to stay and tell the parents?" he offered.

"No." She laughed a bit hysterically. "His father is away on business and I will tell the mother later."

"Let me wake your husband, then. I don't want to leave you alone."

"It's all right. I really need a moment to myself, and then I'll go up to him."

"Are you certain you don't want me to stay?"

Alisa shook her head. "Thank you for coming, for everything. Please go on home."

The old man hesitated a moment and then left wearily.

Alisa sat in a wing chair, hearing the sounds of the servants beginning their day. There were no tears, for within her was such an ugly hatred of her sister at that moment, nothing else permeated her senses.

Alisa stood, her spine straight, her face composed. She climbed the stairs slowly and walked down the long hallway to Ivy's room. She did not pause to knock but opened the door and crossed to the foot of her sister's bed, staring down at her silently.

Ivy woke slowly at first and then with a start. Alisa seemed a wraith looming before her. She spoke coldly, quietly. "You son is dead."

Ivy pushed herself up against the headboard to gather her wits. "It's over then, is it?" she said derisively.

"Aren't you even going to pretend grief?"

"No. I never wanted him, Alisa. He was a nuisance, as all babies are."

Hard midnight-blue eyes bore into Ivy. "I wonder if you realize how contemptible you are."

"What I realize, Alisa," she spat venomously, "is that you can't judge me. You have everything I want, you always did, and until you know what it is to be refused what you most desire, don't sit in judgment of me."

"How could we both have been raised the same yet be such different people? I wonder if you are even human."

"That's laughable. A murderess telling me I'm inhuman."

Alisa watched her, hated her. "Christian has bought a house for you. I was going to wait until he had hired the staff before I told you, but I can't wait another hour. You have to move your belongings out of here today. I can't bear the sight of you."

"Grief makes you brave, does it? Or perhaps just imbecilic. Shall I inform Christian of your past?"

"It won't work this time, Ivy. Either you get out or I will have you thrown out."

Ivy laughed, a high, vicious sound. "Do you know what this means, Alisa? This is where I want to live and *how* I want to live! If I can't stay here with you, I will stay without you."

"This is Christian's home," Alisa answered calmly, her contempt strengthening her to withstand Ivy's threats. "You can tell my secret, and that may end my marriage and my stay here. But not only will you be left evicted along with me, you will also lose the house he's purchased for you and the staff of servants he is willing to pay to appease you.

What will it be, Ivy? Will you leave, or will we both lose?"

Ivy watched Alisa, seeing the strength, the determination in her. She knew that in this instant Alisa would risk all rather than concede again. She recognized that she was defeated. She reassured herself that it was temporary, for she still retained some power by knowing Alisa's secret.

"I'll leave," Ivy said, her tone spiteful, "but I will give you fair warning, dear sister. I want it all, including Christian, and I will do anything to get it. Your days here are numbered, so enjoy them while they last, because soon I will be mistress of everything, and you will discover what it is to want what I possess."

Chapter Fifty

Thanksgiving was only two days after the small funeral for Jonah. Ivy had retreated to the house Christian had purchased for her, and Alisa made it clear that her sister was not welcome in her home again.

Ivy had not bothered to move Owen's belongings when she ordered the servants to transport her things, and this, coupled with the baby's death, brought an end to Owen's tolerance. By December first Owen had packed all he owned and bought a horse to leave New Haven and a wife who wanted no more of him than he wanted of her.

He completed his last day of work, dined with Christian and Alisa and then adjourned to the library with Christian.

Christian poured two snifters of brandy and then sat behind his desk, watching Owen intently as he paced the room.

"You know Jonah was not my son," Owen said without pausing to glance at Christian.

"No. I didn't know that."

"I believed he was mine when I married Ivy. I never really wanted her; in fact, I only turned to her when you married Alisa." He laughed mirthlessly.

"Jonah was born only six months after the wedding, so of course I realized he wasn't mine."

"Why did you stay with Ivy if you didn't care for her and he wasn't your child?" Christian asked, a wave of compassion washing over him for the man.

Owen shrugged. "By then I had lost everything, and being married to her was a way to get to America, to use you to get a start here," he said bluntly. "It was also a way to see Alisa again."

Christian remained silent.

Owen continued, unaware of the dangerous topic he broached. "I was just about to ask Alisa to be my wife when I heard she had married you and left England. God, what a disappointment. I didn't even know who you were, and you had stolen her out from under me."

Christian's voice was deep. "You wouldn't have gotten her at any rate. Her father had plans of marrying her off to one of his old cronies." He cleared his throat, searching for an adept lie and settled on a version of the truth. "We forced her father to agree to the marriage, but it was against his will."

Owen stopped his pacing and turned to Christian with a scowl.

"He had betrothed her to Philip Mathews," Christian went on as suspicion raised its nasty head.

"Philip Mathews died two years earlier," Owen exclaimed. "Aldis Todd berated me often about my tardiness in becoming his son-in-law. He encouraged me when I lamented over Alisa's disregard of my attentions, telling me to press my suit. If he considered Alisa betrothed to anyone, it was to me. He used to introduce me as his future son-in-law."

Christian stared at him, his expression studiedly blank as his thoughts raced.

Owen spared him the need to speak. "She must have wanted you badly to have played on your sympathies with that story. What did she do, beg you to rescue her from becoming an old man's bride?"

"Something like that," Christian mumbled.

"Well, it was a wise move on your part. You have something very special in Alisa. It's my greatest sorrow that I didn't push her when I had the chance. I kept biding my time, hoping she would come to care for me. Instead I ended up with Ivy. What a rude awakening after Alisa!"

Christian was impatient to end this conversation. "Are you certain you don't want more of the money you've earned?"

It took Owen a second to understand the abrupt change of subject. "No. I have enough to get away from here. Use the rest for Ivy. I'm sorry to be dropping her on you like this, but if I stay I may kill her! I'll be in touch when I get settled." Owen emptied his glass and set it on the sideboard. "Actually, I asked to see you now to warn you about Ivy."

"Is there a need for that?"

"I don't know. Maybe it's just my imagination and disgust with Ivy, but I get the feeling she means Alisa harm. I really think she hates Alisa. I know she is bitterly jealous of what Alisa found with you, of all the money, especially. Ivy has fostered her own private war against Alisa for as long as I've known her. Her selfishness can be quite dangerous. She's ruthless in pursuing what she wants, and she wants whatever Alisa has. It's almost a sickness with her." His face sobered as he stared at some invisible spot again. "Ivy was so determined to get here, to get a part of what Alisa has with you that she risked Jonah's life. He was not healthy even at birth; he was small and couldn't hold down his food. The doctors warned us not to travel with him until he was stronger, but Ivy disregarded it. I didn't think he would live through the voyage. Ivy didn't care; nothing could sway her."

Owen sighed after a time, lifting his eyes again to Christian. "Well, that's all past now, isn't it? I don't think Alisa realizes how vicious Ivy is, how selfish and vindictive. She is not above anything, and I don't think Alisa sees that. I doubted that Alisa would believe me if I told her, so I thought it best to warn you. You will watch out for her, won't you?"

"It isn't something I need to be asked," Christian said pointedly.

Owen held out his hand to Christian. "I appreciate all you've done for me. I'll send you what money I can, because Ivy would throw it away on gewgaws."

Owen moved to the door. He laughed wryly before he left. "If you can accomplish it you should send Ivy back to England. I don't think you'll have any peace from her if she is even in the same country."

Christian paid little attention to Owen's last words, his thoughts mulling over all that had been disclosed of Alisa's past. Now, more than ever, he wondered just why Alisa had needed to marry him.

By mid-December, word reached New Haven that Owen had been killed, robbed and shot on a road just out of Hartford.

Ivy's only reaction to his death was a contented smile as she embraced widowhood and its attendant freedom with relish. She turned her sights full swing to Christian Reed.

Chapter Fifty-one

They spent Christmas in the country, which was a welcome respite for Alisa, though it was a sad holiday this year, coming so near to two deaths. Alisa tried to hide her depressed feelings, not wanting to dampen the spirits of the three men who strove to cheer her up.

Nicholas and Scott thought their efforts were successful, but Christian knew better and offered his wife silent understanding and support she drew on often in these difficult weeks.

As the new year approached, Alisa agreed to attend a large party at the home of one of the few families that had stood behind Christian through the scandal of his divorce. Alisa's mood lightened just a bit in preparation, and Christian encouraged it with a gift of a new gown for the occasion.

He awaited his wife in the drawing room with Scott and Nicholas. All three were formally attired, but Christian was the most devastatingly handsome of the group. He wore a black tail coat with a white silk lining that fit tightly across broad shoulders and bulging arms, narrowing at the waist. His vest was dove-gray satin over a white shirt of fine cambric with very small ruffles down the front. A wide neckcloth was wound around his muscular neck, and a black cravat topped that. He looked magnificently dashing, standing with one elbow resting on the mantel before Scott, who wore chocolate brown, and Nicholas, in green.

Alisa's entrance was later than she had anticipated as Ann struggled to contain the tangles of burnished copper hair. It was drawn to the back of her head to leave thick curls cascading from the crown to rest over one shoulder and down her back. She paused for a moment in the doorway, her eyes taking in only Christian, who smiled appreciatively.

The gown Christian had given her was lustrous silk, an iridescent pearl color that picked up highlights of the russet hues of her hair. The bodice cupped her narrow waist closely beneath a full ruffle that rested low on her breasts and off each creamy shoulder, leaving more exposed than anything she had ever worn.

The skirt was full, held wide with fifteen petticoats, decorated by two bands of shirring and a lacy flounce at the hem. She wore no jewelry.

Christian crossed the room slowly to stand before her, his smile intimate as his bluish-green eyes devoured her. He raised one large hand to her temple, teasing the stray curl there. "When I bought that dress, I wasn't aware so much of you would be displayed."

Alisa smiled warmly up at him, enjoying his lightheartedness. "I was curious about that when I put it on. But it's too late now," she responded in kind.

He kissed the bare spot where her neck and shoulder joined, breathing in the sweet scent of her. "You look divine, my love. Please keep in mind my jealous nature tonight."

Alisa laughed. "And you remember mine!"

Scott and Nicholas rode their horses alongside the heavy oak sled that was just large enough for Christian and Alisa amid many petticoats and fur robes. The night air was mild, crystal clear and invigoratingly chilly. Alisa's cheeks reddened, and for the first time in weeks, she grew excited and felt happy.

The ride was short to the neighboring estate of the Franktons' home, a two-story colonial mansion alight with lanterns outside and the warm, golden glow from dozens of windows brightening it from within. Lilting music could be heard as they left the horses to liveried servants. Alisa breathed a cleansing sigh as she anticipated a pleasurable evening. No sooner was her mink cloak removed by Christian's adept hands than any hopes for that were dashed.

Her attention was drawn to the narrow staircase to the right of the entrance by a high, melodic laugh, and then the sound of Ivy's voice.

"Happy New Year, dear sister."

Descending the stairs was not only Ivy, a victorious smirk on her lovely face, but also Ellen, ravishing in a scarlet gown that made Alisa's seem modest in comparison.

"Ivy!" Nicholas's voice rejoiced from behind Alisa as he held both hands out to the woman, complimenting her profusely.

Ellen stood before Christian, her holiday greeting a soft, intimate tone as she presented her lush bosom for his perusal.

Ivy left Nicholas abruptly to stand on Christian's other side, clasping his arm to her breasts and giddily sparring with Ellen over possession of Christian's first dance. To Alisa, they seemed like silly adolescent girls preening for the attentions of a singularly attractive rogue. Flaming jealousy coursed through her.

Scott saw her despair. He offered her his arm and led her away from the scene, which he judged to be as much for Alisa's benefit as for the entertainment of the other two women.

Scott's hand covered Alisa's in the crook of his arm, warm and comforting. He spoke close to her ear. "Breathe deeply, Alisa, or they will know they've won."

He took Alisa into the well-lit ballroom, turning her into his arms for a waltz with smooth grace. She smiled up at her brother-in-law gratefully.

"I thought I was free of Ivy and Ellen in the country. I certainly never expected to find them both here tonight."

Scott's smile was kind and sympathetic. "Ellen was also good friends with the Franktons, but she hated being out of the city so fiercely, she has never before attended one of their parties."

Her smile was pained. "Unfortunately that's little comfort now that I'm here."

When the dance ended, Scott escorted Alisa to where Christian stood, glaring at them from a stormy countenance. He spoke to Scott, "In the future either distract or spirit away those who are mauling me and leave my wife to me. I don't appreciate your taking Alisa and abandoning me to the wolves."

Scott laughed. "I'm sorry, Christian, but I have never enjoyed dancing with you; you always trod upon my feet."

Ivy's voice reached them before another word could be uttered, again entwining her arms with

Christian's. She was apparently adamant in her quest.

"You wouldn't mind if I share just this one dance with your husband, would you, Alisa?" she purred with syrupy sweetness.

"Yes, she would," Christian answered quickly, disengaging himself with firmness. "Alisa has already offended me by granting Scott a dance she had promised to me. If you'll excuse us, Ivy. Scott was just about to ask you for this dance himself."

Christian leered at his brother and whisked Alisa back to the dance floor before Ivy could speak again. He saw his wife's dejection and pressed a warm kiss into her hair. "Smile, my love. We are about to escape this bevy of questionable beauties. Do you think you could bear a much more private party?"

"It seems like an act of cowardice."

"No, merely a wise retreat."

Within moments they had fled the noisy house, and Alisa relaxed back into the seat of the sled, thankful for the hasty rescue as Christian slapped the reins against the horses' backs and headed, not down the road that connected the two estates but into the forest of barren elms and maples, their gnarled branches entwined overhead in a lacy canopy against the star-filled black sky.

Chapter Fifty-two

Spooner's Cottage stood like a dark shadow in the moonlight, barely discernible against the backdrop of massive tree trunks. Alisa smiled to herself when she finally realized their destination, preferring this by far to the company of her sister and Christian's former wife at the crowded party.

The small stone structure was a trifle dusty from disuse, but still it was a cozy respite Alisa welcomed. Christian built a roaring fire in the hearth before either of them had removed their cloaks, spreading the blankets from the narrow cot and the fur robes from the sled on the floor in front of it.

He left the cabin for only a moment, to return with a large bundle wrapped in a linen napkin, and a bottle of French champagne.

"What is that?" Alisa questioned as he set his treasures near the fireplace, ceremoniously untying the knot in the napkin.

"A purloined feast! I couldn't have you fainting from weakness just when I've stolen you away for the night, could I?"

He laid the napkin flat, disclosing its contents of ham, cheese and freshly baked bread. "The Franktons' butler and I are old acquaintances. He was most obliging in my request for a small repast for the journey home."

"Wonderful! I'm starved!"

Christian feigned injury. "To think of what it required to pry that admission from you before, when a mere ham can cause it so easily!"

He shed his jacket, vest, neckcloth and cravat, stretching his neck with relish. Then he kicked off his boots and unfastened his shirt nearly to the waist before he settled down onto the bed of blankets and fur to carve their feast with his pocketknife and open the champagne.

Alisa shrugged out of her mink cloak and peered down at her own very formal dress. It was impossible to sit on the floor with fifteen petticoats and not be drowned in fabric in the process. Besides, her gown was too exquisite to crumple. So, while Christian's back was to her, Alisa hastily removed the gown and then the petticoats. She finished the process by dropping her lacy pantaloons and silken chemise. A silent shiver shook her as she donned her mink cloak to conceal her nakedness, its satin lining an icy mantle around her bare flesh.

She sat beside Christian, feeling a rush of excitement run through her at the deliciously sensual act. Her face glowed with desire at the thought of Christian's surprise. The sensation of cold satin on high, taut nipples made her skin tingle.

Christian handed her a metal cup filled with bubbling champagne, his attention now drawn to his wife. His expression was initially quizzical until he took in the fur cloak hugged much too closely around her for there to be a gown and all of those petticoats beneath it, then one bushy brow quirked upward.

"Eat what you've stolen," Alisa commanded nervously. "I won't be accused of keeping you from a meal."

"Are you joining me?" he asked, his tongue jutting slowly from his mouth as two fingers placed a chunk of ham there.

"I'm not hungry."

Christian finished chewing, his eyes never leaving her. "A moment ago you were starving."

"It's passed." Her lips curled around the rim of the cup slowly, sipping the champagne as her eyes met his.

"I remember another time when you drank without eating. It has a strange effect on you, if memory serves."

Alisa's face colored slightly at that. "I have no intention of getting drunk."

"I wouldn't mind if that's what it takes to find out what's beneath that cloak." Again he took a bite of food, his angular jaw working with exaggerated slowness.

"Nothing," she said innocently.

"I suspected as much, but I will need proof."

"No."

"No?"

"I have no intentions of ravishing you," she said.

"Ah, but I have every intention of ravishing you."

Christian stood then, bluish-green eyes never wavering from midnight blue. He pulled his shirt from his breeches, unbuttoning it without preamble and tossing it on Alisa's petticoats. Next went the trousers, leaving him magnificently hard and naked as he knelt in front of her.

Alisa's breathing was constricted, her body already tight with arousal. Christian reached a hand to the ribbons holding her hair, freeing it to fall in a wild mass of curls. Then he cupped her shoulders, lifting her to her knees before him.

The first touch of his strong, powerful hands on her flesh sent a shiver through Alisa. She raised her palms to press against his chest, playing in the mat of hair, teasing his nipples to tautness.

Christian pulled her to him, his mouth falling to hers softly, a chaste kiss and then another and another, his lips drawing hers, leaving them with deliberate slowness so that they parted reluctantly. His hands moved from her shoulders down each arm, dropping the cloak to a furry heap behind her, leaving her body naked in the golden glow of firelight.

He kissed her neck, feeling the rapid beat of her pulse, the soft creaminess of her shoulder, breathing deeply of the sweet scent that clung there, then the spot where her breast just began its delicate rise from the hollow of her chest, and then the deep valley between her breasts, his tongue flicking lightly before his mouth again rose to hers in a warm kiss that spoke of his own raging passions. His massive arms engulfed her, holding her molded against his length, his hot, hard shaft pushing demandingly at the lowest part of her abdomen.

One of her hands played in the softness of his hair; the other pressed the corded muscles of his neck to deepen their kiss, her tongue meeting his, following it to search his mouth boldly as he did hers.

He cupped her buttocks, holding her hard against him as their mouths seared into each other. His hands traced a firm path along shoulders that stretched wide, and down biceps bulging with rigid muscles, and up again to the steely mounds of his chest. Then she slid silken fingers around his narrow waist to his back and then lower, her own small hands grasping his iron-hard buttocks to draw him even closer against her.

His head fell back in a groan of pleasure, only to come forward again to kiss her neck hungrily as he lowered her on her back onto the fur mattress, with himself half over her. His mouth worked a fiery, urgent path to her breast, one large hand filled with the soft mound, squeezing it to meet his burning lips as he took it fully into his mouth, sucking deeply, sending a straight shot of desire through her middle to that impatient spot between her thighs.

As if in answer, his other hand touched her there gently, but firmly teasing, separating, entering as his thumb flicked against that spot, sending spasms of delight and a more urgent desire racing through her.

She moaned softly, reaching her own soft hand to close about his steely-hard manhood, determined to bring him to as frenzied a need as he had her. His breath drew in harshly; his back arched and his body moved lower, out of her reach, leaving her confused and then shocked as she felt hot lips kissing her stomach, his tongue teasing her naval only to move lower still.

"Christian," she gasped in alarm, "is that . . . right?"

His deep chuckle was her only answer as she felt the warm smoothness of his mouth on her most private parts, his tongue tantalizing her, tormenting her until she cried out for him to fill the aching, pulsating need in her.

He raised above her, fitting himself easily between her open thighs, his long, engorged shaft probing for entry and slipping deeply within the recesses of her body.

His hands held her hips tightly against him as he moved, slowly at first, driving so deeply into her, he was fully engulfed by the moist folds of her body. Each succeeding thrust grew rapid and fierce, striving, fighting for that glorious release, reaching the highest point in an explosion of the most intense, sharp, keen pleasure.

Slowly each muscle relaxed, and their bodies slacked into a soft, close embrace.

It deepened Alisa's suspicion that she was growing to love him. And Christian was panicked at the thought of that feeling overwhelming him for a second time in his life.

He rolled from Alisa, pulling her to rest beside him, toying with the tangled mass of curls falling onto his chest. Silence reigned for a long time as both wrestled with their own emotions. Finally, Alisa spoke, her voice a soft, raw whisper that Christian knew came from more than mere curiosity.

"What does it feel like to be in love?"

Christian hesitated, fearing what she felt, what forced the question. His own tone was low. "It's ecstasy and misery; delight and hatred; beauty and ugliness; searing hot and icy cold; divine rapture and debilitating pain; gaiety, wretchedness, agony . . . and what we just shared."

Silence fell again.

Alisa realized she felt all of those things, but worse yet, she heard the note of disdain in Christian's voice and thought she could not stand it.

He spoke again, a reluctant whisper, as if he did not want to know the answer. "Do you love me, Alisa?"

How could such perfect pleasure of a moment before, such warm, miraculous joy swelling inside of her so quickly turn to the most startling, stabbing pain?

"I don't know." It was a ragged murmur. "I hope not."

This struck Christian a blow as devastating as any Alisa felt. "Why?" The question forced its way from him.

"You won't love me in return."

The words tore through Christian, but he could not refute it. He could not!

The heavy silence enveloped them, but neither could move from the arms of the other as though their bodies could console what their words wrought.

"I wish there had never been Ellen, or any of the pain she caused you."

"So do I."

"I wish we had met before." Her voice was thick, and Christian heard so much more than what she said.

At that moment Christian knew that no matter what Alisa admitted or denied, she loved him, loved him in the same way he had loved Ellen, openly, freely, fully—and it weighed on him. He knew that he had the same power over Alisa that Ellen had had over him, the power to hurt her as badly as he had been hurt. He saw the immense vulnerability she worked so hard to hide, and it hurt him.

His hand ran gently through her hair, caressing the back of her head. "If you did love me, Alisa," he said with profound sincerity, "I would cherish your feelings, protect them as the most precious gift ever given me."

Alisa swallowed thickly. "Perhaps it's too precious a gift to be given when the same is refused in return.

Somehow it seems to me that if you hold yours away from me to protect yourself, the gift is cheapened."

"Ah, Alisa. Give me time yet. What I feel for you is so confusing. It's new and strange, and it scares the hell out of me."

Alisa pushed herself from his arms and Christian let her go. She put her cloak around her, not even feeling the chill of the satin against her bare skin now. She left the small cottage, standing just outside, her arms tightly wrapped around her stomach, her head far back, her face skyward as she fought furiously to gain control of her emotions. She lost the battle to the silent tears coursing down pale cheeks. She did not even hear Christian come to stand beside her.

"Oh, God, Alisa, don't cry," he said desperately. "Not for me!"

"Go back inside where it's safe, Christian. Perhaps when I learn to lock away all of my feelings, we can go on. But it's a sorry prospect you paint for our future."

"Dammit!" He pulled her fiercely to him, pressing her to his chest. "I don't want you to do that! It's not what I want for our future. I want your love. Goddammit, I need it." The words were wrenched from him as he held her crushed against him, his face lowered into her hair.

He breathed deeply to clear his senses. "You've done so much already to mend my wounds, don't desert me now. Don't close yourself off to me. There's a battle going on inside of me, between what I feel for you and all of my damned fears and scars. When we share what we did tonight, the demon that grew when everything happened with Ellen rises up and leaves me as frightened as a child. Don't leave me alone with the demon, Alisa. And for God's sake don't create one of your own."

"Sometimes I think you are my demon."

He laughed mirthlessly. "Never, sweet, never! There is nothing in me that wants to hurt you."

He bent and lifted her into his powerful arms, cradling her as he carried her back into the cottage and laid her on the furry mattress before the hearth. He set another log to burn on the fire and then knelt near Alisa, gently removing her cloak and then his own. He lay beside her, melding their naked bodies into one, but now it was not passion that bound them but a deeper, more binding emotion neither would name as love. The term did not matter, for the flame was there, burning in them both no matter how fiercely it was denied.

Chapter Fifty-three

Christian woke to the muted, far-off sound of Alisa retching. He rolled on his back with a quiet moan, flinging a long arm across his eyes against the glare of early-morning sun reflecting off the late February snow beyond the windows. The room was icy, an indication that it could not be long past dawn or a maid would have already lighted the fire.

Alisa padded back to bed, easing under the covers carefully, since it appeared Christian was still sleeping. She lay flat and breathed deeply, hoping futilely for her stomach to settle down.

"This has been going on a long time, Alisa." Christian's voice was low and gravelly with sleep.

"I didn't mean to wake you," she whispered weakly, fighting the second rise in her gorge.

"Have you had even one day free of this in the past fortnight?"

She swallowed thickly. "No. Surely it can't go on much longer. Yours lasted only a day."

"I was sick over a month ago, sweet. Do you really believe this is the same?" he said dubiously.

"Of course it is. What else could it be?" she asked guilelessly, certain she had the same malady that had plagued most of the household in January.

Christian noted the ashen pallor of her skin, the dark circles beneath thick lashes, and her hollowed cheeks. His bluish-green eyes grew dark as he gently smoothed the hair from her forehead.

"See if you can get some sleep, Alisa. I'll light a fire and leave; you stay in bed until you feel better."

"Thank you," she managed, dropping off to sleep even as she spoke, her words slurred just a bit. "I can't seem to stay awake lately, either," she mumbled before nodding off into a sudden, deep slumber.

Christian, Scott and Nicholas were all sharing a last cup of coffee when Alisa came downstairs. She moved cautiously so as not to jar her irascible stomach and bade the three men a quiet good morning.

She was too miserable to notice Christian's quizzical scrutiny. All of her feeble energy had been spent in the simple tasks of dressing and descending the stairs. Ann placed a steamy cup of tea before her, trying to tempt her with an assortment of delicacies for her breakfast, all of which were met with a slight shake of her head and a wrinkled nose at the very thought of eating.

"Bring her an egg and toast," Christian calmly ordered, to satisfy his own curiosity.

Scott excused himself, offering Alisa his sympathy with a slight, knowing smile.

Nicholas watched Alisa almost as intently as Christian but with far more obvious concern. Ann placed the toast and coddled egg in front of Alisa, who peered down at the food before her, her eyes held by the still slimy white of the egg. With a sudden gasp, she rose, her fingers pressed to her lips, her eyes wide, and ran from the room.

"That was a cruel thing to do, Christian. And totally uncalled for. She said she wasn't hungry!" Nicholas shouted angrily.

"I didn't expect her to eat it, Nicholas. I merely wanted to see her reaction to a meal she has eaten often in the past," Christian answered, unperturbed.

"She's sick. You should be calling a doctor instead of torturing her. Yesterday I went to her studio to ask her advice on a painting, and she had to run from the room twice in half an hour's time. If you don't get her a damn doctor, I will."

Christian was surprised to see the same level of heated anger in Nicholas that he had not witnessed since childhood. "Calm down, Nicholas. There is no need for your concern. I know what ails Alisa, and a doctor cannot help her."

He found Alisa in their bedroom, lying on the day bed on her side, her head resting wearily against the high back. She felt utterly defeated by her persistent nausea. She awakened each morning with the horrid feeling and to make it worse, she was so tired, she could sleep away the entire day.

Christian sat beside her on the bed, a sympathetic smile on his dazzlingly handsome face. "Why didn't you stay in bed?" he asked kindly.

"I may never rise again if I give in to this. I'm beginning to think something horrible plagues me, Christian."

He chuckled lightly. "It will pass, sweet."

"When? Already it has far outlasted what everyone else suffered with it."

"You don't have the same malady."

"Whatever it is, I wish it would just go away."

He laughed. "It will. In a few weeks, you'll feel fine."

"A few weeks! Please don't torture me with even the thought of that!"

"Do you honestly not realize what is the matter?" he teased her, amused.

"It's something dreadful, whatever it is. I think I'm in need of a doctor, Christian. Perhaps you should call one."

His smile was mischievous. "What you will be in need of is a midwife."

Alisa's eyes widened and she swallowed thickly; a surge of the purest panic blocked her throat. "Oh, my God!" Her stomach rebelled as if she had been punched, and she ran for the chamber pot in the next room.

When her stomach calmed, Alisa sank weakly into a nearby chair. Shock and panic and fear coursed through her. It had simply not occurred to her before this that she carried Christian's child. Thinking back, she could not remember suffering her monthly indisposition in January, or in February, either.

Oh, my God! Oh, my God! Her mind whirled with the thought, hearing again all of the disparaging things Christian had said since the beginning of their marriage about having children. Children were nothing but a source of trouble . . . he would pay nannies and nurses to keep any child out of his sight until he could send it away to boarding school . . . babies were too easily passed off onto people who didn't want them . . . they were an unfortunate result of pleasure . . . nothing but a problem.

Would he hate it? Would he punish a mere baby for the scars of his past? Why did it have to happen now? Why couldn't it have waited until she had won his love?

"Are you all right?" Christian's voice interrupted her tormenting thoughts.

"Yes." She forced herself to stand. Trying for a semblance of composure, she walked back into the bedroom, feeling Christian's eyes on her the whole time.

"Haven't you anything to say about impending motherhood?" he asked with a frown, not understanding her reaction.

Her voice was wracked with desperation. "Please, Christian. I'm too sick to deal with it."

"That won't make it go away, Alisa." His confusion was mounting. "Don't you want the baby?"

She sank down on the bed dejectedly. "That isn't the point, is it? Whether I want it or not, you will hide it away somewhere so that it won't bother you."

"What the hell would make you think that?"

"You said it! You said you could afford to pay nannies and nurses to care for it until it could be sent away to school. You've said all sorts of horrible things about it. How can I be happy to give birth to a baby you're determined to hate?"

Christian sat beside her, duly chastised, taking her hands into his much larger ones. "The baby is mine, isn't it?"

"Of course it is. How could you doubt it?"

One curved finger beneath her chin turned her face to him. "It occurred to me a few days ago that my seed had caught you, and since then I've given thought to little else. I will admit to an initial rise of my ugly suspicions. After all, there were several nights alone with Owen in November."

"Oh, Christian," she lamented wearily.

"Shh . . . I'm not finished. I must be winning the battle with my demon from the past, because I fought down that thought without much trouble. I know the baby that grows in you is mine. I can feel it in a way I never did with Ellen. I discovered that I really want this baby. I long to see what we have created, to hold it and marvel at it. I'm sorry you're so sick with it, but don't be unhappy, my love, and certainly don't fret over my feelings, because I'm looking forward to it. In this I am free of the shackles of my past."

"Are you sure?" she asked, filled with her own doubts.

"I want this baby," he said, each word slowly enunciated. "I promise to spoil it heartily! It's about time you and I have a child of our own, don't you think?"

Alisa sighed. "I'm too tired to take care of a baby."

Christian laughed, his broad shoulders curving around her as steely arms encircled her. "It will pass by then. For now you would do better to stop being so damn stubborn and trying to fight it. If you rest, you'll feel better."

He pressed her gently back onto the pillows, pulling a heavy quilt over her. One small hand reached to him just as he moved to leave her.

"It is your baby," she said softly.

His glance was warm in return. "If anyone else had fathered it, it wouldn't be causing you such torture, my love. It seems even in this I have given you a hard time."

Alisa's eyes closed heavily as his lips lowered to her forehead, his bushy mustache tickling her skin as she fell into a more contented sleep than she had found of late.

Chapter Fifty-four

"Christian, I must speak to you before you go up to Alisa!" Scott was waiting in the entrance hall when Christian arrived home for the day.

His brother's tone and expression alarmed Christian. "Is she all right? The baby?"

"She's fine, and so is the baby."

Christian was obviously relieved. Alisa's queasiness had subsided, but he found himself constantly worrying about her health.

Scott's voice drew his thoughts back. "Alisa received a letter today from her father's attorney. Aldis Todd died in January."

Christian shook his head. "Damn! Just when she's feeling better."

"She seems to be taking it well; she's strong. But I thought you should know before you go up to her so she doesn't have the burden of telling you."

Christian patted his brother's arm.

He found Alisa sitting quietly peering from her bedroom window at the green. The first buds and leaves of spring were just beginning to bloom on the huge elms that lined the square.

She turned when Christian entered the room. He saw her sadness but no trace of tears.

"Scott told me, sweet. I'm sorry," he said simply.

"I knew Papa was ill. He wrote me from a hospital bed the last time. Still, it seems so odd that he's gone. I think it will take me a long while to believe he isn't still at home in London." Alisa shook her head and sighed with finality. "But there is a problem."

"I'll do what I can, Alisa. This is not a time for you to be burdened."

"I'm afraid it is something you will have to tend to. Papa's counselor wrote that after Ivy's marriage, Papa changed his will, leaving Owen as executor. With Owen dead, you're left as the only male member of the family to oversee the legalities. Ivy has already sent word that she means to go to protect her interests. And there is the added problem of your aunt. Apparently her state of mind has deteriorated."

Christian absorbed this unsavory news. "Dammit," he breathed, "can't it wait until after the baby comes?"

"He says you must come right away or the estate will be claimed for debts and Deadra will be sent to an asylum."

Alisa's voice lowered, her gaze returned to the window to hide the fear that rose with her next words. "There is nothing else to be done, Christian. You will have to sail for England as soon as possible . . . and with Ivy."

It was still dark when the servant knocked on the door to rouse Christian; the tower clock struck four simultaneously.

It was April 3, 1851, and at dawn Christian's ship would sail, the only other passenger Ivy, who knew

Alisa's guilty secret and who had sworn to win Christian for herself by any means.

Alisa was in such a state of despair that sleep eluded her. Christian's hand ran gently down her side to her hip and back again.

"Goddammit, I don't want to go," he said, his clear tone revealing his own lack of sleep in these past hours.

"You will try to be back before the baby is born?" she asked for the hundredth time.

"Nothing could prevent me from missing it, my love." His voice was deep with regret.

"Be careful, Christian," she whispered.

"There is nothing to worry about."

Alisa hesitated as she had a dozen times in the past week. She could not let him leave without voicing her fears. "It is not only your safety I fear for," she said softly.

"What then, sweet?" He kissed the top of her head, staying there to breathe in her sweet scent, hoping to carry the memory of it with him.

"She wants you, Christian," Alisa said ominously. "I didn't know if I should say it, but when I told her to leave this house after Jonah died, she swore to destroy our marriage, to win you at any cost."

"Do you believe that possible?"

"Ivy is capable of anything."

"I am not some dolt, to be easily deluded by Ivy. I know well what she is. She holds no attraction for me, especially now. Do you think I would leave behind my wife while she carries my first child and cavort like some horny stallion set free in a pasture of easy mares? Regardless of what Ivy intends or desires, I want nothing to do with her. Nothing!"

"She can be very devious. And very captivating when she sets her mind to it."

"I am not a fool, Alisa. And you are overlooking your own charms. It's you I want, not your sister."

"Just beware of her, please."

"Don't worry about it. I promise you nothing will happen."

He sighed heavily. "I have to go, Alisa. I'm already overdue on board ship. I should have slept there last night." He rose, donning his clothing rapidly in the cold room.

Alisa watched, devouring the sight of him, embedding this moment in her mind with a bittersweet feeling. Christian sat back on the bed, after he had dressed, running his hands carelessly through his hair and then taking Alisa's small hands to hold.

"I'll be back before you know it. You'll be so busy getting everything ready for the baby, you won't even notice I'm gone."

"You would be furious to come home and find that true." She managed a smile. "Christian?" Her voice was soft, hesitant. "I want you to know something before you leave."

"What is it, sweet?"

"I'm grateful to whatever fates were at work that night that led me to you. I love you." She pressed her fingers to his lips, stopping his words before they could be spoken. "I waited until now to say it because I wanted to give you a parting treasure to take with you. Maybe in the long months ahead, you will have time to think about what you feel. Don't say anything. I know your demons still haunt you, and this way you will be gone and not faced with me each day waiting to hear the words from you."

"Alisa," he breathed raggedly. "This is unfair."

"Just keep it in mind when Ivy beckons."

"Is that the only reason you've told me? To counter anything your sister has planned?"

"I hope you know better than that. I said it only because it's true."

Christian bent to her, warm lips taking hers gently first, then more deeply, a long kiss filled with emotion.

"You make it hard for me to go."

"And in a hurry to return, I hope," she countered lightly, though her smile was forced. "I love you, Christian. Godspeed."

He kissed her again, all of his reluctance to leave, all of his desires, all of the feelings within him expressed in that parting caress.

Then he left. Alisa stared at the ceiling, feeling an aching void and a deep, devastating fear of what was to come.

Chapter Fifty-five

"Nicholas! That wouldn't be proper!" Alisa laughed, her hands pressed to the small mound of her abdomen.

"It isn't improper. Besides, who will see? There is no one here but us. I just want to feel it move. It's simple curiosity."

Alisa and Nicholas sat in the garden, each behind canvases resting on tall easels, painting the lush scenery beyond the fountain.

"You're embarrassing me, you know." Alisa's face heated, but it was not an effect of the June sun.

Nicholas smiled mischievously, his voice a stage whisper. "I won't tell a soul. I just want to press my hand to that cute little bulge. If I were your brother you would let me."

"You are not my brother."

"We could pretend I am for a moment." He feigned a pout.

Since Christian's departure, Nicholas had been Alisa's constant companion. He seemed to have set himself the goal of entertaining her, filling every hour possible with his charming, teasing, good-natured company. Before Christian had left for England, Alisa had thought of Nicholas as the playful brother she had never had. In the intervening three months, however, she was growing more uncomfortable with their relationship.

What troubled Alisa was nothing more than a feeling, a sense that Nicholas's lighthearted banter was not as innocent as it seemed. She chided herself for her suspicions one moment, but the next found herself plagued with them again. Surely, she reasoned, now of all times, it was ridiculously vain to believe his efforts were anything more than kind, brotherly compassion for her lonely state.

But then she would see an odd glint in his eyes and he stared at her for long moments when he thought her unaware, or he would jest about stealing her away from Christian and making her his own with a bit too much persistence, or his hand would linger too long at her arm when helping her from a carriage. Sometimes he would stand behind her as she painted, his body much too near for propriety's sake, a hand at her shoulder or lightly caressing her cheek as he admired her work.

Now, as he tried to tease her into allowing him to feel the movements of the child she carried, Alisa could not quell the feeling that his interest was not at all brotherly.

There was a sharp edge to her voice. "I think I must play matchmaker and find you a wife, Nicholas. You should appease your curiosity with a baby of your own."

He looked hurt. "I thought you might like to share a bit of it with me, since Christian has abandoned you."

Guilt struck Alisa, softening her tone. "Christian didn't abandon me; he would never have gone if it wasn't necessary."

"He's got a damn lot of money. He could have simply reimbursed Ivy for whatever she would lose by not going; certainly you don't need what's left of your father's estate."

Alisa was surprised at Nicholas's rare criticism of Christian. "It was more than just money. My father's entire life had to be cleared up, houses, debts, businesses, even Christian's aunt Deadra will have to be provided for. Besides, he will be back soon now."

Alisa picked up a sheet of parchment and used it to replace the canvas on the easel, attempting to change the subject and divert Nicholas's strange mood. "You promised to sit for me, Nicholas. Since you've lost interest in your painting, now is a good time."

He started slightly, as if his thoughts had been elsewhere, and smiled charmingly once again. "All right, sweet Alisa. Will this do?" He struck an exaggerated pose.

Alisa laughed. "No, it won't do at all. I want a portrait of you, not some silly dandy. Be natural."

Silence reigned for a time as Alisa's attention was absorbed in her drawing, and Nicholas gazed back at her intently. After a time he spoke again, his voice soft, distant. "Are you lonely, Alisa?"

She answered him without really giving much thought to the question. "Yes, a little. I miss Christian greatly."

"You didn't feel like you belonged here before, did you?"

"I suppose not. I felt a bit of an intruder at first."

"Do you still?"

"No. Now that I think about it, I guess I don't, though I couldn't tell you when it stopped. Perhaps it was just being in a new place, for you and Scott have been kind to me from the start."

"I've lived here for eighteen years, and I'm still not certain where I belong." His tone was sad, serious, drawing Alisa's attention away from her picture.

"Do you still feel that way?"

"It's difficult to be the charity case if you have any pride at all. Not that I wasn't welcome here. But I'm still the poor relation. It's especially hard because I could never compete with Christian's and Scott's good looks, their impeccable characters, winning personalities and money, to boot." He laughed mirthlessly. "Were our positions changed, I would belong because of wealth and heritage, and they would belong just because of the way they are. It would have been much easier."

"Do you really think so little of yourself, Nicholas?"

"I'm realistic, Alisa."

Her heart went out to him, forgetting her recent suspicions of him. "You're wrong, you know. You're different from Christian and Scott, but that doesn't make you inferior. You have qualities that make you special, Nicholas. It is foolhardy to base your value of yourself on the merits of others. You are a warm, kind, caring person in your own right. Why do you think you must compete with them?"

He gazed intensely into her eyes. "Because they have all I want."

"In what way? You live in the same places with the same rights; you work at the same tasks. I think you put too much emphasis on their money."

"The money is not the most important part of it."

"Then what is, Nicholas? I don't understand."

"Christian has you."

Alisa was stunned. She did not know what to say. She finally asked, doubtfully, "Do you feel all of this only because of me?"

"I do now."

"You know that's impossible! It isn't even me you want, if you were honest with yourself!"

"Do you love Christian?"

"Yes, I do. I mean to stay his wife throughout eternity," she said softly, to ease the blow of her words.

"You see. In comparison, you choose him. If I were an equal, you might not be so sure."

"That is simply not true. If your theory made any sense, then Scott would be the perfect substitute. Yet I feel nothing but sisterly affection for Scott, the same as I feel for you. So, you see, there is no validity in your conjecture. To me there is no one to compare to Christian and what I feel for him. Somewhere there is a woman who would think me daft to love Christian with all of his faults, while she will adore you for yours."

Nicholas smiled disbelievingly. He stood and moved to see her drawing of him, and she laughed ruefully. "I'm afraid it's not at all you, Nicholas."

The portrait was undeniably Nicholas, the features a remarkable resemblance, but this man was quiet, pensive, sad, solemn, everything she knew Nicholas was not.

He studied it and then spoke as he moved to leave her.

"Perhaps you've captured more of me than you think."

Chapter Fifty-six

One late July evening in the middle of the north Atlantic, Christian stood at the railing, staring at the star-filled sky and listening to the water lapping at the side of his ship. In England he had found Aldis Todd's debts large but his holdings much more than he had expected. Alisa and Ivy had been left with large fortunes, even after Christian had seen to permanant arrangements for his aunt's stay in an institution.

He pushed himself from the railing and headed for his cabin. He stepped into the well-appointed captain's quarters, turning as the door closed to peer at the occupant of his bunk, his handsome face devoid of expression.

Ivy sat with her back propped against the wall, her elaborately coiffed hair incongruous with her languidly posed, naked body. His eyes moved slowly from her seductive smile to full, ripe breasts, then lower to the pale red triangle between her thighs, and back again to the face that resembled Alisa's.

"Give up, Ivy. You're wasting your time and mine." Christian was unmoved by the sight of his sister-in-law. In fact, he was bored with all of Ivy's attempts to seduce him. He continued contemptuously, "I wouldn't bed you even if my only other choice was a lifetime of celibacy. Get the hell out of my bed and out of my room. I have no intention of using a piece of flesh already gnawed on by my entire crew."

Ivy's lids dropped halfway over unremarkable blue eyes; her lips twitched in invitation, ignoring his rebuff. She drew her hands up her body slowly, cupping each breast to push them upward and outward. Her voice purred. "You're a lying bastard, Christian. You want me and you know it." She slid lower on the bed, her lanky legs parting. "I'm ready for you."

Christian disgustedly picked her silk wrapper up from the chair where she had discarded it, throwing it at her distastefully. "I've never been aroused by a bitch in heat. You turn my stomach. I've seen used-up whores who offered more than you. Now get the hell out of here or I'll call someone to throw you out. I wouldn't even touch you to do that."

Now Ivy stared at him through narrowed eyes, her expression vicious. "I suppose you find dear Alisa more to your taste, is that it?" she spat.

"Eminently."

"You're not alone," she said spitefully. "Owen preferred her, too. In fact, that brat she carries is his. The whole reason we came to New Haven was so he could have sweet Alisa. You're such an ass if you thought they spent that time while Jonah was sick taking care of him. Ha! It's no wonder the poor brat died. Instead of tending him, Owen was sticking it to her right there. I came home late one night and found them, naked, together on the floor. So go ahead and be faithful, Christian; it's a good joke!"

Christian watched her, seeing her game. "It won't work," he said flatly.

Ivy laughed, an evil sound. "You're a fool. I knew it from the moment you came to London. God, how Ellen and I laughed at you when I told her about your pining away for her in England. How easy it is to dupe you. Ellen enjoyed the story of how I had found you such an easy target. And then we have sweet Alisa. Do you know why she married you?" Vicious delight beamed on Ivy's face, watching Christian's expression of bored disgust.

Christian said nothing. He crossed his arms calmly over his broad chest as if he felt only impatience with this performance.

Ivy continued, ignoring Christian's reaction, enjoying herself more than had he accommodated her in bed. "You may not want me, but I wonder how much you will want your little wife when you discover what she really is."

Ivy stood, donning the silk wrapper slowly, prolonging this moment she relished. Seducing Christian had only been a prelude to this, at any rate, an added blow against Alisa before she destroyed her marriage.

"Dear, sweet Alisa . . . is a murderess."

Ivy paused to watch Christian's face. She was disappointed to find it unchanged, his expression still bland.

"It's quite true. On the afternoon before we trapped you into marrying her, she killed my lover. Willis Potts was our neighbor's son at the country estate. He was also Jonah's father. Didn't you think it odd that Alisa fretted so much for a brat that was not her own? It was guilt, you see; she owed him the care since she killed his father."

"The man must have been feeble," Christian said sarcastically. "How else could she have harmed him?"

"She was arguing with him over his discipline of some little heathen. They struggled and he fell on his own knife."

"Then it was in defense of herself and a child," he said calmly. "She would not have been considered a murderess."

"A man died at her hand. That is murder."

"A man died from an accidental fall while she defended herself. No court would have found her guilty of murder."

"She killed him! His father was a Lord High Magistrate with a great deal of power and a vindictive nature. She would have hung for it." Ivy laughed brashly. "I was foolish enough to think I wanted Owen at the time, and he wouldn't have me with Alisa available. So I used the situation to get rid of her."

Ivy walked to the door, smiling wickedly at the frown on Christian's handsome face.

"Your wife is a killer, Mr. Reed. The only way I could convince her to marry you was to threaten the hangman's noose. It was not an easy task, I assure you. Alisa wanted Owen, and she despised you. She saw you as the besotted fool you are. The only thing in the world less desirable to her than marrying you was hanging, for there was no question that was where she would have ended up. Any threat less than the gallows would never have convinced her. You are nothing more than the moronic oaf that saved her neck. And to top it off, now you pine for her and will play Papa to another man's bastard. It's really too delicious. I never thought Alisa was that

lever, but she certainly managed to dupe you. She
lust be smarter than I thought. You are quite a
air, a murderess and a fool!''

Christian did not hear the door close, nor the satis-
.ed laughter that echoed in the corridor behind Ivy.

Christian's thoughts would have surprised Alisa
nd disappointed Ivy, for he did not believe Alisa
arried Owen's child, nor was he repulsed by the fact
hat she had killed a man.

What Christian doubted now was Alisa's true feel-
ng for him. Throughout this trip he had pondered
or long hours what his own feelings were. Ivy's
vords had put a harsh light on the situation, fueling
is apprehension about lowering his barriers to un-
each what he suspected was a love deeper than that
e had for Ellen.

Now he could not help but wonder if Alisa's telling
im she loved him was just a ruse, a contrivance, a
imple form of protection in case he stumbled onto
er secret or Ivy disclosed it. It was obvious she
eared his reaction more than anything or she would
ave told him and freed herself from her sister's
lutches.

Christian fell back onto the bed Ivy had vacated,
is bushy brows pulled by a deep frown, his features
aut with a newly strengthened resolve to keep his
eart hardened. He mentally replaced the locks on
is tender emotions, vowing that nothing would re-
ease them again . . . nothing short of Alisa's con-
vincing him beyond all doubt that her professed love
or him was genuine, given freely and sincerely, and
not just another clever ruse perpetrated by another
leceitful woman.

Chapter Fifty-seven

"No, Nicholas!" Alisa's voice rang with a note of panic. She consciously calmed herself and her tone. "Thank you, anyway. But Scott has already promised to take me to meet Christian. I wouldn't want you to alter your plans."

Alisa's midnight-blue eyes shot furtively to Scott, hoping he would not give her lie away. He had found her in the morning room on this hot August day, to inform her that Christian's ship had just docked. Nicholas had joined them only seconds later, before any plans had been made to meet him.

Scott smiled warmly at her, taking up her story. "You know I've got to go down there at any rate, Nicholas. And you're needed to tend that mess at the carriage works this morning."

Nicholas's face turned angry; his black eyes stared at Alisa, ignoring Scott. "I see you've finished with my company now that your husband has returned. I should have guessed!"

"Oh, Nicholas. It isn't that. Hasn't any of what I've said to you sunk in?"

"What has managed to sink into my thick skull is that I should seek a better woman than you. Perhaps now that Ivy is free she will be a more satisfying partner for me." His words were well calculated, for he was privy to Alisa's feelings about her sister.

"Surely you jest. Ivy prizes only herself."

Nicholas smirked, not realizing Alisa spoke the truth, seeing it as jealousy. "I've always found Ivy enchanting," he said pointedly as he left the room.

"What the hell was that all about?" Scott breathed.

Alisa's head shook. "It isn't as improper as it sounds. Nicholas has confided many things in me these past months. He believes he could only find happiness if I were his wife instead of Christian's. He's been so insistent about it, he has barely left my side in this past month. I've been forced to be rude at times to be free of him. Now I have hurt him." Her joy at her husband's return was dimmed by the turmoil Nicholas had caused.

Scott was sympathetic. "I had noticed that Nicholas was hovering. I'm sorry, Alisa. If I had known, I'd have devised something to divert him."

"I'm just grateful that you saved me today."

"I spared you Nicholas's company, but I don't think you should go down to the pier. Christian will be home in a matter of hours now; surely you can wait."

"No, I can't!"

Scott's glance fell to the enormous bulge of her middle, obviously in the final weeks of pregnancy. "It's unwise for you to be venturing away from this house at all now, Alisa, and especially not on a blistering hot day. Christian would skin me alive if I allowed it."

"I did not ask your permission, Scott," she said kindly but firmly. "I am going, with or without your escort."

He watched ruefully as she tried to lift herself from the chair, and finally offered her assistance. "This is foolhardy, Alisa. Do you want the first Reed heir to be born on the docks?"

"I'm going," she repeated.

Scott remembered the last time she had been determined to go to Christian; he realized again that he would have to accommodate her stubborn will.

The wooden planks of the Long Wharf bowed and creaked beneath the lively bustle of a busy summer's day. The sun's reflection off the green water magnified the already intense heat, but Alisa still refused Scott's pleas to go back home.

The months of Christian's absence had been long, and Alisa's worries about Ivy made her imagination race with a variety of dire possibilities. She had to see for herself how Christian had fared, and she could not prolong the misery by waiting at home.

As she left the carriage with Scott's aid, her eyes searched the deck of the ship looming so high above. The gangplank was lowered, and men moved up and down carrying boxes, crates and trunks.

Alisa caught sight of Christian staring down at her. She smiled, waving her arm over her head. He did not return her greeting, nor did his handsome face ease from the dark scowl that was evident even from this distance. Her heart sank, her worst fears gaining strength.

"Are you feeling all right?" Scott asked, seeing her hesitation and the joy drain from her features.

She forced a smile, straightening her shoulders. "I'm fine. Will you take me onto the ship?"

His head shook slowly in resignation, and he offered his arm.

Christian watched his wife walk up the gangplank and was struck by her loveliness even though he was surprised by her swollen belly. The picture he had carried in his mind was of Alisa as she had been when he left, small and thin still, with only a bare hint of a rounding middle. Now she looked too tiny to be carrying such a large, round stomach; it seemed much too great a burden. He felt a surge of protectiveness once again.

"She does look ghastly, doesn't she?" Ivy's voice came from beside him suddenly.

"I thought you had left." Christian's tone was aloof. Perfectly coiffed and elaborately gowned, Ivy looked unaffected by the heat.

She smiled wickedly and, to Alisa's eyes, intimately at him.

"I'm leaving right now," Ivy purred, her actions timed for and motivated by Alisa's arrival. She placed a hand on Christian's arm. "I merely wanted to thank you for . . . everything." She spoke loudly and insinuatingly so that her sister would hear as she drew near.

"Good-bye, Ivy," Christian said disgustedly, turning his attention to his wife and dismissing Ivy, who laughed gaily.

She smiled serenely at Alisa before leaving, her expression that of a very satisfied, victorious cat.

Bluish-green eyes ran slowly from Alisa's flushed face, down her perspiration-moistened gown to the large mound of her abdomen as he spoke to his brother. "Why the hell did you bring her down here? She is sure as hell not in any condition to be prancing about the docks. Use your head, man!"

Scott's jaw clenched; his scowl was angry. One hand patted Alisa's tenderly to comfort her, knowing how Christian's slight would hurt her. "Use yours, Christian," he ground out.

Alisa's face paled beneath her heat-flushed cheeks and she turned to Scott as if her husband were not there. "You were right, Scott. I should not have come. Please take me home . . . now."

Scott sent one final glance to Christian before leading Alisa away.

Chapter Fifty-eight

"You're a goddam fool, Christian!" Scott spat, having heard Christian's arrival home and summoned him into the den.

"Leave it, Scott. It's not your business," Christian said, his voice low, gruff.

"I don't give a damn what you did these past months with that slut, though if you even touched her, you've lost all of my respect. But you deserve a horsewhipping for the way you treated Alisa today."

"Thank you for the welcome, Scott. It's good to be home," he said sarcastically, moving to leave.

Christian was halted at the door by Scott's voice, equally sardonic. "I didn't know you had learned so much from Ellen. You would be a good match for her now. But have the decency not to hurt your wife more than you already have today. Unfortunately, she is about to give birth to your child, or have you forgotten?"

Christian paused, stung by his brother's words, but without turning, he left him.

Alisa sat erectly in the garden, staring at the fountain, her eyes reflecting her desolation. The white knuckles of each hand grasped the wrought-iron arms of her chair, the only evidence of her fight to control the pain that roiled inside her.

Christian came out onto the terrace, but she did not remove her glance from the water cascading out of a pitcher held aloft by a marble cherub. Her face was no longer flushed from the heavy heat. Her midnight-blue eyes glistened with tears.

Christian leaned one leg onto the brick ledge before her, blocking her view of the fountain. His voice was cold, distant. "I apologize for greeting you as I did today. I was concerned for your health. You should not have been there. In fact, you should be lying down right now, until it's cooler."

Alisa stared up at him. Her voice was strong, proud. "I have managed quite well for myself this whole summer without your advice. I am in no condition to be comfortable at this point, no matter what the temperature. But you seem to have noticed my misshapen form, so that won't surprise you. Then again, after so many months with Ivy, I suppose I am a shock to you. Perhaps you would prefer her house to this until you can bear the sight of me." Her voice sliced through him.

"Don't be absurd!" he said curtly, aching to pull her into his arms, kiss her, caress her, explore that round belly until he had had his fill. But he had nurtured too many doubts since Ivy's revelation, and he held his feelings at bay.

"I was only thinking of your comfort," he added formally.

"How kind of you."

"Have you been well?"

"Perfectly." She turned her eyes to a large vase at the end of the terrace, not wanting him to see the efect of his aloofness. "Should I have your things or nine moved to another room?"

"Neither!" he boomed. "Why the hell would you lo that?"

She shrugged, hoping it appeared inconsequential :o her. "It's often done at this point."

"What point is that?"

"Whichever you prefer as an excuse. We can say that my body is so repulsive to you that it was better :o seek separate rooms or that your taking a mistress left you in need of more privacy."

"Have you lost your wits?" Christian was truly shocked by her words, lost so completely in his own turmoil that he had not seen this as the reason behind Alisa's suffering.

"A woman loses her waistline while carrying a child, not her wits . . . nor her eyesight. Which excuse do you prefer? Or perhaps both would suit."

"Neither, dammit! Nor will we take separate rooms. I am not repulsed by your body, and I certainly have not even considered taking a damn mistress."

Alisa lifted wide eyes to his face, seeing the rage there. In her mind only one answer remained, that he had discovered she was a murderess and that it was this that caused his disgust of her. Her face grew ashen, and she swallowed thickly, intense fear a hard knot in her throat. She played for time, trying to think of what to do.

"Did Ivy not attempt to become your mistress?"

"She tried and failed."

"Am I to believe you don't find my bloated form offensive?"

"I hardly expected to find you hiding the growth of my baby in your pocket."

Another thought struck her, causing more pain than her fear that he had discovered her secret. Perhaps her parting words to him had led in the opposite direction she had intended.

"What is it, then?" she asked, her tone barely audible, suppressed beneath dread.

Now Christian looked away from her, incapable of facing her and hiding his suspicions and doubts. "It's nothing, Alisa. I was surprised by your size . . . not repulsed," he was quick to amend. "You just looked so damned little to be carrying that middle, and you were so flushed, I was afraid the heat would harm you."

Alisa saw that he had seized the first reasonable explanation he could think of, but it was not actually the cause of his attitude toward her. She attempted to stand then, with effort, her head held high. Christian reached to help her, and she slapped his hands away.

Once on her feet, she spoke again. "I can bear deceit no better than you, so don't ask me to pretend to accept that lie. I will have my things taken from your room. I cannot share something as intimate as having this baby with a man whose heart lies somewhere else, whether it be with another woman or not."

Alisa took only two steps before her breath drew in a deep gasp; her body bent forward as her arm clasped her middle, a sharp pain stabbing her. Christian lunged for her, his large hands grasping both of her arms to support her. The pain ebbed, and Alisa pulled free of his grasp with force, gathering her strength and composure once again, to stand erect.

She breathed deeply, willing herself to relax. But after she took three more steps, the pain assaulted her anew, this time harder, doubling her over with its fierceness.

"Christian!" His name was forced from her lips in panic. She reached a hand to him as her other arm circled her hard stomach. "Oh, God, Christian, it's the baby," she groaned, everything forgotten but the misery slashing through her.

Christian scooped her up into his arms, his own face taut and pale with worry. She curled tightly against the pain as he carried her easily through the house, shouting for Scott as he climbed the stairs.

Chapter Fifty-nine

Time stretched out. The midwife and Ann were closeted away in the master suite as Alisa labored in the sweltering heat, her strength sapped by the intense temperature as much as by the pain.

The midwife asked that a doctor be summoned, and the tension in the house grew tangible.

Christian paced the drawing room, all but his perspiration-dampened shirt and breeches shed through the long hours of waiting. His sleeves were rolled, exposing thick, corded arms, his shirtfront left unbuttoned over the sandy-colored hair dotted with drops of sweat.

Nicholas had not returned, so only Scott sat with Christian. They had spoken little in their vigil, the harsh words before leaving a rift between them. Scott saw his brother's torment and believed it to be guilt, deeming it better left unexplored for both their sakes.

The doctor came downstairs after dawn. His coat was removed, his shirt moist; his wrinkled brow was furrowed as he accepted the brandy Scott offered.

"What is it? How is she?" Christian burst out, fear running rampant in him. Alisa's soft, muffled groans still sounded from the bedroom, so he knew it was not yet over.

The old doctor shook his white head wearily, his eyes marking Christian's size. "She's too little."

Christian thought his heart would stop with the words.

"Oh, my God," Scott's voice answered.

"What does that mean?" Christian demanded, drops of perspiration falling down the sides of his face.

Again the old doctor's eyes raked over Christian. "It means she's having a bad time of it. A very bad time."

"Will she be all right?" Christian's agitation was plain.

The doctor stood, shrugging. "I can't say. Only time will tell. A man as big as you are shouldn't marry one so small. You should have picked a woman big enough to have big babies."

The doctor left then, and Scott heard Christian mutter under his breath, "I didn't pick her. She picked me."

Scott's fist crashed into Christian's jaw, sending his head reeling, so that it took several backward steps to gain his balance again.

Christian's hand went to his jaw, his eyes blazed at Scott, and then his lids closed as he sat back into a chair. "All right, I deserved that," he said quietly.

"What the hell has gotten into you?"

"You wouldn't understand, Scott."

"What I do understand is that Alisa loves you in a way I'm beginning to think you're not worthy of."

"Does she love me? I wonder. She said so just before I left for England, but now it seems like nothing

ore than another lie to cover what she's been hid-
g from me."

"You're a damn jackass if you believe that. I don't
now what she's hidden from you, but I know a
oman in love when I see one, and I know how much
u hurt her today for no goddam reason! Yet you ac-
pted the flimsiest lies from Ellen. I watched her
ay you like the best audience for a prime act. And
ow you won't even believe Alisa when she truth-
lly says she loves you. She isn't capable of per-
rming for your benefit, but you are still
etermined to punish her for Ellen's wrongs."

"Dammit, Scott, don't you see?" His voice was low,
rtured. "Don't you see that I would give anything
. . *anything* not to feel this? Not to think it? I want
 believe her, but Ellen's lies taught me too much
ot to suspect Alisa."

"Has she given you any reason to doubt her? Or is
his Ivy's doing?"

"I have reasons. *My* reasons!"

"Not one that's valid, I'd stake my life on it. What
ave you done, Christian? Set out to hurt Alisa as
adly as you were hurt? You couldn't get back at El-
en, so instead you take what Alisa offers you hon-
stly and use it against her?" Scott taunted.

Christian answered wearily. "In the past weeks
here has been more pain because of this than there
ver was with Ellen."

Scott shook his head disgustedly. "That only
makes you a bigger damn fool. You didn't deserve
what Ellen did to you, and now Alisa deserves better
han what she's getting from you in return."

A muted scream tore from Alisa, sounding as if it
choed from the depths of hell.

Scott watched Christian's face drain of all color,

his eyes grow wide. He sat very, very still, his larg
hands like talons on the chair arms as drops of pe
spiration beaded on his handsome face.

They heard another scream of agony. They waite
in the stillness, held by fear greater than if thei
lives were threatened. Another muted scream, weal
weary, defeated.

A cold shiver ran along Christian's spine, held sus
pended in his own hell of uncertainty.

The silence was broken by the loud, lusty wail c
an infant, followed by the old doctor shouting com
mands that Christian and Scott could not discern
Footsteps sounded heavily overhead, rushing in re
sponse to the doctor's orders.

Then all of the noise stopped. No crying baby. No
screams. No commands. No running footsteps. The
only thing Christian heard was the pounding of hi
own heart; suddenly he wished that, too, would cease
if Alisa were dead. He sat transfixed, his misery
abounding.

The bedroom door opened and closed softly, and
slow steps descended the stairs. The doctor crossed
the room to Christian and extended his hand.

Only then did he smile. "Congratulations, Mr.
Reed. You have a son."

Christian waited, unable to speak, to ask the question.

"Your wife has come through it, too, on pure stubborn will, I think. She's weak and needs a great deal
of care, but she should be fine."

Christian breathed then, collapsing back into his
chair for only a second before springing to his feet. "I
have to see her."

The old man chuckled. "Give them a minute to
clean things up. If she's sleeping, don't wake her, she

needs the rest. From the look of you, you could use sleep yourself. I know I certainly can; this has been a long one!"

Scott led the doctor to the door, offering the appropriate words while Christian stood at the stairs, his foot on the first step, staring up at the closed bedroom door, unable to move.

Scott returned to his brother, a long arm extending the width of Christian's back, a hand clasping his shoulder. "Give in to it, Christian. This time it's real."

Christian sat on the bed, one knee bent to nearly touch her. He took her hands into his own, his thumbs rubbing them lightly. She looked so frail, it sent a fresh wave of fear through him.

Alisa's eyes opened heavily, a weak smile on her pale lips.

Christian pressed a kiss to her brow; his voice was quiet. "You gave me quite a scare, lady." His eyes grew misty.

"I didn't mean to," she answered, touched by what she saw in his face, in his eyes. "I haven't seen the baby. Is he beautiful?"

Christian smiled. "Not beautiful exactly. His head is a bit misshapen, but the midwife tells me that is normal. He's not the big, strapping son I expected to see after his birth being so hard on you."

A small hand lifted to Christian's jaw, caressing it gently. "What happened to you? Where did you get that bruise?"

He chucked. "It was a well-deserved gift!" Then he sobered. "I missed you, Alisa. I'm sorry yesterday was so disappointing. I didn't mean for it to be."

"How did you mean it to be?"

"I wanted to hold you and kiss you and feel that big belly, feel the baby kick from inside of you. I feel as if I've missed something I wanted so badly to experience."

At that moment she saw no sign of his emotions of the previous day, and she thought them all past, resolved with the birth of the baby. Her eyelids closed with a will of their own, and she sank back into exhausted slumber, her hands falling limp in Christian's large, powerful ones.

He kissed her again, fighting hard against flames burning through him, wondering if he would be engulfed by them regardless of his efforts to gain control.

Chapter Sixty

"Not married?" Alisa shrieked from her bed, sitting upright with the shock of her sister's words.

Ivy's expression was smug as she stood before Alisa, dressed beautifully in yellow and white sprigged poplin, a large-brimmed straw hat at a jaunty angle on her head.

"That's right. You and Christian are not really married." Ivy's visit, on the pretext of seeing her two-day-old nephew, had been unannounced and uninvited, but it was nothing to the shock she had delivered with this news.

"Explain to me what makes you say such a thing, Ivy." Alisa was irritated but not convinced. She had seen too many of Ivy's dramatic performances develop into nothing more than attention-seeking lies.

"It's quite simple; I paid a man to pretend to be a minister when, in fact, he had no credentials at all. He was an old sot who called himself an actor. You're no more married to Christian than I am." She laughed, enjoying herself.

"How do I know you aren't lying, Ivy?"

Ivy shrugged carelessly, "You don't. But just think about it, Alisa. Try to picture the minister that married you. Remember how he stumbled over the words? He couldn't even read them clearly. A real minister would have been able to perform a wedding ceremony by memory.''

Alisa did recall thinking the preacher odd; she remembered his ill-kept appearance, his sparkling white collar that appeared new.

Ivy continued, ''What a shame I didn't think of it while Christian and I were in England so he could have tried to find the old sot. But then we were well occupied. It actually slipped my mind until I heard of your new son. My first thought was that the child is a bastard.''

''What do you hope to gain by this?'' Alisa's anger was hot.

''Why, Christian, of course. This makes him a free man. After our lovely trip, I find I want him all the more.''

''You have enough money now, Ivy. You don't need my husband.''

''He is not your husband. Besides, I don't want his money; as you said, I have all I need. I discovered on that long, lovely voyage that he's the man I want. He's quite the best lover I have ever had . . . but then you already know his talents in that area, don't you?''

''I don't believe you, Ivy.''

''Don't you?'' Her eyes narrowed to slits of vindictiveness. ''That's your prerogative. However, it's all very true. It makes sweet, pure little Alisa a bit of a whore, doesn't it? And that is the most divine part of it all. After all the years you judged me immoral, it turns out you're no better. Bearing bastards, tsk, tsk, Alisa, and all the while thinking yourself so much better than I.''

"Why would you have done such a thing? What purpose did it serve to hire a bogus minister?"

"It amused me at the time. I found it delicious to think of high and mighty Alisa being bedded illicitly, bringing little bastards into the world. As time has passed, I've thought of several things about the situation that were to my advantage because of it. Had I arrived on your doorstep to find you had told Christian about your crime, I intended to use it then. I suppose it was just a means of gaining a hold over you, Alisa, and entertaining myself in the process. My reasons are really unimportant, though, aren't they? The only thing that matters is that you and Christian are not married . . . and Christian is fair game. Beware, Alisa. Very soon now I may have even more news for you. Remember that I warned you that Christian would be mine one day." Ivy's wide skirts brushed the floor in a swirl as she turned on that note and left.

Alisa regretfully handed her seven-week-old baby, David, to his wet nurse, watching with concern and jealousy as the woman put him to her breast.

Alisa's milk had come in a day after David's birth, and she had enjoyed feeding him, though most of her contemporaries preferred to leave that job to a servant or a hired wet nurse. But within two days of Ivy's visit, she had stopped lactating. After days of trying every remedy and concoction the midwife could think of, she admitted defeat and allowed this woman, whose own baby was thriving to nurse her son.

Alisa alone knew what had caused her milk to dry up, and in the following weeks, she sank deeper into despair. For, within days of her son's birth, Christian's subdued mood had returned. Though he was continually kind, compassionate and understanding, she still detected that remoteness about him. His eyes watched her as though he were seeking a clue to something Alisa was ignorant of. Each night they lay side by side in bed, separated by a chasm Alisa could not understand. She could only conclude that Ivy's revelation that Christian was her lover was true.

Alisa gently put David in his cradle, tucking his blankets cozily about him. She kissed his downy head and left him to the care of his nurse for the night. She climbed the short staircase to her attic studio, her spirits dark and low. How could she tell Christian that there existed the possibility that they were not married when he was nothing more than formally polite to her? If he were simply tolerating her now, this news would destroy whatever remained between them.

She lit a fire in the hearth against the chill from the large windows. She had not found the time since David's birth for painting or drawing, but with this first trip to her studio, thoughts of Nicholas invaded, adding to her dreary mood.

In these past weeks, Nicholas had become abrasive, flaunting his affair with Ivy, tormenting Alisa with comparisons between the two sisters when he was alone with her. She worried that he was headed for so much more heartache, but her warnings brought a thunderstorm of anger from him.

She pushed away thoughts of Nicholas at last, deciding she had her own problems to deal with. She set about sorting through a stack of drawings she had piled in a corner, hoping to summon the comfort and respite her artwork had always given her.

Engrossed in her task, she did not hear Christian's entrance. He came up behind her, clad only in a heavy robe, his hands pushed into pockets at the sides.

"So this is where you are."

Alisa jumped with fright. "You frightened me to death," she breathed, turning back to her work.

"When you didn't come to bed, I was afraid something was wrong with David. You weren't in the nursery, so I thought I might find you here. I wondered when you would go back to it."

"I'm just sorting through some old pictures."

"You have all day to do that. Come to bed now."

Alisa was tempted, beckoned by the deep tone of his voice. She wanted him. But she knew it wouldn't matter. "What difference does it make when I come to bed? I won't wake you." Her tone held a sharp edge.

She was tired of this game, whatever it was. She ached to have him touch her, just reach a hand to her hair or her shoulder, but Christian only moved to her side, looking down at the sheets of parchment on the floor.

"These are all of me!" He laughed harshly, ignoring her words.

She was so lost in misery, she hadn't realized that the majority of the drawings were, indeed, of Christian, at various stages of their relationship. He crouched down beside her, spreading the large papers so that each could be seen separately.

There were those she had drawn when they first came here, his face distorted with an expression of feral attack; some showed avid rage, others disgust, and then there were those more complimentary, portraying his kinder, more gentle side; some with

his handsome face pensive or deep in thought, and
even one of him asleep. But when he took out a picture that showed him looking like a cold, aloof
stranger, Alisa could not help saying, "It's hard to
believe this was done so long ago when it so accu-
rately portrays you now."

Christian saw that she was not going to be diverted this time. "We're going to have it out, aren't
we?" He stood, towering above her as she kneeled on
the floor.

"Yes, we are. I think it's about time." She stood,
too, refusing to allow him the advantage of added
height.

"Well? What is it?" Christian had no intention of
revealing the real reason behind his sore spirits.

"Somehow that innocent tone doesn't fit you,
Christian. I didn't understand your mood that first
day back from England, but when the baby was born,
you seemed your old self. It was short-lived, though,
wasn't it? I think you should tell me what is going
on." Alisa preferred almost anything to this pro-
longed state of limbo.

"What do you think is going on?"

"My sister tells me that she knows firsthand what
a talented lover you are."

"That's ridiculous, Alisa, and you should know
it."

"Why should I know it?"

"Because you know how I feel about your sister."

"What I don't know is how you feel about me. Or is
your present treatment supposed to let me in on that
bit of information?"

Now Christian was wary, treading between lies
and truth. "You have combined two different things,
Alisa, and come to a mistaken conclusion. I was

urly when I first returned because Ivy plied me with
tories of your having an affair with Owen. I'm sorry
o say she was very persuasive, and until I actually
aw David, I nearly believed he was not mine."

"You said you didn't believe that."

"I didn't. But Ivy said it over and over again in
very descriptive tones. It opened old wounds. I have
no doubt that David is my son. But that was what
was wrong then."

"And now?"

"I haven't been irascible."

"No, you haven't. You are as courteous as if I were
your dowager aunt. And not nearly as affectionate."

"What exactly is your complaint?"

"Are you bedding my sister?"

"No, dammit. I told you that."

"Then who?"

"I told you once that I was faithful to you, Alisa.
That is still true."

"Is something wrong with you?" she persisted.

"Of course not."

"It's just that you've discovered that you don't
want me."

Christian hesitated, knowing she was going to
make this more difficult than it already was for him.
"It isn't that I don't want you, Alisa," he said slowly.
"And it sure as hell isn't because I'm bedding someone else. You had a bad time giving birth to David."

"I'm well now."

"You nearly died. The doctor berated me for marrying you; he said you were too small to have my babies."

"Then that doctor is a ninny."

"Have you forgotten what you went through? Do
you know how many women die in childbirth?"

"Do you mean for us to live platonically, then?"

"Yes, dammit. There is no other sure way of pre venting it."

"How long will it be before you take a mistress?"

"All I know is that there can be no more babies!" he shouted, remembering too vividly his own tortur that night.

"It doesn't frighten me. Why should it matter?"

"Do you want to die?"

"I won't die!" she screamed back.

"No!" He walked toward the door. "I won't risk it Alisa. And that is final, dammit."

Alisa stood in her studio, staring at the empty space. She accepted Christian's reasons, understand ing the rise of his old doubts as well as her sister's talents at persuasion. She even believed that he was not having an affair with Ivy. But she was still plagued with the fear that there was more on Chris tian's mind than he admitted to. For now, however, she must discover whether he still wanted her and only rejected her merely out of fear of conceiving an other baby.

Alisa left her studio, determined that tonight Christian Reed would be bedded.

Chapter Sixty-one

The hour was late, and the servants grumbled at
Alisa's request for a bathtub filled with steamy
water in front of the hearth, only a few feet from the
foot of the high bed in which Christian sat propped
against pillows, watching.

Alisa ignored her husband's presence in the room,
her expression innocently beguiling. She undressed
leisurely, removing her gown and petticoats, folding
them carefully and putting them in the pile at the
bottom of her wardrobe to be laundered. She then removed her undergarments, seemingly heedless of
her naked body, lifting her arms to pin the wild, burnished mass of curls atop her head. Before entering
the high-backed tub, she bent far over, trailing a
long-fingered hand to test the water.

Christian adjusted his seat in bed as Alisa lifted a
slender leg over the side, clearing his throat uncomfortably. Alisa paid him no attention.

Christian could not pull his eyes from the vision of
his wife. Her silky shoulders and just the tops of
well-curved breasts were visible above the side of the
bathtub. She closed her eyes and let her head fall
back to expose the creamy column of her throat; her

soapy hands caressed it and then splashed clear water to wash away the suds.

She slowly lathered each arm in turn with a soapy sponge, drawing it over her shoulders and across her chest, dropping between her breasts to soap the crevice there.

Christian's eyes widened, following the sponge. He swallowed with difficulty and felt himself harder, achingly.

Alisa lifted one leg high, pointing her toes as she washed it, squeezing clear water from the sponge to send streams down the length to rinse it. Christian's glance followed the trail of droplets, from ankle to knee to thigh to . . . Again he fidgeted in agony, the skin across his neck and shoulders tight, a wave of heat washing over him.

Her bath complete, Alisa stood, again bending forward to reach a waiting towel. From Christian's angle, it was a perfect picture of tantalizing breasts falling forward, the shadow of a triangle of copper curls evident in the space between them.

Alisa did not wrap the towel around her body; instead, she rubbed herself dry, drawing the towel languidly, but with intense concentration, over her body. It was more than Christian could bear.

"This won't work," he said, his tone raw with desire.

A sensuous smile curved her lips. "I beg your pardon?"

"I will not make love to you."

"I haven't asked you to," she said carelessly, her arms again raised high to slip an extremely filmy gown over her head to slide in a bare whisper down her body, adding nothing more than an alluring veil to her exposed charms.

"I have lived too long not to recognize a seduction when I see one, Alisa."

"Whatever you say, Christian," she answered easily. She walked to the lamp that lit the room, her body silhouetted against it with a halo, the glow outlining her perfect curves and luscious mounds before she blew it out to leave only a dim light from the dying fire in the hearth.

She climbed into bed, sliding close enough to Christian for their sides to touch just barely. She pretended not to notice the telltale rise in the blankets across Christian's lap as he remained sitting. Again her mouth curved into a smile. Christian always slept nude, and her own pulse raced with the thought of his lean, hard body beside her.

"Should we simply shake hands good night, then?" she teased. "I wouldn't want to be accused of leading you astray with a kiss."

"You find this all very amusing, don't you?" he growled.

"Very." She laughed lightly, a lilting sound to Christian's ears.

"Do you mean to torture me?"

"Certainly not!" She feigned shock.

"Well it's ineffective!"

"My bath was quite effective. I feel wonderful." She smiled innocently up at him. "Are you going to kiss me good night or not?"

"I am not!"

Alisa shrugged. "All right, then. Sleep well." She turned to her side, curling as she did each night, her backside pressed firmly up against Christian. She closed her eyes contentedly, wiggling a bit to insure her comfort was just perfect, and sighed as if awaiting nothing more than the arms of Morpheus.

Christian's own eyes closed; his head fell back to the headboard as he remained sitting, desperately working to gain control of the pulsating throb in his loins, the ache in every inch of his body for hers. He consciously relived the long hours of his son's birth in his mind, again experiencing each moment to remind himself of his vow. It was a desperate battle, and as he reached its apex, the climactic fight of passion and sanity, he felt Alisa's small rump rub against the hard length of his thigh again, as her voice whispered softly, "I want you, Christian."

"Goddammit, Alisa!" he shouted as the battle ended, passion the victor.

He slid low beneath the quilts, one hand pushing Alisa's shoulder to lie flat on her back, her exquisite face smiling up at his dark, tormented frown.

"This is insanity," he said harshly.

"Then it's divine madness." Her arms snaked up around his thick neck, pulling his face near enough so that she could lift hers to kiss him, her lips slightly parted, soft and warm.

Her light, short, nibbling kisses drew his lips to hers. Her tongue slipped into his mouth, beckoning wantonly until, with a guttural groan, Christian surrendered. He pulled her to him with force, crushing her against his hard chest as his lips ravaged hers with an urgent hunger. His hand cupped the back of her head, pressing the unruly tangles of her hair, holding her captive beneath the onslaught of his mouth.

She met his demanding kiss with an urgency of her own, as if desperate for the assurance that he wanted her, burned for her.

Ungentle hands tore the filmy nightgown from her shoulders, lowering to her freed breasts, kneading,

ressing, tormenting. Her hand ran down his chest
the hard muscles of his flat stomach, then lower,
ithout hesitation or inhibition, slowing as she
ught the long, steely length of his manhood, reas-
ured yet again by its silken, throbbing, hot need of
er.

He reached between her legs, finding her already
oist and open to him, her hips arching up against
im in silent longing. He could not delay longer, ris-
ng above her, easing himself up into her carefully,
owly now, feeling the warm folds of her flesh envel-
ping him in her exquisite velvety depths.

Alisa's breath drew in, long and deep, nearly
eaching her own peak with the wondrous sensation
f him filling her completely, perfectly. Their bodies
oved in unison, each thrust met, each movement a
ew wave of ecstasy, every nerve alive with bright,
ot, tingling excitement, racing, rushing to the top,
he very highest peak of pleasure as wave after wave
f rapture washed over them.

Afterward they lay quietly entangled, loath to
art, to lose the intimacy that bound them so magnif-
cently. Alisa's heart felt as if it would burst with
ove for this man, thinking now that she had loved
im from the start but had been too stubborn to rec-
gnize it. At that moment, she would have given
nything in life to hear Christian say he loved her,
nd his silence left this hour of lovemaking bitter-
weet.

Chapter Sixty-two

David's christening party was a large one. Not since before Christian's divorce had there been so many people gathered at the Reed house. It seemed that his marriage to Alisa and his son's birth had made Christian once again acceptable in New Haven's conservative society. The christening party had been Alisa's idea; she insisted that everyone who had sent gifts and cards of congratulation be invited.

Christian had agreed to the party, but there remained a wary expression on his face throughout the day; he was not particularly fond of so many of these fine snobs but reasoned that for the sake of Alisa and David he would allow the truce.

Alisa had pointedly not invited Ivy, having no desire to see her sister. She had still not told Christian of Ivy's contention that they were not actually married. Therefore, the gaiety of the occasion was diminished when Nicholas strolled proudly into the gathering with Ivy on his arm; she was gowned splendidly in orange taffeta, a smug smile on her lovely face.

Alisa watched her sister warily, refusing to offer her welcome. Ivy looked regal. Her nose was slightly tilted as she seemed to bestow greetings on only the

most worthy, all the while holding Nicholas's arm a
if he were no more than a servile escort.

Conversely, Nicholas's eyes never left Ivy, thei
black depths shining with more than love; it was bet
ter termed worship and a swaggering pride that sh
was gifting him with her attentions. Alisa's hear
sank at the sight of Nicholas's feelings, so raw anc
vulnerable.

Christian was unaware of his wife's lowered spir
its as he carried the small bundle of his son, dis
playing him proudly to those people he counted as
friends. Alisa smiled at him as he approached her
touched by the sight of the large man gently tending
their baby.

"I think it's time David escaped this crowd for a
nap," he said to Alisa.

"I'll take him up to the nursery."

Christian cleared his throat, discomfited. "I think
it's better if I do it, sweet. He seems to have wet his
father's best suit, and if you remove him, I will be
left with the embarrassing evidence that now lies
concealed beneath him. I will put him to bed and
change my clothes."

Alisa's midnight-blue eyes sparkled with warmth.
Christian thought her exquisite with her thick mane
of burnished curls pulled to a loose knot atop her
head, her pale-peach velvet gown with its high, lacy
neck.

"All right, then, but don't be long. I don't know
most of these people."

She turned to the sound of Nicholas's voice, his
arm unadorned by Ivy for the first time since his arrival.

As Nicholas bade Alisa to follow him into the cold,
early winter's afternoon, Christian handed David

er to his waiting wet nurse and entered the master
edroom through the door that connected the two.
e quickly discarded his soiled clothing, standing
ad in tight-fitting breeches when he heard the door
nob turn. Thinking Alisa had followed him, Chris-
an turned to the slowly opening door, only to find
vy boldly entering, a seductive twitch twisting her
ps.

"Oh, Nicholas, you can't mean that," Alisa said
nhappily.

"Can't you overcome your jealousy of Ivy long
nough to congratulate me?" Nicholas accused with
isgust.

"Has she agreed to marry you?"

"Not formally, but she will. I was hoping to an-
ounce it today, but she wants to wait until she's ab-
olutely certain. It won't be long."

"Reconsider, Nicholas. At least give it a good, long
ime before you marry her."

Nicholas's face was angry now. "I should have ex-
ected this from you. You didn't want me, but you
don't want Ivy to have me either, do you?"

"She can't love anyone but herself."

"That's a dirty lie, Alisa. I wanted to tell you first,
o share my happiness with you to make up for how
I've treated you recently, but I see now that you deserved it. I don't know what I saw in you before. You
can't hold a candle to Ivy in looks, and you are as
hateful and jealous as Ivy said you were. This time I
have the best, and Christian comes up short. It's
wonderful justice that, after all these years, he
should have you when I will have Ivy."

Nicholas bowed mockingly. Alisa was left feeling
disheartened.

She spent a long time trying to compose herse
When she returned to the party, her eyes scann
the crowd for Christian, but he was nowhere in sigl
Instead Alisa's gaze was caught by Ivy, standing
the entrance to the ballroom as if she were just i
turning. She shivered at the sight of her siste
though she did not understand why. Her mood w
not eased by Ivy's determined approach.

"Are you happy, Alisa?" Ivy said snidely.

"I would be a good deal happier if you werei
here, Ivy. But since you are, I have a request to mal
of you."

Eyebrows arched and pale-blue eyes widened i
dramatic surprise. "Pray, what could you want fro
me?"

"I don't want you to hurt Nicholas," Alisa a
swered bluntly.

Ivy laughed in vicious delight. "Nicholas is
grown man. He can look out for himself. You, on tł
other hand, should take great care in the near fi
ture, dear sister, for all is not going to continue a
you want it."

Alisa sighed disgustedly. "What is that suppose
to mean?"

Again Ivy laughed evilly. "I wouldn't think c
ruining all of the surprises you have in store for yo
Alisa. Why, it would take all of the fun out of it, an
I've worked so hard!" Ivy's glance took in the large
formal room slowly, a wicked smile twisting her lips
"Enjoy everything you can, Alisa."

Ivy walked confidently to where Nicholas waited
She clasped his arm to her full breasts possessively
Alisa watched as Nicholas beamed at Ivy, kissin
her neck intimately as he swept her from the room

Just as Alisa decided to go and find Christian, h

appeared, dressed handsomely in a deep-blue suit at darkened his eyes. Even from a distance, Alisa ought something was wrong with him; his bushy ows were drawn together, his angular jaw enched hard. When his eyes found her, there was amistakable fury blazing in them.

Alisa's heart pounded and her blood ran cold in er veins, for she knew that Ivy's threats were not ade in vain.

Chapter Sixty-three

The doors closed on the last of the guests. Christian's large hands rested for a moment on the solid panel before he turned to Alisa, his expression alive with white-hot anger.

She stood behind him, her body rigid with tension, her beautiful face pale as she waited for the storm to break, her dignity and pride not allowing her to cower before the onslaught.

"Upstairs," he grated through clenched teeth, climbing the steps two at a time before her. He stood beside the bedroom door, slamming it viciously behind her.

She started slightly at the sound, fighting for courage. She turned slowly to face him, awaiting his wrath.

"I understand," he said, each word grinding harshly with sarcasm, "that you and I are not married, nor have we ever been married. You can imagine my surprise."

"Ivy," Alisa murmured.

"Of course Ivy! Who else can wreak such havoc with my life? She equals Ellen's best efforts. Where shall I place you, Alisa? The third in the set?"

The little remaining color drained from her face "What do you mean?"

"Don't play me for a fool!" he shouted. "You knew the minister was a fraud. How could you have allowed your own son to be born a bastard?"

Midnight-blue eyes widened to their limits. "What did Ivy tell you?"

"Dammit!" His fist slammed into the bureau beside him. "She told me the whole story of your bogus minister."

"My bogus minister? I had nothing to do with that."

"No?" he challenged. "It was not your idea to have a fake wedding so that you would be left free to seek your future? That once here, seeing all that I could offer you, you decided to play out the ruse?"

"I didn't even know about it myself until two days after David was born."

Christian watched her now, searching for a sign she was lying. "You did not know the minister was an imposter when we were wed?" he asked suspiciously.

"No. Ivy came to me with the story, as I said, not two months ago."

"Why the hell didn't you tell me about it then?" he raged.

"I hoped it was a lie, that it was another of Ivy's vindictive acts to cause trouble."

Bushy brows drew together. "Then why the hell not tell me? Would you have let David grow up never knowing if he was legitimate? If anything happened to me, you and David would risk losing everything. Did you intend never to tell me?" His angular jaw was hard, the creases in each cheek deep; his mouth was a thin line beneath his bushy mustache.

"I don't know. It has weighed on me since she revealed it. I had hoped . . ." She could not bring herself to say she had planned to wait until she had won his love to disclose it.

"You had hoped what?" he pressed.

Alisa sighed, trying to clear her racing thoughts. "You have been so preoccupied, Christian," she blurted out. "I was afraid if I told you now you might seize the opportunity to be rid of me."

"I see. So after two years of supposed marriage and a son we share, you thought so little of me that you were convinced I would toss you out into the streets, happy to be free of you both?" His tone was knife-edged and snide.

"I didn't know what to hink," she murmured honestly. "It would also free you of Ivy's interference. After all, this was not a union of your choosing. That is something I can never forget. I had no way of knowing what would happen if these ties suddenly did not exist."

Christian studied her, seeing her fear. "When will you realize it is better to come to me with the truth than to keep secrets that can only hurt you more than anything I would ever do?"

Alisa's expression became suddenly alert, sensing something more in his words. Surely he could not know the other, graver deceit? She swallowed thickly, too afraid to pursue it.

"Now that you know, what will happen?" she managed.

Christian saw the drastic change in her face and knew her thoughts. Disappointment that she did not confess all and free them both cooled his anger. He breathed a long, slow sigh of blighted hope.

"As soon as you change your gown, I intend to

marry you again, *legally* this time. And then I will do whatever is necessary to insure that David is recognized irrefutably as my first, legitimate heir."

Alisa's face erupted with joy; her dark eyes glowed with such warmth and love, it was almost enough to convince Christian of her feelings.

"Will you marry me again, Alisa, for no reason other than to have me?"

"You know I will! The question is, will you marry me for no other reason, or will David be the deciding factor now?"

Christian crossed to her, his arms going around her narrow waist. "I love our son, but I will marry his mother *only* because I want her as my wife. Forcing us together is the single thing Ivy has ever done that was inspired, and for that alone I am grateful to her."

Alisa's eyes lowered from his piercing bluish-green gaze, her teeth tugging on her bottom lip in indecision. She spoke hesitantly, resolving at last to reveal her secret.

"I must tell you something, Christian. I can't bear to enter into our marriage yet again with anything hidden between us."

Christian's hopes rose high. "What is it, sweet?"

"I was not honest with you when I explained the reasons behind my trapping you into marriage." She paused. "I killed a man that day. I struggled with him, he fell on his knife and died. As Ivy so often reminds me, I would have hanged if I had remained in England. That is the real cause for our wedding. Ivy devised the plan to hasten my escape from the gallows."

Alisa's cheeks burned with shame, staring at Christian's broad chest. She could not believe she

ieard him chuckle, and felt his arms pull her near to
iim.

"I know, Alisa," he whispered.

Her head shot back in horror.

"I realized when we were still in the hunting cabin
that something more serious was behind all of this
than marriage to an old crony of you father's. Just
before Owen left here, he told me your proposed
groom had been dead for two years before our wedding. On the voyage home from England, it was Ivy
that told me about the man's death. I've known all of
the details since then."

"Then that's the reason for your mood since your
return, isn't it?" she said dejectedly.

"No." His voice was reassuring. "Without meaning to, I'm sure, Ivy told me enough of the circumstances for me to know you are hardly a murderess.
It was an act of defense."

Now confusion reigned. "What is it that bothers
you, then? Have you tired of me?"

He stared down into her eyes, his brow furrowed.
"Would I marry you again if I had tired of you?"

"To gain your son, yes. Surely you know better
than anyone what hell lies in holding secrets. Please
don't prolong my torture more. I cannot marry you
again thinking it is only for the baby's sake."

His tone was a bit harsher. "What was the exact
purpose behind your words just before I left for London?"

"You doubted them?"

"I wondered if perhaps you lied, out of fear that I
would discover what you suffered so much to hide.
When I came back, I waited for you to prove you
meant it, but I have not heard it again."

Alisa's temper was sparked. "Did you expect a declaration of love in response to your coldness, your aloof formality? I had no idea if the cause of your attitude was love for another woman, hatred of me or God knows what. Your logic escapes me. I tell you I love you, and you can think only that it is a ruse? Surely my feelings could not protect me from your opinion of my past deception. No, my love could only leave me more vulnerable to you. Were I wise, I would have kept my feelings to myself."

"Am I to believe you still love me?" he asked with a crooked grin.

"To my shame."

"Shame?"

"It is demeaning to love a man who offers only to hold my feelings as if they were a possession . . . like some prized pig! Allow me the dignity of your not forcing the words to be said again."

Christian laughed uproariously, pulling her tightly up against him. "First you will become my bride, and then tonight, after our new marriage has been sealed, I will spend a long time explaining my feelings to you, Alisa."

"I prefer to know before I agree to marry you again."

Christian's eyes sparkled with bliss and mischief. "It's much too long a story, and I'd rather tell it in bed with you in my arms. For now, I will only tell you that you are the wisest woman in the world, and I suspect I have loved you for longer than either of us knows."

Chapter Sixty-four

"Not on our wedding night, Alisa! David's nurse will tend to him. Your husband and this new marriage are in desperate need of consummation, and that comes first tonight."

Alisa hesitated only a moment before walking from the nursery door into Christian's arms. She felt as if the past two hours had been a lovely dream through which she had moved in a blissful trance.

As Christian undressed her leisurely, her senses awakened to the reality that this was no dream. She and Christian had once again exchanged vows in a ceremony that was an affirmation of their equal decision to be together, so unlike the first, bitter, guilt-ridden joining.

They made love slowly, quietly, almost as if it were the first time. Words of love flowed freely, the sweet nectar that all other encounters had lacked. Christian knew without question that no other woman could ever give him all that Alisa did.

Alisa had no experience for comparison; to her it was an instinctive knowledge that only here, in Christian's arms, could her passion, her love, her body and mind find such perfect satiety.

They lay closely entwined in the aftermath,

basking in contentment that neither had ever felt before.

"I believe you promised me a long story about your feelings, Mr. Reed," Alisa prodded, settling in the circle of Christian's powerful arms.

He laughed lightly. "It's not such a long story. I doubt if it will surprise you. I think you've known me better than I've known myself since we met. You have scared the hell out of me through most of this, Alisa."

"Yes, I am a fearsome beast."

"You are not, but what you made me feel was. It was more frightening than even the simple worry of repeating all the pain that I found with Ellen. My feelings for you were so much stronger, so much deeper in comparison, that all I could think was if it hurt so damned bad to have that destroyed, how would I ever survive the destruction of this?"

"Didn't it occur to you that our marriage might survive?"

"I was a bit slow to trust, I'm afraid."

"You're a master of understatement, sir."

"These past years since Ellen seem like an extension of my adolescence. Today you married a man. I'm not sure what you married before; it seems I was something in between, a portion of me was still too much child to avoid punishing you for another's wrongs and for my own mistakes. I'm sorry for that."

"Am I forgiven, then, for all my misdeeds?"

"I only regret that you suffered so much in keeping secrets from me. I would not have judged you as harshly as you thought had you told me. That's why I think you struck something in me even before our first wedding."

"I can't believe that. You were formal and cold then, too. You avoided me at every opportunity."

He laughed. "Because you were the dreaded demon . . . woman!"

"Then it took one demon to chase away the others!"

Christian propped himself up beside her, a lecherous glint on his handsome face. "Ah, but what a method this demon used."

His mouth fell to hers, once again hungry for her. Alisa met him eagerly, her own appetite for him awakened. Soft fingers held the back of his neck, playing with the silky waves there as his massive hand cupped her breast, his thumb teasing the taut nipple, tracing circles just around its sensitive outer edge to drive her mad, as only he could.

She felt the long, iron-hard length of his manhood pressed to her thigh as one sinewy leg lay over her, and she moved up against it, feeling his pleasure in the action.

Insistent knocking at the bedroom door drew an angry groan from Christian. "Go away!" he shouted, his voice low and gravelly with passion.

"I'm sorry." Scott's tone was urgent. "This can't wait."

Christian pulled one of the blankets from the bed to conceal his all too obvious desire, and opened the door only a crack. "This is getting very annoying, Scott!" Christian barked.

Scott's face was deadly serious. "You'd both better come with me, Christian. Ivy's been badly beaten. The doctor has sent for her next of kin."

* * *

Alisa sat at her sister's bedside. Christian stood behind her, offering silent support in the comforting hand at her shoulder.

Ivy was a gruesome sight, broken and bloody. The doctor had done what little he could to ease her suffering. Her face was barely recognizable in the swollen purple flesh, both eyes unable to open. Her nose was at an odd angle, and her lips bulged and bled over broken teeth. Dark bruises in the shape of fingers coiled around her throat. She struggled to speak through spasms of racking coughs that sent trails of blood bubbling from the corner of her mouth.

Her voice was a raspy whisper, responding to Alisa's presence. "I didn't think you would come."

Alisa swallowed thickly to allow her own voice to pass. "What happened to you, Ivy?" she asked compassionately.

"Nicholas." Ivy's tone was filled with contempt. "That bastard. He tried to kill me!"

"Why, Ivy? Why would he want to kill you? He loved you."

"Because I'm pregnant." Ivy managed a short painful chuckle, and Alisa wondered at her sister's sanity when she spoke again, sounding victorious. "It's Christian's child, you see. We had an affair through the trip to England . . . and since." Ivy was unaware of Christian's presence in the room, for only Alisa had spoken. "It's me Christian loves, you ninny. I told Nicholas about it when he tried to push me into marrying him. The ass thought the baby was his. I told him about our affair. I told him Christian was not really married to you and that he would marry me soon. Nicholas went wild. He said Christian would not claim another of his children. He's insane. He tried to kill me."

"Oh, Ivy." Alisa sighed, knowing her sister lied, seeing the ugly, twisted irony of Ivy's deceit ending her life.

Ivy managed another perverse laugh. "You're such a fool, Alisa." A paroxysm of coughing took her.

Alisa gently wiped the blood from her sister's lips.

"I really was happy that you killed Willis Potts, did you know that? I detested him after a while, and our little accident left me in the perfect position. It was such a good plan. I could have Owen, and it left me with such power over you. Everything was always so easy for you; Papa loved you, while he couldn't abide me. Even my beaus were more interested in you. I hated you for it. You always had what wanted. But now I will have dear Christian. You can see how you like losing what you want most." Again Ivy was racked with agonizing coughs, that jarred her abused body harshly.

Alisa felt overwhelming pity for her sister, seeing clearly for the first time the depth of her demented jealousy.

Ivy uttered a dreadful choking sound as she fell limp and lifeless, a macabre ending for one whose most cherished possession was her beauty.

Christian led Alisa from the house, his strong arm supporting her as he explained to Scott all that Ivy had said. The three traveled in silence back to their home where Christian remained with Alisa until she slept.

Then he and Scott went in search of Nicholas.

Chapter Sixty-five

he door to a small furnished room in a boarding
ouse near the wharves was unlocked when Chris-
an and Scott arrived. The brothers' eyes met before
hristian opened the door without knocking.

Nicholas's head jerked toward them, his expres-
on turning from startled fear to disgust when he re-
lized who his late-night guests were. He wasted
nly a second before continuing his task of stuffing
othing and money into a large carpetbag.

"How did you know about this place?" Nicholas
sked contemptuously.

The door closed behind the two tall, large men.
cott answered, "I overheard you talk about it not
ong ago. You weren't difficult to find; you're well
nown, Nicholas."

A short, derisive chuckle sounded from the much
maller man. The change in Nicholas was a shock to
oth Christian and Scott, for gone was the easygoing
nan they had known.

"Yes, I'm well known in this fair city. The Reeds'
charity case." His disgust was thick as he finished
is packing and stared at them through black eyes
glittering with barely controlled rage. His silver-

blond hair was matted to his brow with sweat, a
blood splattered the front of his jacket.

"Did you think that I would never tire of playi
the buffoon for the two of you? Having to entert
and please you both wore thin."

"There was no need for it, Nicholas." Christi
spoke quietly.

"No need? How else was I to keep my place but
making myself your 'private jester'? That is h
Scott introduced me to Alisa the first time. The p
vate jester. Neither of you ever understood what
was like to live on someone's charity. Never to fe
you could expect anything but second-best. You gr
up belonging. Part of a family that was well r
spected, admired, accepted everywhere, while I w
'the ward'! I was left scraps!"

Christian saw there was no reason to refute Nich
las's words, it was clear he believed all he said, felt
all more strongly than anyone could ever realiz
These were Nicholas's convictions from boyhoo
and nothing now could change them.

Nicholas's lips curled with hatred. "I was doome
to a life of wanting what I could not have. Somethin
you have never known; especially you, Christia
Did you know I loved Ellen?"

Christian's bushy brows rose in surprise, pleasin
Nicholas.

"I loved her long before you came back. She ha
agreed to marry me but why should she settle for m
when she could have all you could offer her? Even i
the baby she carried was mine." Nicholas watche
Christian intently. "You never guessed, did you
She swore he wasn't, that she was being bedded b
more than just me. But I always thought he was my
baby. Those four months that you pranced about

owing off your son, I wanted to kill you. I sent you
a note about Ellen that day. You never knew that,
her. I decided if I couldn't have her, then you
uldn't enjoy her, either, or my son. I knew where
e was . . . and with whom. I always knew. I fol-
ved her, watched her. But even when you dis-
rded her, she refused me. Even then she wouldn't
mit that Nat was mine, and she wouldn't have me.
e said after you I was like some little boy and she
uldn't bear me. You don't know how I wished you
d killed her instead of divorcing her," he spat.

"Did Alisa tell you I loved her, as well?" Nicholas
ded, as if the final irony.

Christian shook his head.

Scott's voice rose loudly. "That's enough, Nicho-
s. None of this has anything to do with what you've
ne tonight."

Christian's hand on Scott's arm quieted him. "Let
m go on," Christian said ominously.

"There's nothing to tell. Alisa was just another
ing I couldn't have. I decided to hurt her with Ivy.
y was second-best, but I came to love her, to want
r as much as I did Alisa. She was like a replica of
isa, and so many admired the fact that Ivy was
ine, it made up for it. She led me to believe she
uld marry me. She was pregnant, too. Then to-
ght she said she wouldn't have me, the bitch. She
id she would say the baby was Christian's, that
e would destroy Alisa's marriage with it. She said
e had money of her own, and freedom, and she
uld never take me as her husband, so I could feed
f of her like I had fed off of the Reeds all these
ars."

Pain softened Nicholas's vehemence. His tone was
fter, apologetic. "I didn't mean to hurt her. I

wasn't thinking straight. She taunted me; even af
I had hit her, she goaded me as if it entertained l
to see me that way." His black eyes ran to th
pleadingly now. "Don't you see that I was desper
to have something of my own? Something tl
wasn't loaned to me or given out of charity? I wan
something everyone else valued. Neither of you ev
wanted my knowledge. You would go to talk bu
ness and leave me always to entertain the ladies
thought having Ivy would give me that. She w
beautiful. Men wanted her."

Nicholas laughed in self-contempt. "I guess it w
a way of proving even now that I was as much a m
as you, Christian. If I couldn't take your wom
away, at least I could win the next best. But
couldn't sit by and watch the same thing happen
second time. It seemed that not only was I refus
what you had, but even my own two children were
be yours as well. Didn't you have enough that w
yours without taking the only things that we
rightfully mine?"

Nicholas's hand rose quickly from behind his ca
petbag; he held a revolver leveled at Christian. F
sighed, resigned. "You are not going to take me in
the law. I didn't mean to hurt her."

"You killed her, Nicholas," Christian said.

"You won't take me! No court would understan
that I've suffered enough! That she deserved wha
she got!" His eyes glittered with malice, as if wisl
ing Christian would give him the slightest excuse t
shoot.

"They'll hunt you down, Nicholas," Scott sai
evenly, hoping to draw his attention, but Nichola
merely smiled an ugly grin.

"It's better than just giving up. Especially to th

two of you. I'd rather kill you both." He stepped nearer to the door. "Will either of you try to take me and risk the life of the other? I don't think so. Your affection for each other always did grate on me, but now I think it will serve me."

Nicholas dashed wildly for the door, his small size giving him the advantage, and made it out of the room, the door slamming closed behind him before Christian or Scott could reach him. They heard the key in the lock on the outside.

Scott turned his side to the door, ready to charge it, but Christian's hand stopped him. "Maybe it's terribly wrong, but I think we should let him go. He wouldn't believe it, but I can't be the one to bring him in, any more than I could do it to you."

Scott stared at Christian, puzzled for only a moment before his stance relaxed. His voice was grave. "I don't think I could, either."

Chapter Sixty-six

"Christian?" Alisa spoke softly from the doorway of the den where her husband worked at his desk.

Christian's face raised to her, piercing bluish-green eyes quizzical.

"I just wondered if you would take me upstairs and hold me and make love to me and tell me you love me."

Bushy brows rose in surprise. Two weeks had passed since Ivy's death and Nicholas's escape. In that time, Alisa had been very quiet and removed, spending hours alone in her studio, working at a frenzied pace well into each night. Christian had offered his comfort and support but accepted her explanation that she needed to be left to her own thoughts, to work through her feelings for her sister.

So this request from Alisa as she stood before his desk stunned Christian.

"It would be my pleasure, but are you sure?"

Alisa smiled at him, and he thought how beautiful she was, loving the untamed mass of thick, burnished curls like a halo around her face.

"I'm quite sure."

Christian needed no further urging; his passion for her was always close to the surface and roused by

her nearness. He took her small hand in his large
one and led the way to their bedroom.

He complied with her request, making love to her
slowly, tenderly, carefully, almost as if offering a
balm to her abused senses. Afterward, he held her
closely to his long length, breathing in the clean
scent of her tousled, tangled hair.

"Are you all right, Alisa?" he asked quietly, stroking her arm.

"I am now. I love you, Christian. I hope you know
that."

His lips curved into a broad smile beneath the
dusky-colored mustache; deep indentations in each
cheek marked his intense pleasure in her words.
"I'm afraid I need to hear that often. I find myself
slipping back into doubts about it if you fail to reassure me."

"Never doubt it. My love for you has become my
source of strength. I think I would cease to live without it."

His voice was low with emotion. "I understand
that well, for it is how I feel about you, my love. I'm
amazed at how stubbornly we fought it all that
time."

"I've spent so much time thinking about Ivy . . .
and Nicholas. I think I understand their envy. If I
were refused you and your love and what we have together, I think I might be inclined to use any weapon
to gain it for myself."

"I've come to much the same conclusion. I also realize that I must never take you or David for
granted, though I believe I could be perfectly content
with nothing else but you and the baby."

One curved finger raised her chin so that his lips
could reach hers, his mustache tickling her. When

e kiss ended, Alisa's cheek nestled in the hollow of s muscular shoulder again. Her tone was once ore serious.

"Do you think they will ever find Nicholas?"

"I don't know, love," he answered simply. He had t told her that he and Scott had let their cousin es- pe.

"I hope they don't," she said softly.

"Why is that?"

"I felt so sorry for him. He deserved much better an Ivy, though he wouldn't believe it."

"It was you he wanted, Alisa."

"Not really. He wanted whatever was yours. Be- ause of that, I don't think he will ever find happi- ess, but I could not have stood for him to be hung or nprisoned. In thinking about it all these past weeks ve realized that Ivy was a little mad. And I knew nly too well how much she could hurt people. In a vay, Nicholas was defending himself. He was the nost vulnerable person she ever manipulated." She hivered. "I don't know if she was exactly evil or vicked, but very near to it. Perhaps such selfishness lways borders on that."

"Ivy and Nicholas were more mismatched than any two people ever could have been. Both of them always wanted what belonged to someone else; nei- her was ever able to prize what they had." Chris- ian squeezed her tightly. "It's all over now, Alisa, and best left in the past."

She smiled up at him. "Weren't those my words to you some time ago?"

He grinned sheepishly at her. "I told you you were the wisest woman I ever met."

Alisa's expression turned more quizzical. "Is your past left behind now, Christian?"

He kissed the top of her head. "Blessedly. I feel like a burden has been lifted from my shoulders." He paused. "God, how I love you, Alisa. If for nothing else, we can remember Ivy kindly for bringing us together and be grateful to Nicholas for giving me cause to rid myself of Ellen."

"Does that mean I can relax and not worry that our next baby will raise your doubts anew?"

"Are you pregnant?"

"No." She laughed. "But I wouldn't mind if I was." She rubbed her cheek in the mat of hair covering his chest. "It will be all right, you know. I won't allow anything to take me away from you."

"You're sure you're not?"

"Positive."

He pressed her onto her back with a playful growl. "Good, because I'm not finished with you tonight and I wouldn't want you pleading a delicate condition."

"As if I ever would!" She laughed, feeling wonderful for the first time since Ivy's death. Her midnight blue eyes suddenly grew moist. "I do love you," she whispered.

He smiled at her, kissing each eye slowly. "And love you, Alisa."

His warm lips took hers, first softly and then with a new urgency she welcomed as they savored at last the love each had longed for and the perfect contentment each had earned.